continued ...

"Deborah Cooke has only touched the surface about these wonderful men called the *Pyr* and their battle with the evil dragons. . . . I am dying for more."

—Romance Junkies

Kiss of Fire

"Cooke, aka bestseller Claire Delacroix, dips into the paranormal realm with her sizzling new Dragonfire series. With a self-described loner as a hero, this heroine has to adjust to her new role in the supernatural and establish bonds of trust. Efficient plotting moves the story at a brisk pace and paves the way for more exciting battles to come."

—*Romantic Times*

"Wow, what an innovative and dazzling world Ms. Cooke has built with this new Dragonfire series. Her smooth and precise writing quickly draws the reader in and has you believing it could almost be real. . . . I can't wait for the next two books."

—Fresh Fiction

"Deborah Cooke has definitely made me a fan. I am now lying in wait for the second book in this extremely exciting series."

—Romance Junkies

"Paranormal fans with a soft spot for shape-shifting dragons will definitely enjoy *Kiss of Fire*, a story brimming with sexy heroes; evil villains threatening mayhem, death, and world domination; ancient prophesies; and an engaging love story. . . . An intriguing mythology and various unanswered plot threads set the stage for plenty more adventure to come in future Dragonfire stories."

—BookLoons

Also by Deborah Cooke

WINTER KISS

KISS

A DRAGONFIRE NOVEL

DEBORAH COOKE

A SIGNET ECLIPSE BOOK

SIGNET ECLIPSE
Published by New American Library, a division of
Penguin Group (USA) Inc., 375 Hudson Street,
New York, New York 10014, USA
Penguin Group (Canada), 90 Eglinton Avenue East, Suite 700, Toronto,
Ontario M4P 2Y3, Canada (a division of Pearson Penguin Canada Inc.)
Penguin Books Ltd., 80 Strand, London WC2R 0RL, England
Penguin Ireland, 25 St. Stephen's Green, Dublin 2,
Ireland (a division of Penguin Books Ltd.)
Penguin Group (Australia), 250 Camberwell Road, Camberwell, Victoria 3124,
Australia (a division of Pearson Australia Group Pty. Ltd.)
Penguin Books India Pvt. Ltd., 11 Community Centre, Panchsheel Park,
New Delhi - 110 017, India
Penguin Group (NZ), 67 Apollo Drive, Rosedale, North Shore 0632,
New Zealand (a division of Pearson New Zealand Ltd.)
Penguin Books (South Africa) (Pty.) Ltd., 24 Sturdee Avenue,
Rosebank, Johannesburg 2196, South Africa

Penguin Books Ltd., Registered Offices:
80 Strand, London WC2R 0RL, England

First published by Signet Eclipse, an imprint of New American Library,
a division of Penguin Group (USA) Inc.

First Printing, November 2009
10 9 8 7 6 5 4 3 2 1

For Kara Cesare—
with many thanks for her energy and enthusiasm

Prologue

Chicago
February 9, 2009

Erik was pacing the floor of his renovated loft. The
building had been reconstructed since the fire a
year before, and though it was similar to his former residence, the presence of Eileen and their daughter had
transformed the space. It was more than just baby toys
and items scattered in the kitchen, new toiletries in the
bathroom, the closet filled with feminine clothing, and
the invasion of knitting wool—the once-austere space
now possessed a more welcoming air.

Erik's living accommodations had finally become a
home and he was glad of the change.

Zoë had been colicky since midnight and Eileen had
remained up with her. It was just after nine in the morning, a day that Eileen didn't have to go to the university,
but so overcast that it was still dark. Erik walked with
his daughter, taking his turn in what seemed like a futile
effort to soothe her.

Erik was restless himself. He felt as if his body hovered on the cusp of change, but he couldn't understand why. There was no threat to his family or home, no presence of other *Pyr* or *Slayers* within proximity. It was true that he needed sleep, but this sense was different.

Maybe it was just that he was worried.

It had been a year since there had been a full eclipse. His own firestorm had been presaged by a full lunar eclipse, as had those of Donovan and Quinn before that. But Erik had checked, and there would be no total eclipses before December 2010.

Did that mean there would be no firestorms for the other *Pyr* in that interval?

Or did it mean the firestorms were less critical to the survival of the *Pyr*? The Wyvern had foretold that those three firestorms were critical for the *Pyr*, that they had to be negotiated successfully for the *Pyr* to have a fighting chance in the final war with the *Slayers*. Were subsequent firestorms less important?

Erik didn't know, and he had no one to ask.

The *Slayers* were quiet, almost absent from Erik's sense of the world, and he distrusted that. Magnus hadn't surrendered, and he wasn't dead or gone.

Magnus was scheming something somewhere. Erik both wanted to know what it was and dreaded that truth. In times past he would have sought out his old foe, but now Erik had a mate and a child.

More than that, Erik and Eileen had a *daughter*, which meant the next Wyvern was his child to raise and defend. It also meant he couldn't access the Wyvern's wisdom until Zoë herself learned to talk.

He might not be able to consult with her until she passed puberty. That was when male *Pyr* came into their powers, after all. Erik didn't know how it worked for the Wyvern, and there was nothing in the paucity of literature about the Wyvern and the *Pyr* to reference.

Eileen had looked.

Erik had no information and no one to ask. It wasn't his favored state of affairs.

So he paced with an irritable Zoë and tried to ease his own anxiety.

"I've been thinking," Eileen said, her voice surprising Erik.

He turned to find her in the bedroom doorway, her hair loose and beautiful, her nightgown flowing around her knees. "I thought you were asleep."

"I was." She took a bottle of juice out of the fridge and poured herself a glass, glancing up at him with a smile. "Did you know there's a penumbral lunar eclipse this morning?"

"No, I only look for the total eclipses." Erik guessed, though, that the partial eclipse might be the reason for his restlessness. He'd never been sensitive to partial eclipses before, but much was changing in the world of the *Pyr*.

Was that why Zoë wouldn't sleep, either? How much *Pyr* was in her already? How much had yet to come?

Eileen sipped her juice, watching Erik so carefully that he knew she had more to say.

"You have an idea," he prompted.

"There are three penumbral lunar eclipses in a row this year. One today." She flicked a glance at the clock. "In about fifteen minutes, it'll be total. Then there's one in July and another in August."

"So?"

"What's a penumbra but a shadow? What if these eclipses are about shadow dragons?"

"That's ridiculous. *Slayers* don't have firestorms. . . ."

"But one of the shadow dragons isn't a *Slayer*, is he?"

Erik stared at her, astonished as he understood. "Delaney."

"Delaney," Eileen agreed, and finished her juice. "I'm

not sure he counts as a shadow dragon, actually. Maybe he's just in the shadows."

"He was a dead *Pyr* when forced to drink the Dragon's Blood Elixir that raises the dead and turns them into shadow dragons. . . ."

"But not dead long enough that his soul had abandoned his body." At Erik's look, Eileen shrugged. "I mean, in *Pyr* terms, the divine spark within him hadn't yet returned to the Great Wyvern."

"Magnus couldn't corrupt him," Erik said. "Delaney wasn't a *Slayer* choosing to drink the Elixir, either, and he refused to become one."

"Where is he?"

"I'm not sure."

"Can't you feel his presence?"

"I haven't looked."

Eileen watched him and he felt compelled to say more.

Erik sighed. "I know that he liquidated all of his assets. He sold his car, his home in Seattle, and sold half of the eco-travel business he started with Niall to Niall at a bargain price. He hasn't returned to Sloane for further treatment or advice, either. He responds to no query in old-speak." He met Eileen's gaze, knowing she didn't like his answer. "Delaney doesn't want to be found. I have to respect his desire for privacy and his knowledge of his own reality."

When Eileen spoke, her tone was so carefully neutral that Erik knew she had strong feelings about his choice. "What about defending his firestorm?"

Could Delaney have a firestorm?

Erik found his daughter watching him with wide eyes. At three months of age, she was too young to really make sense of what she saw and Erik knew it, but still he couldn't deny his sense that she understood a great deal more than anyone expected. Now she watched him so solemnly that she might have been reading his thoughts.

Questioning his choice, just as Eileen did.

It was at moments like this that Erik believed Zoë was already the Wyvern, that her soul was old and already up to the task, and that it was simply her body holding her back from active participation. He decided to take a chance on his instinct.

Maybe there were other ways to access whatever she knew.

"Will you help me, Zoë?" he murmured in old-speak, that form of speech that humans could not hear. The baby blinked once before she fixed her steady stare on him again.

Had she heard him? He thought so.

"There's a weird connection between you two, that's for sure," Eileen said softly.

"Does it bother you?"

She smiled. "It fascinates me. But then, I have a tendency to believe stuff about old souls finding each other time and again." Their gazes met and locked as Erik smiled at his wife and partner. She had taught him that not everything was logical, and that there were benefits to taking chances.

"Let's fill the sink with water," he suggested impulsively. "The Dragon's Egg is shattered beyond repair, but sometimes a bowl of water is just as good."

"Or an ocean can be a dark mirror," Eileen agreed. She filled the kitchen sink, pulled the blinds, and turned out the lights. They stood side by side in the darkened kitchen, the baby perched on Erik's hip between them.

Zoë had stopped fussing.

Erik kissed the baby's forehead and whispered in her ear. "Come on, Zoë. Conjure me a vision that will tell me what to do." Then he switched to old-speak. *"Aid me, Wyvern."*

Erik watched in amazement as the baby extended one plump hand toward the water's surface, fingers outstretched.

Then he caught his breath as the surface of the water swirled with dark clouds. He leaned closer, bending his attention upon the emerging vision, his heart leaping as a scene became clear. He watched avidly as the ebony clouds parted to reveal swirling red liquid.

"The Dragon's Blood Elixir," Erik murmured, remembering the glimpse he'd had of it in his dream of Sigmund.

The baby stretched her hand closer, almost touching the surface of the water. The Elixir flowed and a massive red dragon talon floated into view. Erik had only a glimpse of it before it disappeared into the murk of the Elixir again. He shuddered in understanding of what made the Elixir.

The clouds parted further, revealing a cave, with the Elixir contained in a massive vial against one wall of the space.

"It's the sanctuary where Magnus has the source of the Elixir secured," he murmured.

"Is that where Delaney is?" Eileen asked.

The scene spun, then the point of view rocketed through a labyrinthine entrance and out to a parked car. A tall auburn-haired man sat in the driver's seat, and Erik recognized Delaney immediately. He looked determined.

"He thinks he can eliminate the Elixir alone," he said.

"Magnus won't like that plan much," Eileen murmured. "Where exactly is the Elixir?"

"In a sanctuary, but I don't know where. We'll have to find it."

The clouds covered the surface of the water again and Erik thought the vision was over. He kissed his daughter, convinced that she had brought him this gift, but she squirmed and stretched out her hand again.

To his wonder, a gold line, similar to the ones that had once appeared on the surface of the Dragon's Egg, danced over the surface of the water. It outlined the continent of North America in gleaming gold.

"Whoa," said Eileen, who had never seen the Dragon's Egg.

Erik didn't even dare to blink, lest he miss a detail. His heart was pounding. Zoë was already so powerful! A line of longitude and one of latitude were drawn to triangulate a position.

"Ohio," Eileen said, leaning forward to look. "In the south."

"Let's go," Erik said, heading for the door to the roof. He felt the change build within him, rising to a crescendo that he might not be able to deny. He was calculating, certain that he could fly to Ohio within hours, perhaps in time to stop Delaney from making a mistake. . . .

Eileen put a hand on his arm to stop him. "Not so fast, Mr. Sorensson. Don't you remember how Delaney tried to harvest Sara's son and Alex's son while both women were still pregnant?"

"That wasn't Delaney's intent. Magnus had planted that command in his subconscious and he couldn't deny it."

"That's why he exiled himself." Eileen was grim. "To protect the children of the *Pyr*." She reached and plucked the now-sleeping baby from Erik's arms, then glared at him. "You have to find a way to aid Delaney's firestorm without risking Zoë."

Her point was well taken. Erik's heart clenched. If the *Slayers* gained possession of the new Wyvern—well, Erik wouldn't even consider the possibility.

He couldn't leave the baby alone with Eileen, not without his personal defense of them both. And he didn't dare take them closer to Delaney. He frowned, caught between his two responsibilities.

Eileen, as was so often the case, had a solution. "Remember that the mark of a great leader lies in his ability to delegate."

"I can't send Quinn or Donovan. . . ."

"Because Quinn won't go without Sara and baby Garrett, and Donovan won't go without Alex and baby Nick," Eileen concluded, following his thoughts perfectly.

"Sloane," Erik said. "The Apothecary might be able to help Delaney through this challenge."

"What about Niall?" Eileen suggested. "They were partners and friends. He can send you updates on the wind."

"Niall does have a cell phone." Erik felt compelled to note this fact. "We all do."

Eileen laughed. "Don't give me that. You *Pyr* love your old-speak too much to surrender the chance to use it."

"It's tradition," Erik insisted. He felt the eclipse slide toward its totality, even the penumbral eclipse making his body resonate with the urge to shift.

Eileen smiled at him, reaching up to press a kiss to his cheek. "Do what you need to do, then come to bed with us." She met his gaze, her eyes flicking over him as the urge to shift grew even stronger. He knew she understood. "Soon."

Erik couldn't argue with that. He shut the blinds, plunging the loft's main room into darkness, then surrendered to his body's urge to change shape. It felt good to let the power flood through him, to let his body do what it did best. He felt powerful and invincible, strong in his lair. He recalled that the Wyvern had been able to deny the moon's call, even on the full eclipse, and wondered whether such a skill could be learned.

Then Erik closed his eyes and concentrated, trying to pinpoint the respective locations of Sloane and Niall. Niall was with Thorolf—probably arguing—but Erik thought they could do this together.

It might improve their tolerance of each other.

Or it might not. He could only try to foster better relationships between members of his team. To be fair, he shared some of Niall's irritation with Thorolf's tendency to demand little of himself.

Erik sent his summons in old-speak, waiting until all three had replied. He checked the smoke perimeter mark around his lair, then scanned for a hint of any of his fellows in the vicinity. It was a habit, one that wasn't as reliable as it had once been, but it reassured him all the same.

It wasn't long before Erik felt the moon slide from the shadow of the eclipse. He shuddered as he let his body change back to human form. He took a moment to compose his thoughts before joining Eileen.

If nothing else, he had complete faith in the *Pyr* who followed him. It wasn't quite as good as taking care of everything himself, but he was learning to accept it as good enough.

Delaney was driving through the Ohio countryside when the assault came. He began to shift shape suddenly and without any decision to do so.

He couldn't stop the change.

The dragon within him had gained ascendancy and that reality terrified Delaney. He lost control of the rental car in the transition, his talon leaving a long scratch on the dashboard as the car slid sideways from the road. It came to a halt, tipping into a snow-filled ditch. He was out the door just before he shifted shape completely, the change rolling through him with unrestrained power.

What was happening to him?

And why?

It was dark, too dark for morning, and Delaney abruptly remembered why. There was to be an eclipse on this day, only a partial one, but his body was obviously responding to it.

And how. The beast within was completely unleashed, raging with a fury that was terrifying.

Lusting for the Dragon's Blood Elixir.

The yearning was so violent that his body shook—he was like a junkie being denied his fix. His gut gnawed, he ached and he burned and he *wanted*, as he had never wanted before.

Was it because he had come close to the Elixir's sanctuary?

Or had something changed within him? All *Pyr* felt the urge to shift under an eclipse, and felt it most strongly under a full eclipse. It should have been comparatively easy to deny his body's urge under a partial eclipse.

But it wasn't.

Worse, his body demanded that he go to the Elixir, that he seize it and drink it.

There was no way Delaney was going to do that. He gritted his teeth and fought his own body's demands. He threw himself into a snow-dusted field of corn stalks. He rolled, battling his own body, trying to inflict pain on himself, a pain that might recall him to his senses. He fought the imperative to take flight, to go to the Elixir, to drink deeply.

To lose his soul forever.

The nightmare came to him then, assaulting him in daylight as it had every night he'd dared to close his eyes and sleep. He had endured it a thousand times already. In a way, it was more horrific to be awake and see its threat.

Delaney saw the earth in its verdant infancy and tried

to force the vision from his thoughts. He knew where this nightmare led, what fate it assumed for the planet and the humans who lived upon it, and he didn't want to see it again.

But the nightmare was relentless. It had a hold on his mind and wouldn't let go. It showed the spread of industry across the planet's surface, devouring the pristine wilderness it had just displayed to him. It documented fallen rain forests and oil spills, species eliminated and birds covered in fuel oil. It showed him plumes of pollution rising into the sky; it showed him mercury slipping into the bodies of fish. It showed him rivers of trailings that ran crimson, like the blood of Gaia herself spread across her land.

And that was the effect upon nature herself. It also displayed the malaise in the hearts and minds of men. It showed him injustice and genocide; it showed him violence and hunger and poverty. It showed him polluted water and wells gone bad; it showed him air too toxic to be breathed; it showed him nuclear fallout. It documented birth defects from exposure to contaminants and children living in garbage dumps. He saw humans sicken and die; he saw selfishness become ascendant and individuals condemn others for their own profit.

Delaney saw the selfish perspective of the *Slayers* grab hold in the minds of men and was sickened by it all over again. The trouble ran deep, deep in the hearts of men and the soil of Gaia.

And he saw Gaia retaliate in an effort to save herself. He witnessed floods and tornados, tsunamis and earthquakes. The planet was in her death throes, prepared to do anything to preserve herself, and humans were destroyed by her mighty power.

But still the shadow spread. He struggled as he was pulled back to view the earth from afar, as if he sat upon a distant planet and was apart from the entire ordeal. But Delaney's heart was on the earth, with Gaia, with the humans who called the planet home, and his responsibility as a *Pyr* was to protect the treasure of both of them.

So he despised the sight of the shadow sliding across the surface of the earth. It was like watching an eclipse, except that the earth was cast in shadow instead of the moon. On this day, he felt its chill right to his marrow, and knew that the Elixir was the toxin at work. The darkness spread across the planet, and he recalled the old idea of the dragon in the sky devouring the moon during an eclipse.

But these dragons, the *Slayers*, devoured the earth itself.

He heard wind and he heard rain and he heard the calls of humans in distress. He heard hurricanes thrashing against shores and he heard the despair that comes in the night, fed by the terror of the unknown.

The shadow deepened, claiming more of the earth's surface, gradually moving across its face. Delaney was cold, colder than he'd ever been, and in his vision, the earth was being plunged into a deep freeze. He watched hoarfrost grow along coastlines, saw trees and buildings encased in ice. He saw the ice spread relentlessly across the earth, moving like quicksilver, stealing life and vitality from everything it touched. It claimed everything in its cold grasp.

When the eclipse was complete, when the earth was completely devoured by the shadow, the planet glistened in the darkness. The shadow passed, as the light would return after an eclipse, but the earth that was revealed was utterly changed. Its rivers were frozen. Its mountains were buried in snow. The forests were frozen icy white.

And it was silent.

There was no motion upon it. No life. The sheen of ice reflected the light of the sun, sparkling and glistening with horrific import.

The Elixir had consumed the planet, exterminating everything upon it and preserving what was left forever.

Dead.

And it was all because Delaney had not taken the initiative to destroy the Elixir.

The duration of that morning's eclipse was four hours and three minutes. Delaney felt every second of it. He spent that entire morning thrashing in a farmer's field as the snow fell steadily, his mind haunted by a vision of what could be.

No one saw him triumph over his body's need, not in that remote field in the middle of a snowstorm. No one saw him shift back to human form and stand up, panting and exhausted, in the snow. No one saw him wipe the sweat from his brow, shaking from his ordeal.

And no one saw the resolve harden in Delaney's eyes.

He wouldn't fight that battle again. A vicious monster had awakened within him, one that he couldn't control and didn't trust. He'd come too close to losing this fight, and he was determined to never surrender to the *Slayers* and their Elixir.

He was close, very close, to the Elixir's hidden sanctuary. If nothing else, the bit of it in his body allowed him to sense it more accurately. He'd find it and eliminate it, no matter what the price to himself.

He climbed out of the field and checked the road for possible observers. When he saw none, he shifted shape and pushed the car out of the ditch. He felt normal again, his dragon form tame and easily controlled.

Delaney wasn't fooled. The next eclipse would be worse.

The car started right away, giving him only a moment to note the long scratch on the dashboard from his talon. It was a potent reminder of the involuntary change.

Never again. By the next eclipse, Delaney would be dead and the Elixir would be destroyed.

Chapter 1

Delaney decided to attack the sanctuary of the Dragon's Blood Elixir on Saturday morning.

There was no question of his sleeping on Friday night. Magnus's dragonsmoke perimeter mark on the sanctuary was almost cursory, and it had certainly broken. There would be no issue in getting into the sanctuary of the Elixir.

And Delaney didn't have to worry about coming out.

Delaney couldn't summon the *Pyr* to help him, couldn't risk that Magnus would compel him to turn against them or that they would be imperiled in his last mission.

He was on his own.

He had sensed Magnus's presence in Ohio, as well as that of Magnus's current favorite, Jorge. The *Slayers* seemed to have gathered, maybe to fortify themselves with the Elixir.

He'd spent the week observing Magnus's external security measures, which weren't worth concern. Unfortunately, he wasn't sure what he would find within the sanctuary—how the Elixir was stored and how precisely he would destroy it—which made it hard to formulate a plan of attack. Delaney had been unhappy with this lack of information, but more unhappy with the doubt it fed within him.

Once he had been bold. Once he had been confident. Once his brother, Donovan, had called him a daredevil. Once he would have simply charged into the sanctuary and dealt with whatever confronted him, assured of his own success. But the Elixir had cast a shadow on his heart, making him doubt his abilities and his success, making him delay. His chronic lack of sleep didn't help.

He despised what he had become.

It was time to resolve the matter.

Delaney knew that he was on a suicide mission.

He didn't care. Dying had to be better than living as he had these past years, and if he could accomplish something with his death, all the better.

He'd destroy the source of the Dragon's Blood Elixir so that Magnus couldn't make more shadow dragons of dead *Pyr*. *Slayers* wouldn't be able to drink the Elixir to become stronger, either. And no one would ever have to suffer what he had endured, being forced to consume the Elixir against his will.

No *Pyr* would ever have to be afraid to fall asleep again.

Delaney had spent a year preparing, mastering his fighting skills, and getting his body into prime condition. He'd sold everything and made his will, prepared for his own demise.

Delaney was between the forms, so to speak. He hadn't embraced the Elixir, so it hadn't turned him *Slayer*. He hated how the shadow seed that Magnus had planted in his heart refused to be banished, hated how he had been unable to stop himself from attacking Donovan's pregnant mate, Alex. His action had been disgusting and reprehensible.

Exiling himself from his fellows had been the only choice.

Delaney drove his rental car aimlessly on Friday night, fighting his exhaustion. The recurring nightmare pressed at the back of his thoughts, threatening to consume him if he succumbed to the need to sleep. Its bleak vision always left him shaking and disheartened—he couldn't risk it on this night.

He drove on country roads, past fields lying fallow, past snow under moonlight and forests of bare branches. Just when he was sick of his own company, he saw lights.

Delaney pulled into the parking lot of the roadhouse on instinct, and realized he was craving the company of the humans he and the *Pyr* were charged to protect. He didn't give himself time to think twice.

He strode into the noisy bar, savoring the sounds of laughter and music, the sight of people dancing and celebrating, and appreciated the point to his sacrifice. They would all be oblivious to what he did, just as humans were always oblivious to the efforts of the *Pyr*, but their optimism would carry on.

That made it worthwhile.

He had ordered a beer and a tequila shooter before a woman rapped him on the elbow. "Hey, this is a private party," she began, falling silent when a spark leapt between her fingertip and Delaney's elbow.

He felt his own eyes widen as an unfamiliar heat spread through him like wildfire. Even though he'd never felt it before, Delaney knew exactly what it was.

His firestorm.

His last chance to do something right. It was a gift and a sign—*Slayers* didn't get firestorms, so Delaney knew that the Great Wyvern was blessing him with a chance.

He was going to use it.

His blood seemed to sizzle and he became keenly aware of everyone around him. He felt a desire so sharp and hot that it nearly took his breath away, and he knew the role of this woman in his life. This was how his body was supposed to work, and that predictability made him bold.

It didn't hurt that the petite redhead at his side was the cutest woman he'd ever seen. She was as small and delicate as a fairy, but more curvy than any fairy could have been. Her hair was a mass of coppery gold— long and curly and thick—and her eyes were blue and bright with curiosity. She looked on the verge of laughter, reminding him of a beam of sunlight dancing on the sea.

She was as different from him as a human could possibly be.

She wore a black sparkly camisole that highlighted the curve of her breasts and a flirty black skirt that danced around her hips. Her dangly earrings were set with amber, one of his favorite stones, and they swung against her cheeks as she talked. She was wearing very high-heeled strappy black sandals, but even with them, she stood only as high as the middle of his chest.

She was also a bit unsteady on them, as if she wasn't used to wearing such high heels.

She pursed her lips, flicked him a look, and touched her fingertip to his elbow once again.

He liked that she wasn't afraid.

The spark of the firestorm flared right on cue, lighting her features with golden splendor. She stepped backward in astonishment, caught her balance by grabbing the edge of the bar, but didn't run away.

Instead, she whistled in admiration, licked her fingertip, and made a hissing sound. Then she laughed.

It was the most enchanting sound Delaney had ever heard. Her laugh was lower than he would have expected, the laugh of someone who loved life and made the most of the moment.

He could admire that.

She wasn't spooked by him or the firestorm, which had to be a good sign. Delaney held her gaze and knew with utter clarity how he'd be spending his last night. He'd make one more play for the team. He'd consummate his firestorm and give Erik another *Pyr* for the ranks of his warriors.

It would be the right thing to do.

"You're a real firecracker," he said quietly, and she smiled. Her smile lit her face, and Delaney sensed that she smiled often.

He found himself smiling at her pleasure, the expression feeling unfamiliar upon his lips.

But good.

"You stole my joke," she complained, not looking offended in the least. "I was going to toss you out, but maybe there's more to you than meets the eye." She gave him an appreciative survey and her eyes shone with mischief. "Maybe I should say you're hot stuff."

"Maybe we should find out just how much sparks fly."

She laughed again and Delaney felt less burdened. "Or whether those who play with fire have to get burned."

"Now you stole my joke," he complained.

"Turnabout is fair play." She laughed again, then put out her hand. "Ginger Sinclair. Eternal bridesmaid, go-to party organizer, best chef in four counties."

"And the light of the night," Delaney said, wanting only to make her laugh again. She did and he felt triumphant.

Alive.

Daring.

"Delaney," he said, taking her hand. When his fingers

closed over hers, the firestorm's heat surged through his body from the point of contact, leaving him shimmering in its wake.

Leaving him unable to think of anything except peeling Ginger out of that camisole and skirt. There were freckles in her cleavage, a smattering of them that would extend across her breasts and over her shoulders. He wanted to find them all, caress them all, kiss them all.

Meanwhile, Ginger's eyes widened and she caught her breath, a flush launching over her cheeks as she stared up at him. She swallowed visibly. "Delaney what?"

"Just Delaney."

Her eyes sparkled again, a sign that she wasn't daunted by him. "All this and mystery, too. That could be too much for a little country girl like me."

"I think you can handle anything I've got."

Her smile turned coy and she let her gaze slide over him again. "Maybe."

"*Everything* I've got," he corrected.

Her smile broadened. "Maybe."

"Maybe a little chemistry is all we need."

"Maybe." Ginger nodded, and her gaze flicked to their interlocked hands. Delaney let his thumb slide across her skin, savoring its silky smoothness. A trail of embers followed in the wake of his slow caress.

Ginger stared at it, then licked her lips. "I think I've had too much to drink," she said, and fanned herself. "Do you find it hot in here?"

"It's only going to get hotter," Delaney promised softly, and she blushed a little. The bartender brought his beer and shooter, but Delaney wasn't interested in drowning his sorrows anymore.

He was interested in seducing tiny, perfect Ginger. ASAP.

The DJ put on a slow song, perfect timing. Delaney paid for the drink and left it behind, spinning Ginger toward the dance floor. "Come on, they're playing my tune."

She spared a glance over her shoulder at him, tilting her head to meet his gaze. "My gran told me not to slow dance with strangers." She was smiling, so he knew she was teasing him.

Flirting, maybe.

It felt good.

Light.

Closer to happy than he'd been in a long time.

He was going to make the most of the moment.

"I only slow dance. Are you turning me down?" He let his fingers slide up her bare arm and Ginger shivered with what he knew was desire.

"My gran also said you only live once," she said firmly, and took his hand in hers. She pivoted on the edge of the dance floor to face him, anticipation in her eyes. The dance floor was old, with pulsing lights in the floor, and the red and blue lights made intriguing shadows as her skirt flared out.

"Show me your best moves, Delaney No-Surname," she challenged, and Delaney didn't need a second invitation.

He knew they'd be doing more than one slow dance together before the night was through.

When he pulled Ginger into his arms and the firestorm shimmered between his chest and her breasts, she caught her breath and looked up at him in awe.

That was when he knew that she knew it, too.

"Only if you show me yours," he murmured.

The mischief in her smile made his heart skip. "You've got a deal, hotshot."

Delaney No-Surname was hot.

Not only was he the handsomest guy on the dance floor, not only could he dance, but he made Ginger feel like a queen. She knew her friends were checking him out, didn't doubt that they were wondering where he'd come from, but she didn't care. He was completely fixated on her and it felt good.

They could have been alone.

Ginger was starting to wish they *were* alone.

He was tall, more than just taller than she—everyone was taller than Ginger, but Delaney was taller than most of the men in the bar. He was lean but broad through the shoulders, and his jeans showed his legs and his butt to advantage. He looked as if he worked out all the time.

Maybe he had a job at a gym.

He wore a striped polo shirt and a leather jacket, the forest green in the shirt making his hair look more auburn. His hair was cut short, so short that the haircut and his trim build made her wonder whether he was in the service.

He had that taut authority, as well, his expression so impassive that his sudden smile felt like a gift. She liked the silver Celtic cross that he wore on a silver chain around his neck—it was both beautiful and spoke of their having a shared faith in something greater than themselves. There were shadows lurking in his eyes, all the same, and it took an extra beat for him to smile, making Ginger think he'd seen more than any person should.

Back from war, then. Not physically wounded but emotionally scarred. Ginger could relate to that.

Suddenly it didn't seem so depressing not to have had a date for the party she'd arranged for her two best friends.

It seemed more like kismet.

Delaney was a perfect gentleman, spinning her and making her look good, his eyes gleaming with admiration when she flaunted her stuff. He wasn't a predator or a violent person: Ginger could sense that sort of thing. He was scarred, but not bad.

He'd lied about only dancing slow dances: once they took to the floor, they kept dancing, regardless of what the DJ played. Ginger was hot and knew she was flushed—not the best look for a redhead, but she'd never have guessed by Delaney's obvious fascination with her. His attention made her feel gorgeous.

Sexy.

Daring.

The music changed to a slow beat again, the lights dimming, and Delaney swung her into his arms with no doubt that she'd be glad to be there. He was right. It was easy to fall against his chest, to be held close, to just enjoy a man treating her well. Ginger felt heat radiate from him and caught a whiff of his scent, masculine and clean. The little flurry of sparks that danced from every point of contact tickled and sizzled, making her laugh.

"How do you do that?" she asked, tipping her head back to watch him.

"Do what?" he asked, but she knew he was putting her on.

"Make the sparks."

"I thought you were the firecracker," he said, his voice dropping low as he smiled down at her. His intent expression made her heart skip a beat. "I thought you were the one who was hot stuff."

Ginger laughed. She wasn't so drunk that she'd lose her head, but she was feeling impulsive. She'd followed her heart for a long time and it had never steered her wrong.

And there was something about Delaney No-Surname that caught her attention and held it fast. He was a keeper and she knew it, maybe down on his luck, maybe a little lost, but she sensed his integrity and honor.

They moved slowly to the music, fitting together better than she could have expected. Her breasts brushed against his chest, the casual touch leaving her simmering.

Ginger was well aware of how long she'd been alone. Dancing with Delaney gave her one good idea what she could do about it.

Delaney's hand rested on the back of her waist, resolute and proprietary. She liked its weight there, liked it even better when his fingers began a slow stroke.

She was already hot, but his caress stoked the heat in her veins. Desire was kindled and coaxed to a flame. Ginger didn't believe in coincidences. She didn't believe that people came together by accident. She believed in destiny and kismet, and finding what—or whom—you needed right on time.

Her intuition told her that Delaney needed her, and she had a strong sense that she needed him, too. Stone-cold sober on a Tuesday morning, she might have waited to see. A little bit drunk on a Friday night—at yet another stag-and-doe, for yet another wedding of people she had introduced to each other—Ginger surrendered to impulse.

She moved closer to Delaney, putting her cheek on his chest. He hesitated only a moment before pulling her tighter into the circle of his arms.

A gentleman.

Ginger smiled. She'd read him right. She felt surrounded by his strength and exhaled with pleasure as his fingers slid into the hair at her nape. She swallowed when he rested his chin against the top of her head and closed her eyes as his breath slipped through her hair.

They moved together easily, keeping the beat of the music, as if they'd danced together a thousand times. As if this was meant to be. Ginger kept her eyes closed and listened to the pulse of Delaney's heart, content for the first time in she didn't know how long.

She would have been happy for the song to last forever, but of course, it didn't.

"Let's liven it up, people!" The DJ's voice boomed

abruptly through the bar, followed by the strong beat of a dance song. The lights began to pulse brightly and the dance floor suddenly became crowded.

Delaney and Ginger parted reluctantly and she saw an echo of her own surprise in his expression. She saw desire and she saw that he would wait for her to make the first move.

She did.

Ginger reached out and took Delaney's hand, giving his fingers a squeeze. There was a blaze of light between their hands, an orange flame that she halfway thought was a manifestation of her desire.

"There's something between us," Ginger said, raising her hand to his chest. Those sparks danced again, flickering yellow and orange around her fingertips, then settling to a glow that outlined her hand. She stared at them in awe, unable to explain their presence. The strobe lights came on, disguising the sparks from casual view, but Ginger could feel their sizzle. "It feels like magic."

"Not quite magic," Delaney agreed quietly. His eyes were dark, filled with mystery and shadow. He was solemn and intent, watchful, letting her set the pace. "But maybe close enough."

"You feel it, too?"

He nodded. "I felt it as soon as you tried to throw me out." His reluctant smile made her heart skip a beat. "As if you could."

Ginger laughed at the truth of that. "Points for effort?"

"Points for guts." He sobered then, his gaze admiring. "There's something very sexy about people who believe in themselves."

His hand slid along her jaw then, easing into her hair and cupping the back of her head. It was a possessive caress, one that made her tingle to her toes and left her mouth dry. Ginger knew what he was going to do and on one hand, she wished he would hurry.

On the other, it was delicious that he moved so slowly.

So deliberately.

It made her yearn.

Delaney studied her and Ginger simmered with the conviction that he was really looking at her. Ginger had been a substitute for another woman's affections before, and she was touchy about going that route ever again. Delaney, though, seemed to marvel at her, seemed determined to let her know that she was the one he wanted.

If that weren't sexy enough, if it weren't enough that he actually liked the outspokenness that some men found annoying, there was his kiss. He bent his head slowly toward her, giving her lots of time to evade him if that had been her plan.

As if.

Ginger slid her hands over his shoulders.

Delaney cupped her head in his hands, tipping her face upward. His mouth closed over hers with surety, leaving no doubt that he was claiming what he wanted.

Her.

Ginger melted. His kiss was firm and persuasive, his hands gentle and strong. It was a kiss as Ginger had always thought kisses should be: confident not tentative, resolute, honest. As intent upon giving pleasure as getting some.

It was Ginger's kind of kiss.

She let Delaney know she approved. She leaned against him, her breasts crushed against the hard strength of his chest as she locked her hands around his neck. She felt only solid muscle beneath her hands and knew he was stronger even than she had guessed.

But he was tender with her, tempering his power. Ginger would never have called herself fragile, but she liked being treated like a treasure. Delaney didn't try to curtail her passion, didn't disapprove of her desire or her communication of it.

He simply deepened his kiss. Ginger was captivated. She shivered as she ran her fingers over his short hair and felt his erection against his stomach.

Delaney wanted her, just as she was.

There could be no aphrodisiac more potent than that.

Delaney spread one hand across the back of her waist, lifting her to his toes as their tongues tangled and danced. Ginger felt the heat of desire burn within her, felt her body lust for more than just a kiss. She kissed him with fervor, encouraged that he responded immediately to her touch.

"Whoa!" Tanya said from close at hand. "Take it outside, Ginger, or keep it legal."

Ginger jumped at the sound of her best friend's voice. Her face heated as she blushed, but Delaney closed his arms protectively around her.

To her surprise, she and Delaney stood in a warm glow of light, as if they were in the middle of a bonfire. Some jerk must have turned one of the yellow spotlights on them.

If it bothered Ginger, it didn't bother Delaney. He brushed his lips across her forehead, then bent to whisper in her ear. His murmur was low enough to resonate in her veins, his intent expression enough to eliminate her reservations.

"I have a rental car," he said softly. "Let's drive."

"No," Ginger said, speaking so firmly that he met her gaze with surprise. "Come home with me."

He hesitated, looking deeply into her eyes. "Are you sure?"

"Are you turning me down, hotshot?"

Delaney shook his head, as if surprised that she could

imagine such a thing. "You said you'd had too much to drink." His gaze turned warm, as his fingertip slid across her cheek so slowly that Ginger shivered at the trail of heat. His words turned husky before his confession. "I won't regret anything we do, so I don't want you to, either."

His touch would have dissolved her knees, if his words hadn't done so first. Ginger had been matchmaking for a while, and she knew a good fit when she saw one.

"Let's go home," she said, placing her hand in his and heading for the door.

To Delaney's surprise, Ginger directed him away from the bright lights of the roadhouse and down a network of unlit roads. The power lines ran beside them, looping from pole to pole, occasional lights burning in the darkness from houses set well back from the road. They rode in silence, the warm glow of the firestorm between them. It was snowing, the white flakes spinning out of the sky in an endless dance. The world seemed quiet, pensive, on the cusp of a profound change.

When Delaney glanced Ginger's way, she smiled at him. He liked that her confidence in her choice never faltered.

His certainly didn't.

At her instruction, Delaney turned into a driveway beside a large sign that he couldn't read in the darkness. The house was several hundred yards from the road, on the left, and was an old two-storied house with ornate gingerbread trim hanging from the rafters. There was an old barn just behind it, then a large modern barn several hundred yards beyond that. A massive light illuminated the space in between house and barns. He could see the silhouette of solar panels on the roof of the new barn, although they couldn't have been effective with so much snow.

He parked outside the kitchen door beside a large faded red pickup truck.

Ginger got out of the car before he could open her door, bouncing up the steps of the wooden porch. She didn't teeter on her heels quite as much as she had in the bar.

Delaney took his time following her, gathering a sense of who she was from her home. The house was old, made of clapboard. It was in good shape, well-maintained, the shutters on either side of each window intact and straight. He smelled manure and straw in the crisp air, earthy scents of cultivation.

Delaney had missed farms, not the hard work that he'd found on them in the past, but the integrity and sense of unity with the earth. He felt a stab of regret at selling his own land, then dismissed it as irrelevant.

Maybe Ginger's connection with the earth was part of what he found so alluring about her.

She pivoted before the unlocked door and flashed him a smile. "Too long in the city," she said with an apologetic shrug. "I even lock the doors out here."

"That's only sensible."

Ginger laughed, a merry sound that lightened Delaney's heart. "Crazy city stuff, according to my gran." She mimicked a stern tone. "*No point in living someplace where you aren't safe or you don't feel safe.* That's what she always said."

Delaney understood that Ginger's grandmother had passed away. "Do you feel safe here?" he asked, curious.

Ginger's gaze flicked over the fields, sky, and barn, then she smiled at Delaney. "Depends. There's something to be said for the sound of others close at hand. It was strange to come back here, back to the quiet."

"Back to the earth."

"That part I like a lot." She seemed about to say more, then glanced at him. "Did you grow up on a farm?" He sensed that she was changing the subject, maybe to hide some of her own story.

"I worked on a farm for a long time." Delaney omitted the detail that he had later owned the farm. "The owner told me that once I got the earth under my nails, I'd never get it out." He shrugged. "He was right."

"He was," Ginger agreed softly. "I could never stop missing this place." She sighed. "It's just good, knowing where your food comes from and seeing your connection to the earth every day."

"You grow crops, then?"

"Well, not enough. I want to take the farm organic, to raise market vegetables, all organic, mostly heirloom varieties." She winced. "It's a ton of hard work, but I can taste the difference."

"Is that common here?"

Ginger laughed. "No! Everyone thinks I got crazy in the city. They're waiting to see me fail."

He saw her lips tighten as she looked across the fields and knew then the depth of her determination. "You won't fail," he said softly.

She met his gaze with a smile, an appealing conviction in her eyes. "No," she said with confidence. "I won't. Ten years from now, maybe twenty, they won't be able to believe they ever did anything different. I'll find a way to get it done. For now, there are the girls and they're a lot of work."

"The girls?"

"Sinclair Farms has always been a dairy farm. I have a hundred cows in the barn, most of them pregnant." She smiled. "We always had Guernseys, but I'm adding other heirloom and endangered breeds."

"They're easier on the land."

She smiled at him. "Exactly! Tanya went to chef school with me and followed me back here to become an artisan cheese maker. Then she met Steve and that was that."

"So you set them up."

"Yes and no." She flushed a little. "People tease me about matchmaking, but it's like putting the right ingredients together for a soufflé. You just know when you've got something special."

Delaney understood exactly what she meant.

"I love it here." She looked across the fields again, this time with pride, and Delaney followed her gaze. He sensed her bond with the land and her resolve to make a difference. He admired her certainty and wanted to know more about her plans for her own future.

To his own surprise, he felt a sense of common ground with her, so to speak, one that only enforced his sense of union. He could have lived like this, followed the same objectives. Delaney listened to the night and inhaled of the cold air, knowing that his senses would be sharper than hers.

He smelled *Slayer*, at a distance, and *Pyr* at a greater distance. He smelled the Dragon's Blood Elixir, not so far away that it could be forgotten, then cattle and compost and wildlife. He smelled coffee grounds in Ginger's kitchen, fresh laundry, her perfume, and was beguiled by the combination of Ginger with the earth he so loved. He concentrated on the scents more closely associated with humanity, with those linked with Ginger, and looked down into the vivid sparkle of her eyes.

She was his destined mate. The firestorm didn't lie.

But even the faint scent of *Slayer* lent an urgency to his reaction.

She was so fragile.

So vulnerable.

So oblivious to danger.

Delaney's protective urge shook him with its urgency, but despite its power, he knew what he had to do.

The conviction that sating his firestorm would be the last thing Delaney did in this life lent a potency to the moment. He felt a lump in his throat as he stood beside Ginger.

"What kind of farm did you work on?" she asked abruptly.

"A horse farm." He followed her to the porch, pausing beside her.

She tipped her head back to study him, intent upon the nuances of his answers. He didn't doubt that she'd see them. "Arabians?"

Delaney shook his head, hearing a doubt that echoed his own. "Not racehorses. The owner didn't like how they were treated in the racing world. More like machines than animals. I didn't like it much, either."

Ginger was watching them, understanding in her eyes.

"We bred workhorses."

"Belgians and Clydesdales?"

"Among other working breeds."

She put her hand in his and watched the little flurry of resulting sparks with a smile. "More glamorous than dairy cows."

Delaney squeezed her hand, feeling how small it was. "Doesn't everyone like milk?"

She smiled up at him. "I do." She wrinkled her nose. "And I like the girls. They have a serenity about them that's nice." She sighed. "Or maybe I'm just used to them. I can't imagine being here without cows in the pasture."

They stood for a moment, hand in hand on her porch, Delaney's heart pounding with what they were about to do. He felt the glow of the firestorm between their palms, a warmth that he could imagine was a resonance of the similarities in their perspectives.

He wanted to see her farm and hear her plans, meet her cows and talk about the future.

He couldn't do that, couldn't ask for more from her than she was already going to give him.

She was going to bear his child, after all.

"Are you sure?" he asked again, his words riding a white puff into the cold night.

Ginger grinned up at him. "You wouldn't be here otherwise, Delaney No-Surname."

"Shea," he said, reminding himself of the darkness within him when it might have been easily forgotten. "Delaney Shea." It was the first time he'd claimed the surname of his father. He'd always used his mother's name, Connaught, because his father had surrendered to the *Slayer* side. Using Shea now was a potent reminder of what Magnus had done to him.

But the confession of his name made Ginger brighten. "Delaney Shea," she repeated with satisfaction. "A good Irish name."

"It is Irish," Delaney agreed, bending to kiss her before he revealed more. It was too easy to give to Ginger, too easy to say things to make her smile.

It was better that Ginger know less about him rather than more. It would be easier for her to accept his disappearance if she didn't know where to look.

He should have made up a surname, but it was too late for that.

Then Ginger slipped her tongue into his mouth and Delaney forgot about everything but the lady in his arms.

Chapter 2

The heat surged through Delaney's body from every point of contact with Ginger, making his lips sizzle and his blood heat. The firestorm was a golden blaze, lighting his desire and coaxing it to an inferno.

Ginger's eyelashes fluttered down, her expression rapturous. Her fingers grasped the back of his neck, her back arched, and he felt the taut peaks of her nipples. She could have been made of firelight, all sparks and passion and heat. She was warm and giving, golden and gorgeous. He saw her as the source of the light of the firestorm, a radiant spark that warmed him to his darkest corners.

She was the dawn that awakened him from a long nightmare.

He had to make this night one of pleasure for her.

Delaney deepened his kiss, loving how Ginger moaned. Sparks shot into the air around them, falling into the snow beyond the porch, lighting the night. Delaney hauled open the kitchen door, then caught Ginger up in his arms, kissing her again. He carried her over the threshold, never breaking his kiss, and kicked the door shut behind them.

She framed his face in her hands and kissed as if she couldn't get enough of him.

Delaney could relate to that. He had a hard time believing that once with Ginger would be enough. She kicked off her high-heeled sandals and he heard them fall down the stairs behind them.

The bedroom she directed him toward had a hand-made quilt on the neatly made bed. A simple pine dresser and matching chair were the only other furniture in the room. The floors throughout the house were wide-planked pine, polished to a gleam.

Delaney fell onto the bed in the darkened room, his arms full of the sunshine that was Ginger. She rolled on top of him, and sat up, straddling him. Her hair was mussed, her cheeks flushed, and her lipstick smeared. Her earrings danced against her cheeks. She looked rumpled and alive, sparkling and animated. The desire in her eyes was enough to make Delaney catch his breath.

"Too many clothes," she said, wrinkling her nose in a gesture that made her look young and cute. She peeled off her jacket and cast it onto the floor, then bent over him to steal a kiss. Delaney gripped her buttocks and held her closer, liking how he was enveloped by her perfume. She moaned into his kiss, rubbing herself against him, and even with their clothes on, he thought he'd lose his mind.

His desire wasn't at fever pitch because it had been so long since he'd been with a woman—it raged because he had spent a lifetime without a woman like Ginger.

"Your turn," she said, rolling from his side breathless moments later.

Delaney didn't need a second invitation. He got up and tugged off his jacket, hanging it on the back of the chair.

"Sure," Ginger teased at his neatness. "Show me up."

She propped her chin on her hand to watch him, her

eyes dancing. She was lying on her stomach, and the angle let him see deeply down her cleavage. Delaney glimpsed a rosy nipple and the sight made his jeans tight. Her skirt had risen up, revealing the ripe curve of her bum, and she kicked her feet playfully in the air.

He could have devoured her.

He bent down, bracing his hands on the mattress and touched his nose to hers. "That's not what I'm going to show you," he teased.

She smiled, a glint of challenge in her eyes. They were as blue as a midnight sky, filled with twinkles that could have been stars. "Promises, promises." Then she sighed and examined her fingernails, supposedly bored by the delay.

Delaney wasn't fooled. Her playfulness, though, was infectious. He caught one of her feet, his hand closing around her ankle so that she couldn't squirm away. He ran his fingertips over the arch, then tickled the bottom of her foot.

As he'd expected, Ginger was ticklish. She whooped and struggled, squirming so that her skirt worked its way around her waist. Delaney was merciless, capturing the other ankle and repeating his teasing so that she writhed.

"Uncle, uncle!" Ginger cried, and he found himself amused by her antics. He held her feet against his chest and looked down the length of her legs, letting her see that he was surprised by the sight. She wore lacy black panties, black stockings, and a matching garter belt. The black against her creamy skin was dramatic and very sexy.

This woman was his fantasy come to life.

"Stockings and garters?" he asked, desire making him nearly incoherent.

Ginger blushed even though she sighed with mock

concession. "Call me an optimist." She giggled then, not in the least contrite for her choice of sexy attire.

"I like stockings and garters," Delaney admitted, his words falling low. That was the understatement of the century and he suspected that Ginger heard as much in his tone.

Her cheeks burned vivid red. "Then optimism has paid off."

"Not quite yet," he murmured. He kept her ankles captive in one hand—she was tiny enough—and bent over her. He caught one garter in his teeth, then met her astonished gaze as he unfastened it.

Ginger gasped and stared at him, a flicker of sparks dancing between Delaney's mouth and her skin. He felt the fan of his own breath against her skin, felt the answering heat rise from her flesh. He eased his tongue across her scented skin, knowing he'd never forget the smell of her lotion.

He repeated his trick with the other garters, taking his time unfastening her stockings. Then he released her ankles, locking his hands around her thighs. He eased his fingers beneath the stockings, tickling and caressing her smooth skin. She was soft and strong, compliant and excited. He was assailed by the scent of her perfume.

And her desire. Delaney slowly slid his hands down the length of Ginger's legs, easing the stockings toward her feet, the sheer fabric catching on his palms.

A shimmer of golden heat followed his hands, crackling against her skin, leaving her both flushed and gasping.

He caught her lacy black underwear with a fingertip and tugged it down toward her knees. Ginger caught her breath, but she didn't move away. He flung her underwear over his shoulder, then dropped to his knees, her legs on his shoulders. He inhaled deeply of her scent, savored the softness of her thighs, then bent to touch his tongue to her slick heat.

A spark leapt from his tongue to her, making her gasp. Delaney closed his mouth over her, teasing her to pleasure. She writhed and he locked his hands on her hips, holding her captive to the pleasure he was determined to give.

He felt the heat build between them, felt desire rise to a crescendo. He heard Ginger's heart pound and her pulse race, felt her quick intake of breath as surely as if it had been his own. He coaxed the firestorm to burn hotter between them, urging it to be more insistent with every passing moment, with every caress.

He felt Ginger hover on the cusp of release and felt a wave of tenderness for this woman, this spark who would bear his son.

This fascinating woman he'd never see again.

He paused, let her squirm, exhaled so that his breath made her cry out in frustration.

"Tease!" she gasped, and reached for his shoulders.

Delaney flicked his tongue across her heat, deliberately and firmly, grazing her clitoris with his teeth.

Ginger cried out in her release, twisting on the bed before him as he prolonged her pleasure. He wasn't entirely sure who enjoyed her orgasm more. When she shuddered and stilled, he pressed a kiss to the inside of her thigh, ran a hand over the soft length of her thigh, then eased her to the mattress. He straightened, drinking in the sight of her.

"Oh," Ginger said softly, astonished to near silence.

"Oh," Delaney echoed. She laughed. It was easy to banter with Ginger, and he wished for a heartbeat that he could stay with her.

Seduce her even more slowly.

Even build a future.

But he didn't have that right. He'd take what he could have and be glad of it.

Delaney shook out Ginger's stockings, looped them around her ankles, and tied them in a lazy knot to the bedpost. "Don't move," he said, knowing that she could easily slip away. He liked the look of her, though, rumpled and half bare, surprised and pleased.

"Are you going to make it worth my while?"

"What do you think?"

She laughed again. "Well, based on recent experience, I'd say the chances of that are pretty good." There was no doubting her satisfaction and her warm smile made Delaney feel good.

As if he'd finally done something right.

As if he had his old verve back.

Ginger lounged on the bed, looking disinclined to go anywhere.

Delaney peeled off his shirt and folded it on the chair, then kicked off his boots and jeans. Socks and underwear and the T-shirt he'd worn beneath the rugby shirt joined the folded pile, and then he turned to regard his pleased mate. He wore only his mother's cross, because he'd vowed never to take it off.

Ginger's gaze slipped over him, as surely as a caress, and dropped to his erection.

"Oh," she said again, smiling with a familiar enthusiasm.

Delaney unknotted the stockings slowly, letting his fingertips slide over her skin. She shivered as the sparks danced between them. "You didn't move," he whispered.

"Do I get a reward?"

"Didn't you already have it?"

"That's backward," she laughed at him. "I want another."

Delaney rolled her over and knelt on the mattress beside her. He unfastened the back of her glittery camisole and the zipper in her skirt. She rolled to her back, kicking off the skirt and tossing it on the floor.

"Old habits die hard," she said, then her smile broadened as her gaze fell to his erection again.

He removed her camisole in one smooth gesture, revealing the lacy black of her strapless bra. He shouldn't have been surprised—it matched her underwear—but he was momentarily awed by the splendor of his mate.

"Too big?" she whispered, the first quiver of doubt in her tone. Delaney wasn't going to let her imagine there was anything less than splendid about her.

"Too perfect," he said firmly, then cupped one breast in his hand. He liked the ripeness of it, the fullness and abundance of it. Her curves spoke to him of passion and life, of pleasure, and all the things he was doomed to leave behind.

The things that Magnus and his Elixir had stolen from Delaney.

He bent, wishing things could have been otherwise, and pressed a reverent kiss to Ginger's breast. He slipped her nipple free of its lacy confines and flicked his tongue across it, making her moan again.

Within moments, the bra was on the floor and there were just the two of them, naked in Ginger's bed. They caressed and whispered, explored and savored, finding each other's sensitivities and exploiting them over and over again. They teased each other, the firestorm's loving light playing over both of them.

And when he was finally buried inside her, looking into the dancing lights of her eyes, Delaney's awe was complete.

"Oh," she whispered, her hands on his shoulders and her blue gaze locked on him.

"Oh," Delaney echoed, not troubling to hide that he was overwhelmed, too.

She reached up and kissed his cheek, her breath sliding across his skin and making him simmer. "I knew I was right about you," she murmured.

Delaney didn't have time to ask what she meant. She was too tight, too hot, too perfect. Ginger pulled him down for a kiss, even as his pulse became as loud as thunder, and he claimed her mouth triumphantly. He moved within her, astounded that lovemaking could be so glorious and intimate.

Ginger was vital and passionate. She was honest and outspoken. She was everything Delaney had sought all of his life.

She was more than enough.

But she wasn't his to keep.

He wished with heartfelt intensity that things could have been different between them, that they could have had a chance, that they might have met in another time and place.

When he had been whole.

Then the tide of desire swept through him, pushing reasonable thought aside, leaving only sensation and yearning. They moved together, his awe reflected in her eyes, amplified by the yellow blaze of the firestorm. They pushed each other higher and harder, their hearts pounding in unison, the connection between them drawing tighter with every stroke.

It got hotter in the room, perspiration sliding through Delaney's hair, between Ginger's breasts, lighting on their lips and mingling in their frantic kisses. The inferno of the firestorm burned brighter and hotter, brighter and hotter than Delaney could have believed possible, until suddenly, they climaxed as one.

The room was showered in brilliant yellow sparks. Delaney had to close his eyes against the light and Ginger shouted before she moaned.

Delaney leaned over her, bracing his weight above her even though he was spent. He had the seductive sense that he'd finally come home.

Just in time to leave forever.

*   *   *

Delaney lay in the darkness as Ginger slept beside him, once again fighting his body's urge to sleep. It would have been easy to doze in Ginger's bed, easy to believe that his life had changed and that everything would be different because of his firestorm.

Delaney knew better. He knew the nightmare was waiting to claim his thoughts and destroy his confidence. He knew that this moment, however precious, was an illusion. He was spooked by the memory of the eclipse's effect upon him and the conviction that something evil lurked inside him. It could awaken at any time. There was no future, for him or for the *Pyr*, so long as the Elixir existed.

It was still snowing, the snowflakes falling fast and thick outside the window. He watched them spiral out of a fathomless dark sky, knowing that the world would be blanketed in white silence by the morning.

He was reluctant to move. He wanted to stay with Ginger, learn her secrets, know her as well as he knew himself.

But Delaney knew that this moment was just an interval. It had been stolen from his destiny, only because the Great Wyvern had seen fit to give him the chance to reproduce before he died. Delaney was grateful for that gift and grateful for this night, but it didn't really change anything. It couldn't. He had a mission, one he had chosen himself, and he had to fulfill it.

Delaney couldn't let himself think of what Ginger would think of him the next morning, when she awoke to find him gone without a word. He wouldn't think about her annoyance when she realized he'd left her pregnant. She was resilient and smart—she'd come to terms with what he was compelled to do, and she'd raise their child well.

If anything, being with Ginger redoubled his determination to destroy the Elixir. He knew that he wouldn't ever betray this woman who had shared so much of herself with him. He had to make the world safe for her, and for the son who would result from this night. He had no real choice.

But Delaney had plenty of regret. He watched the snow fall for longer than he should have. With Ginger beside him, he felt a peace within himself that he hadn't experienced since his imprisonment. He felt optimism, and a sense of possibilities. He felt the return of his old confident self, a self he had almost forgotten. He reminded himself that this moment couldn't last, that it was stolen.

He still wanted it.

It was the realization that the *Slayers* would sense the firestorm that jolted Delaney to action. They were already close at hand. He was frightened then, frightened that he had already put Ginger at risk.

He sent a message in old-speak to Erik, terse and urgent. *"Defend my mate in my memory."*

"Wait for me." Erik's reply was tinged with more than an increment of irritation.

"No. Promise me."

There was a pause, a hesitation that made Delaney glad he wasn't in Erik's presence. Erik might change Delaney's mind with persuasive arguments, might weaken his determination.

The words came finally, sending relief through Delaney's body. *"You know I will. But wait for me."*

Delaney heard reluctance in Erik's concession, but it heartened him all the same.

"You know that I can't." He gave Ginger's name and location to Erik, knowing the details were unnecessary. Between the heat of the firestorm and Erik's powers of foresight, the leader of the *Pyr* probably already had a good idea of her location.

But Delaney had to be sure.

When Erik would have continued the discussion, Delaney closed his mind against the persuasiveness of old-speak, willing himself not to hear it.

He had to focus.

Erik would find Ginger. Erik would come. Erik would ensure that Delaney's son was raised by the *Pyr*.

Erik could answer Ginger's inevitable questions.

Erik would see the son Delaney never would.

Delaney had done what he could.

Now he had to do what needed to be done.

Delaney breathed smoke as he lay beside his destined mate, breathed an unbroken stream of dragonsmoke. He guided it to encircle her house; he wove it into a barrier that traditionally would have been regarded as an impenetrable barrier to any other *Pyr*.

He knew, even as he breathed his protective smoke, that the old perimeter mark was less reliable than it had once been. He knew that Magnus and his minions had found a way to breach a dragonsmoke barrier, even without the permission of the *Pyr* who had created it. It was a violation of how the *Pyr* world had worked for centuries and a bad portent for the future.

It was a development that came from the Dragon's Blood Elixir. Drinking the Elixir gave *Slayers* these unnatural powers, powers that should have been reserved for the Wyvern. Delaney's determination to destroy the source of the Elixir grew with every breath of dragonsmoke he exhaled.

If nothing else, though, the resonant ring of a complete dragonsmoke territory mark would summon Erik directly to Ginger's location.

He knew it was an excuse, that breathing a dragonsmoke perimeter that might not make any difference gave him more time in Ginger's presence. He savored every second of it, while she slept, curled against him.

When Delaney was done, when the smoke was as thick and deep and interwoven as he could make it, Delaney pressed a kiss into Ginger's tangled hair and was startled at the spark that leapt from his lips to her temple.

It must have been only the last vestige of the firestorm, its dying embers. The firestorm was satisfied; Delaney knew it. He and Ginger had been intimate and she would bear his son.

Maybe he had imagined the spark.

Maybe it was a manifestation of his temptation to stay, to talk to Ginger, to explain.

But if he waited one more minute, Delaney would lose his will to do what had to be done.

He forced himself to leave the warm bed, to ignore how Ginger rolled into the hollow where he had been and sighed contentment. He dressed quickly, knowing there was too much at stake for hesitation. He left the house silently, hoping the sound of the car engine wouldn't wake up Ginger.

It was cold enough to stop his heart when he stepped outside—or maybe it was something else that made his heart clench when he crossed the threshold—but Delaney knew what he had to do.

He owed his son a future.

Lingering wouldn't change anything.

In fact, delay only diminished the chance of his success.

Ginger awakened with a sense that the world was good. She stretched, letting herself awaken slowly. Three of her grandmother's quilts were piled on top of her bed, as light as a feather but warm enough to tempt her to stay put.

Of course, there were other reasons to stay in bed today.

One big reason was named Delaney.

She'd been right about him, absolutely right. Once again, her instincts had steered her straight and she was glad to have listened to them.

Ginger kept her eyes closed for a long moment, wanting to hold on to her sense of warmth and goodwill. Delaney was an amazing lover, one who left her both sated and hungry for more. It had been a while since she had greeted the day with such a positive attitude. Gran's death had shaken Ginger and uprooted her usual optimism, made her wonder whether a world in which she was left alone could truly be a good place.

Of course, she had pinned a smile on her face and gone about the business of living, but she didn't know how many friends she had fooled. It wasn't in the Sinclair genes to break down in public, to surrender, or to admit to a weakness.

In private, there was no one to witness that truth.

Ginger acknowledged there had been a reason, just as Gran had always insisted. She recognized that solitude had sharpened her instincts and made her more prepared to seize opportunity when it—or he—strode through the door. A year ago, she would have let Delaney walk away. A year ago, she would have waited—and hoped—that he'd approach her.

But now, Ginger knew that life was what you made of it, and that there was always a clock ticking somewhere. When Delaney had walked into the bar the night before, she'd felt as if she'd recognized him on sight. Maybe it was her heart that recognized him. Either way, she'd had to talk to him, even if it meant making the first move. She'd felt good flirting with him.

And what had come after that had been even better.

Best of all, it was just the beginning of something Ginger knew would be good, would be exactly what she'd been waiting for. She knew, right in her bones, that she'd made exactly the right choice.

Maybe she knew it in her genes.

She stretched, then reached across the mattress, her hand moving under the layer of quilts and over the smooth cotton sheet, her eyes still closed.

But there was no one there.

The bed was cold.

She awakened abruptly, rolled over, and stared around the room. Delaney was gone, and not just down the hall. There was no sound of another person in the house, no smell of coffee brewing, no spatter of the shower running.

Delaney's clothes were gone.

There was nothing left but his scent on the pillow and her memory of his seductive touch.

Ginger realized belatedly that she'd been awakened by the sound of a car engine. She got out of bed faster than she ever had in her life and rubbed the frost from the inside of the old window.

Two tracks in the snow were all that marked the presence of Delaney's rental car.

They hadn't filled with snow, even though the flakes were falling fast.

He couldn't have gotten far.

He wouldn't get much farther without answering to her. The good news was that the girls were in transition and didn't need to be milked this morning. The chickens could take care of themselves. There was nothing to stop her from pursuing Delaney Shea.

Ginger wanted some answers before he disappeared from her life. Great sex didn't happen by accident— she knew that—and her instincts had never yet been wrong.

If nothing else, Delaney could look her in the eye when he dumped her.

He owed her that much.

If not a whole lot more.

Ginger pulled on a pair of jeans and layered a fleece vest over a cotton turtleneck and T-shirt. She grabbed a thick pair of socks on her way out the bedroom door, spent a minimum of time in the bathroom, and trotted down the stairs with her hair tied in a ponytail. Her boots and jacket were beside the back door, her hat and gloves jammed into the jacket's pockets.

The pickup was as cold as ice and she said a little prayer as she turned the key. The old truck was getting increasingly finicky, and cold weather brought out its worst.

The engine started on the third try, then sputtered. She gave it a teeny bit of gas, just the way Gran had taught her, and it settled into a choppy purr.

Ha! Ginger swept the snow from the windows and roof, then scraped the ice from the windshield. She glanced down the long lane before getting back into the truck, and decided it would be a good day to travel prepared.

She ducked back into the kitchen, leaving the truck running, and rummaged in the purse she had dropped on the counter the night before. Her cell phone could have stood to be recharged, but it wasn't that surprising that she'd forgotten about it the night before. She took it anyway. Her wallet and keys went into her pockets. She grabbed the emergency flashlight as well as an extra blanket. She was heading out the door when she saw Gran's rifle leaning in the corner, just as it always was.

She remembered her determination not to use it, and the way Luke, the neighbor's son who came to help with the girls, had mocked her.

"What kind of chef doesn't know where meat comes from?" he'd asked. "What kind of chef doesn't get blood on her hands?"

There was something irritating about Luke and it was more than his assumption that Ginger should go out with him, just because.

Luke had shown her coyote tracks around the barn the previous winter, and she'd suspected he'd been trying to frighten her.

"A coyote can't take down a cow," she'd insisted, knowing she was right.

Luke had smiled, his condescension making Ginger want to deck him. "You can't always count on wild things knowing the rules, city girl."

"Even in the city, wild things follow their instincts," Ginger had retorted.

Luke's smile had faded. "Around here, sometimes you've got to solve things yourself, city girl." He'd leaned closer. "Sometimes, you gotta get your hands dirty."

It had been Gran, unable to rise from her bed, who had set Ginger straight. "A coyote can't take a cow," she'd said, coughing in between each word. Then she'd shaken a finger at her granddaughter. "You're right— Luke is trying to see what you're made of. But a coyote can take a calf, especially a sickly one or a young one. You can't risk that predator being here come spring."

It had been the first time Gran had said "you" instead of "we."

That was when Ginger had known her gran was going to die, and that her gran knew it, too.

She'd recognized that she had to prove herself, not just to Luke but to her gran. She'd gotten the rifle from the corner, cleaned it just the way she'd been shown by her grandfather, loaded it, and stalked that coyote.

She'd shot it right through the heart, a one-shot kill.

Clean, just as Grampa had taught her.

Then Ginger had dragged the carcass to the spot where Luke always parked his truck in the morning. It had left a long trail of red blood in the snow.

Luke had never said a thing, although she saw him looking that next morning after he parked and before he went into the barn. Ginger didn't know what had happened to the carcass.

But she did know that Luke had never called her "city girl" again.

And her gran had nodded with satisfaction when told of the news.

She'd died three days later.

The fact that she had even noticed the rifle this morning told Ginger that she might need it. She couldn't imagine why, but she went with her gut instinct, grabbing it and putting a box of ammo in her pocket, just in case. She took the shovel from the porch, too, and put it in the back of the truck, just in case she got stuck.

The snow was still falling fast, piling up with alarming haste.

The truck had warmed up and the windows were clear. Ginger slowly backed up. The big tires got traction, despite the depth of the snow, and the headlights picked out the trail of Delaney's tire tracks. She put the big red truck into four-wheel drive, not even thinking about what it would do to her gas consumption, and drove.

At the end of the driveway, Ginger got out and looked more closely at Delaney's tire tracks. She studied the distance between the tires, the width of each tire, the amount of snow in each one.

Then she headed onto the road. On her quiet side road, Delaney's tracks were the only set, but that wouldn't last.

Ginger Sinclair was going to get her man.

Chapter 3

The scent of *Slayer* and Elixir had led Delaney to the Serpent Mound the week before, and that was his destination of the morning. He'd done a lot of research since locating the site, and could have walked the site blindfolded.

He certainly didn't have a hard time finding it in the snow.

The Serpent Mound was an earthwork, an effigy of a snake winding alongside Brush Creek. The snake figure was four or five feet tall, made of mounded earth and stone, and almost a quarter of a mile long. At one end, its tail wound in a curl; at the other, its mouth was open. There was an oval shape before the mouth and people had argued over its meaning. Was that oval a platform for some forgotten ritual? Was it representative of an egg? Of the sun?

Current scholarship dated its construction as roughly nine hundred years ago, but the identity of its builders was as uncertain as its meaning.

But then, Delaney reasoned, archaeologists had never asked the *Pyr* what they knew of the Serpent Mound.

It had been noted that the head of the serpent was aligned to the summer solstice sunset and some had declared other intersections between the tail and coils with equinoxes and solstices. Some had suggested connections between the Serpent Mound and other massive earthworks, like Stonehenge. There were theories that its construction was in reaction to observation of Halley's Comet in 1066 and the Crab Nebula's light in 1054. Others speculated that the Serpent Mound was allied with the stars in the constellation Draco.

Draco. The dragon.

Delaney knew that last detail wasn't a coincidence.

He guessed that Magnus Montmorency, leader of the *Slayers*, had deliberately chosen this ancient work—protected as a state park for more than a hundred years—as the marker for the sanctuary of the Dragon's Blood Elixir. It had been the Romans, after all, who had named that constellation Draco and Magnus had never been able to resist a reference to his own origins.

Perhaps he had also liked that his treasure was hidden beneath a protected piece of land. The Serpent Mound might be excavated, but the work would never be deep enough to unearth the truth.

The Serpent Mound was also located in an area of strange geology for the region. The Serpent Mound crypto-explosion structure was roughly five miles in diameter and comprised of faulted bedrock, unusual for Ohio. This kind of bedrock was found at sites of meteorite impact or volcanic eruption, and opinions were divided as to which caused this rock formation—recent scholarship favored a meteorite.

Delaney knew it had been a meteorite. He knew there were heavy metals buried deep in the earth beneath the effigy, metals with vibrations he could sense. Rafferty, he suspected, would have been highly aware of the presence of these alien minerals, given his strong affinity for the earth. Rafferty would have been able to name them individually, like old friends.

What Delaney didn't yet know was that the meteorite's impact also had opened fissures, crevasses, and faults that stretched deep into the earth. Water had had millions of years to widen those faults, to erode the rock, molecule by molecule. Where once there had been cracks, there were caves.

A labyrinth.

And at the core of the labyrinth, directly beneath the mysterious oval mound and deep in the earth, was the sanctuary where Magnus had secured the Dragon's Blood Elixir.

Delaney didn't know any of that, and he didn't care. He only knew where he was going and why. The Serpent Mound State Memorial wasn't open to visitors so early in the morning, but Delaney parked his car in the lot anyway.

He had some walking to do.

The snow was fluffy, obscuring the landscape beneath its gentle white drifts. The sun was a pale orb in an overcast sky, offering no warmth and little more illumination than the snow itself. It was cold when Delaney stepped out of the car, colder when snow slid inside the collar of his jacket and landed on his bare hands. Delaney shivered. He wasn't dressed appropriately for the weather, but he wasn't worried.

By midday he'd be dead, anyway.

Delaney trudged toward the Serpent Mound with purpose, the snow as deep as his knees. The gate was easily breached, and there was no one present to challenge him. He was struck by the magical aura of the place, the sense that it was potent and special. The wind seemed to still as he drew nearer to the effigy itself, if more piercingly cold.

The headache erupted between Delaney's ears as

soon as he left his car. It throbbed with an insistence he remembered from his recurring nightmare, and he refused to let its dark promise invade his thoughts.

He didn't have the luxury of letting his resolve be weakened.

Delaney followed the song in his blood, the siren's call of the vestige of Elixir in his veins being drawn to its source. Delaney didn't like the place, much less his sense that its purpose had been subverted and twisted by Magnus.

The sooner he could destroy the Elixir, the better.

Delaney passed the Serpent Mound, following the footpath. He slid down to the river when he tried to take the narrow path he'd used the other day, filling his jeans and boots with cold snow. He pulled himself to his feet with the help of a pair of sturdy cedars, then followed the course of Brush Creek upstream.

He could have shifted shape, but Delaney knew that Magnus's awareness of him would be sharper when he took that other form. He didn't expect to arrive unannounced, but stayed in human form longer than might have been ideal.

Maybe it was a way of delaying the inevitable.

He climbed the fence that marked the boundary of the land owned by the historical society. He caught the first whiff of dragonsmoke and sensed a break in the territory mark.

Was Magnus losing his edge?

No. Delaney had sensed other breaks in the dragonsmoke perimeter mark around the sanctuary and he guessed they were deliberately left. Magnus wasn't interested in keeping *Pyr* out of the sanctuary, not if they came for that first sip of the Elixir that would leave them beholden to the old *Slayer* forever.

Delaney continued to the point where the river slid underground, the hole almost hidden by the thick growth of cedars. He'd found this spot earlier in the week, but it marked the full extent of his exploration.

His head was pounding, the headache growing stronger with every step he took closer to the sanctuary, and he winced against the brightness of the snow. He didn't know what he'd find inside this hole, except that the Elixir was there. The scent of *Slayer* was strong and Delaney guessed that several of them had also come recently to this spot.

He lifted his gaze, scanning the horizon, and eyed the house perched in the snow, not far across the fields. It was the closest residence. Delaney wondered whether that person owned this land, whether he or she had any idea that an access to another world lurked on the property. The house looked new, of low and broad construction, and its driveway was gated as few driveways were in the area.

The scent of *Slayer* emanated from it in such strong waves that Delaney suddenly guessed who owned it. He narrowed his eyes and worked through the individual scents, not surprised at the identities of the *Slayers* in that house.

Balthasar.

Mallory.

Jorge.

Three of Magnus's henchmen.

And three other *Slayers* whom Delaney couldn't name. They might have come and left, or they might still be in the house, hidden in its depths. Their scents were faint yet worrisome.

There was no scent of Magnus himself, but Delaney knew that some of the older *Slayers* had learned to disguise their scent. He had no doubt that Magnus was present and accounted for.

The scents that approached the point where the river dove into the earth were overwhelmed by the smell of the Elixir. Its scent was overwhelming, intoxicating, spicy and exotic. Seductive. Promising. Deceptive. It tickled Delaney's senses, teasing him with false possibilities and empty promises.

And the nightmare vision that had tormented him sharpened, shoving its way into his thoughts. He saw darkness and ice, saw the shadow devouring the earth in the same way as an eclipse appears to consume the moon.

But the earth would never emerge from the Elixir's shadow.

Delaney shoved the dream out of his thoughts and glared at the distant house. Magnus needed to watch the elimination of his source of power. It was a dare the old Delaney would have made, a bold gamble that he would have offered before he had been imprisoned.

It was the right choice, to die as once he had lived. Delaney sent three words toward the quiet house, dispatching them to Magnus in old-speak.

"Come stop me." It was a taunt, one he knew Magnus would take.

Delaney didn't wait for an answer. He scrambled to the lip of stone, slid into the hole, and let the river take him down into the earth. It was like a waterslide, albeit a bumpy one, and he braced himself for his arrival at its foot. It was dark, as dark as pitch, the light of the morning disappearing behind him quickly as he slid downward.

And it was as cold as ice.

He sensed a pulse of red light before he saw it, the scent of the Elixir growing impossibly strong. His body tumbled out of the access route, and he rolled across hard stone. The river danced and gurgled, carving its underground course. Delaney stood and eyed the red glow coming through the opening before him, the one that the water had abandoned. His headache pounded in time with the red pulse.

As if he were already a part of the Elixir's toxin.

There was an iron grate locked over the opening, one that would provide a formidable barrier to a human intruder, but was no more substantial than a gate of straw to a dragon.

Delaney shifted shape with lightning speed, motivated by the Elixir's shadow growing in his mind. He felt large and strong, more powerful and determined than he had in a while. It was a gift of the firestorm, a surety born of his conviction that his legacy would continue.

Delaney would make a difference and he would make it now.

He reared back, hovering before the gate, and released a stream of dragonfire. The iron heated to red, then white, then began to melt. He ripped the weakened steel loose with one claw, broke the hinges and the locks, and cast it aside.

Nothing would stop him now. He flew into the labyrinth, moving with all the speed he could muster, determined to put his destiny behind him.

The destruction of the Elixir's source was long past due.

The Serpent Mound parking lot was the weirdest place for Delaney to have stopped and the last place Ginger would have expected to find him.

But the car tracks had led her directly there, and the rental car was the same brown Pontiac that she'd ridden in the night before.

It even had that big scratch across the dashboard.

Ginger eyed the footprints that made a trail from the car into the snow. Why on earth would Delaney come to a park before it was open, and in the middle of a blizzard, as well?

She admitted there could be a great many things she didn't know about her sexy lover.

And maybe she was about to find out one of them.

The snow fell steadily, cloaking the park in silence. The wind was almost nonexistent, and the stillness combined with the relentless cascade of snow might have been soothing under other circumstances.

As it was, Ginger was nervous. She didn't know why, couldn't name her fear, but didn't like this development one bit.

She followed Delaney's tracks. She remembered there was a footpath running between the effigy and the river, intended to give visitors a good view of the mysterious earth mound.

She strode through the deep snow, trying to remember whether she'd last been to the park in sixth grade or seventh. Maybe Delaney had missed his school trip.

Ha. It was better, Ginger told herself, to discover that he'd come to a national monument than to find he'd gone to another woman's home, or back to his halfway house, or . . .

She stopped when she saw Delaney's footprints veer from the footpath to continue alongside the creek. There was nothing but bush along there, at least as far as she knew. A cedar branch had been broken and it looked as if he'd slipped on the snowy slope, sending a spill of fresh snow down to the frozen surface of the creek.

The tracks carried on, though, unmistakable. There was no one else in the park. Why would Delaney go down there? Why now? Ginger nibbled her bottom lip, her bad feeling suddenly amplified.

Was Delaney doing a drug deal, out where it couldn't be witnessed? That would explain his secrecy and the imperative of making the meeting. People who bore scars could get themselves into all kinds of complicated situations, without really understanding what they were doing.

Ginger couldn't think of a single other plausible explanation. The snow fell, piling on her hood and her shoulders, dusting the backs of her hands, filling his tracks. It might be foolish to continue, but there was no question of Ginger abandoning her quest now. She was too curious to leave without knowing the truth.

Whatever it was. If she was wrong about Delaney, she wanted to know what mistake she had made, and just how wrong she was. The only way anyone ever learned anything, her gran had taught her, was to review a bad choice.

Even if she still had a strong sense that Delaney was a keeper. Was her intuition that far wrong? Ginger needed to know for sure.

But she wasn't going to follow him blind and unprotected.

Ginger went back to the truck, loaded the rifle, and retraced her footsteps. She took a deep breath, then followed Delaney's trail, albeit with a little more caution than she'd used before.

She hoped that curiosity didn't have to kill the cat.

Things didn't get any more promising as Ginger progressed.

Delaney's tracks followed the creek. She knew that he had headed upstream, even though there was a thin coat of ice on the creek that obscured its moving surface. The ice wasn't strong enough to support much weight, probably because of the current running beneath. Ginger saw where the paws of raccoons had broken through to the cold water.

The last thing she wanted was a soaker, so she didn't step on the ice. Even so, Ginger had a hard time keeping her footing on the sloped bank. She saw that Delaney had held on to cedars and brush as he went—their boughs were occasionally bent and many were devoid of snow—so she did the same.

She paused for only a moment where he had climbed the fence that marked the perimeter of the property held in trust for the protection of the monument. The property beyond would be private, and she would be trespassing.

On the other hand, Ginger doubted anyone would follow her on a day like this one.

She climbed the fence herself.

There were open fields visible beyond the brush that lined the creek, and she could see several houses. The closest one was new, a low-slung, large bungalow, complete with a gated drive. A lazy swirl of smoke rose from its chimney on this chilly morning.

The others, farther afield, were old farmhouses like her own. She thought that maybe the next one was the Van Vliet farm. They kept dairy goats, brown ones. She narrowed her eyes and was sure she saw brown animals moving beside the barn behind the old house.

Her gaze flicked back to the newer house as she recalled Paul van Vliet bragging about the sweet price he'd gotten for selling a piece of land to some businessman from down east.

That had been on one of her visits to Gran, maybe ten years ago. She recalled everyone joking about Paul giving this businessman their number. Cash was never easy to come by in Adams County and there had inevitably been those who resented the Van Vliets' sudden good fortune.

Was this house Delaney's destination? It made a kind of sense that he as a stranger might have a connection with the only other stranger in the area.

If so, why not just drive there and knock on the door?

Maybe she was seeing connections that didn't exist.

Ginger followed Delaney's tracks, noting that they continued to cling to the same side of the creek, the side opposite the house. How far would he go? She rounded a bend and saw the tracks slide into a hole in the snow.

The water burbled and bubbled there. Closer inspection revealed that a part of the creek went underground from this point and that a hole had been worn in the rocks. Ginger brushed away some overhanging snow and peered into the tunnel that looked like it fell toward the center of the earth. It was about three feet in diameter, dark and wet.

She looked around, but there was no doubt of what had happened. There were no departing tracks.

Delaney had gone into the hole.

He hadn't come out yet.

But another set of tracks came up from the creek's edge, partly obscuring Delaney's tracks. They, too, were the size of a man's boots, like Delaney's but with a different tread. They had less fresh snow in them than Delaney's tracks.

Someone else had followed him into the tunnel.

Did Delaney know?

Was this the person he'd planned to meet?

Ginger intended to find out.

She was in the hole, sliding down the wet tunnel on her backside before she realized the pursuing tracks had materialized from nothing. The tracks began at the lip of unbroken ice over the creek. The man hadn't marred the snowy surface by crossing the creek or broken the ice by coming from the water. He hadn't followed the same trail as Ginger and he hadn't come from any other point.

It was as if he hadn't existed before he left his boot prints not twelve feet from the entry to the tunnel. He could have parachuted down from Mars.

Except there was no parachute.

Maybe he had been standing there, waiting for

Delaney, as the snow filled the tracks that marked his arrival.

But then, why was there so much difference in the amount of snow in the two men's tracks? If he'd been waiting for Delaney, surely they would have entered the hole together?

Ginger's bad sense got stronger, but it was a bit late for that.

She slid on the wet stone, gaining speed like a child on a slide in a water park. She couldn't stop; she couldn't see where she was going in the darkness; she didn't know how far she'd already fallen or where it would stop.

Until she tumbled—ass over teakettle, as Gran would have said—into a small antechamber. The water leapt into a bed it had carved into the floor, gurgling and splashing into darkness. The floor of the chamber was dry and the walls had been carved from rock.

Ginger stood up and winced at the wetness of her jeans. She shivered at the chill against her skin. That was when she realized she could see, because the chamber was lit with a dull red light. The light seemed to pulse.

It gave her the creeps.

Her cell phone made the perky little combination of beeps that meant it was out of juice. Ginger pulled it out of her pocket, only to confirm that it really was dead.

She was on her own.

Ginger checked her rifle. The red light came from a fissure on the far side. There had been a gate locked over the gap, but that piece of metal had been torn from its hinges and cast aside.

Ginger approached with caution, laying her hand on the discarded grate. The metal was so hot that she quickly pulled her hand away.

Whoever was with Delaney, whoever was melting steel gates, wasn't too far ahead of her.

Great.

Ginger told herself that she wasn't hearing the spooky organ music that always played in horror movies, the music that always accompanied the heroine's bad decision to go down the basement stairs and find out what was lurking there. It was the music that indicated the heroine was heading straight for trouble, serial killers, and nasty situations.

There was no music in the cave.

Because, because going forward was the sensible thing to do.

Uh-huh.

Ginger didn't believe it, but she went anyway. She had to know. She took a deep breath and eased through the opening. She stepped silently, as she had when stalking that coyote, except that this time she had no idea who or what was her prey.

She hoped the victim wouldn't be herself.

Delaney halted before the repository of the Dragon's Blood Elixir and stared at it in horror and awe. He didn't know what he had expected, but it hadn't been this.

His body responded to its proximity, that gnawing hunger taking hold of him.

It would be so easy to drink of it.

So easy to surrender.

Delaney took a step back, shaking his head.

When he had been imprisoned in Magnus's dark academy, the Elixir had been brought to Delaney in a cup or a syringe, forced down his throat or injected into his veins when he was incapable of resisting.

It had been dark and cold in the academy, with no hints of day or night, no sense of time's passage. But the Elixir had made his moments darker yet.

Delaney remembered the icy collision between the Elixir and his body, the shivers that had rocked him as it spread its vile darkness through his veins. He'd been given it three times and he'd never forget how each administration was more horrific than the last. He remembered the dissociation from his own nature, the phantasms and nightmares, the brief moments of clarity and the accompanying conviction that he was losing his mind.

What he had been losing under the Elixir's influence was his heart.

The third and last cavern, after the third iron gate, was distinguished by its size. The floor of the cavern was uneven, scored with the passage of water and liberally embellished with mineral deposits. The ceiling dripped with stalactites, some of them white and others ochre, all of them bathed in the red light that emanated from the far side of the cavern.

The light came from a massive rock crystal vial that seemed part of the opposite wall. Delaney couldn't tell if it had been formed naturally—which was unlikely— or so cunningly carved and installed that it looked to be part of the cavern's natural development. A set of stairs had been carved from the rock crystal and spiraled around it from foot to lip. The crystal was cloudy and obviously thick, its surface gleaming dully.

It wasn't so thick, though, that its contents couldn't be discerned. A cloudy red liquid filled it to the brim, emitting a bit of steam into the chamber. It was humid in this cavern, the chilly air smelling of decay and blood and destruction.

The distinctive scent of the Elixir.

It wound into his nostrils and made his gut clench. He felt the shadow slide over his thoughts, felt the monster within awaken with a roar. A ravenous hunger, one that would only be sated by the one thing Delaney would never willingly ingest, claimed his body and left him shaking with need.

Delaney had to destroy the vial, immediately. He

knew that rock crystal could shatter and he could see the flaws in the stone.

Force would win this day.

Delaney had already shifted shape and he took flight with purpose. He flew toward the vial at top speed, breathing dragonfire. It was harder to breathe fire, but maybe that was part of the Elixir's effect. He blew harder. As he drew closer, spewing fire, he saw the rock crystal shimmer a bit beneath the assault of heat.

He breathed fire until he was almost upon the vial, then threw his shoulder against it, slamming his weight into the crystal. He hit it with everything he had, the beast within him bellowing at the injustice of his choice.

The vial shuddered, but didn't crack.

Delaney repeated the exercise three times, until his breath was coming in spurts and he was feeling the exertion. Each time he drew near it, that desire increased and his power over his body diminished slightly.

But his assault made no difference. Other than the Elixir swirling within the vial at greater speed, nothing changed.

He could simply drink some. That would help.

The thought slid into his mind, coming from everywhere and nowhere, threatening to pervert his knowledge of what was right.

Delaney attacked the vial again, again to no visible effect.

One sip. It would take only one sip.

Delaney felt a moment's panic as the thought became more persuasive. He couldn't have come this far and challenged Magnus to meet him, only to fail.

Energized by the chance of failure, Delaney lunged at the vial again. He thrashed it with his tail; he threw his weight against it; he clawed the surface with his talons. He breathed smoke and fire. He grasped the sides of the vial and tried to shake it loose of the cavern's walls, his efforts only managing to make the cloudy Elixir roil behind the crystal.

Then Delaney glimpsed an eye, right before his own. The eye was wide and staring and red, the eye of something submerged in the vial. And not just any eye—it was an eye of a dragon. The pupil was a vertical slit.

That eye seemed to stare directly at him before disappearing into the red murk.

Delaney was disgusted at the import of what he'd seen. The Elixir moved in silence, concealing what it had just revealed. Delaney had never seen the source of the Elixir, never glimpsed the origin of the dreaded substance. He'd never truly thought about what created it, but in that moment, he understood.

And was appalled all over again.

It was, after all, called the Dragon's Blood Elixir.

He roared in fury and dug his talons into the crystal. He tried to unmoor it from its seating, slamming his shoulder into the vial over and over and over again. The floor of the cavern shook with the force of his efforts, but the crystal showed no flaw.

"Surely you can't imagine sheer force will work," Magnus mused, his old-speak echoing in Delaney's thoughts.

Delaney spun, knowing he wasn't alone any longer. He had a glimpse of Magnus in human form before the leader of the *Slayers* shifted shape and leapt into the air to attack.

The chamber seemed instantly smaller. Magnus's antagonism was intense, but it had nothing on Delaney's fury. This was the *Slayer* who had put poison in Delaney's body. This was the *Slayer* who had tormented and nearly destroyed him. This was the *Slayer* Delaney hated above all creatures.

It was time for Magnus to pay.

Magnus flew directly at Delaney, his eyes bright with

anger. The pair locked claws in the traditional fighting pose, colliding with a vengeance. They tumbled from the force of Magnus's attack, Delaney spinning to slam Magnus into the vial.

The cavern shook with the impact. Other than the Elixir swirling a little faster, the vial remained pristine.

"Tougher than it looks," Magnus mused, clearly unsurprised.

"Like many of us."

Magnus smiled as his grip tightened. *"Sure you wouldn't rather have a sip?"*

"Not a chance."

"I'll drop you right into it," Magnus threatened, chuckling at the prospect. *"Hold you down until you surrender."*

The prospect was horrifying. Delaney slashed at the *Slayer*'s belly with his rear claws, twisting free of Magnus's grip when he recoiled. He hit the *Slayer* with his tail, sending Magnus rolling through the air.

It was clear that Magnus relied upon his help to do the dirty work. Delaney raced after the *Slayer*, knowing he could take him down.

"Go ahead and try," Delaney taunted. Magnus turned and flew for him again. They locked claws once more, biting and slashing with a vengeance.

Their entwined bodies fell toward the floor of the cavern. Magnus bit Delaney and twisted out of his grip just before they hit the floor. He broke a stalactite as he turned, leaving a dusting of ochre rock on his wings. The stalactite shattered when it fell, making the floor vibrate.

The Elixir sloshed.

They lifted their talons and circled again, their expressions grim. The flap of their wings stirred the dust on the floor of the cavern and the light from the Elixir created long, ominous shadows from their silhouettes.

As they circled each other and Magnus moved into the light, Delaney saw the missing scale on the *Slayer*'s chest. It was hard to believe that Magnus could ever have loved anyone more than himself, but maybe that self-adoration was the weakness indicated by the lost scale.

Delaney didn't care. He knew where to hit to hurt, the missing scale being the place of Magnus's sole vulnerability.

"You're slow," Magnus murmured, his smile predatory. *"Maybe you have mixed feelings about me."*

"Maybe not."

"Dead or alive, I'll take you and make you mine," Magnus threatened, his eyes glittering yellow. *"By coming here, you've made it easy for me to claim you once and for all."* Magnus's conviction in his own invincibility was clear, but there was no way Delaney would let him succeed.

It was Magnus who would die.

"You'll never claim me," Delaney retorted. *"I'll destroy you first."*

Magnus laughed, but Delaney attacked, the frenzy of his assault clearly taking the ancient *Slayer* by surprise.

That was nothing compared to what Delaney would do.

Chapter 4

There was someone ahead of her.

Ginger heard rustling, like footsteps on stone, then a mighty thump that made the floor of the underground cave shake.

A second thump was less vehement but still powerful.

What she heard next sounded like men fighting. There was an occasional grunt, the sound of a blow connecting with flesh, the crack of a bone. Stone broke, the floor shook, and there was a flash of fire.

Delaney was in trouble! Someone or something roared with anger, which was all Ginger needed to encourage her to get involved. She'd never been one to stand back and watch when she could make a difference, and she didn't see a reason to start now.

She hefted the rifle, stepped through the last opening, and froze in shock.

It wasn't the eerie red light that stopped her, even though it pulsed as it bathed the chamber in light the color of blood. It wasn't the huge rock crystal container of cloudy liquid on the far side of the chamber that halted her, or even the fact that it seemed to be the source of the weird light.

It was definitely the two fighting dragons that surprised Ginger.

She blinked and stared, certain her eyes were deceiving her, but the dragons continued to fight overhead.

They were massive creatures, just the way one would expect dragons to be, coiled with ferocious strength. They possessed a dangerous beauty.

One had scales that could have been carved from emeralds, each faceted to catch the light. His scales—it was impossible to think of these monsters as female—could have been edged in copper. His muscled and scaled stomach was copper, as were the talons on each of his four claws. His eyes shone green and his teeth were both numerous and sharply pointed.

His opponent had scales in all the cloudy colors of jade, ranging from almost white to deep green. His talons were gold, and he seemed larger and thicker than the copper and emerald dragon. They both had massive wings that could have been made of leather, although the jade one had a gold talon at the end of each wing.

They fought viciously, apparently ceding no rules. Ginger had seen enough bar fights to understand that the loser would die.

But where was Delaney?

There was no sign of him.

Had one of the dragons eaten him?

She couldn't see any other way out of the cavern than the tunnel she'd just used, and Ginger knew it wasn't wide enough that anyone could have passed her without her knowing it.

She eyed the bellies of the dragons as they battled above her and wondered whether one was more rounded than the other. Could a person survive being swallowed by a dragon? It was frigid in this cavern despite the fact that it seemed to be filled with steam. All the same, Ginger felt a different kind of heat in her veins.

It reminded her of the sparks she'd imagined leaping between herself and Delaney the night before. Certainly, the slow burn of desire was the same as what she had felt the night before. Ginger felt a shimmer on her skin, a vibration of lust in her veins, and marveled that she could feel excited by the presence of fighting dragons.

But she did.

They were muscled and beautiful, purely masculine, but it was more than that. She was definitely aroused— just as she had been with Delaney.

It was hardly the time for such thoughts.

The emerald dragon struck the other with his tail and the jade dragon rolled through the air, barely missing a beat. He roared back toward the emerald one, breathing fire. The emerald one ducked, but the jade one caught him by the end of the tail. He flung the emerald one against a wall of the cavern, making it shudder again, and inhaled audibly.

Ginger guessed he was going to breathe fire, maybe roast the emerald one.

The emerald dragon had other ideas. He dove at the jade one, winding his tail around the jade dragon's tail to hold it down. They wrapped around each other, biting and grappling for supremacy, like boa constrictors each trying to squeeze the life out of the other.

They fell, landing heavily and launching a cloud of red dust. The jade one rolled and bit, digging his talons into the emerald one's wings. Red blood flowed over the gold talons.

The emerald dragon twisted and snapped at the jade one, freeing himself from the larger dragon's grip as he tore the jade dragon's flesh. He threw the jade dragon against the large column of red liquid and again the floor jumped. The emerald dragon dug his claws into the jade dragon's mailed chest.

The jade dragon screamed as the talons tore. His blood ran as black as pitch over his glorious scales as he writhed out of the emerald dragon's grip. "You can't truly injure me," he taunted. "Not when the means to recovery are so close."

"Let's try," the emerald dragon muttered with grim determination.

Ginger blinked. She had to be imagining that he sounded like Delaney.

The emerald dragon ripped the chest of the jade one, leaving his opponent gasping in pain. The emerald dragon hit his opponent hard with his tail, then he slammed the jade dragon into the massive vial.

The jade dragon slid bonelessly down the smooth crystal, catching himself on one of the steps carved into its face. He pivoted, leaning his back against the crystal, and seemed to smile at his hovering opponent.

His gaze flicked across the chamber. Ginger's heart leapt in terror. She knew he'd seen her when his eyes gleamed. A puff of smoke came from his nostrils and his smile widened.

"Oh, look," he said, launching into flight with surprising speed. "Luncheon is served."

Ginger didn't wait for introductions. She raised her gun and shot.

Her shot got the jade dragon in the knee, but he didn't seem to notice. She wasn't entirely sure that the shot even penetrated his scales. It didn't stop him or even slow him down.

If anything, it only annoyed him.

He breathed fire as he bore down on her, fearsome and closing fast. Ginger shot again, but her shot went wild. She pivoted and ran toward the passageway that led back to the surface and sanity.

The emerald dragon bellowed, but Ginger didn't bother to look. She would have preferred to have evaded them both. The jade dragon was fast, faster than she'd expected, and he snatched her with his talons before she got to safety. Ginger dropped her rifle as she was lifted above the ground.

The jade dragon raised her high, his smile all the more malicious at close proximity.

He had a lot of teeth.

And they looked sharp. Had he eaten Delaney? If so, they might be together sooner than Ginger had expected.

If not in any condition to chat.

Ginger struggled, but to no avail. She kicked and fought, even bit the dragon's fingers. It made no difference. He breathed another puff of smoke, then opened his mouth slightly. She saw the flames flickering deep in his gullet, and closed her eyes when he exhaled. Smoke surrounded her, the smell of fire and ash, and she struggled with new force.

It made no difference.

Ginger had time to hope that she gave him indigestion before the first of the flames licked her skin. She smelled her jacket burning and knew she'd be next.

Then salvation came from the most unlikely of places.

Delaney was shocked to see Ginger in the cave. He'd felt heat, but had attributed it to his efforts in fighting Magnus. It had felt like the firestorm, but he'd been sure that was impossible.

His firestorm was over. They'd sated it.

But Ginger was here and he was sizzling all over again.

She was a fool to have followed him, but that didn't mean she should die for her mistake.

Magnus had already snatched her up and loosed his dragonfire. Fortunately, he was focused on torturing a human and not obviously paying attention to Delaney. Delaney didn't doubt that it was a lure, and that Magnus would try to awaken some embedded command in Delaney's thoughts.

Ginger's presence infuriated him as nothing else could, and the prospect of her being injured sent a jolt of adrenaline through his body. The dark threat of the Elixir faded from his thoughts, its power over his confidence eliminated as he found purpose.

He had to save Ginger.

Delaney fell upon the ancient *Slayer* in a flurry of talons and teeth. He didn't care where he inflicted damage on Magnus, so long as he did. His blood lust would have frightened him in other circumstances, so violent and powerful, but Magnus deserved no less. The beast was loose and this time, Delaney was glad.

"Join me," Magnus murmured in old-speak even as he was battered.

"Never!" Delaney cried aloud. He steeled himself against Magnus's inevitable attempts to control him.

Ginger's gaze flew to him, her astonishment clear. Had she recognized his voice?

"Acknowledge that humans are the vermin that plague the planet," Magnus continued. *"Take this one as your first victim, a commemorative prize for joining the* Slayer *side."* He breathed fire at Ginger and she screamed as her jacket began to burn.

Delaney was livid. He ripped at the tendons at the top of Magnus's wings, then sank his teeth into the *Slayer*'s shoulder. Magnus shouted, breaking his stream of dragonfire, and spun to fight.

Delaney tore Ginger from the *Slayer*'s grasp, passing her to his back claw and smothering the flames with his grasp. He was shocked at the large spark that leapt between them, at the hum of desire that settled within him.

The firestorm was undeniable, the radiant glow from his claw that grasped Ginger leaving no question.

"Nothing like a firestorm," Magnus said with glee. "How very, very interesting."

Delaney dove for the missing scale on Magnus's golden chest, sinking his fang into the skin revealed there. Magnus roared with pain, his black blood spewing over Delaney. Ginger screamed.

Magnus began to chant a low chorus, an ancient tune that resonated deep within Delaney. Delaney felt that impetus to serve Magnus's will, he felt the desire to do what the leader of the *Slayers* wanted of him, but he also felt the agitated pulse of his mate. His heart thundered, his brain filled with a red rage that insisted he destroy.

"*Kill her*," Magnus commanded, lower and more insistent than old-speak. Delaney slammed the *Slayer* into the stone wall and Magnus shuddered as a bone cracked within him. *"Kill her now."*

Delaney didn't heed the command. He'd kill Magnus instead. He ripped the *Slayer*'s carcass open with a violence that had been alien to him, hooked a talon into Magnus's guts, and compelled them to spill forth.

Magnus roared in pain.

"*Kill her!*" Magnus bellowed.

Delaney caught the *Slayer* and spun him in the cavern, not caring that Magnus's body broke stalactite after stalactite, not caring that the falling stone filled the chamber with dust. He was enraged. Magnus's blood spilled on the cavern floor, burning whatever it contacted.

Ginger swore softly, her heart skipping before it settled. Delaney noted that she had passed out in his grasp, her face pale.

"*You cannot deny me!*" Magnus shouted in fury as he struggled.

"I just have." Delaney dropped the *Slayer* on the floor of the cavern, noting how he didn't immediately rise.

Magnus's guts spilled from the open wound, his black blood spreading rapidly across the floor of the cavern. Delaney could smell the filth that ran in the *Slayer*'s veins, the hatred and the darkness, and he wanted them to have nothing in common.

And he enjoyed Magnus's defeat. Delaney felt a savage glee as Magnus fell, as his guts spilled and his blood flowed. He could have shredded the *Slayer*. He could have tormented him with pain, just as Magnus had tortured him. It would have been justified.

It would also have made him just like them.

Delaney saw the hatred in himself and was horrified. He could have surrendered to it completely, to its call for brutality under the false banner of justice.

But he became aware of a radiance in his claw. The firestorm burned hotter and more insistent, its light searing his heart. Its brilliance filled him, banishing the beast within and his thirst for destruction. It reminded Delaney of the value of temperance, of the need not to act in vengeance.

Ginger was captive in Delaney's claw, frightened but alive. Her presence clarified the situation for Delaney, made him keenly aware of the stakes. He felt his own heart synchronize with the frantic pace of her own, felt his breathing match her frightened huffing. The connection strengthened him, filled him with light and power.

It made it easy to deny Magnus, the *Slayers*, and the Elixir.

It made it easy to step back from his anger.

Delaney chose not to let the beast win. He wouldn't become a mindless and heartless killing machine. He wouldn't let Magnus do that to him.

That was the true triumph.

When Delaney backed away from Magnus's bleeding

body, the allure of the Elixir dimmed. His body didn't yearn for it as vehemently.

His body yearned for Ginger, instead. His true nature was drawn to the light of the firestorm and its promise for the future.

Magnus writhed, bracing himself on his front claws and breathing dragonfire mingled with smoke. He couldn't fly anymore, couldn't rouse himself from the floor, but he spewed his venom as far as he could. He again tried to dispatch his command into Delaney's thoughts, but he was easier to ignore each time.

The air became thick with dragonsmoke and smoke from Magnus's dragonfire. The Elixir seemed to churn with greater agitation in the crystal vial, as if it responded to Magnus's distress.

Magnus began to shift between forms, almost certainly against his will, flicking between human and dragon. Delaney was surprised to glimpse a green salamander periodically appearing as a transition phase.

So, Magnus had mastered that ability of the Wyvern as well.

Delaney knew that Ginger wouldn't be able to breathe much more of the foul air Magnus was creating, the dragonfire stealing the oxygen from the cavern. He had to make this visit count.

Plus he sensed other *Slayers* coming to Magnus's aid.

Ginger had brought him the gift of denying Magnus's subliminal commands and the key to banishing the beast fed by the Elixir. Ginger had to survive.

Even if it meant that the Elixir did, too.

Delaney mustered all of his strength and dove one last time at the massive vial. He thundered into it with all the force he could muster, driving his shoulder into the rock crystal. The entire cavern vibrated with the impact.

A single hairline crack appeared in the vial.

Silver beads formed on the crack and dripped toward the floor. They were odd, like liquid silver, and Delaney couldn't understand what they were.

He might have collected one, but Ginger moaned and stirred.

As close as victory might be, Delaney had to ensure her safety first and foremost.

The Elixir would wait.

He realized abruptly that shattering the vial now would send its balm cascading over Magnus. Let Magnus drag himself up those many stairs for his restorative sip instead.

Delaney left the cavern and Magnus, shifting back to human form in the last minute to slip through the small portal. He carried Ginger with care, scooping up her rifle en route, and made his way hurriedly through the labyrinthine passage.

He'd figure out how they'd get up that last chute to the riverside when he had to. At least the air was clearing. The warmth of the firestorm settled around them, lighting his way with its golden glow.

Delaney couldn't understand its presence, but it was undeniable.

Why hadn't it been sated? What did the firestorm's persistence mean? And what was he going to do about it? He couldn't leave Ginger without creating a son, not without abandoning his duty to his fellow *Pyr*.

First things first—they had to get out of the cave alive.

And if he had to frighten Ginger into not following him again to ensure her own safety, so be it.

Ginger awakened to a persistent and gentle tapping of fingertips against her cheek. She heard sparks crackling and saw bright light through her lashes. She felt warm, even though her jeans were still wet. The languid heat rolling through her body told her who was holding her against his broad chest.

"Come on, Ginger," Delaney said, and she felt like purring at the sound of his voice. "You've got to wake up so we can get out of here."

His urgency was clear.

Ginger opened her eyes, half expecting to find dragons in the vicinity. Instead, she was in what looked like the first cavern at the foot of the chute where part of the creek went underground. She sat up, aware of Delaney's watchful presence but not quite ready to meet his gaze.

She reached toward his hand, then jumped at the spark that arced between them. She wasn't drunk anymore. What was going on?

Where had he been?

"That's better," Delaney said with satisfaction, as if the spark hadn't happened. He pulled her to her feet, clearly not inclined to talk. "Come on. Let's go."

Ginger didn't move, because she realized that she *had* heard his voice emanate from the emerald and copper dragon.

Except that that was impossible.

She might have thought she had dreamed the whole thing, but the front of her coat was burned black. Her face felt flushed, as if she had a sunburn rising.

And the barrel of her rifle, close at hand, was warm.

"What's going on? Where were you?" Ginger wasn't the kind of person to have hallucinations. She wasn't possessed of a vivid imagination. She was, in fact, known for her sharp observational skills and her ability to call things as she saw them.

Which was usually how they were.

That didn't explain the sparks.

Or the dragons fighting.

"Later," Delaney said. "We'll talk about it later."

How could Delaney's voice have come from one of them?

"Now works for me," Ginger insisted. She thought of Jonah and the whale, then met Delaney's gaze. She saw concern in his eyes as well as a bit of wariness. There was no point in beating around the bush. "Where were you? Did he spit you up whole?"

She knew she didn't imagine that Delaney eased away from her slightly. "Who?"

She heard in his tone that he knew exactly whom she meant but was pretending otherwise. Indignation made her rise quickly to her feet and jab a finger in his direction.

"You know who! The emerald and copper dragon. I heard your voice come from him. Did he swallow you whole and then spit you up?"

"No." Delaney's tone was flat and he headed for the chute. Clearly, he didn't want to talk about it further.

Ginger didn't move. "Then what the hell happened back there?"

"We'll talk about it later." His expression was grim. "Let's get out of here first."

Ginger folded her arms across her chest. "I'm not going anywhere without an explanation. If you think I find this whole mystery man thing attractive, you can think again."

"Now," Delaney said, the single word low and forceful.

Ginger would have argued, but there was something odd about him. He turned to face her, his intensity stopping the question that rose to her lips. He seemed suddenly larger, more dangerous and determined. More predatory and powerful.

For the first time, she was a little bit frightened of him. Delaney's body shimmered blue around the edges, as if he weren't entirely there. The hair prickled on the back of Ginger's neck, her body more wary than the rest of her. He took a step toward her and she backed up, afraid of what he might do.

Delaney's eyes, though, were the really strange part of him. They shone a brilliant green, shone as if lit from within.

But his pupils were vertical slits, like the eyes of a reptile.

Like the eyes of a dragon.

Time to go.

Ginger didn't wait to see anything more. She clutched her rifle against her chest and scrambled up the slope, using only one hand. It wasn't easy but she wasn't going to leave her weapon behind.

Ginger climbed up the slope with record speed, never looking back. She heard Delaney behind her and that only made her move faster. She tore her palm on the stone and got soaked to the skin on the way.

She felt heat on her cold butt, as if Delaney were a bonfire racing right behind her. She felt that stupid lust again, untimely and unwelcome as it was, and ground her teeth in irritation at her own weakness.

He might be the sexiest man she'd ever known, but there were issues that demanded review.

"Faster," Delaney murmured from right behind her, his voice low enough to make her shiver. "They're too close."

She didn't ask who.

She wasn't entirely sure she wanted to know.

Ginger emerged into daylight, blinking at the bright whiteness of the snow. She had time to see two dragons descending out of the sky, and two unfamiliar men on the riverbank close at hand. Then Delaney pushed her aside, jumped over her, and leapt into the air.

By the time Ginger looked up, a dragon was ascending quickly.

A copper and emerald one.

And, once again, there was no sign of Delaney.

Ginger heard the rush of wind and the flap of wings. The two men on the riverbank were gone when she glanced their way, the sound coming from two dragons gaining altitude right behind the emerald one.

Five dragons.

One of the dragons following the emerald one could have been made of amethyst and silver. The other appeared to be scaled in all the colors of tourmaline, shading from green to purple and back over his length, each scale edged in silver.

Ginger stared. She was wet and cold, but too astonished to care. She felt suddenly light-headed and sat down in the snow, telling herself it was a choice but knowing her knees would have given out on their own.

She cradled the rifle in her hands and savored its familiar weight. It felt good to hold something solid, something that was precisely as she had always known it to be and showed no signs of changing. The rifle was reassuring and real.

Even if it had been useless against dragons so far.

One dragon that approached was agate, his russet and gold and green scales lined like ancient stone, and accented with gold. The other was remarkable, as red as garnets, with gold and what looked like embedded pearls.

The dragons looked even more like fabulous jeweled beasts in the light, but they were far from ornamental. The copper and emerald dragon attacked the agate one with a vengeance. Ginger had the odd sense that he was defending her. The pair locked claws, then tumbled through the air, slashing and thrashing.

Did dragons take sides? Or did the emerald one just want her for his own lunch?

The amethyst dragon took on the garnet dragon,

breathing fire so that the garnet dragon recoiled. Meanwhile the tourmaline dragon had flown behind him and attacked from the other side. The garnet dragon screeched and spun, caught between two opponents. It was a violent and rough fight, but Ginger couldn't tear her gaze away.

"This'll be short and sweet."

The sound of a man's voice behind her made Ginger jump to her feet again and pivot, rifle at the ready.

Chapter 5

Ginger was afraid of him.

Delaney told himself that was good.

He hadn't started to shift on purpose, but his body had been responding to the presence of a threat to his mate. He hadn't intended for Ginger to see his truth, but now that she had, he told himself to be glad of it.

It would be easier to leave her if she feared—or even despised—him. Delaney knew she was smart and resilient, and the heat of the firestorm made him want her in a very basic way.

But she was afraid of him.

And he could ensure that she became more afraid of him.

Maybe after she witnessed the fullness of his truth, she wouldn't mind him abandoning her.

It would then be easier to do what he needed to do.

Even if Ginger's fear did prove that his mother had been right.

Even if he did regret that he had frightened her. Ginger was too giving, too stubborn, too damn attractive. If he couldn't defend himself against the promise of the firestorm, he'd frighten her and make her the one who declined him.

Delaney had been an outcast for a long time, long enough that he knew the shadows were where he belonged.

Still he resented his truth as he never had before. He raged at the injustice of his birthright as he lunged at Mallory. The only kind of creature less worthy of respect than Delaney was a *Slayer*. That defeating the *Slayers* was essential to protecting his mate was just an added bonus.

They gave him a release for his anger.

A tall man stood before Ginger on the edge of the scrub, his hands braced on his hips as he avidly watched the battle overhead. Ginger guessed that his indifference to her was an act, and that he was completely aware of what she did.

He obviously had been the one who had spoken.

His long, dark blond hair was tied back in a pony-tail, his tight jeans revealed that he was buff. The black down-filled vest only made him look bigger, and his grim manner convinced Ginger that he, too, had seen a number of bar fights.

Even participated in them.

Without looking directly at her, he reached to push the muzzle of the rifle with his fingertip, directing it away from himself. The dragon tattoo on the back of his left hand snared Ginger's eye, made her think.

Persuaded her to shut up for the moment.

It was impossible for men to become dragons, wasn't it?

Then where had Delaney gone?

And where had the copper and emerald dragon come from?

Ginger eased away from the stranger, keeping the

muzzle momentarily averted. It didn't make a lot of sense to tick off this guy, whoever he was. He had to be three feet taller than she and looked as if he could take her on with one hand.

Overhead, the garnet dragon screamed as the tourmaline one slashed his claws across that pearl-embellished face. Black blood spattered down and the tall man pulled Ginger out of the way. The blood sizzled where it fell in the snow and loosed a little bit of steam.

"I'm only here to protect you," he drawled, not taking his gaze from the battle overhead.

"Not if I say otherwise."

He flicked her a look. "It's Delaney's call whether you need to be beguiled, but don't imagine that you'll just walk away."

Ginger didn't know what he was talking about, although she had to admit that Delaney had charmed her the night before.

"I'll run," she said vehemently, and she meant it.

"Delaney will find you." He spoke with such confidence that Ginger believed him.

Where was Delaney? Ginger watched the copper and emerald dragon overhead, fighting the obvious answer as determinedly as the emerald dragon battled the agate one.

Surely he hadn't become the dragon? She thought about his pupil being a vertical slit and shivered.

Impossible.

Meanwhile, the fight continued. The garnet dragon might have retreated, but the amethyst one leapt on his back. He buried his teeth into the garnet dragon's shoulder as the tourmaline one breathed fire at the garnet dragon. The garnet dragon screamed in pain and struggled, but seemed unable to break out of the pair's deadly grip.

The copper and emerald dragon was thumping the

agate dragon, landing blow after blow on him with his tail. He fought more viciously than the others, clearly seeing every battle as being to the death. The pair spiraled around each other, the agate dragon trying to scorch the emerald one or tear his wings.

The emerald one was faster and more agile, maybe more motivated. He attacked the agate dragon, one talon catching the agate dragon's eye. That dragon bellowed in rage and pain, then launched himself at the emerald one.

It was a bloody, dirty fight, so vicious that Ginger understood the losers could die.

"Where *is* Delaney?" she asked, finding herself unable to look away from the carnage overhead. She suspected the answer, even though it was crazy.

Let someone else say it out loud.

The tall man did. "He's the copper and emerald dragon." His gaze was amused as he looked at Ginger. "We're dragon shape shifters. Didn't he mention it?"

"No. Oddly enough, it didn't come up in conversation."

The tall man chuckled.

Ginger didn't say anything more. What other rational explanation could there be for Delaney's voice coming from that dragon in the cave below?

Although "rational" could be considered a stretch.

"You might notice that he's defending you from Mallory and Balthasar," the tall man noted.

"He might be defending you."

Her companion laughed again. "I can take care of myself."

"So can I." Ginger gripped her rifle a little more tightly. Could she duck past this guy and run? He was a formidable obstacle and seemed to think it his responsibility to keep her right where she was. He'd be faster than her, too, given his height.

She stayed put, waiting for her moment, and looked skyward again at the sound of distant thunder.

It was an odd time for thunder.

The emerald dragon roared as he flung the agate one through the sky at his fellow. The tourmaline and amethyst dragons must have guessed his intention, because they spun the garnet dragon, who was bleeding profusely, and cast him at the agate one.

The two dragons collided with a heavy thud, their heads clunking together. Ginger winced, even though she wasn't cheering for those two.

The garnet dragon fell out of the sky, his eyes closed.

"Look out!" the tall man said, dragging Ginger backward instead of giving her a chance to follow his instruction.

He moved fast, she'd give him that.

The garnet dragon's body crashed through the trees, breaking branches as he fell into the creek. The ice on the surface cracked and broke immediately, and his body fell through the ice into several feet of water.

He didn't move.

The tall man kept his hand in front of Ginger all the same, and she noticed he was shimmering blue around his edges, just as Delaney had done in the cave below.

Was he intending to protect her, too?

Why?

Ginger had to admit that having a defender in the face of fire-breathing dragons sounded like a good plan, even if she didn't understand what was going on.

The copper and emerald dragon joined forces with the tourmaline and amethyst ones to fight the agate dragon. The agate dragon didn't engage, though—he pivoted and retreated, breathing slowly and deeply as he stared at the trio.

"Dragonsmoke," the tall man said under his breath.

"I don't see any smoke," Ginger said.

"I do. Our senses are sharper than yours." He twitched involuntarily and urged her farther back into the woods. "It burns, that shit." He shuddered again and urged Ginger to move away from the fallen dragon's body.

Ginger chose not to argue with him. Putting distance between herself and dragons, whether there was burning invisible smoke or not, was a good idea in her books.

The trio of dragons in flight retreated with such care that Ginger understood there was something nasty about dragonsmoke. The amethyst one moved toward the agate dragon but was suddenly repelled by something that made him scream in pain.

"Stupid," her companion muttered, and the amethyst dragon glared at him.

Meanwhile, the agate dragon descended steadily toward his fallen comrade, hovering just above his body. He breathed slowly and steadily, his manner almost meditative.

"What's he doing?"

"Defending the corpse with dragonsmoke," the tall man said, his tone grim. "Defending himself with it, too."

"Why?"

"He's making sure we can't take the corpse and ensure that Mallory stays dead."

Ginger eyed her companion, who appeared to be serious. "Is that supposed to make sense?"

"It will." He cast her a crooked smile, then his eyes narrowed and he looked at the sky again. "Another *Slayer* incoming."

Ginger barely glimpsed a dark shape in the distant sky before the tall man grabbed her elbow. It could have been a bird approaching, but she knew it wasn't.

It was much, much bigger than a bird.

And she was sure it breathed fire.

It paused and hovered in the distance, as if deciding what to do.

"Time to go." The tall man tugged Ginger toward the parking lot, setting a pace she struggled to match. The deep snow made it hard to run, especially given her height, but Ginger was motivated. She was glad when she saw her trusty red pickup truck, so reassuringly normal, dusted with a generous layer of snow.

"I'll just be heading out, then," she said, marching toward her truck, sanity, and the real world.

"Not so fast," the tall man said, although he didn't touch her.

Ginger turned to look, wondering what he meant, then saw three dragons spiraling out of the sky. They were graceful despite their size, moving like prime athletes. They were enormous and the sight of their approach made her mouth go dry.

It also excited her in an odd way. She felt a tingle, like flames licking at her toes, like desire unfurling in her belly, and decided she really needed some breakfast.

But she couldn't move away. She was transfixed by the sight of the copper and emerald dragon. He led the way, the tourmaline and amethyst ones right behind him, and headed straight for her.

Was it really Delaney?

There was purpose in every beat of the copper and emerald dragon's massive wings as he flew closer. Ginger caught her breath at the weight of the dragon's gaze. He was staring at her, his gaze fixed upon her as he flew closer.

His eyes were green.

Just like Delaney's.

And his manner was intense in a very familiar way.

Ginger swallowed, but held her ground. There was

a challenge in his eyes, as if he dared her to keep looking, to make the connection, to understand what he
was.

Ginger had never in her life backed down from a
dare. She stared directly back at the dragon and waited
for the worst. She felt that tingling heat grow as he came
closer, that unruly desire that had made her surrender to
impulse the night before.

Lust roiled within her, shorting her circuits, making
her forget everything except the sexy quirk of Delaney's
smile.

"You ought to close your eyes," the tall man advised.

"Not a chance." Ginger gripped her rifle but kept it
at her side.

"The transformation is hard for humans to witness,"
he insisted.

If there was a transformation, Ginger wanted to see
it all. It was the only way she'd believe it possible. She
stared unblinkingly at the copper and emerald dragon
as he descended to the parking lot.

"Just sayin'," the tall man added, but Ginger ignored
him.

She forced her eyes to remain open, staring at the
dragon as he drew closer. He seemed to hesitate for a
second, as if he, too, would warn her of the perils of her
choice, but Ginger wasn't interested in being deceived.

She wanted the truth.

And she wanted it now.

Whatever the hell it was.

She lifted her chin and squared her shoulders.

His eyes gleamed.

Then the copper and emerald dragon landed grace-
fully before her, launching a flurry of snow as he did so.
Ginger halfway wondered what a hunter would make of
those tracks, then she felt the desire weaken her knees,
and forgot everything else but the dragon.

He was watching her with those odd green eyes, staring so steadily at her that Ginger almost shivered. The snow melted around them, leaving a round space of bare ground.

Then Delaney's voice came from the dragon's mouth. "Don't try to make sense of it," he advised, the familiarity of his voice wrenching Ginger's heart. "Maybe it's just a dream."

"I never got burned in a dream before," Ginger retorted, plucking the blackened mess of her jacket.

"Look away if it upsets you," he said, but she heard the dare in his tone. If he thought she was some weak girl who couldn't take the tough stuff, he could think again.

"Not on your life," she said.

"It won't come to that."

Ginger didn't ask about her own life.

The dragon shimmered before her eyes. It was strange but one minute, he was clearly a dragon; in the next minute, the perimeter of his body shone with a strange blue light. His edges flickered, like a gas flame, there and yet not. The precise distinction between him and the world around him became more cloudy, less readily discerned. His form morphed and grew less clearly defined, changing before her very eyes.

Ginger tried to see all of the transformation at once and that was maybe her mistake. Her gaze darted over the dragon, watching for changes, noting differences, observing how one form morphed into the other.

Impossible.

She saw the reptilian dragon eyes become Delaney's eyes, saw the sharp talon change to a finger, noted how the wings folded upon themselves and disappeared into his back.

Impossible.

She saw the sharp teeth fade away, saw him shrink

to human size, saw his tail disappear as if it had been absorbed.

Impossible.

Ginger saw his clothes appear, seeming to be unfolded from beneath one of his scales, so that his human form was never nude in an Ohio parking lot in the middle of a February snowstorm.

Impossible.

But happening right before her eyes all the same.

Ginger forced her eyes to remain open when they might have closed. But when he was almost completely shifted, when the creature before her was snapping into the Delaney who had spent the night before in her bed, Ginger's brain abruptly refused to accept any more sensory data.

The change was occurring quickly, too quickly for Ginger to accept what she observed, so quickly that Delaney was able to catch her in his human form when she fainted.

"Smooth," Thorolf said when Ginger fainted. Delaney didn't know whether the newest member of Erik's team of *Pyr* was being sarcastic or admiring, and he didn't much care.

He should have felt more triumphant than he did, given that he'd succeeded in frightening Ginger again.

Instead, he felt like a jerk.

It was strange, but he felt the familiar combination of potency and confidence again today. He sensed that the firestorm had helped him find his old self once more. He'd hit Magnus hard enough to take the ancient *Slayer* down, however temporarily. He'd gotten Ginger out of the sanctuary and he'd defeated the *Slayers* come to do Magnus's dirty work.

There'd be more of that before it was over. It was time to get Ginger farther from danger.

He scooped Ginger up before she fell and cradled her against his chest, surprised again by the persistent spark of the firestorm. He was doubly surprised by his own protectiveness toward her. She should be simply a means to an end for him, the vessel for his child, but Delaney could already sense that Ginger wasn't a woman he'd easily forget.

He was also aware of *Pyr* disapproval of his decision to frighten her.

"She wanted to see," he said, hearing defensiveness in his tone.

"Sometimes humans are wrong about what they want and what's good for them," Sloane said, shifting smoothly as he landed beside Delaney. The Apothecary of the *Pyr* was a tourmaline dragon in his alternate form.

Delaney bit back a sharp retort, knowing that it was Sloane who had helped him to heal as much as he had. He was glad that the *Pyr* had come to help him, but his firestorm was his own business.

Both Sloane and Thorolf were eyeing the sparks that leapt between Ginger and Delaney, but Delaney wasn't going to talk about the persistent golden glow.

It didn't make any sense that the firestorm still burned, but he wasn't going to turn its satisfaction into a team effort.

The amethyst dragon landed and shifted shape, becoming Niall, the *Pyr* with the greatest affinity for the element of air. Niall had also been Delaney's business partner for years in the eco-tourism company the pair had founded. Delaney was glad to see him, glad when Niall offered him a gruff nod.

Just like old times. They'd argued when Delaney had insisted on selling his half of the business to Niall earlier in the year, and Delaney had feared that he had ended a good friendship forever. He'd told himself then that he didn't care, and wasn't really surprised to learn that conclusion was wrong.

It was good to see Niall again, good to have the *Pyr* come to fight with him.

"So, it is your firestorm," Niall said. "I wondered why it burned so strongly for me. Congratulations."

"Thanks." Delaney felt that familiar sense of being part of a team. He'd missed that feeling. He knew that the *Pyr* often felt most strongly the firestorms of those with whom they had a personal connection. He and Niall went way back, but he still hadn't expected anyone to feel his firestorm.

Much less come to help in defending it.

"Why didn't you sate it yet?" Niall asked, as blunt as ever.

"I thought I did."

Thorolf grinned. "You don't know?"

Delaney shot a killing glance at this new recruit. "Something weird is going on."

Sloane pursed his lips and folded his arms across his chest, and Delaney could see that he was thinking furiously. "Figures," he said quietly, but Delaney didn't have time to chat about it. He had to get Ginger out of the vicinity of the *Slayers*. He headed for her red truck.

He held Ginger, checked that she was breathing normally, and steadied his own thumping heart. He couldn't believe that she had followed him and was grateful that she was uninjured. She was as light as a feather in his arms, and fit there just as well as she had the night before.

He felt caught again between the mission he'd pledged to fulfill and his firestorm.

"Wait a minute, you can't just walk away," Niall said. "What were you thinking, entering the sanctuary of the Elixir alone? If you were injured or even killed, any of the *Slayers* could have made you one of them right then and there."

Delaney slanted a glance at his old friend. "I intended to die in there."

"How would you have made sure you were really dead?"

"I would have done it, somehow." Delaney spoke with grim conviction, hating that Niall's objection made some sense. "I have the motivation to make it happen."

"You should have called for help," Niall argued.

"And see you killed, too?" Delaney shook his head. "No, I know too much to ever put any of you into that situation by choice."

"We fight best as a team," Niall insisted. "I would have answered your summons."

As glad as he was to hear that, Delaney knew he would never have asked that of a friend. "I have to destroy the Elixir alone," he said, hearing resolve in his own voice. "It's the only way." He glanced down at Ginger and felt a niggle of doubt.

"That's a crazy plan. Magnus will never allow it," Sloane said.

"Magnus is down hard," Delaney said. "I left him with his guts spilling all over the floor of the sanctuary."

Niall whistled through his teeth. "So much for your not being much of a fighter."

"I've got a cause now," Delaney said, and Niall nodded his understanding.

"Are they coming?" Thorolf asked as Sloane glanced back with narrowed eyes.

"They're tending Mallory, probably taking him to the Elixir."

Meanwhile, Niall's gaze dropped to Ginger. He said nothing, just met Delaney's gaze steadily, his own expression thoughtful. *"You can count on me,"* he said in old-speak, and Delaney knew that Niall would watch out for Ginger in Delaney's absence.

It was a good feeling.

Sloane trudged over to the others, his expression grim. "You left Magnus wounded close to the Elixir, right?"

Thorolf snorted. "Just what we need—Magnus tougher than ever."

"And Mallory dead with friends close enough to give the Elixir to him," Sloane said with a sigh.

"That wasn't his plan," Niall said, defending Delaney.

"But that's how it shook out, anyway," Thorolf charged.

"I had to get Ginger out of there," Delaney said. "I'll go back and finish what I started."

"Alone?" Sloane asked.

"Alone." Delaney felt the *Pyr* exchange glances, but wasn't interested in their opinions. He was glad they had come but knew what he had to do. They wouldn't change his mind, even if they were his friends. He put Ginger into the passenger seat of the truck with care.

"Is she injured?" Sloane asked.

"No," Delaney said, not hiding his relief. "Just shocked."

"Because she didn't know the truth," Thorolf supplied. "I had to tell her."

"You shouldn't have!" Niall charged. "It's just one more truth to beguile her out of believing."

"I didn't have a choice." Thorolf threw up his hands, Niall's censure obviously hitting a nerve. "Delaney shifted shape right over her head. She asked where he went. She's not stupid—I think she'd halfway figured it out already."

"Great," Niall said again, shoving a hand through his fair hair and leaving it disheveled. "You do have a gift for complicating things."

"I just tried to help," Thorolf said, his manner petulant.

"Wait a minute," Sloane said slowly, addressing Delaney. "You consumed the Elixir, which moves you a step closer to being *Slayer*—you shouldn't have even had a firestorm."

Delaney fixed Sloane with a steady glance. "Whom are you calling *Slayer*? My blood runs red."

The *Pyr* froze in shock at this.

They all knew that Delaney's blood had initially run black after his release from the academy, then had changed back to red when Delaney had chosen to sacrifice himself if necessary to save his brother Donovan's mate. It had mingled since, predominantly red but sometimes tinged with black. Its changing hue had been an ongoing source of frustration to Delaney, and a cause of his despair.

He knew what he'd seen in the sanctuary, though.

"No darkness in it?" Sloane asked, his tone as sharp as his gaze.

Delaney was resolute. "None." He shrugged out of his jacket and peeled back his T-shirt, letting Sloane see the wound that Magnus had inflicted on him. The scab was as red as a ruby.

Sloane glanced down at Ginger, then frowned in thought.

Delaney saw that Ginger's lashes were fluttering. Her eyes opened, her gaze fixing on Delaney. He saw her surprise, her quick glance over him as if she'd confirmed that he was a man again.

To his surprise, she did a credible Desi Arnaz imitation. "Okay, hotshot, you've got some 'splainin' to do."

"Hotshot?" Niall asked, his confusion clear even in old-speak.

"We met last night and consummated the firestorm," Delaney replied. He felt the shock of his fellows.

"In one night?" Niall said.

"Not wasting any time, were you?" Sloane teased.

"No wonder she calls him hotshot," Thorolf added, and the three *Pyr* chuckled together. Delaney felt the back of his neck heat and he saw Ginger glance between them. She pushed herself out of his embrace and sparks lit where her fingers landed on Delaney's arms.

The *Pyr* caught their breath as one. *"Except it wasn't sated,"* Sloane murmured, his eyes gleaming. *"How strange."*

Ginger glared at the four men. "What's so funny?" she asked. "What did I miss?" She flung out a hand in the direction of the *Pyr* and turned to Delaney. "Who are these guys and why are they here? What happened down by the creek? Were there really dragons?" She cast an accusing glance at the sky, her frustration clear. "And why on earth is there so much thunder?"

"Looks like you *do* have some 'splainin' to do." Niall put out one hand. "Give me your keys, hotshot, and you can set the lady straight while you drive her home."

"Whose home?" Ginger demanded, her eyes narrowed.

Delaney didn't blame her for being uncertain about the arrival of the *Pyr*. They'd shown up all at once, after all. "Could we go back to your place?" Delaney asked. "I can explain things to you, but it will take a while."

"And them?"

"They're part of this story."

"So they're your friends?"

Delaney met Niall's gaze and found a glimmer of unexpected humor there. The other *Pyr* understood Delaney's hesitation, his conviction that he was too different to expect camaraderie from his former fellows.

Yet the *Pyr* had come to aid his firestorm. Sloane and Niall had fought alongside Delaney, just like old times, and Thorolf had stood guard over Delaney's mate. The bond between them was strong and their loyalty undiminished by the darkness that had made him act against his own urges in the past.

It was more than he deserved to expect of them, and he was glad of their presence.

"Yes," Delaney said with satisfaction, feeling that the change Ginger had made within him made it possible for him to claim his allegiance to the *Pyr* once more. "Yes, they're my friends."

Chapter 6

Delaney had introduced the other men quickly, then tossed the rental car keys to Niall. Ginger was still trying to make sense of their all being dragon shape shifters, not men. She'd only tried to witness Delaney's change, but she had seen Sloane and Niall as men beside her in one moment and as dragons the next.

Plus, she'd heard and felt that garnet dragon fall, shaking the earth so hard that her teeth had rattled. She'd felt the fire breathed by the jade dragon and if she'd doubted her memory, her blackened jacket was telling evidence.

She was definitely wide-awake.

On one hand, she wanted to go back and see that fallen dragon again, the one they called Mallory. She wanted to prod him, make sure he was dead, and confirm that he was really a dragon. On the other hand, it seemed smarter to let dead dragons lie.

She insisted on driving, needing to do something normal to put her thoughts in order. Delaney sat calmly beside her, looking more at ease in her battered truck than she felt.

Ginger supposed she should be more afraid of Delaney than she was. She was afraid of what he could become, but he *had* protected her. There was also that distracting shimmer of desire. Her memories of their night together and his tenderness overwhelmed her doubts.

For the moment.

Maybe it was because the heat between them was stronger than ever and impossible to ignore. It turned her thoughts in a very basic direction, which made it tough for Ginger to be logical. He cast a look her way, his expression knowing and secretive and intimate.

Ginger tingled. Was this what it meant to be beguiled?

Ginger looked back at the road. She liked how Delaney's presence made her feel, though, sexy and powerful. She caught herself admiring the lean strength of Delaney's legs, the shape of his jaw, the glint of red in his hair. She should have been thinking of what he had just done, but instead she was recalling how considerate a lover he had been.

He'd left her tingling.

And wanting more.

She could smell his skin and the cab of the truck seemed much smaller than she remembered. She thought of everything they had done together, and how Delaney had fought as a dragon—fair but hard—and felt her interest in him redouble.

There was something alluring about a man who was both a lover and a fighter, a man who could use force when necessary but be gentle in other moments. That was exactly the kind of man Ginger had always hoped to find.

The dragon bit defied belief.

But she'd seen most of it.

Incredibly enough, his explanation was the one that made the most sense.

Dragon shape shifters.

Ginger gripped the steering wheel and told herself to focus on driving. She drove with care through the snow, comfortable in the familiarity of her vehicle and knowing that few people would be on the roads this morning. Most would have the sense to stay home, put on a pot of coffee, and wait it out.

Her awareness of Delaney's presence beside her grew with every moment of silence that passed. She could hear him breathing. Heat emanated from him and seemed to grow between them. She turned off the heater, but it made no difference—the cab was filled with a golden glow and the snowflakes melted the moment they touched the windshield.

Delaney waited with a patience that Ginger appreciated. He must have known that his reality wasn't easy for someone to accept. She stole the occasional glance at him, as struck by how handsome he was as she had been the night before.

"Tell me," she invited, once she'd turned onto the highway.

He settled back in his seat and she realized he'd been uncertain of what she'd say. "There's a lot to tell," he said, but she knew from his thoughtful tone that he wasn't avoiding the discussion. "Ask me a question to get me started."

"What's the deal with the cave? And who was the jade dragon?"

Delaney frowned. "I need to start earlier than that. We're dragon shape shifters, as you saw, and we're called the *Pyr*."

"Why?"

"It's ancient Greek for 'fire.'"

"You were around to be named by the ancient Greeks?"

"Our species was. I'm not nearly that old."

She flicked him a look, curious, and found him watching her. He held her gaze, inviting the obvious question. His eyes were normal human eyes, and a warm shade of green.

His gaze made her even more aware of his presence and left her feeling both feminine and aroused.

Even knowing what she did about him.

Gran had always said that it was incredible what a person could learn to accept and Ginger saw the truth in those words again. Just a few hours ago, she'd had no idea that there even were dragon shape shifters, let alone that she'd brought one home. Not long ago, her brain had been unable to process Delaney's change, but now she was prepared to accept his advanced age.

She would have bet that she'd be able to watch the whole transformation now, knowing what was coming, but wasn't quite ready to volunteer.

Yet.

"How old *are* you?" she asked instead.

"Four hundred and fifty years, give or take." Delaney said it so matter-of-factly that Ginger believed him. It wasn't, after all, the first impossible thing she'd heard that day. "I was born in 1564."

Ginger blinked. "Not here."

"No. Ireland." He gazed out the window at the fields they passed. "In a way, this reminds me of it. Your farm brings back memories."

Ginger supposed that Ireland must have been completely agrarian in the sixteenth century. And that was where he had worked on a farm that bred and raised workhorses. It was easier to accept what he told her when she considered each fact individually. "Are you immortal, then?"

"No. We just age slowly." He waited, but Ginger just nodded, chewing on that detail. She was sitting with a man who was four hundred and some years old.

Not a man—a *Pyr*.

A dragon shape shifter.

The road was becoming harder to discern with every passing moment. Ginger supposed that the plows hadn't been out yet—but then, what would be the point, when the snow was still falling so thick and fast?

Delaney continued to speak. "Our task is to protect the treasures of the earth and that's where it gets tricky. The *Pyr* traditionally included humans among those treasures, as well as the four elements and the earth itself. A long time ago, some *Pyr* decided that humans were too destructive, and that humans had to be exterminated to protect the planet. Those *Pyr* became known as *Slayers*."

"Because they slaughter humans?"

"Yes, as well as the *Pyr* who defend humans."

Ginger nodded, understanding a bit of what she had witnessed. "Good guys and bad guys. I'm with you so far."

"Traditionally, turning *Slayer* was a choice. It was said that *Pyr* were born and *Slayers* were made."

"I heard a 'but' in that."

"But," Delaney ceded, casting her a smile that made her heart go thump, "the *Slayers* found the Dragon's Blood Elixir. We were just in the sanctuary that holds the source of the Elixir."

"That big rock crystal vial with the red juice in it."

Delaney nodded. "And the jade dragon was Magnus, leader of the *Slayers*, who defends the Elixir as his own."

"Why?"

"Because a lot of *Slayers* want a sip of the Elixir. It's supposed to confer immortality, and it does help a wounded *Slayer* to heal more quickly than is normal."

"The *Pyr* don't drink it?"

He shook his head, resolute. "It's evil." Ginger said

nothing. She could believe that. That murky red substance had just looked nasty. "It also gives those who drink it willingly the capability to learn some other powers."

"Like?"

"Changing into shapes other than dragon and man." He sighed. "Passing through a dragonsmoke perimeter mark."

Ginger understood that not all dragon shape shifters found that dragonsmoke burned. "So, why were you there?"

"To destroy the Elixir forever." Delaney spoke with unexpected heat, his passion for his quest revealed in those few words.

"Why?" He looked at her, all blazing determination, and Ginger felt the urge to clarify her meaning. "I mean, it's evil, but it seems as if you have a personal stake."

"I have the most personal stake of all," Delaney admitted, his voice falling low. He sounded dangerous and deliberate, and Ginger stifled a shiver, even though she knew his animosity wasn't directly toward her. She didn't want to see his eyes. "You see, I have tasted the Elixir."

It was the last thing Ginger would have expected him to say.

Ginger's head snapped to one side as she stared at Delaney, and she inadvertently jerked the wheel to one side. The truck swerved, skidding on the road, but Delaney reached over and grabbed the wheel, straightening their course.

Ginger told herself that her heart was jumping, because she'd nearly gone into the ditch. She knew, though, that it was Delaney's proximity that had made her pulse leap.

Never mind his confession. Had she missed something in his explanation? Wasn't it only the bad guys who drank the Elixir?

Was Delaney a *Slayer*?

The seductive heat that made her blood simmer didn't help Ginger to think straight. Even as she tried to make sense of what he had said, she thought of Delaney's tongue coaxing her response, his fingertips sliding across her breast, his lips against her ear. Lust raged within her. She thought seriously about letting the truck slide into the ditch just so she could jump his bones.

But the other *Pyr* were right behind them.

Ginger liked a bit more privacy than that.

She swallowed and gripped the steering wheel, telling herself to get her mind out of the gutter. She was in her truck with a guy who could turn into a dragon, a guy who might be one of the bad guys, and all she could think about was sex.

She tried to find a logical reason why Delaney—who she was sure was a good guy—would join the bad guys. "You drank the Elixir to become immortal like the *Slayers*?" she asked when the truck was safely back in the middle of the road.

"I was force-fed it, against my will." Delaney spoke with bitterness.

Ginger was reassured that he hadn't made the choice to turn bad. "How?"

Delaney frowned. "Let's backtrack a bit. The Elixir, you see, can raise the dead."

"Be serious."

"I am. The bodies of those *Pyr* who die but are not exposed to all four elements within half a solar day—twelve hours—can be raised if the Elixir is administered to them. They have no souls, because their spark has returned to the Great Wyvern, so their bodies are simply machines. They have no morals and can be commanded to do anything."

"Ghouls," Ginger said, negotiating a turn with care. She'd seen lots of late-night movies during her sleepless nights since Gran had died. "Zombies."

"Shadow dragons we call them. They have memories of their lives but no emotion, no morals, no soul. They're hard to destroy." He fell silent then, and she understood that they were close to the nut of the matter.

"That's why the agate dragon defended the body of the garnet one," she said, seeing again the sense behind what she had witnessed.

"Yes," Delaney said flatly. "We would have ensured that Mallory was exposed to all four elements, but Balthasar preferred to protect his body. Mallory's probably already been given the Elixir."

He was probably already a shadow dragon.

Ginger shuddered. "Isn't Magnus dead, though?"

Delaney grimaced. "Probably not. He was close enough to the Elixir that he's probably had more."

"And is stronger than ever." Ginger saw Delaney nod and understood why his mood was grim. "You didn't finish him off."

"It was more important to get you out of there."

Oh. Ginger felt a little tingle of pleasure. Delaney had abandoned his quest to ensure her safety. Even if that made his quest harder in the end, it was difficult not to be pleased by his need to protect her.

She flicked a glance his way and found him frowning at the passing fields. Probably trying to figure out how to save his mission.

She asked a question to get him started again. "How do you destroy a shadow dragon?"

"You dismember him and incinerate the pieces, then scatter the ashes to the wind." Delaney winced. "They keep fighting, no matter how badly their bodies are injured, so it's not easily done."

Ginger drove. She didn't really want to think about

facing a foe like that, one that didn't lose a step when it was decapitated. They probably had vacant stares, just like the zombies in movies, and were relentless in their determination to fulfill the commands given to them.

How many *Pyr* had died over the centuries? How big a force of ghouls had Magnus been able to raise?

Ginger chose not to think about it yet.

The snow swirled against the windshield, making it look as if she drove into a screen saver. The road was impossible to distinguish from the ditch, so she just drove in a line parallel to the power lines.

She could see the lights of the rental car following behind them and figured that, if nothing else, the *Pyr* would be able to pull her truck out of the ditch if she miscalculated where the road was.

Delaney still didn't continue, so Ginger tried to prod him. "But I still don't understand how you were fed the Elixir."

Delaney straightened, as if the memory made him restless. "I was injured badly in a battle and the *Slayers* took my body so that it couldn't be exposed to the elements."

"You were killed?"

"Yes. They imprisoned me and fed me the Elixir, but my soul hadn't departed my body."

"What does that mean?"

"It means that I was an experiment. Usually shadow dragons are made of corpses that the soul has vacated. Usually *Slayers* who have already turned against the *Pyr* drink the Elixir by choice."

"But you were *Pyr* and still had your soul."

"Exactly." Delaney smiled, but there was no humor in his expression. "Which meant the battle that raged within me for dominance over my body nearly drove me insane."

He glanced down, frowning, and Ginger gave him

time to collect his thoughts. His expression was drawn, and she was reminded again of vets who came home from war, not physically injured but not quite the same psychologically as they had been, either.

It was strange that she had initially assumed he was a serviceman. He had the same discipline and drive as men she'd known who joined the military, but was in the service of a different force.

It was still one fighting for good, though.

Delaney continued softly after a minute. "They released me and I thought I had triumphed over the Elixir's wickedness, but Magnus had submerged commands in my subconscious while I was in captivity. Each time the *Pyr* fought the *Slayers*, Magnus triggered those buried impulses and made me act against my own will."

"That's evil."

"It is." He looked up at her, his expression haunted. "I even tried to attack the mates of my brother and his friend, tried to steal their unborn babies." He swallowed, the shadows in his eyes more clear than ever. "I didn't want to do it, but I couldn't ignore Magnus's command."

Ginger could see how the memory pained him.

She also noticed that none of the *Pyr* she had met had been introduced as Delaney's brother.

Ginger frowned at the road. Delaney's confession made her believe that the Elixir hadn't managed to turn him *Slayer*. It bothered him that he had been compelled to act that way.

He was with the good guys.

Her instincts had been right.

Ha.

"Your brother isn't here, is he?" she asked quietly.

Delaney shook his head. "He doesn't trust me. I haven't trusted myself. I don't want to do anything to

Alex or little Nick. It's been better not to be in each other's presence."

Ginger understood that Delaney missed his brother but was afraid of what Magnus had done to him, was afraid that he might be compelled to do something against his will again.

It tore her heart that someone—Magnus—had put this poison in his mind. She reached across the cab and caught his hand in hers, giving his fingers a quick squeeze. He closed his hand around hers, seeming to welcome the sympathy she offered. Those sparks jumped from the point of contact, sending a glow over Ginger's skin and making her mouth go dry.

Her thoughts headed straight for earthy possibilities, right on cue. This guy had some effect on her libido. It wasn't a dragon shape-shifter thing, because the other *Pyr*, while attractive men, didn't make her heart jump.

Just Delaney.

He continued quietly, his manner intense. "You have to recognize that the strongest urge for a *Pyr* is to defend his mate, against anyone or anything."

Mate. There was a strong old word, one that made Ginger quiver. She could understand that primal urge, though. She'd dealt with enough testosterone in her time on the farm to recognize the power of biological demand.

And to respect it.

What were these dragons but raw testosterone in action? Was that why Delaney had protected her? Because he considered her to be his mate? They certainly had mated the night before—and how. The idea of his being possessive of her made that roar of desire grow.

That was exactly the kind of distracting thought Ginger didn't need.

Delaney gave her fingers a squeeze. "Something changed, Ginger."

"What do you mean?"

"In the sanctuary. Magnus tried to command me and it didn't work."

"What did he command you to do?"

"Kill you."

Oh. Ginger couldn't think about dragons roasting her, shredding her, or eating her. She didn't dare let herself remember the view down Magnus's gullet or the heat of flames burning her coat. If she did, she'd run screaming from the truck, from Delaney, from all the strange things happening in her life this morning.

She thought about snow instead. She thought about real life. She thought about the barn needing to be mucked out, cows needing to be checked, and coffee needing to be made. She felt Delaney's expectation that she would ask more questions, but she needed a minute to digest what she'd already heard.

He gave her that minute, and his understanding made her warm to him all over again. The snow squeaked under the truck tires as they rode in silence. Ginger saw her mailbox and pulled into her own driveway. She parked in her usual spot and turned off the engine. The *Pyr* parked Delaney's rental car beside her truck, but they didn't get out of the car, either.

The silence in the truck cab felt charged, erotic, dangerous. Ginger decided she needed more than those couple of minutes to review her plan.

"I guess everyone is hungry." She reached for the door handle, sparing a glance at Delaney. He was watching her with an intensity she was coming to associate with him. His eyes were green but normal. The admiration in his gaze made her heart go thump and her reservations dissolve.

She belatedly remembered what he'd said. "You never told me why you didn't do what Magnus commanded you to do."

Delaney smiled just a little, a playful curve appearing at one corner of his mouth. Ginger's mouth went dry at the memory of how that mouth could kiss, where he had kissed her, how he had made her feel. "You," he murmured. "I met you and that changed everything." His gaze danced over her, as if he was amazed by her.

Ginger tingled. This man had a dangerous power over her, an ability to make her forget everything about him.

She really should put some distance between them.

But instead, she let go of the door handle and her voice dropped to a whisper. "Be serious."

"I am. I think it's the magic of the firestorm." He slid his hand over hers, interlocking their fingers with possessive ease. She felt that heat rise beneath her skin, desire making her pulse leap. His hand felt strong and warm, protective and reliable over hers. She liked that his hand was so much larger than her own, that he was tall and broad and handsome.

And he wanted her.

"What's a firestorm?" she whispered.

"This," he said, the single word low enough to make her blood simmer. He lifted her hand to his mouth, pressing a kiss into her palm as he watched her. The kiss sizzled, shooting sparks into the cab of the truck, sparks that illuminated his features and made her chest go tight.

Ginger swallowed. Delaney pressed her hand against his chest, trapping it between his palm and the thunder of his heart. She felt the power of his heartbeat, her eyes widening as it matched its pace to her own. Their hearts seemed to beat as one, pounding golden light out from beneath their entwined fingertips, a light that melted her reservations. Ginger felt a little dizzy, a little lost in the bright green of Delaney's gaze.

Yet, at the same time, she couldn't imagine being anywhere else.

She found herself easing closer to him, putting her other hand on his shoulder. She watched him smile, satisfaction warming the light in his eyes even further.

"The firestorm marks the meeting of a *Pyr* and his destined mate," he whispered, and she felt his voice as much as she heard it.

Mate. There was that word again. "How many mates do you get?"

"Just one." Delaney bent and brushed his lips against her temple. He smiled quickly. "One is really all any *Pyr* needs."

Ginger caught her breath at the wave of desire that swept through her, the sizzle that slid over her skin from his touch. She liked to think that she wasn't easily charmed, but Delaney Shea had her wrapped right around his little finger.

Even if he was a dragon shape shifter.

Wrapped around his talon, maybe.

His hand slid to her nape, pulling her closer, and as much as she wanted his kiss, Ginger tried to be the skeptical city girl she'd always been.

"Why should I believe that?" she asked.

"You've seen the firestorm," Delaney said. "You've felt the heat of it and now you know what it means." He arched a brow, looking powerful and knowing and sexy. There was a little bit of the dragon in his confident expression and it made Ginger's heart skip with desire. "A firestorm only happens once in a lifetime. It can't be missed because sparks literally fly."

"I thought I'd imagined that."

"You thought wrong." Delaney bent down to her, his expression filled with intent. Ginger caught her breath and she shivered when he touched her cheek. There was that tenderness again, that light caress that could make her blood sing. The awe in his eyes made her heart pound. "You are the only one."

"How many women have you told that to?" she asked lightly, trying to hide how powerfully his words and his touch had affected her.

"Only one," he said with force. She looked up to see his eyes brighten as his gaze danced over her features. Ginger could have sworn he was telling her the truth. "Only you."

Delaney's words thrilled her, made it impossible for her to move away. Rational thought surrendered the war to sensation and desire, knowing the battle was long lost. Ginger's heart skipped as he bent to kiss her.

She knew what he was.

But she still thought he was the sexiest man she'd ever met.

And she wanted his kiss, this kiss, even if it wasn't the most sensible choice she'd ever made in her life. Sometimes, even Gran had said, a woman has to follow her instinct.

Ginger was running on pure intuition with this man.

And it felt right.

As right and as good as his kiss.

Delaney didn't appreciate that Thorolf rapped his knuckles on the window of the truck. It wouldn't have mattered when the *Pyr* had chosen to intervene—it would have been too soon. Ginger's kiss was sweet and hot, well worth savoring, and Delaney wasn't happy with the interruption.

He was starting to understand why Niall found Thorolf so irritating.

"Hey, I could do with some coffee," Thorolf shouted, knocking on the glass again. "It's cold out here." Delaney heard the newest recruit to the *Pyr* team stamp his feet and was sure he heard Niall and Sloane chuckle.

Delaney broke his kiss with reluctance, then smiled for Ginger. She was flushed, her lips redder than they had been. "They're not the most subtle guys on the planet," he said.

"No." A fleeting smile touched her lips. "I guess not." She flicked a glance over Delaney, exhaled, then opened her door. She jumped out of the truck. "I could use a coffee, too, actually." She slammed the truck door, then strode so quickly to the kitchen door that he halfway thought she was trying to escape him.

"Trouble in paradise," Thorolf said in old-speak, and Delaney ignored him. He got out of the truck and followed Ginger.

Was she overwhelmed? He could respect that she might need a bit of space to come to terms with all he'd told her, and knew that he found the firestorm distracting, too. Her kiss had shaken him, left him raging with desire and unable to think of much except heading back to her bedroom for another attempt to sate the firestorm.

"I thought it looked like a good kiss," Niall added, his tone teasing, but Delaney ignored him.

"Nice smoke boundary," Sloane mused, obviously trying to restore the balance between them all.

"For all it's worth, now that the Slayers *can cut smoke,"* Thorolf muttered. Delaney knew that the relatively recent addition to Erik's team of *Pyr* had yet to master the art of breathing smoke.

"It's better than nothing," Niall said, showing some of the same irritation Delaney felt at the judgment. *"Better than you could breathe, certainly."*

Thorolf's eyes flashed, then he and Niall glared at each other. Their mutual animosity was well established, and of no interest to Delaney. He saw Ginger glance over her shoulder and up at the sky, frowning.

"You going to beguile her?" Thorolf asked.

Delaney shook his head. *"No. I'm telling her the truth."* He followed Ginger to the porch then, ending the conversation because he didn't want the *Pyr*'s advice on how to manage his relationship with Ginger. He still knew what he had to do, he still expected to die doing it, and he wanted her to know at least that he had been honest with her.

Even though there was a whole lot more truth to be shared.

Ginger pushed open the kitchen door and passed the weight of the storm door to him, starting to shrug out of her jacket before she glanced toward the table and froze.

"Coffee's on." Rafferty, one of the oldest of the *Pyr*, sat at the table, his long legs outstretched and crossed in front of him. He had his hands wrapped around a steaming mug of coffee, and Ginger looked from him to the pot still on the stove. "I hope you don't mind my making a pot. I figured you all would need it."

"Who are you and what are you doing in my house?" Ginger demanded.

Rafferty rose to his feet, all of his courtly charm on display. "Rafferty Powell, at your service." He bowed slightly. "The door was unlocked, and I thought it smarter to wait out the storm inside."

Ginger glanced to the driveway, then back at the table. "I forgot to lock the door," she recalled, speaking almost to herself before she looked at Rafferty again. "But there's no car and there are no tracks."

Rafferty smiled. *"I heard the smoke,"* he said in old-speak.

"Thunder again!" Ginger said with obvious frustration.

"He's a friend of mine, actually," Delaney said.

Ginger's eyes narrowed. "Another friend? Or another *Pyr*?"

"Both," Delaney and Rafferty said in unison.

Ginger closed her eyes for a minute as she took a deep breath. "How many of you are there?"

"Not enough," Rafferty said, and it looked as if Ginger might challenge his conclusion.

Delaney stepped forward and touched her elbow. The spark made Rafferty's eyes widen. "Sit down and I'll get you a coffee."

"Black, please," she said, sinking into a chair. "I need the strongest hit I can get this morning."

"And that's not thunder," Delaney continued as he poured her coffee. "You're hearing old-speak."

The *Pyr* hung back, standing around the perimeter of the room except for Rafferty who took his seat again. They were waiting for him to reassure his mate, and although Delaney appreciated that courtesy, he was beginning to wish they weren't so good at making trouble for him.

"What's old-speak?"

"It's how we communicate with one another. Our senses are more sensitive than human senses, so we can hear sounds at lower frequencies. When we communicate with old-speak, it sounds like thunder to humans."

Ginger arched a brow as Delaney put the mug of coffee on the table in front of her. "So, now you have secrets from me, too?"

Rafferty hid his smile behind his mug as he took a sip of coffee. His twinkling eyes gave away his amusement.

"Why is that funny?" Ginger asked.

"Because mates never take well to old-speak," Rafferty said. "I'm always interested in the explanations and rationalizations of the individual *Pyr* before the inevitable result."

The tension eased out of Ginger under the influence of Rafferty's calm demeanor. He had that effect upon humans, with his slow speech and mellow manner. It was his affinity for the element of earth that gave him a reassuring aura.

"What's the inevitable result?" Ginger asked.

"The *Pyr* always give up old-speak in the presence of their mates," Rafferty said with complete confidence. He smiled at Ginger. "Don't be fooled—mates have a dangerous power over the *Pyr*, despite their fire-breathing ferocity."

Ginger made a sound of approval and glanced at Delaney, her manner expectant. It was such a small concession to make.

He could return to scaring her later.

It was the firestorm undermining his conviction. Delaney knew it, yet he couldn't stop himself.

"I don't see any reason why we shouldn't speak in tones that Ginger can hear," he said, and was rewarded by her smile. The sight made his heart skip a beat and he was shocked at the power this woman already had over him.

"Absolutely," Niall agreed, quick to support Delaney. Sloane and Thorolf nodded; then Ginger's smile broadened.

Delaney felt relieved that the moment had been saved, but that sense wouldn't last long.

Chapter 7

"I expect everyone is hungry," Ginger said, and there was a general murmur of assent. Delaney enjoyed the sight of her satisfaction and thought that giving up old-speak—for the moment—was a small price to pay.

She took a swig of coffee, then got to her feet. She crossed the kitchen, quickly ensuring that each of the *Pyr* had a mug of coffee and putting on another pot. He followed her as she opened a door on the far side of the kitchen and was surprised to see a large, stainless steel fridge and matching freezer.

"They didn't look good in the kitchen," she said with a smile. She opened the freezer and he was surprised by how full it was. "Tanya and I have been making the food for the wedding reception ahead of time. Those two thousand appetizers are the last of it." He remembered what she had said about being a trained chef and was intrigued.

Ginger, meanwhile, pulled out a pound of frozen bacon.

"Heirloom pigs?" he guessed, and she smiled.

"Raised organically in the next county," she agreed.

"Let me do something to help," Delaney said, and she let him begin to fry the bacon. He was impressed by how efficiently she moved and knew she'd made a plan for preparing the meal. He stayed out of her way as he started the bacon, but watched.

Niall, Sloane, and Thorolf tried to become invisible and failed—they stood around the kitchen and nearly filled it with muscle. Rafferty watched with amusement, sipping his coffee as Delaney and Ginger worked together.

Delaney felt Ginger stop beside him. She held two cartons of eggs but knew she wasn't just assessing the progress of the bacon. "Why are your friends here?" she asked him in an undertone. "Is it because you were going to destroy the Elixir?"

Delaney tried to warn her in time. "They can still hear you."

"It's because of the firestorm," Rafferty said, proving that Delaney's claim was true.

Ginger turned to consider the older *Pyr*, clearly surprised that he had heard her words.

"Those sharp *Pyr* senses," Delaney murmured, and she nodded in understanding.

"We can also sense the firestorm," Rafferty said, calmly continuing his explanation. "No matter where we are." He put out one hand, spreading his fingers as if savoring the heat from a bonfire. "We can feel the heat, possibly because it's our obligation to our own kind to facilitate firestorms when we can."

Ginger flicked a look at Delaney, her skepticism clear. "You help one another get lucky?"

"That's not what the firestorm is about," Rafferty declared.

"I know that the firestorm marks a *Pyr* meeting his destined mate," Ginger said, clutching the cartons of eggs. "Delaney just explained that."

Rafferty's gaze flicked to Delaney, who shrugged.

Ginger caught the exchange and turned on Delaney. "There's more, isn't there? What else does the firestorm mean?"

Delaney licked his lips. The *Pyr* waited in silence, having already given him plenty of rope to hang himself. Rafferty looked expectant. Niall was smothering a smile. Sloane had developed a fascination with his own fingertips and Thorolf was grinning. Delaney would have liked to have had this discussion with Ginger on his own schedule.

Or maybe not at all.

And Ginger sensed that.

He already knew she wasn't the kind of person to pretend otherwise. Ginger put the eggs down and placed one hand on her hip. "What aren't you telling me? Come on, cough it up."

"The firestorm also means that the mate conceives the *Pyr*'s son," Delaney admitted.

Ginger made a dismissive wave of one hand. "No such chance. I take the pill." She would have turned to the stove, but Rafferty spoke.

"That doesn't matter," he said, and Delaney wished he hadn't.

"Excuse me?" Ginger turned on Rafferty again.

"The pill is known to have a small failure rate in preventing conception." Rafferty shrugged. "I guarantee you that the firestorm will ensure that is what happens between you and Delaney."

Delaney winced to have that detail aired. As much as he was glad to have the support of his fellow *Pyr*, they did have a tendency to be annoying.

Life would have been a lot easier if they had just shut up.

Ginger's eyes flashed as she turned to Delaney again. "You *knew* that?"

He felt the back of his neck heat. "Well, yeah. That's the point—"

Ginger interrupted him. "You *intended* to get me pregnant without talking to me about it first?" she demanded, her voice rising. "Don't you think that I might have had other plans for the next twenty years of my life? Don't you think you ought to have *asked*?" She threw out her hands. "Oh, no, that's right—you *left* this morning without even talking to me!"

"Ginger, I . . ."

She shook a finger at him and he took a step back from her anger. "You planned a one-nighter to knock me up! You *planned* to leave me pregnant. Just who in the hell do you think you are?"

Delaney didn't have a good answer for her. He'd thought only of his duty to the *Pyr*, not of the implications for Ginger, and felt foolish as a result. "It's my responsibility—," he began, but she interrupted him again.

"Responsibility? What am I? Just a womb for the taking? I can't believe I thought you were a gentleman." She practically growled as she opened one carton of eggs. "I can't believe I thought you were a keeper."

"Ginger, I—"

She turned on him again. "You really think it's that easy for a woman to raise a child alone?" Ginger flung out a hand. "Never mind a child who's going to be a dragon shape shifter . . ."

"We *Pyr* don't come into our abilities until puberty," Rafferty interjected softly.

"Great!" Ginger said, facing the older *Pyr*. "That would give me twelve or thirteen years to figure out how to explain that to the school." She glared at Delaney, her hands on her hips, and he thought again that she was a little spitfire. "What was in your head? Or maybe your planning was being done a bit lower down."

Delaney shuffled his feet, feeling as he did whenever he'd been called on the carpet by Erik, leader of the *Pyr*. "I guess I wasn't thinking clearly...."

"Well, neither was I." Ginger growled in irritation, then whirled and headed for the stove. She dropped a second cast-iron skillet onto the burner so hard that he feared one or the other would crack.

She was furious and every *Pyr* in the kitchen knew it.

Delaney didn't look at his fellows. His firestorm wasn't going well and he wasn't sure what to do about it.

He wasn't even sure why it was still burning.

Could Ginger be right? Was the pill working?

It was one thing for Delaney to be a dragon shape shifter.

It was quite another for him to be a dragon shape shifter who had unilaterally decided she should bear his son, had tried to impregnate her without discussing it first, then had planned to disappear forever without telling her the truth.

Men!

Or maybe *Pyr*!

Ginger cracked eggs so hard that each and every yolk broke. The *Pyr* would get scrambled eggs for breakfast, which was a damn sight more than they deserved, given the way they'd shown up uninvited with lofty expectations.

Maybe being a dragon shape shifter made a man presumptuous.

Maybe the details didn't matter.

Delaney was smart enough to keep out of Ginger's way. In fact, the *Pyr* all kept a low profile, murmuring quietly to one another at the table. They didn't use their old-speak, though, and Ginger could hear their words.

Niall came to her side and offered to help—she pointed him to dishes and cutlery, preferring not to be close to Delaney just yet.

She had to collect her thoughts first.

A child.

Delaney's child. The prospect had a dangerous appeal, which just proved she wasn't thinking clearly, either. As much as Ginger would have liked to have had children, as much as she was attracted to Delaney, a one-night stand with her left alone and pregnant wasn't her preferred way to begin a family.

She hoped Rafferty was wrong about the pill.

No, she *prayed* that Rafferty was wrong about the pill.

When the table was set, Ginger put Niall to work making toast. Ginger figured they'd need the better part of a loaf of bread, and the toaster only took two slices at once. Thorolf set the table at her instruction, the *Pyr* who towered over her leaping to his feet when she asked for help.

At another time, she would have been amused by how they were all spooked by her. In this moment, though, Ginger was too angry to care.

Delaney had planned to leave her pregnant. Ginger was beginning to seriously question the reliability of her intuitive trust of him. Had her instincts led her wrong? There would have been a strange irony in the best regional matchmaker being unable to make a decent match for herself.

Doubtless she'd find that funny another day.

Maybe the day that her next period started, right on time.

"Let me see those wounds again," Sloane urged from the other side of the room.

"I'm fine," Delaney said, with obvious impatience. Ginger could feel him watching her, but she pretended to be oblivious to him. She whipped the eggs to a froth, then dumped them into the sizzling butter in the pan.

It was patently unfair for her to still find the man sexy. Her body was on his side and that was just wrong. She jabbed a spatula into the eggs.

"It's my job to decide that," Sloane argued, and Ginger heard Delaney make a sigh of concession. She saw him move from the corner of her eye and glimpsed that rugby shirt falling on the kitchen chair she'd abandoned.

If there was eye candy, it only seemed fair for her to have a sample.

Ginger glanced over her shoulder and her heart stopped cold. Delaney was bare chested in her kitchen, as buff as she recalled, and he was staring directly at her. He was tanned and muscular, as magnificent in the daylight as he'd been at night. He looked taut, irritated, and as sexy as any man she'd ever seen.

He had a nasty cut on his chest and Sloane was frowning as he daubed at the wound. That silver cross was even more beautifully detailed than she recalled and it shone against his tanned skin. Delaney seemed to be indifferent to Sloane's murmuring—although he winced when Sloane got some salve from his satchel and rubbed it into the wound.

Delaney's attention was so fixed on Ginger that she felt snared by his gaze. She stared back at him, even as she smelled the eggs burning a bit. His expression was grim and she wondered whether he was more annoyed with himself or with her. She was usually less impulsive than she had been the night before.

He raised a hand toward her as if he'd make a plea on his own behalf, and Ginger felt her resolve weaken. She spun to move the eggs around the pan. She told herself not to care that they were too brown on one side, but busied herself with keeping them from burning again.

Delaney had expected her to have his child.

Was there more to the story than she already knew? The look in his eyes made her think she had condemned him without a trial—shouldn't she learn all of the facts first?

Was she crazy to even think about giving him a chance to explain?

Her imagination began to conjure possibilities. Maybe she was wrong that he'd intended to leave this morning. Maybe he'd meant to come back. How permanent were the *Pyr*'s relationships with their mates? Ginger knew on some level that she shouldn't even be curious—curiosity was one step closer to forgiving him—but she was.

That was probably a bad sign, but Ginger couldn't help it. She *was* curious and there was no point in denying the truth.

"Red, red, red," Sloane was saying with approval, which made no sense to Ginger at all. "There's not a drop of black in your blood anymore."

Ginger glanced over her shoulder again, seeing Sloane daub at Delaney's wounds.

"I told you that." Delaney frowned, his attention fixed on Ginger. She turned her back again before he could catch her eye.

She knew her weaknesses. Listening wasn't the same as surrendering all reason, but if Delaney touched her, she'd be a goner.

Maybe a pregnant goner. Yikes. Was Gran rolling in her grave because Ginger had been so impetuous?

"Since when?" Sloane demanded.

"I told you."

"Tell me again." Sloane sounded impatient as well. "This is big, Delaney. I need to try to understand what's happening to you."

Delaney made a sound of frustration. "Okay. Since yesterday."

"The firestorm," Rafferty said with undisguised satisfaction. When Ginger peeked, she saw that the other *Pyr* looked impressed as well, but their admiration was for Delaney.

Or his good fortune.

She supposed that if you waited four hundred years to meet your match, it might be a pretty special moment.

Delaney had given her the credit for his ability to deny Magnus. Did he mean her personally, or the firestorm in general? Ginger much preferred to think that she had had a powerful impact on Delaney—maybe as powerful as the impression he'd made on her—than that a force of nature was responsible for the change.

"So, your firestorm finished what Donovan's firestorm began," Sloane mused. "It makes a certain sense, since our own firestorms are said to burn the hottest of all."

"And are best at cauterizing our wounds," Rafferty said.

Ginger cleared her throat. She kept her tone cool, as if she were less interested than she was. "If you're talking about Delaney's firestorm, shouldn't you include me in the discussion?"

"She's right," Niall said quickly, and Ginger was glad to have an ally.

She noted the glances the *Pyr* exchanged, then put the eggs in a serving dish and carried the dish to the table. Niall got the bacon and pushed down the button on the toaster once more. The *Pyr* hesitated a minute, then she gave Thorolf the serving spoon.

"Eat while they're hot," she said, and he needed no further encouragement to dig in.

"This is really good," Thorolf said a moment later.

"It's what I do," Ginger said, more interested in the *Pyr* than in her cooking. At Thorolf's glance, she elaborated. "I'm a chef. I cook. Those are organic eggs from my chickens, and bacon from Smith's organic pork farm, whole grain bread from the natural-food store in town."

"The butter is phenomenal," Sloane said.

"Tanya churns it for me, from my girls' milk. She runs a small artisan cheese operation and uses milk from me and from the Van Vliets' goats."

Rafferty smiled and saluted her with his coffee. "It's good not to be the only one attuned to the songs of the earth. Thank you for your hospitality, especially as we are uninvited."

The *Pyr* joined him in thanking Ginger and she found herself blushing a bit that they were so fulsome in their praise. "It's just bacon and eggs."

"I've never had bacon and eggs like this," Thorolf said.

Niall nodded, then eyed Delaney. "I can't believe you went after the Elixir after feeling your firestorm. You had to know that you might not come back."

"Or might not come back the same," Sloane clarified.

Ginger looked to Delaney in alarm. It was one thing to take on a noble quest, quite another to expect to die doing it.

Delaney remained standing with his back against the wall, his arms folded across his bare chest. His eyes were dark and his expression impossible to read. "Don't you guys have somewhere else to be?"

"I don't think so," Niall said with resolve. "Not if you're so determined to undertake a suicide mission."

Ginger set down her fork, unable to eat in her dismay.

"Ginger and I need to talk." Delaney was grim. "Alone."

Ginger was in complete agreement with that, but the *Pyr* stayed put.

"We all need to talk," Sloane said. When Delaney might have argued again, Sloane fixed him with a look. "Destroying the Elixir is too big a task for a single *Pyr* to take on alone."

"It's my responsibility!" Delaney argued.

"Says who?" Rafferty asked softly.

Delaney ignored him. His mouth set into a stubborn line that reminded Ginger of her grandmother.

"Look what happened when you tried," Sloane countered. "Mallory is probably sipping of the Elixir as we speak."

"Another *Slayer* who is tough to defeat," Thorolf said, rolling his eyes.

Niall shook his head. "Sit down and eat already."

Delaney kept standing.

"And Magnus at the foot of the Elixir, ready for more," Thorolf added. "It's a fuckup, no matter how you look at it." He picked up the serving spoon in the dish of scrambled eggs. "If you're not eating, I'm going to finish this."

"I'm trying to remember why I'm friends with you guys," Delaney complained. "Why don't you say what you really think?"

"Don't shoot," Sloane said lightly. "But we like you alive." The others chuckled while Delaney glowered.

"We should have gone in together," Niall argued. "We should have made a plan. . . ."

"And at least one of you wouldn't have come back," Delaney retorted. "I'll take care of it myself, in my way and on my time. It's my responsibility."

"Why?" Rafferty asked again.

"How?" Niall demanded.

Delaney glared at them both in obstinate silence. Ginger had to admit that Delaney's friends were making more sense than he was.

"Didn't you just try? Didn't your plan fail?" Niall

continued, his manner adversarial. He stabbed at his eggs with his fork. "And for what? Your chest ripped open and nothing good achieved. You used to be smart enough to admit when you were wrong, never mind when you needed a new plan."

"No one but no one is going to go through what I went through," Delaney said, his tone harsh. "You have no idea what hell the Elixir plays with your mind. I'll take care of it."

"How?" Niall asked again.

"Somehow," Delaney said with force.

The *Pyr* fell silent then, their expressions grim as they ate. As much as Ginger could respect Delaney's determination to protect his friends, she didn't like the idea of his dying in their defense.

"Sit. Eat." At Rafferty's gruff command, Delaney finally pulled on his T-shirt again and joined the group. Rafferty commandeered the spoon from Thorolf. Niall gave Delaney a playful punch in the shoulder, but Delaney didn't acknowledge the gesture.

The silence was oppressive. Ginger ate but didn't taste her food, her thoughts swirling with all she had learned.

"Why you?" Rafferty asked again, his quiet words unattended while Delaney finished his meal.

"Why not me?" Delaney asked with annoyance.

"I can think of a lot of reasons," Niall began, but Delaney glared at him.

He pushed aside his plate. "Look. Whoever destroys the Elixir won't come back. That's a given." He spoke with a conviction that made Ginger glance up at him, horrified. Those shadows were back in his eyes again. "It has to be me."

"Why?" Rafferty asked again, his tone still mild.

"You're going to tell me you've got nothing to live for?" Niall asked. Ginger felt the *Pyr* looking at her. "I tried to believe that six months ago, but I won't buy it now."

Delaney ignored that comment, too, although Ginger's heart skipped a beat. "The vial should have shattered," he said with force. "I hit it with everything I had."

"What vial?" Sloane asked, his eyes lighting with curiosity.

"The Elixir is stored in a massive vial, one that looks like it's been carved out of rock crystal," Delaney said. He grabbed a napkin and drew the layout of the sanctuary on it, plus a sketch of the vial. The *Pyr* leaned close to study it as he worked. "There are stairs winding around the vial to the summit. It's in the third and last cavern after you enter the sanctuary." He started to say something else but frowned and fell silent. "It should have shattered."

"So, it can't be destroyed with force," Rafferty said. "Interesting." He began to twist an unusual ring that he wore on his left hand. It could have been made of black and white glass wound together. The *Pyr* watched his gesture and she noticed that they became disconcerted.

What was the deal with the ring?

Was Rafferty sending them some other message she couldn't hear?

"That's just more proof that we have to work together." Sloane pushed his empty plate aside and templed his fingers together as he regarded Ginger. "And that means *all* of us." The *Pyr* nodded and looked at Ginger again. She felt like a bug under a magnifying glass. "The firestorm has brought you into this, but you must find some of it confusing." His expression was serious and his manner thoughtful. "Did Delaney tell you about the Elixir?"

Ginger nodded. "That he was forced to consume it and it almost made him go nuts."

"Right." Sloane nodded. "Because he wasn't *Slayer* in the first place, it didn't make him immortal as it does for those *Slayers* who drink it by choice. Because he wasn't dead, it didn't make him into a shadow dragon. As near as I can figure, he's been caught between the living and the dead." Sloane indicated Delaney's wound. "*Slayers* have black blood. It's said that the darkness of their blood is a reflection of the darkness in their hearts, and a sign of the withdrawal of the Great Wyvern's favor."

"Why?" Ginger asked. She felt the tension between the *Pyr* lessen, as they turned their attention to explaining the situation to her. She could feel the bedrock of their familiarity with one another, the root of their old friendship, and knew they were angry only because Delaney was putting himself at risk.

She could respect that.

Rafferty, meanwhile, took Delaney's sketch and turned it over. He began to write across the back of the sheet of paper and Ginger assumed he was making notes. The other *Pyr* ignored him, so maybe it was a habit of his.

She liked that they knew one another well and had some tolerance for their friends' quirks. That was what made friendship work, in Ginger's opinion.

She also liked that they had come to help Delaney's firestorm, even if it meant arguing with him to do so.

"*Slayers* have black blood because they choose self-interest over the collective good," Niall explained.

"Because they choose the shadow over the light," Sloane said.

"Why is that important?"

"Because Delaney's blood has kept changing. When first he returned to us, it was dark and his eyes were empty." Sloane frowned and Ginger thought again of zombies in B-movies. "It was as if his spirit had been banished to a hidden corner of himself."

That adhered to Ginger's impression of Delaney having endured some ordeal. She nodded in understanding. Delaney pushed himself to his feet and paced her kitchen, clearly restless.

Was he that anxious to die?

Or did he just dislike having his weakness discussed so openly?

"But then he was drawn to the heat of Donovan's firestorm," Rafferty added, pushing the sheet of paper aside and laying the pencil atop it. "The light pierced his darkness, summoning him like a beacon."

"We always feel the heat of the firestorm," Delaney added. She appreciated that he was trying to help her understand their world. "But we feel it more keenly when it's that of someone we know well."

"I was drawn to yours, for example," Niall said, then smiled for Ginger. She understood then that he and Delaney were good friends, and that was why he was trying to ease the situation. "Not quite like a moth to the flame."

"That was Delaney's role," Rafferty said, his tone joking.

"But close to it," Niall concluded.

"So, what happened with Donovan's firestorm?" Ginger asked, intrigued by the story they were telling her.

"He's my brother," Delaney said.

"And exposure to his firestorm turned Delaney's blood red again," Sloane said.

"Clarified it," Rafferty said.

Niall pointed a fork at Sloane. "When Delaney protected Alex—"

"Donovan's mate," Rafferty supplied, "doing so potentially at his own expense—"

"He was wounded in the fight that followed," Niall said, nodding.

"And his blood ran red," Sloane concluded with satisfaction. "But since then, it's wavered back and forth, the red ascendant but the black staining the flow. There was a change, but not a complete recovery."

"It's depressing." Delaney glared out the window. He looked tormented again, burdened by the memory of some ordeal, and Ginger felt sorry for him.

"But you said something changed," Ginger reminded him. "You said you were able to deny Magnus's command in the sanctuary."

He smiled at her, the change in his expression making her heart skip. "I was, and that's because of you." He held her gaze, letting her see his conviction. "That was no lie, Ginger."

She couldn't stop herself from smiling back at him.

Which just proved she was a complete sucker for this man.

And maybe not as bright as she'd always thought she was.

Ginger sobered and averted her gaze from Delaney's smile, focusing instead on a piece of cold toast. It tasted like sawdust—organic sawdust—but she ate it anyway.

"Because of the firestorm," Rafferty said. "His ability to deny Magnus is like his blood running red again. It's a sign of healing."

"The firestorm heals our wounds," Niall said.

Sloane frowned. "But what I don't understand is why the firestorm is still burning."

"How long does it usually burn?" Ginger asked, and each *Pyr* developed a fascination with his plate. Delaney's neck was ruddy again, but he was the only one who would meet her gaze. "What did I say?"

"Something I said, I'm afraid," he admitted gruffly. "The firestorm burns until the *Pyr* and his mate are intimate. That's when they conceive."

Ginger knew enough about biology to argue the

point. "That doesn't happen instantly. It takes at least a week for the embryo to implant in the uterus."

Delaney's jaw set. "It happens immediately for us."

"First time, every time. A *Pyr* and his mate only have to have sex once to get the job done," Thorolf said cheerfully, cocking a finger at Ginger after helping himself to more eggs. "And hey, we know why you call him 'hotshot.'"

Delaney had told his friends that he and Ginger had had sex. Why had she imagined he'd be more circumspect than that?

"Thorolf!" Delaney protested, but Ginger was already on her feet, leaving the table. She knew her face was scarlet. She spun around when Delaney touched her elbow. Sparks leapt from his touch, but she backed away until her butt collided with the counter.

His expression was unrepentant and that finished her.

"You *told* them?" she demanded. "How *much* did you tell them?"

Ginger held up a hand before Delaney could answer. She had made a mistake and she was going to fix it immediately. "No, wait. I don't want to know. That's enough. You try to get me pregnant; you intend to destroy the Elixir and get yourself killed; you're going to leave me pregnant and alone; you tell your friends about your *score*, and I nearly get killed by dragons on top of it all." She pointed to the door. "That's it! The kitchen is closed. All of you, out!"

"Ginger, it's not like that ...," Delaney said, beginning to make an appeal that Ginger didn't want to hear.

"There is nothing you can say to save this situation," she told him, and meant every word. "In fact, you can leave first and lead the way."

"They asked why I hadn't satisfied the firestorm before going after the Elixir," Delaney argued, his own voice rising as he got to his feet. "I had to defend my decision! I had to tell them I had fulfilled my responsibility to the *Pyr.* . . ."

"What about your responsibility to me?" Ginger demanded. "What about my choices? What about *my* privacy?" She slapped her forehead. "Oh wait, that doesn't matter. I'm just a *mate*." She pointed to the door again. "Out!"

Chapter 8

Ginger thought that Delaney would just surrender the fight, but instead, he got a determined look. He came after her, pursuing her right across the kitchen. He was so intent on arguing his case that she was surprised.

Wasn't he the one who'd planned to just leave? Why should he care what she thought of him?

But he did.

Ginger hated how appealing she found that fact.

His eyes shone. "I had to tell them that I'd fulfilled my responsibility to the *Pyr*, to sate the firestorm. I admit that I wasn't thinking further than that. . . ."

Delaney reached for her, but Ginger interrupted him. "Let me explain something very basic to you," she said. "I believe in love and I believe in romance. I believe in two souls finding each other and making a future together, one based on choice and mutual respect. I believe in creating a family out of love, not out of biological urges, and I believe in waiting for a match that is worth having. I believe that nothing of merit comes for free."

Delaney folded his arms across his chest to watch her, but he didn't interrupt.

Ginger took a deep breath. "Your firestorm makes sense to me, as a kind of kismet thing. You seem to view it as a reproductive necessity, like a bitch that has come into heat being in the same pen with the stud."

"I never said that!"

"You didn't have to. I got the subtext. And if you're not interested in making a permanent relationship, then I'm not interested in having a child, firestorm be damned."

"The firestorm is a mark of destiny," Delaney said.

"Well, I believe in free will, too," Ginger retorted. "You had no right to make that kind of choice for me. You were absolutely, totally, out of line, and since you don't understand that, there is nothing to talk about." She pointed to the door. "Out."

Rafferty began to applaud, a gesture that earned him a ferocious glance from Delaney. "I like feisty mates," Rafferty said, his tone teasing. "It keeps things interesting."

"But the firestorm shouldn't still be burning," Sloane reminded her. "As Thorolf said, it should have been sated as soon as, well, you know."

"Ginger . . ." Delaney took a step closer and Ginger felt that predictable flush of heat. Her toes curled in her boots and she was keenly aware of the breadth of Delaney's shoulders.

And the appeal in his eyes.

This man was dangerous. He could make Ginger forget everything she knew to be true, and act against her own best interests. "Wait," she said when he might have come closer and eliminated her ability to think clearly. "If the firestorm burns until a conception is made, then I'm not pregnant, am I?"

Rafferty shook his head.

Ginger took a deep breath. "Well, then, there are only two possibilities, aren't there?" she said. "Either my pill is working"—she pointed at Delaney—"or you're shooting blanks, hotshot."

Delaney's eyes flashed green fire.

Sloane's expression turned pensive. "Now, that's an interesting idea," he mused.

Ginger wasn't interested in his conclusions. She reached for her jacket and hauled on her boots. "I've got stock to check. When I get back, you'd better all be gone."

"Ginger, we need to talk."

The way Delaney said her name was seductive and sexy, reminding her of the way she had shivered beneath his touch the night before. It would have been easy to listen to his explanation and find it plausible. It would have been easy to surrender to him again, to drag him back to her bedroom for another round.

The man had an ability to mess with her own clear thinking and she was right to toss him out.

Even if it felt wrong.

The only good news was that she evidently wasn't pregnant. She'd gotten lucky, and she wasn't going to count on that happening again. If putting distance between herself and Delaney was the only way to achieve that, she'd do it.

"I think you've said plenty." Ginger paused at the doorway. "It'd be nice if you did the dishes, but I know better than to expect too much."

Niall winced.

"Ouch," said Thorolf. "No point letting this go to waste," he added, and loaded his plate one more time.

Sloane was lost in thought, as if he was trying to remember something.

Rafferty was utterly still, except for his gaze flicking over everyone in the kitchen in turn. Ginger knew he was noting every nuance of response and had the sense that he had enjoyed her outburst.

Ginger didn't look at Delaney. She didn't dare. She

simply left, letting the kitchen door slam behind her. It wasn't often that she was in the mood to muck out the barn, but she was sufficiently fed up with the *Pyr* to be looking forward to evicting bullshit.

From her barn and from her kitchen.

Ha.

Well, that had gone well. Delaney turned on his so-called friends and let his lousy mood show.

"Thanks for nothing," he said. He knew he had to pursue this quest alone and even with the firestorm's appearance, he'd known he could handle it. There was a puzzle to be solved about breaking the Elixir's vial, but he'd solve it.

As well as the mystery of why his firestorm continued to burn. The last thing he needed—and the one thing that could condemn his chances of success, at least with Ginger—was the *Pyr*'s collective presence.

"Again, I have to ask whether you guys don't have some place better to go."

Rafferty settled back to savor his coffee. "I always insist on ringside seats to a firestorm."

"This isn't a group effort!"

"But your success with Ginger concerns all of us, dude," Thorolf said. "Like Erik always says, we need more *Pyr*."

"I could stand having fewer *Pyr*, at least in the vicinity," Delaney retorted. "Why don't you all leave? I'll call if I need you."

"Right." Niall watched Delaney with affection. "The boy learns to fight and thinks he can kick the whole world's butt by himself. Wait till I tell Donovan."

Thorolf jabbed his fork through the air at Delaney. "You need help with those *Slayers*. Without Niall and Sloane, you'd have been drinking the Elixir yourself by now."

"And I'd be staving off its effects again," Delaney replied. "I'm tougher than I was, and I can handle this."

"Your plan sucks and you should be smart enough to know it." Thorolf ate with gusto even as he criticized. His attitude only made Delaney more angry.

"My plan is the only plan," Delaney insisted.

"Delaney's right," Sloane said abruptly, pushing to his feet. "I've got other things to do than stay where I'm not wanted."

Delaney wasn't the only one surprised by the Apothecary's change of heart. Rafferty watched Sloane with consideration.

"Like what?" Thorolf challenged.

Sloane smiled. "I want to catch up on my reading."

"Ah!" said Rafferty, as if this made perfect sense. He emptied his mug of coffee with satisfaction, then set it aside and stood. "I suddenly recall that I also have errands to run."

"You really don't want us around?" Niall asked Delaney. He was still seated at the table and looked reluctant to leave.

"No." Delaney was adamant. "I need to talk to Ginger. Alone."

"You need to *seduce* Ginger, man," Thorolf corrected.

Delaney glared at him. "Which also isn't going to happen with an audience. You heard the lady. Out."

"You've got to promise not to go after the Elixir again alone," Niall said.

"I don't have to promise anything," Delaney argued. "I know what I have to do, and I know what I'm up against. You don't."

"Delaney . . ." Niall began to argue again .

"Look, could you maybe respect my insight on this?" Delaney demanded, knowing his tone was sharp. "I don't want help. I don't need help. You all need to leave. Now."

Thorolf and Niall exchanged a look and rose to their feet in turn. "If you insist," Niall said with obvious reluctance.

"I do."

The *Pyr* headed for the door, their strides revealing their respective levels of enthusiasm for departing, but Rafferty halted in front of Delaney.

"You'll see that it's not as simple as you believe," he said with confidence. There was wisdom in his dark eyes, and understanding. His words were low and fell slowly from his lips.

Delaney braced himself for advice from the ancient *Pyr*, who was the most enamored with the idea of the firestorm. He didn't doubt that Rafferty had a comment or two, and he knew those comments wouldn't change his mind.

"You have to recognize that the Great Wyvern chooses a mate for each of us who can best help us learn what we need to know," Rafferty said. "*Pyr* and mate can be two halves of a whole, partners working together, the better to fulfill their respective destinies."

Delaney ran a hand over his hair. "Okay, I should have talked to her. I understand that now. . . ."

"More than that," Rafferty interrupted with quiet force. "The Great Wyvern will demand far more of you than that." He held Delaney's gaze steadily for a moment, then pivoted and strode to the door. He held up his left hand, letting the white and black ring catch the light. That ring was all that remained of Nikolas and Sophie, and just the sight of it stole the breath in Delaney's lungs. "There are many kinds of sacrifice, and sometimes the one that appears to be greatest isn't the greatest after all."

Delaney was impatient with Rafferty's tendency to make enigmatic comments. "What's that supposed to mean?"

Rafferty smiled. "That choosing to live can be harder than choosing to die."

Delaney didn't know what to say to that. Nikolas and Sophie's mutual sacrifice had been key in destroying Magnus's dark academy, after all. They had died to cleanse the earth of that foul place and that had been no small accomplishment.

How could it be wrong for him to choose to make a similar sacrifice, and surrender his own life in exchange for eliminating the Elixir? How could it be wrong to surrender everything he had to make the world a safer and better place? How could it be wrong for him to guarantee that his son or his fellows never had to suffer what he had endured?

It couldn't be. Rafferty just didn't understand the stakes.

Rafferty had never felt the Elixir try to claim his body.

Rafferty had never known the despair of realizing that his body was tainted forever and that the only way to make his life worth anything was to die as Sophie and Nikolas had.

Delaney held the older *Pyr*'s gaze without flinching, completely convinced that he was right. "That's not the case here."

Rafferty studied him for a long moment, then turned away with a shrug. "No point remaining where we aren't welcome," he said with a heartiness Delaney didn't trust. The *Pyr* left the kitchen and paused to survey the sky from the porch.

Niall murmured something, but Rafferty silenced him with a touch on the shoulder. The gesture was so quick that Delaney might have missed it if he hadn't been paying attention.

As it was, he wondered what his friends were up to.

He'd believe they were leaving when they left.

Rafferty glanced back from the porch. "Thank Ginger again for breakfast and the coffee, please." He smiled. "We'll leave the dishes for you."

"That's not the only mess you're leaving me," Delaney complained, and Rafferty laughed.

Then the four took flight, shifting in shape in unison as they leapt off Ginger's porch. The snow quickly obscured the sight of them as they ascended.

At least the neighbors wouldn't see them.

At least they were gone. Delaney grabbed his coat and headed for the barn, following the line of Ginger's boot prints.

All he had to do was figure out how best to apologize to her.

He'd worry about persuading her to try to sate the firestorm again once she would stay in the same building with him. He felt the press of time, and knew he had to attack the Elixir again soon, before the *Slayers* recovered from this morning's assault.

First things first.

Ginger threw open the door of the barn, pushing it hard against the heavy snow. It slid enough for her to enter the barn, and she left it ajar to save herself effort later. The barn was humid and warm, anyway. She was simmering with anger, but she forced herself to settle down before she approached the animals.

They could always sense when she was agitated and the last thing she needed was a bunch of riled-up bulls giving her trouble.

She'd already put up with enough garbage from males on this particular day.

Ginger's family's farm was long established, but she had changed the focus of its business since giving up her city job and coming home. They'd always raised dairy cattle and sold the milk, Ginger's most long-standing memory being the arrival of the silver milk tanker every single day of the year, independent of weather or holidays. She'd learned about milking and breeding and herd management from the time she could walk, listening avidly to her grandparents' accumulated wisdom whenever possible.

When Ginger's grandfather had died, Gran had decided to stay on the farm but manage the workload. She'd rented the workable fields where Grampa had grown fodder, letting Silas Hargreaves at the neighboring farm till that acreage in exchange for enough fodder for the herd. The bottom land had been used for pasture and grazing, as always. And without a man around, Gran had begun to automate functions on the farm. She would never have left the farm—it was a part of her identity—so Gran found ways to stay.

Ginger respected and admired that.

Ginger had yearned for city life until she got there. She'd missed home every minute she'd been away—even though she loved chef's school and adored cooking. When Gran had admitted that the dairy farm wasn't doing well financially, Ginger headed back to Ohio as soon as she hung up the phone. Her plum restaurant job had no longer been able to compete with the allure of rural Ohio and the challenge of putting Sinclair Farms into the black. Under Ginger's leadership, the automation had picked up speed. Ginger had negotiated better terms with Silas, and had employed his son Luke to help with the work on the dairy farm.

Her experience as a chef had made Ginger passionate about finding local sources for food, about organic methods of production, and about preserving heritage varieties. All of those interests came together in the new Sinclair Farms. She'd inherited a prime herd of Guernseys, the established stock of Gran's herd and a breed with an active breeding registry, and had been approached by the registry to sell semen. Ginger had since branched out to other varieties. She had three of the few Kerrys in the United States, and a small herd of Milking Shorthorns.

She loved them all. Cows were serene, their presence giving Ginger a tranquility she'd never felt in the city. She was passionate about her breeding protocols, about ensuring quality and tracking bloodlines. Bull semen kept her farm solvent, and she'd just had a new barn built with a high-tech dairy parlor and solar panels on the roof. Tanya paid a premium for the milk from the Guernseys for making her artisan cheese, too.

Ginger had to fight Luke over every change to the running of the farm: he was resistant to change, but she needed help with the physical work and he was close at hand. Luke was skeptical about everything she did, which meant that Ginger had yet to get more land being tilled with organic methods. Luke just wouldn't do it.

She simply had to persist, like Gran had always told her to do. It would have been nice, though, to have had a supportive partner instead of an obstructionist employee. It would have been nice to have been lucky like Tanya, to follow her heart and find her soul mate on the way.

On this day of days, Ginger stepped into the barn with a sigh of satisfaction. She kicked the snow off her boots and took a deep breath of the steamy air, of the scent of manure and straw and cow. She heard the girls low to one another in announcement of her presence, and move toward the center aisle to see her.

Then she grabbed the broom, left just inside the door. The chickens chattered in their pen, Reginald, the rooster, giving a crow of complaint. The rooster had spectacular plumage, heritage breed prize that he was, but he also had attitude to spare.

And he defended the barn most effectively.

Ginger, however, had zero tolerance for male territory disputes on this particular day.

"Coq au vin!" Ginger cried as usual, lifting the broom.

Reginald crowed, as if to argue with her. The rooster flew at Ginger, all talons and beak, his feathers spread in a majestic display. He was going for blood.

Ginger swung the broom and connected on the first hit. If he'd been a baseball, he wouldn't have been hit out of the park, but it was enough of a blow to be insulting. Reginald was batted into the pen where the hens were clucking. He tumbled, then squawked at the indignity. The hens moved away from his rolling path, clucking. Ginger always thought they sounded like they were laughing at him. Reginald looked so disheveled and insulted by the time he got on his feet that Ginger almost felt sorry for him.

But not quite. He'd rip her eyes out, given half a chance.

"Quiet, you old troublemaker," Ginger said, "or your time in the stewpot will come sooner than expected."

He clucked and strutted, as if he had been the one triumphant.

Reginald was good for one assault, then he usually gave it up. On this particular day, he was true to form—he started to peck at the ground, as if oblivious to Ginger's arrival.

Ginger left the broom beside the pen in case she needed it on the way out. She grabbed a couple of handfuls of feed and tossed it into the chicken pen, watching the hens scrabble and peck.

The barn was a new building, sleek and gleaming, a major investment. The walls were made of a translucent plastic, which was tough, but admitted light to the barn. It was also made of recycled materials, which Ginger liked. The solar panels on the roof kept the lights on in the barn, and ran the coolers for the dairy equipment.

For these six weeks, though, there was no milk. The girls were pregnant or dry, so the barn was quiet. Ginger liked this six weeks before the calving began, as it gave her schedule a bit of a break.

Those translucent wall panels could also be slid open to improve ventilation. Some farmers left their cattle inside all the time in these new barns, but Ginger still liked to send the herd out to graze. The sunshine, Gran had always insisted, was good for them and their milk production. Ginger agreed.

Darian, the Kerry stud in the first stall, gave his usual bellow of welcome. Ginger smiled as she reached over the bar to scratch him. He was small and black, more mellow than any bull she'd ever known. His temperament didn't affect his ability to get the job done, though, and there were two calves sired by Darian due this spring. One pregnant Kerry was in the next stall in Ginger's barn, while the other was in North Dakota. Darian rubbed his snout on the edge of the stall as she scratched him, showing such obvious pleasure that Ginger's smile broadened.

"I gotta muck out the girls first," she told him. "You know how they are." She grabbed some fresh hay for him and put it in his stall to keep him busy. "I'll be back."

He gave a low moo, as if he understood perfectly, and stamped a hoof. His tail flicked as he lowered his head to nibble at her gift.

The two Kerry cows, one pregnant and one not, were lying down at the back of their stalls, ruminating. Ginger left them to it.

Ginger grabbed a shovel and strode down the center aisle of the barn, enjoying how the Guernsey girls all turned at her presence. They began to moo as they eased toward the aisle, their tails swishing. They were a tranquil breed, even for cows, and excellent milk producers. Gran had always been able to sell the Guernsey milk at a premium because of its high butterfat and high protein levels. Tanya raved about it. None of the girls were lactating at this time of year, many of their bellies rounded with soon-to-arrive calves. Others were too young to be bred and Ginger had found herself with a rare interval with a break in the twice-daily milking routine.

In the last stall on the right were the pregnant Milking Shorthorns. One of the benefits of this heritage breed was not only their prolific milk production but their reliability in conceiving every year. Ginger's girls had proven that adage correct and the studs seemed smug to Ginger.

She wondered whether the Milking Shorthorns knew any *Pyr*. First time, every time. Hmm.

Ginger greeted the girls as she strode down the center aisle of the barn. Even though she had a herd of roughly a hundred cows, she named all of the calves each spring. She used Gran's convention of naming all the ones born the same year with names that began with the same letter. The information was recorded on their microchips and ear tags, but Ginger tried to remember each cow's name. The computer displayed their names when they entered the milking parlor twice daily, as well as the free stall barn, and that was a good prompt.

She addressed them with names she'd used, knowing that she probably got one wrong once in a while. The girls didn't seem to mind.

"Hey, Jessie and Jasmine and Jessica," she said, touching noses as she strode past.

The daily routine was to move the girls either into the far section of the barn or the pasture, then muck out the area in which they'd spent the night. It was familiar to the cows and the girls trailed along behind Ginger as she headed for the far gate.

Usually Luke took care of this job, but Ginger knew he wouldn't turn up in such weather. If she was lucky, the Hargreaves would plow her driveway when they did their own. That would be plenty of help.

If not, she'd do it herself.

Gran had taught Ginger self-reliance beyond that of most people.

"Germaine and Gertrude, how's it going? Bess and Bethany, Barbara and Beulah, did you sleep well?"

Ginger noticed that the Guernsey bulls, in individual pens at the far end, didn't turn to watch her approach.

That was odd. They were usually even more curious than the girls.

"Dolores and Dorothy and Dotty and Desirée, how are my girls this morning?" Ginger kept up her greetings, her eye on the bulls. What were they watching? Their tails weren't even swishing, they were so intent. "Nadine and Nancy and Natalie, you look beautiful today."

The bulls didn't even glance her way, their gazes fixed at a point she couldn't see, beyond the end of the last stall.

Ginger had that bad feeling again.

But her instincts were proving to be unreliable. Ginger shook off her feeling of dread and rationalized. It was probably a rabbit or a groundhog. And really, she couldn't be surprised by a wild creature wanting to get out of this weather.

The boys, though, didn't take well to changes in their routine.

"Teresa and Terrilyn, love those lashes." Ginger was about three-quarters of the way down the central aisle when Thomas stamped his hoof and exhaled a puff. His stall was closest to where the bulls were staring, and he was the least tolerant of anyone in his space.

Even bunnies.

Thomas gave a low bellow, one that Ginger knew

was filled with irritation. The other bulls echoed his complaint, lots of hooves stomping on the barn floor. Micah lowered his head and pawed one hoof on the floor.

Uh-oh.

The girls looked in that direction, easing away from the bulls with characteristic caution.

Great. Now she was going to have a stampede.

All over a cold bunny.

Ginger strode to the end of the aisle with purpose, swinging her shovel. "Who's there?" she shouted, not really expecting an answer. She kept talking though, assuming it would spook the bunny into flight and save her a job. "There's no room in this barn for wild critters," she said as she rounded the last corner.

And stopped cold.

A man stood there, a stranger. He was almost as tall as Delaney, but his hair was fair and his eyes were blue. He was smiling, but his smile gave Ginger the creeps. There was something about his eyes, something that made him look predatory and dangerous.

He had a serial killer smile.

His smile broadened at her obvious surprise. "How accommodating of you to cross the smoke boundary," he said, and Ginger couldn't identify his accent beyond the fact that it was foreign. "Surely your injunction against wild *critters* doesn't apply to me?"

She took a step back, wondering how he had gotten into her barn without leaving any tracks. She wondered how he'd gotten past Reginald. Her bad feeling got worse.

"How did you get in here?" Ginger demanded, hoping she sounded tougher than she felt.

"A little trick of the Wyvern's that I've been working on," he said, which made absolutely no sense.

Then he laughed and it was the most malicious sound

Ginger had ever heard. Thomas gave a bellow, but Ginger had other concerns.

When the man's body began to shimmer blue around its edges, Ginger knew exactly what was going to happen.

She dropped the shovel and ran.

Chapter 9

They might as well all be cows.

That was Jorge's thought as he shifted shape and snatched for Delaney's mate. Humans were all placid, stupid, and predictable, just like cows.

A great many of them were also timid. Just as Delaney's mate ran—a stupid choice, given that she could never outrun a dragon on the attack—the cows raced away from the center aisle of the barn. They jostled one another against the exterior walls, lowing and stamping, clustering at the perimeter and as far away from Jorge as possible.

He shifted shape in one bound, savoring the extra surge of power that the Elixir sent through his veins. This last sip had made him stronger than ever.

He was one step closer to replacing Magnus as leader of the *Slayers*.

Magnus didn't need to know that. Let him trust Jorge. Let him share his vast store of knowledge with Jorge. Let him empty his mind and what was left of his heart, and when there was nothing left that Magnus could contribute, then Jorge would eliminate the ancient *Slayer*.

Theoretically, the Elixir conferred immortality. In reality, everyone had a weakness. Jorge believed that everyone could be murdered, and he was willing to test his theory. He'd seen how Magnus had come close to dying, when Erik had injured the ancient *Slayer* so thoroughly and left his carcass far from the healing balm of the Elixir. It had suited Jorge to make a deal to help Magnus then, but that situation might not repeat itself.

Especially if he was the one to fell Magnus, having deemed the old *Slayer* useless.

The Elixir repaired and replenished, but even those who had sipped of it always needed more. Immortality was thus dependent upon not just a permanent supply of the Elixir, but ready access to it.

Particularly in times of injury.

Jorge had a plan to ensure his own longevity, one that still needed some tweaking. He had time to finesse the details, time to let Magnus become bold and absorbed in his own growth of power.

When Jorge seized the leadership of the *Slayers*, the role would be one worthy of his abilities.

For the moment, though, he played the role of Magnus's willing minion.

He'd been sent to collect the mate.

Jorge laughed as he snatched up the small woman in his talons, and enjoyed how she struggled against him. Her every effort was as nothing to him—he held her captive easily in one claw.

He flew directly for the roof, bursting through it and leaving a gaping hole. He liked destroying things that humans had built and enjoyed the shout of frustration Delaney's mate made. The snow swirled around him in a maelstrom of white, but his sense of direction was as unerring as his sense of smell. He ascended, well aware that he was being followed.

And by whom.

"I just had this barn built!" she cried, and kicked at him with new fury.

Jorge laughed. "I wouldn't worry about it," he said, and her eyes widened in dismay. "You have bigger problems right now."

She glared at him. "If you eat me, I'll give you indigestion."

Jorge laughed again. "By tomorrow, you'll wish I had merely eaten you," he said, leaving her to worry about that.

Delaney came raging through the air behind him, precisely as Jorge had anticipated. Jorge pivoted in midair and the woman cried out in fear. Even though they were less than a hundred feet above the ground, there was nothing but flying snow visible in every direction.

"Look familiar?" Jorge dangled the struggling mate before the livid *Pyr*, then tossed her to his back claw. She didn't scream, which was disappointing. She did try to kick him when he caught her. Jorge gave her enough of a squeeze to make her gasp.

"Leave her out of this!" Delaney shouted, but Jorge just laughed.

He tossed the mate to his other back claw, waiting a beat longer before he caught her. She had an instant to believe that he'd let her fall, and this time, she did yelp with fear. Jorge snatched her out of the air. Delaney flew toward him and the pair locked front claws in the traditional fighting pose.

Delaney didn't breathe fire, probably in an effort to protect his mate, but Jorge had no such concern. Magnus had decreed only that she had to be alive. Wounds were optional, as was consciousness.

Jorge belched a vicious stream of fire at Delaney and the *Pyr* winced as his shoulder was singed. His emerald scales turned dark, but Delaney pivoted and swung his tail at Jorge. He caught the *Slayer* across the back and Jorge spun out of range, hiding how much the blow had hurt.

Delaney was stronger than Jorge had expected. But he had a key weakness, one present and accounted for.

The mate.

Jorge tossed the mate again, then just for fun, breathed a little fire at her. She yelped as her coat caught fire, then slapped at the flames even as she tumbled through the air.

Delaney bellowed and charged. Jorge caught the mate in his talons, set her aflame on the back of her jacket, then flung her as far as he could.

This time, she screamed most satisfactorily.

Delaney, as anticipated, chose to save his mate. He raced after her falling form, giving Jorge a clear view of his back.

Jorge didn't waste time. He launched himself at Delaney, and latched on to his back with all four claws. Delaney roared when Jorge dug his front talons into Delaney's wings, but writhed free and spun to fight. He struck Jorge hard with his tail and ripped Jorge's belly with his back claws. Delaney sent Jorge tumbling backward with the force of his assault.

Jorge's blood ran black, stinging his own scaled hide with its corrosive heat. That his coat might be damaged made Jorge angry. In that moment, he decided he cared more for defeating Delaney than for fulfilling Magnus's command.

Let the mate fall to her death. It was more important that Jorge dispatch Delaney. It was unthinkable that his own beauty had been marred, and Delaney had to pay for that.

"You'll never defeat me," Jorge taunted Delaney. The pair had locked talons again and Jorge held fast, ensuring that Delaney couldn't pursue his falling mate. He laughed as the *Pyr* fought against his grip. "I've drunk more of the Elixir than you. I'll heal from my wounds."

"You're preserved, not alive," Delaney retorted as they wrestled. "It's not the same."

"I'm as alive as you."

"You're just *pickled*." Delaney bared his teeth and bit Jorge right in the throat, burying his teeth deeply and giving the *Slayer* a shake. He ripped open Jorge's chest, then cast him aside when Jorge's grip slackened slightly.

Jorge was as shocked by the viciousness of Delaney's assault as his condemnation.

Pickled?

Delaney rocketed toward his mate, abandoning Jorge. Jorge roared in irritation, then exhaled a stream of dragonsmoke. He targeted the smoke at his opponent, but Delaney had anticipated the move. He flew in an erratic pattern, evading the burning touch of the smoke. His course led directly to his falling mate.

To Jorge's disappointment, Delaney would arrive in time.

Delaney snatched up his mate when she was just twenty feet from the ground, then soared upward again with her safely in his claws. She cheered and Delaney pivoted in midair, his eyes glowing and his tail flowing as he eyed Jorge. His wings beat steadily as he hovered.

Despite his wounds, Jorge was no easy target. He dove at Delaney and hit him hard, making him lose the rhythm of his flight. The pair thrashed each other with their tails, tumbling through the sky as they battled. Jorge desperately sought Delaney's missing scale—he had to have lost one, as the *Pyr* routinely loved their mates—but Delaney's scaled hide was perfectly intact.

Had the Smith already repaired Delaney's armor?

Jorge didn't care. He could make this come right with

might. He attacked Delaney with vigor. He locked talons with Delaney, holding fast to one foreclaw and not letting go. Delaney tried to pass his mate to his back claw, but Jorge breathed a thick stream of dragonsmoke to intervene.

Delaney flinched from the smoke's touch and Jorge seized the mate. She struggled against his grip, but she was too feeble for her efforts to matter. Delaney snatched after her, but the smoke made him draw back his claws. He was persistent, though, shouldering through the smoke farther than Jorge would have anticipated.

Jorge breathed smoke thick and fast, cocooning the mate with his boundary mark. He held her fast in his back claw, slashing and attacking Delaney with his other claws.

Jorge flew higher, making his escape, and Delaney fell back, snarling, clearly unable to retaliate because of the smoke. Jorge breathed more smoke, targeting Delaney, intending to enshroud him in the lethal substance and suck him dry. He could let Delaney watch him injure the mate. That would add spice to the moment. Jorge had time to feel triumphant in his plan before Delaney revealed his feint.

Jorge was attacked from below. Delaney flew straight up, fast and hard, right through the dragonsmoke, the *Pyr*'s talons digging deeply into Jorge's genitals. Jorge bellowed in pain and rolled through the air to fight, impressed how Delaney narrowed his eyes against the smoke and kept on the attack.

Delaney wasn't immune to smoke.

He was ignoring it.

Delaney's scales were shriveling and turning dark, but he didn't back off. In fact, Delaney's talons pierced deeply into Jorge's privates, his grasp sending excruciating pain through Jorge. The pain distracted Jorge for a fatal moment.

Delaney slashed at Jorge's back claw at that moment, severing Jorge's foot from his body.

Jorge was appalled to see his own foot fall toward the earth, Delaney's mate still securely within its grasp.

The pain was searing.

Jorge was empowered by his rage. He thrashed at Delaney and pummeled him. He vented his fury upon the *Pyr* who had dared to mutilate him, anger giving him savage power.

Delaney went limp and Jorge let him fall, hoping that the impact shattered his bones. Maybe he'd delay in notifying Magnus of the *Pyr*'s fall. Maybe he'd forget to ensure that Delaney got more of the Elixir.

Delaney dropped far enough to be out of Jorge's range, then awakened so abruptly that Jorge knew he'd been deceived. The *Pyr* caught his mate and set her on the ground, where she promptly wriggled out of Jorge's severed claw and kicked it aside. Jorge fell on the *Pyr*, snatching him up and flying high into the sky.

He loosed everything he had on Delaney, not trusting his sense that the *Pyr*'s strength was fading. He ripped Delaney's shoulder, hating how the blood flowed red; he severed the *Pyr*'s wings at their roots, burned him, and beat him. Then he threw the *Pyr*'s body at the earth, panting at his own exertion, watching until his opponent landed hard.

Delaney didn't move again. His blood ran red in the snow, the stain growing larger as the mate stared. She started toward him, making some pathetic human noise. Delaney shifted back to human form, looking broken and battered and pale against the snow.

He still didn't move.

Jorge didn't think he'd live long.

That was good enough for Jorge. Unfortunately, in his current state, he couldn't challenge Magnus. He'd have to fulfill his errand instead, and keep himself in Magnus's favor until he healed. Jorge swooped down and snatched up both the mate and his own claw. He held them together, enjoying her revulsion.

"I told you that you'd have bigger concerns," Jorge said lightly, then laughed as she battled him. He ascended again, barely aware of her struggles, and set a course for Magnus's home.

He knew exactly what reward he'd demand of his so-called superior for the indignities he'd suffered on this errand.

Magnus would have to pay big for this.

"It's as if he has a death wish," Niall complained. He and Thorolf and Rafferty had adjourned to a diner down the road from Ginger's farm, Thorolf having insisted that he needed a piece of pie. Thorolf was on his second piece, since he'd been unable to decide upon apple or cherry.

The waitress, Mary, was apparently charmed by Thorolf's appetite. It couldn't have been Thorolf's own excuse for charm, not in Niall's view. Niall figured it took all kinds to make a world.

"Isn't it, though," Rafferty said. He barely sipped his coffee, and Niall had the sense that the old *Pyr* was sorting his memories of old stories.

"What do you mean?"

"Nothing really," Rafferty acknowledged, tapping the handle of his mug with a frown. "I'm sure that Sloane will bring us some better answers when he returns with that ancient treatise."

"That's going to take the better part of a day," Niall complained, watching Thorolf put away pie with gusto. "He's got to go all the way to his place in California and back."

"They have sixteen kinds of pie," Thorolf contributed. "I'm good here for a while."

"You'll get fat."

Thorolf's disdain for the notion was clear. "In your dreams. I am metabolism man. Bring on the pie." He raised his voice and waved his fork. "Hey, Mary, can I try the blueberry, please?"

Niall regarded the tall *Pyr* with irritation. "The air is thick with the scent of *Slayer*. If we hang around here, I guarantee there'll be more to do than eat pie and flirt with waitresses."

"Good," Thorolf said. "I like a fight, the dirtier the better."

Niall had to admit that the *Pyr*'s newest recruit was an effective fighter. It was Thorolf's sole talent, as far as Niall could see. Even though he had been the one to find Thorolf, there was something about the other *Pyr*'s casual attitude that irritated Niall. He'd never thought of himself as straitlaced, but Thorolf's language and manner made Niall feel as unbending and constrained by protocol as his father had been.

The last thing Niall had ever wanted to be was a younger version of his uptight and unapproachable father, and he'd never felt that he was until he met Thorolf. It wasn't a comparison that put him in a good mood, and he blamed Thorolf for unwelcome reminders of the past.

Rafferty was drumming his fingers on the table, an unusual expression of urgency for the old *Pyr*. "I think we should leave," he said carefully. "As Delaney requests of us."

"That's crazy," Niall argued. "There are too many *Slayers*, and he's got this nutty idea that he can destroy the Elixir alone. . . ."

"And why does he have that idea?" Rafferty asked softly.

Niall flung out a hand. "I don't know. He was pretty grim when he sold me his share of our partnership. He said life wasn't worth living with the Elixir's darkness in his veins."

Mary brought the pie and set it down before Thorolf. "I put ice cream on it this time, too," she said with a smile. "Is that okay?"

"Great," Thorolf said with appreciation. "You know, this pie is amazing, the best I've ever had."

She smiled. "Maybe you'll come back to try the other thirteen kinds."

Thorolf grinned at her and Niall rolled his eyes. "Maybe I'll just stay here, eating pie, until you get off shift."

"Oh! I'm only working until six today."

Thorolf exhaled and squared his shoulders. "Good thing you have sixteen kinds of pie."

Mary flushed and smiled. "You gentlemen need more coffee?"

"No, thanks, we're fine," Niall said, his manner less encouraging than Thorolf's had been. Mary hurried back to the counter as Thorolf dug in.

"You didn't have to scare her," Thorolf grumbled, but Niall ignored him.

"He said he couldn't live with it," Niall continued his explanation to a watchful Rafferty. "I thought that was a bit ominous at the time, but figured he'd snap out of it. He certainly didn't want to talk."

"And he sold everything?" Rafferty asked.

"He told me he was doing a complete liquidation." Niall frowned. "I would have bought that house in Seattle, but he'd already sold it. I loved that place."

"So did he," Rafferty said. "What interests me is that Delaney has never been inclined to despair."

"But the Elixir . . ."

"Exactly. What did the Elixir do to him?"

"Stole his confidence, gave him nightmares, made him miserable." Niall shrugged. The list was long, but each item on it had a similarity with the others. He saw no point in continuing.

Rafferty's eyes gleamed. "Made him susceptible to Magnus's commands," he added.

"Right, like the whistle Magnus used when Donovan's mate was under attack, or the subliminal command to snatch Alex and Sara when they were pregnant."

"Or Magnus's command that Delaney kill Ginger," Thorolf added, gesturing with his fork. "The command that he denied today."

"He's denied all three of those commands," Rafferty observed. "Either by refusing to fulfill them directly or by removing himself from the scene."

"So, Magnus's strategy is ineffective," Niall concluded. "That's good news."

"Maybe not so good." Rafferty shook his head at Niall's surprise. "What if those are just distractions?"

Niall met the older *Pyr*'s gaze. "You mean that Delaney can deny them because they're less important, because they're not really what Magnus wants him to do?"

Rafferty nodded.

Thorolf looked between the pair, his fork in midair. "Then what does Magnus want him to do?"

Niall leaned back in his seat, feeling sick at the implications of Rafferty's idea. "What if Delaney believes he has to destroy the Elixir alone because that's what Magnus told him? What if that's the real subliminal command?"

"And it's one he can't deny, because he doesn't even recognize it as coming from outside of himself," Rafferty concluded.

"But why?" Niall demanded. "Magnus gets his power from the Elixir."

Rafferty shrugged. "Maybe the answer is in the treatise that Sloane went to retrieve."

Thorolf blinked. "Then why would we leave Delaney alone? Doesn't he need backup if Magnus is after him?"

"Because it's the only way to reveal Magnus's plan fully," Rafferty said. He rose to his feet and threw a twenty on the table. "We don't have to abandon Delaney, but we have to give the appearance of leaving. I'm going to go to Erik in Chicago and bring him up to date."

"What about old-speak?" Thorolf asked.

Rafferty shook his head. "This is too complex for old-speak. I'd like to consult with Donovan and Quinn as well. . . ."

"But they won't come this close with their mates, not until we're sure that Delaney won't attack," Niall said, seeing Rafferty's plan. "I'm staying, though. I don't care what it costs me. Delaney's my friend."

The older *Pyr* nodded, unsurprised. "I thought as much. We'll convene at Erik's, then send you updates as necessary." He smiled slightly. "I know you won't leave, Niall, but I doubt that the *Slayers* will be troubled by one *Pyr* in the vicinity."

"And Sloane will be back," Niall agreed. "I'm going to try to disguise my scent, the way they do."

"What about me?" Thorolf asked, looking between the two. He'd polished off another piece of pie and Mary had been cutting generous slices.

"You'll be busy eating pie," Niall charged as he also rose to his feet.

"I'm staying, too," Thorolf said. Niall was both irritated by this decision and relieved by it. As annoying as he found Thorolf, he was glad to have more backup in the vicinity in case things went badly for Delaney.

"I'll give Delaney some time with Ginger, then go back and see if I can talk some sense into him," Niall said.

Rafferty nodded. "Be careful. Make no assumptions."

Thorolf put another twenty on the table, then waved to the waitress. "Later, Mar," he said.

"Promise?" she said, her manner flirtatious as she came to pick up the cash. She started to make change, but Thorolf touched her hand quickly.

"Keep the change. Looks like a slow day today."

She smiled. "Thanks! You'll be back?"

Thorolf winked. "You bet."

"Good," she said, watching the three of them leave.

"I'm not going to ask the real reason why you're staying," Niall said in old-speak, and Thorolf grinned.

"I'll cover your ass, and that's all that should matter."

Rafferty gave them a look. *"You might try to accomplish something constructive."*

"Breathing smoke," Thorolf said immediately. *"I need some pointers and practice."*

It wasn't an unreasonable exchange for Thorolf's presence in battle, and Niall was glad of something to do. *"Okay, we'll walk farther into the country so Rafferty can shift, then find a place to breathe some smoke."*

"The ring will resonate, drawing Slayers *to whatever site you choose,"* Rafferty reminded them.

"Then we should fortify Delaney's boundary mark at Ginger's place," Thorolf suggested.

Niall had to admit that it wasn't a bad plan.

Maybe there was more to the newest *Pyr* than met the eye.

There were days when Magnus Montmorency was astounded by his own intelligence and cunning.

This was proving to be one of them.

He sipped his second glass of the Elixir, this one in the comfort of his bungalow, and watched Delaney's mate pace the length of the room where she had been confined. He had one-way glass installed in many of the walls of this house, and could spy into all of the rooms without being observed.

She was frustrated, clearly. She had worked the room over a dozen times, but naturally she hadn't found anything. It was a tastefully decorated prison and Magnus was content to let her tire herself over the futility of seeking an escape.

Her restlessness amused him, as well as her confidence. She was small and delicately built, which meant that she would be more feeble than most women. Yet she had this conviction that she could ensure her own freedom. That spirit was attractive in a way, but her quiet style was not the most alluring one for him. He preferred brash women, those who flaunted their assets and painted their faces.

The mate, however, was so very vulnerable.

Magnus liked that part best of all. He liked that she was powerless within his house. He took another sip, savoring the cold collision of the Elixir with his wounds. He grimaced as he stood, even though the pain in his midriff was diminished. He'd be healed by nightfall, but that wouldn't be quick enough.

As much as he disliked delay, as much as he resented prudence, he knew that in this case, it would be wise to let himself heal fully. His pawn was proving to be more resilient than he'd anticipated.

"You could coax Delaney with old-speak," Jorge suggested, ever attentive and never trustworthy.

Jorge's left foot was in a cast and he was limping, a result of his battle with Delaney. The dismembered foot and stump of Jorge's ankle had been dipped in the Elixir before the two were wrapped together and encased in a cast. Jorge's blond hair had also been burned away on one side, and the *Slayer* had immediately shaved his hair short. It made him look even more merciless, his eyes more coldly blue, but the limp detracted from his menacing look.

Magnus suspected there was another reason Jorge limped, an ache somewhat higher than the top of the cast, but it was indelicate to inquire after groin injuries. He'd seen a wince or two that told him everything he needed to know.

Magnus hadn't been impressed by the extent of Jorge's injuries. After all, Jorge had faced only Delaney, and Delaney had already been wounded. Either his new protégé was a less effective fighter than he'd imagined or Delaney had been more motivated.

The second possibility was an interesting one.

It was one worth planning for.

Magnus also hadn't been amused by the avarice and desperation in Jorge's eyes when he'd demanded more of the Elixir than Magnus had been inclined to grant. He wouldn't be making assumptions about Jorge, no matter how unctuous the younger *Slayer* became.

Perhaps he would be more cautious as Jorge became more charming.

Magnus lifted a hand to dismiss Jorge's idea. "Manipulation requires a subtle hand. There can be no hint that the idea is not his very own."

Jorge looked as if he would have liked to have argued the point, but decided against it. Magnus particularly enjoyed when Jorge restrained his instincts in an effort to gain favor. His newest acolyte was far more transparent than he guessed, which suited Magnus well.

"Let us entertain our guest," he said, summoning his most gracious smile as he moved to the door between the two rooms. "It would be unforgivable to me to allow her to become bored."

Jorge chuckled and Ginger spun at the sound of his amusement as the door opened. She folded her arms across her chest and narrowed her eyes as she watched the pair enter the room. Her expression was filled with resentment and frustration, a sign that she was even more transparent than Jorge.

Good. Her gaze flicked over Jorge and her eyes narrowed. So, he'd revealed himself to her in human form.

Foolish.

Magnus smiled. "I do apologize for the delay in my welcoming you to my home," he said, oozing hospitality. "And Jorge has not even taken your coat!"

"That's fine." Her tone was hostile. "I'll keep it on, thanks."

"No, no, I must insist. There's a burn on the sleeve as well as one on the back. I'll have it mended while we visit." Magnus flicked a hand at Jorge, letting his index finger shift to a dragon talon. The red tinge on the nail was slightly more vehement than it had been the last time he had treated himself to a restorative sip.

But it was no matter. All would be resolved shortly.

Meanwhile Ginger stared at his hand in horror. Her shock was sufficient that Jorge was able to lift the coat from her shoulders before she could stop him.

"Isn't that better?" Magnus asked as Jorge limped from the room with the coat. He gestured to a pair of divans near the glass wall facing the inner courtyard. The snow fell in a silent symphony outside the windows. "Come, have a seat."

"I don't intend to stay."

Magnus ignored that foolish comment. "Shall I order you some refreshment?" He lifted his half-empty glass, fully expecting her to recognize the cloudy red liquid within it. Her eyes widened slightly. "A little Elixir for whatever ails you, perhaps?"

Ginger shuddered and Magnus allowed himself a chuckle. "No, thank you." She looked at him, eyed his talon and the glass, then took a breath. "Weren't you hurt this morning? Badly?"

"Yes." Magnus smiled and lowered himself to one divan. He didn't try to suppress his grimace at the twinge of pain across his gut. He sipped, watching her over the rim of the glass.

She considered him for a minute, then marched around the other divan and sat down facing him. "What is the Elixir, anyway?"

She had spunk, Magnus would give her that.

"Do you know the full name of it?"

"The Dragon's Blood Elixir. And there's something in that vial."

"Something?" Magnus invited. "Or someone?"

"I don't understand." Her eyes hinted that she did.

Her curiosity interested Magnus and tempted him to tell her more than was absolutely necessary. It didn't matter, anyway: she'd be dead within hours and he would find it entertaining to share his brilliance with an avid audience. "Let me tell you a story, about a dragon who came to be known as Cinnabar."

"That wasn't his name?"

"Not initially. He was a slave, a foreigner." Magnus couldn't completely hide his sneer. "Ignorant of his body's powers in a most regrettable way."

"Where was he from?"

"I don't know! Somewhere in the desert, where he was raised by savages."

She said nothing to that.

Magnus warmed to his story. "When first he came to Rome, he was known as Sahir. He lived on the street, by his wits, until someone showed him a great kindness." Magnus's voice hardened in remembered resentment. "He didn't understand how gracious it was of that *honestior* to take him in, much less to give him a decent Roman name."

"Which was?"

"Sylvanus Secundus." Magnus still loved the sound

of the name, still loved that it was evocative of a history that his slave hadn't possessed. There had never been a Sylvanus the first. There certainly had never been a legitimate Roman father of that slave.

"What happened to the slave?"

"A regrettable situation. He was convicted of the sacrilege of a corpse." Magnus left out the pertinent details of how his slave had been commanded to do precisely as he had done, and how his capture had been prearranged. He fixed Ginger with a look that he knew was filled with innocence. "Caught red-handed, as it were. It was disappointing and shocking, especially for his patron."

"Uh-huh," Ginger said, so obviously biting her tongue that Magnus found himself liking her more.

"We Romans had no sense of humor about such sacrilege, and he was immediately condemned to labor in the mines. As his was not a first offense, he was sent to Sisapo."

She watched him carefully. "Should I know where or what that is?"

"It's called Almadén now, in Spain." He eyed her but she shook her head. "It remains one of the largest deposits of cinnabar in the world, and is still a working mine."

"What's cinnabar?"

Breathtaking stupidity. Magnus stifled a sigh. "Mercury sulfide. A red stone, which can be used to make the pigment vermilion. The Chinese used it to stain lacquerware. The Byzantines used it for coloring ink." Magnus took the final sip of Elixir from his glass, a long swig that he savored as the mate watched him with disgust. "It was also used medicinally, to promote immortality. Oh, and its colloquial name was Dragon's Blood." He smiled.

Ginger averted her gaze. "Isn't mercury toxic?"

"Yes, which is why criminals were assigned to labor in

the mine. They worked until they died of mercury poisoning, doing service for the good of the Empire in their last days." Magnus carefully put down the glass on a side table. "The oddity was, though, that Sylvanus Secundus never died."

She blinked and he could almost see her thoughts fly. "Because he was a *Slayer*?"

"No, no. The schism between *Pyr* and *Slayers* occurred almost a thousand years later, my dear. To make such distinctions would be anachronistic."

"I see. My dragon history is a bit shaky."

Magnus smiled. "And forgivably so. Sylvanus Secundus was *Pyr*, albeit a *Pyr* who knew little of his abilities or his fellows." Magnus made the necessary point for her, so that she could not miss it. "A primitive *Pyr*, but his blood ran crimson red."

"I don't understand."

"The *Pyr* are not affected by mercury poisoning in the same way as humans. Perhaps the theory of cinnabar's power to create immortality comes from observing us under its effects. I can't truly say, but when Sylvanus did not die, in twenty years, forty years, fifty years, I had to find out why. I went to Sisapo, only to discover that he was virtually in charge of the place. Few overseers were eager to expose themselves to poison, so they paid him extra to do their work, never imagining that he'd outlive them all."

"I see."

She saw only a tiny percentage of the story, though. "Not only did his blood run red, but his skin was flushed and his hair had turned auburn. When he shifted to dragon form, his scales, which had once been the glorious yellow of citrine, were becoming scarlet. The red tinge spread from the root, the lip or corona of the scale remaining yellow. He was quite magnificent, if not the *Pyr* I recalled."

"How did you know it was him?"

Magnus smiled. "I knew."

"How?"

"Each *Pyr* has a distinctive scent. We recognize one another's presence at great distance."

"Because you have keen senses." She eyed him. "His scent didn't change?"

Magnus smiled, appreciating that he didn't have to explain everything. "It altered, it became colder, but the base note was the same. Think of the difference between the body lotion and the eau de toilette in the same fragrance."

"Fresh tomatoes versus preserved ones—still tomatoes but slightly different."

"Yes! Exactly." Magnus was pleased that she showed some cleverness. "You see, he had become so infused with mercury that it had changed his metabolism, and that put me in mind of an old notion, that an Elixir could be created from the blood of a *Pyr* who has undergone such a radical poisoning. Understandably, there had been few volunteers to test the old tale."

"You tested it with him."

Magnus smiled. "One could suggest that by staying at the mine for so long, Sylvanus effectively volunteered."

"But he didn't know what you knew."

"Of course not. His inclination was to serve, not to inquire." Magnus sighed and returned to the core of his tale. "He might have come under greater scrutiny over time, but the Romans lost control of Baeticia—now Spain—by that time and chaos reigned. He continued to run the mines for the Visigoths, calling himself Cinnabar as if he were a different person. They asked few questions so long as the ore was mined." Magnus sneered. "Mercenary barbarians, every one of them."

He saw the flicker in the mate's eyes and read her thoughts. "I may not be an altruist," he said, "but I like to think I have a certain refinement."

"Of course," she murmured, her doubt clear.

Magnus eyed her for a moment, debating whether she should pay for her skepticism, then decided she was more useful alive.

For the moment.

"It was the Moors who had questions, the Moors who guessed the truth and wanted to know the secret that had prolonged his life." Magnus shrugged. "They were rather persistent in their studies."

"They discovered the truth?"

"They suspected that something was different about Cinnabar. They were an inquisitive lot. I had to act before they had the proof. I had to intervene before Cinnabar told what he knew." Magnus pushed the glass aside with his talon. "I had to act to protect our kind, so I did what had to be done."

"You killed him so he couldn't talk," she guessed.

"I acted in my own defense." Magnus smiled. "I persuaded him to trust me, and he did."

"You did kill him!"

"He is not dead. Not technically. He is preserved in that vial, exuding the juice that gives immortality to all who drink it."

The mate shuddered, failing to share Magnus's satisfaction with the story's ending. "He can't come to life again, can he?"

"Regrettably, no," Magnus ceded, no true regret in his tone. "You see, the Elixir draws its power from his life force. He has been slowly bled dry, so to speak, over the centuries."

Her gaze fell on the empty glass. "So, you've been drinking his life force, a serving at a time. You deceived him to check on the truth of that old story."

"And it proved to be true."

"Does he know?"

"I don't care. The important issue is that he pales from

the surrender of his life force," Magnus said quietly. "His time of usefulness is passing, and he must be replaced in the font of the Elixir by a new source."

"With what?" She caught her breath as she made the connection. "With *whom*?"

Magnus rose to his feet, pleased that the Elixir had diminished his injury even further. "Come with me. We must go into the courtyard for the next chapter of the story."

The mate followed him to the door, preceding him into the courtyard at his gesture. She had time to shiver and pivot to face him before Magnus slammed and locked the sliding door. She was sealed in the courtyard while he was inside the house, perfectly poised to watch anger claim her features.

"Hey! I need my coat!" She was clever enough to realize she wasn't going to get it. She pounded on the glass with her fists, making almost no sound at all.

There was no end to the benefit of buying quality. Magnus heard the distinctive rhythm of Jorge's return, his cast hitting the floor without grace as he limped closer.

"Double glass?" Jorge asked.

"Triple," Magnus said. *"And tinted."* He sighed with satisfaction as the mate marched around the perimeter of the courtyard, trying every door and pounding on every pane of glass. So frail. She'd be dead by nightfall, whether Delaney came or not.

But Delaney would come. The firestorm would compel him to come, and then he would be trapped. Magnus's plan was proceeding perfectly. He was quite enamored of his own brilliance.

"Shall I get you another drink?" Jorge asked, picking up Magnus's empty glass.

"No, thank you." Magnus smiled at his minion, knowing precisely what Jorge wanted. *"Did you have a second yourself?"*

Jorge dropped his gaze. *"Of course not, not without your permission."*

It was a lie but one that Magnus felt inclined to indulge. *"Then please do have a sip, as a reward for a day's work well done."*

The pair smiled at each other, each as distrustful as the other. Then Jorge limped across the room, moving with new purpose.

Magnus drummed his fingers, considering his options. He needed a bit of rest to let the Elixir do its best work, all before Delaney was brought to the sanctuary again. He would leave Jorge in charge of Delaney's inevitable attack on the house and capture, in order to ensure his own strength.

The mate could cool her heels, so to speak, for the moment.

In the meantime, he felt the need for a backup plan. Time was of the essence and Delaney was proving to be elusive. Magnus could ensure that there was another candidate, another red-blooded *Pyr* infected with mercury poisoning.

But Jorge would not be the one Magnus sent upon this errand. There was no reason for this student to know everything.

And he was so easily manipulated.

"I trust that I can leave you in charge of Delaney's capture," Magnus said just as Jorge reached the door.

The younger *Slayer* glanced back, unable to hide his predictable pleasure. *"Of course."*

Magnus yawned and stood, rubbing his stomach and grimacing as if it hurt more than it did. "I have need of a rest. I'll be in my suite." He shuffled across the room, feigning a feebleness he did not feel, aware of Jorge's ambitious gaze. "Send Mallory to me. I have a task for him to fulfill."

"I can do it," Jorge said, his ambition clear.

Magnus turned to look at him. "Even you cannot do everything for me. I must save your expertise for the more important details." He smiled.

Jorge hesitated only a moment before he also smiled.

Fool.

Once Mallory understood the challenge given to him and had left to ponder his course of action, Magnus locked the door of his suite. Confident that he wouldn't be disturbed again, Magnus moved more quickly.

He opened the hidden door in one wall, which revealed a flight of stairs. Tucked into a niche opposite the door was a funerary urn with the name AURELIA inscribed on the base.

Magnus smiled to himself as he lifted the lid from the urn. Ah, Aurelia. His wife was long dead and occasionally he missed her.

Of course, Aurelia's ashes were not inside the urn, not after all these centuries. What he kept in the jar was a more powerful talisman. He tipped the urn and a rounded stone the size of an egg tumbled into his hand.

A bloodstone. And not just any bloodstone but one inscribed with ancient symbols for the four elements guarded by the *Pyr*.

Aurelia had tempted him with this stone. She had found it and recognized it for what it was—or at least for the token of power it was. A sensitive and beautiful woman, one possessed of both arcane knowledge and ambition, she had targeted Magnus years before, sensing his truth and seeing his wealth. He had been content to savor the feast she offered, for Aurelia had been an inventive and passionate lover. And discreet.

But one night, one night after he had again partaken of the pleasures she offered with no promise in exchange, she casually showed him the bloodstone.

Magnus had recognized the stone instantly. It could only be the one thing he sought and though he tried to hide his excitement, Aurelia had known him too well.

And she had been watching him closely. Aurelia had manipulated him brilliantly after that and Magnus had married her in exchange for a promise of the blood-stone's surrender. That had only been the beginning of the games between them, the beginning of his quest to possess both lady and gem. Magnus yearned for the way Aurelia had been able to trick him and surprise him and keep him fascinated for decades on end.

She had been a worthy adversary, his sorceress, and Magnus had lost his heart to her cunning and manipulative powers. He had loved and he had lost, and the species responsible for the death of his beloved would never earn his forgiveness.

That humans had been manipulated by Magnus in order to finally give him uncontested possession of that bloodstone was a detail he chose to forget.

He also chose to forget that the bloodstone was what Sylvanus Secundus had been dispatched to retrieve from Aurelia's corpse. Magnus had claimed the stone before condemning his slave.

Flooded with bittersweet memories, Magnus touched his lips to the ancient bloodstone. Its time to serve him had come again.

He pocketed it as well as a loaded syringe from the niche. He then entered the secret passageway, inhaled deeply of the smells of rock and water and the faint tickle of the Elixir, then secured the door behind himself. Even the scent of the Elixir quickened his steps, made him anxious for a restorative bath.

By the time Delaney was escorted to the sanctuary, Magnus would be ready to preserve his prize and secure the future.

And if Plan A failed, his strength would be rebuilt

for the execution of Plan B. He fingered the stone in his pocket and smiled.

Perfect. His plan was perfect.

He was impossibly brilliant, was Magnus Montmorency.

Chapter 10

The nightmare seized Delaney before he had a chance to fight its approach. He tried to force himself awake, to open his eyes, but it already had him in its clutches. He saw the earth being claimed by shadow and then by ice, and knew that everything upon the planet was dying as he watched. The vision moved quickly, destroying Gaia at record speed, then revealing the damage to Delaney's gaze.

Dead.

Everything and everyone was dead.

Delaney cried out in horror as he had every time he had had this dream. He flew toward the earth in his dream, fearful and agitated, only to find that he was completely alone. He found the *Pyr*, one at a time, just as he always did, their bodies frozen beneath rivers or trapped within the earth. He broke them free, but there was no breath in their lungs, no fire in their thoughts. Each and every one was dead, but preserved.

This time, he even found Ginger, trapped in the ice that had claimed Brush Creek. Her blue eyes were wide and staring, and no breath fell from her lips. Delaney shattered the ice to break her free, but she was stiff and cold.

Dead.

He heard her accusation that he'd been out of line, and knew she was right. He'd been unfair. He'd tried to force his own objectives upon her, without any concern for her own ideas. He had to explain himself to her. He had to ask her to bear his son, to increase the ranks of the *Pyr*.

Delaney only hoped that he had the chance. Who knew what fate Magnus had planned for her? The leader of the *Slayers* would do anything to interfere with a firestorm.

Delaney was devastated by his failure to protect Ginger, by his inability to fulfill the promise of the firestorm, by his betrayal of his fellow *Pyr*, by his incompetence in following the creed of the *Pyr* to defend the earth and its treasures.

In his nightmare, he was the last of his kind, the only one cursed to know the fullness of their defeat.

The one who had failed to act, and make a difference.

It was Delaney's fault.

His heart raced, his breath came quickly, and he fought against the nightmare's clutch.

He awakened suddenly, his heart pounding and sweat running down his back. He was lying in the snow outside Ginger's barn.

Jorge was gone.

Ginger was gone.

He'd failed her.

Being awake wasn't much better than his nightmare. Delaney fought the urge to shout in rage again.

"Take it easy," Niall said irritably, leaning back into Delaney's field of vision. "You're a mess and I'm not very good at this, anyway. I wish Sloane were here, but no, you had to send him away."

Delaney was stunned to see his old friend back to help him. "I thought you left."

"Just because you told me to?" Niall rolled his eyes at the idea and Delaney fought a smile. "Like I ever listened to you."

Delaney was relieved not to be alone, yet knew that he couldn't draw his friends and fellow *Pyr* into this quest to destroy the Elixir.

It was his responsibility.

"You should have left. It's my fight."

"I should have been here," Niall said flatly. "Then you might not be so badly hurt." He gave Delaney a hard look, but Delaney dropped his gaze.

He winced as Niall cleaned his wounds, but he tried to remain still. The other *Pyr* frowned in concentration, his fair hair gathering fresh snow. He tended the cuts on Delaney's shoulders, the result of Jorge's attack on Delaney's wings, grimacing in sympathy as he did so.

"It's not so bad," Delaney said.

"Liar," Niall charged, a familiar twinkle lighting his eyes.

"Well, it's not."

"Right. It must hurt like hell."

"It's nothing compared to . . ." Delaney bit back his reply, that there was nothing that could do injury to his body that compared to the agony inflicted by the Elixir.

Niall sobered, and he guessed that his friend had read his thoughts.

Thorolf arrived then, his moonstone and silver dragon form almost ethereal in the snow. He shifted shape more smoothly than he had the last time Delaney had watched him do it, but was still clumsy with the unfolding of his clothes. Delaney shut his eyes, keeping Thorolf's secrets.

"Ouch. I hope you got a few good hits in," Thorolf

said, his pale face telling Delaney all he needed to know about his own condition.

"Who was it?" Niall asked. "Jorge?"

Delaney nodded. "I hacked off his back claw."

"Ha!" Niall's smile was fleeting. "Bet it hurt until he got some Elixir."

Thorolf eyed Delaney. "Here's what I don't understand. You hacked off Jorge's claw just now. This morning you spilled Magnus's guts for him and then thumped Mallory. How did such a primo fighter get taken captive by the *Slayers* in the first place? Did they team up on you?"

"The fighting is new," Niall informed Thorolf before Delaney could answer. "Delaney used to get his way with audacity."

"Charm," Delaney argued.

Niall grinned. "Balls and bullshit. Donovan used to call him the daredevil."

Thorolf nodded approval of the concept. "Gotta love that, especially if you're now primed to fight."

"In the past year, I've taken every class on fighting I could find, and logged more time in the gym even than Niall does."

"That much?" Niall asked lightly. They all knew Niall spent the better part of each day in the gym.

"That much."

Thorolf gave a low whistle.

"Good thing, seeing as the *Slayers* are so determined to take you down." Niall gave one last wipe to the one shoulder cut, then frowned at something on his fingertip. It glistened silver.

"What's that?" Thorolf asked, leaning closer.

"Looks like quicksilver." Niall held it higher. "Mercury."

"I saw some of that in the sanctuary," Delaney said, sitting up to take the glistening bead on his finger. His skin immediately flushed on that hand. His nail, right under the bead of mercury, took a crimson tinge at the root. "It was on the outside of the vial of the Elixir."

"Hey," Niall said, checking his own hand. "That stuff's toxic."

Delaney examined the mercury, noting how quickly his body was responding to it. "Your skin didn't change, did it?"

Niall shrugged. "Maybe it wasn't enough exposure. I wasn't in the sanctuary this morning."

Delaney gave his friend a hard look. "You were never forced to drink the Elixir."

"Do you think your body is responding to the mercury because of the Elixir?"

"I know its shadow is still within me," Delaney said with care. "I wonder whether the mercury is an active ingredient in it."

"And they drink it?" Thorolf shuddered. "How much of that crap has Magnus drunk?"

"It could be a lot," Niall said. "He's had the Elixir for centuries, I think."

Thorolf shrugged. "Why doesn't it kill him? Mercury poisons people all the time. If he's drinking it, he ought to be dead by now."

Niall looked at the mercury bead. "It has to be a coincidence, then," he said, but didn't sound any more convinced of it than Delaney was.

"Sloane might know," Delaney said, wishing for the Apothecary's presence and knowledge. "But it's not that important now. We need to find Ginger." He put the mercury bead on the stone windowsill of Ginger's kitchen. There were plant pots in the snow on the porch and he turned one overtop of it so they'd be able to find it again.

"You're not going after her alone," Niall growled. "So don't argue with us."

"You shouldn't be heading into a fight at all with those wounds," Thorolf said.

"At least leave the risky stuff to us," Niall said.

"They have my mate," Delaney said firmly. "Don't imagine you can stop me." Before they could argue with him, he pulled his shirt collar down, letting them see his rapidly healing skin. "The Elixir is good for something: I heal faster than you two because of it."

Niall rolled his eyes. "Just don't assume you can charm your way out of anything."

"It's worth a try," Delaney said, and leapt into the air, shifting shape as he took flight. He took the scent of the wind, not surprised that Jorge's trail led toward that new house near the entrance to the sanctuary. The scent of Jorge's blood was impossible to miss, redolent as it was of rotten meat and mold.

"Balls and bullshit," Thorolf muttered behind him. *"Just like you said."*

"We'll see how far that combo gets him with Ginger," Niall said and, just like old times, there was anticipation in his tone. Thorolf snorted with laughter.

Despite his conviction that this mission was his alone, Delaney found himself glad to have their company. Jorge wouldn't be alone in Magnus's house, and Delaney might need help. He certainly wanted to ensure that Ginger didn't pay for him entering her life.

He owed her more than that.

Delaney had every intention of winning on every front. He'd save Ginger, charm her all over again, sate the firestorm, and then figure out how to destroy the Elixir without giving Magnus whatever it was that he wanted.

His to-do list was getting longer, but that didn't mean he couldn't finish it all before he died.

Gran had taught Ginger to take care of herself, to be independent, and to stand on her own two feet. Gran had insisted that everyone should be self-reliant, and that it was a mark of poor planning to become cornered or left without choices. That philosophy of independence had led Ginger well.

But it showed its limitations in Magnus's atrium. Gran, Ginger was forced to admit, had never had to deal with dragon shape shifters trying to kill her.

Ginger maybe hadn't shown a lot of foresight in telling off the *Pyr* before banishing them.

Ginger, though, wasn't prepared to surrender.

The air was frigid in Magnus's central atrium, colder than it had any business being. It couldn't have been because the courtyard was shaded, as there was no sun during the snowstorm, anyway. It might have been because every surface was faced in stone or glass, but Ginger had never felt stone radiate cold the way this patio did.

She had a suspicion that the cold had to do with the big bowl in the middle of the courtyard. She had a bad feeling about that bowl, about the way it seemed to have a malignant presence, but she tried to ignore it while she checked every door and window again. She pounded on the glass, knowing that neither Magnus nor his employees would let her into the house again.

And really, she didn't want to go into the house. She wanted to leave the courtyard and the house and go home.

Where it was quite possible that more dragons awaited her.

Ginger had to admit that there were dragons she wouldn't have minded seeing in this particular moment, but she doubted they'd be inclined to help her, after her dismissal. How fast could dragons fly? They might be halfway to some Florida sunshine already.

Delaney, though, had defended her against Jorge, despite her words and her attitude. There was more to his commitment to her than she had realized.

Maybe more than he had realized.

Not that it mattered now. Ginger rubbed her arms, shivering against the chill, and tried not to think about Delaney lying motionless in her barnyard.

Bleeding.

Was he dead?

Or just badly injured?

The memory made Ginger feel a bit sick. The prospect of being trapped here without any chance of assistance—because she had tossed out the *Pyr*—made her feel sicker. She tried instead to think of a way out of the atrium.

There wasn't one. The square was maybe forty feet on a side, open to the sky and falling snow overhead, framed by tinted glass all around. Every wall looked the same. Her tracks went around and around the perimeter, but she could still see which door she'd left.

There were no pillars or means of climbing the walls. Any hinges and hardware were on the inside of the house. Smooth glass began at the patio and stretched high over Ginger's head. She eyeballed the glass doors and guessed they were at least ten feet tall, with another four feet of smooth glass transom windows overhead. There was no chance she could reach the lip of the roof that began fourteen feet up.

She jumped and tried, even knowing it was futile.

If only she'd been born tall.

Although someone would have to be really tall to leap fourteen feet into the air and grab the edge of that roof.

Dragon-sized, maybe.

Ginger was cold, more chilled than she would have believed possible. The outdoor temperature was never that low when it snowed, always hovering around freezing. Although that still wasn't a lot of fun, Ginger was becoming too cold too quickly.

Something was radiating frigid air in this space. She glanced over her shoulder and eyed the big dish with trepidation. It had to be six feet across, mounted on a pedestal, both made of pale stone. The liquid that filled it glistened red and there was pink-tinged hoarfrost clinging to the perimeter of the bowl.

Ginger had a pretty good idea what the red liquid was.

The Elixir.

She grimaced at the recollection of Magnus tossing back a swig of it, as if he savored a cocktail before dinner.

A Bloody Dragon.

Ick.

She remembered the big vial in the sanctuary with the dragon inside and thought about the story Magnus had told of Cinnabar. She wondered how much of the story was true—or how much of the truth Magnus had surrendered to her. She would have bet that he had arranged his slave's arrest and condemnation—it was something a swell guy like Magnus would have done.

She recalled the last thing he had told her and shuddered again. Cinnabar was outliving his usefulness, and Magnus needed another *Pyr*—whose blood ran red— to take Cinnabar's place, to become the source of the Elixir. She considered her situation and the fact that she was Delaney's mate—which all of these dragon dudes seemed to know—and understood Magnus's plan.

Delaney was his candidate of choice.

And she was trapped here as bait.

The very idea infuriated Ginger. She'd played a lot of roles in her life, but being the sacrificial victim destined to lure a hero to his death had never been one of her choices.

She wasn't going to play that part now. If Delaney wasn't dead, she had to warn him of Magnus's plan.

Even if he was dead, she had to tell the *Pyr*, because Magnus would probably choose another candidate from the company of red-blooded dragon shape shifters.

Which meant she had to get out of this courtyard. Somehow, she was going to outsmart Magnus, and do it before she froze to death.

The trick was figuring out how. Ginger considered the broad, shallow dish of Elixir and had an idea.

The dragonsmoke was thick around the house, the one Delaney was convinced belonged to Magnus. Niall and Thorolf hung back from the smoke's biting sting, but Delaney gritted his teeth and flew closer. The pain of the dragonsmoke was nothing compared to the anguish he'd feel if Ginger was hurt because of his choices.

He caught the scent of Ginger, and was surprised that it was as strong as it was. Could she have escaped already? He would have expected the scent to be muffled by the house.

He narrowed his eyes as he flew closer, fighting his urge to flee from the smoke's dangerous bite. It was sliding beneath his scales, burning every increment of flesh it could find. The sensation was pure torment, but Delaney had to learn more.

He saw that the house was built around a central courtyard, a large square open to the sky. He saw a broad basin filled with red liquid in the middle of that atrium, and knew instantly what it was.

He also saw a small red-headed woman circling the basin. His heart leapt in recognition of Ginger as relief flooded through him. She didn't have a coat on, though, never mind a hat or mitts. She must be freezing.

In the same moment, Delaney felt the sizzle of the firestorm. Ginger looked to be unharmed, if cold and irritated. He couldn't blame her for that. Ginger was pacing quickly, as if she meant to dispel the cold, but she looked up suddenly at him.

Delaney realized she had felt the firestorm, too. She took a step toward him, but Delaney couldn't dive all the way down to the ground. The smoke got thicker and more ferocious with every beat of his wings. If he descended to the house, he wouldn't manage to leave alive. The dragonsmoke was stealing his life force, creating a conduit between his body and the *Slayer* who had breathed it.

The longer he stayed, the more of his strength the *Slayers* would steal for their own.

He had to help Ginger, though. He circled the house three times, gritting his teeth against the burn of the dragonsmoke. He hoped that she was warmed, but couldn't endure much more.

He heard the *Slayers* stirring within the house and knew they would have sensed the firestorm as well. He couldn't linger.

He turned and wheeled out of the thick ring of dragonsmoke, racing back to Niall and Thorolf. All the way, he berated himself for not telling Ginger more. He hadn't explained dragonsmoke to her, so she would believe he was abandoning her.

He really did have some 'splainin' to do.

First he had to ensure her safety.

Ginger approached the Elixir cautiously. She would never have believed that a bowl of liquid, however nasty, could exude such a malignant presence. This bowl, though, gave her the creeps.

She felt colder as she moved closer to it and a knot tightened in her stomach. Ginger kept going, kept forcing herself to take one more step. The scent of the Elixir teased her nostrils, a scent evocative of exactly what the Elixir was. She would have expected the juice of a dragon that had been rotting away for a millennium or two to smell just as bad as this. The knot in her gut tightened and she put her hand over her mouth.

But she took another step closer.

The Elixir was cloudy, like milk mixed with blood, and she refused to think about what the white part of the solution might be. It swirled in the large bowl, moving relentlessly even though there was no obvious source for a current. It emanated cold, a chill that slid right into Ginger's marrow. She shivered, but stepped closer.

That was when she saw the silver beads on the lip of the bowl. There was a thick rim of hoarfrost, white at the perimeter and gradually more pink as it grew thinner over the surface of the Elixir. And on the perimeter of the bowl, outside the crust of ice, were silver beads.

It looked like the mercury that had fallen out of a thermometer her grandmother had dropped and broken decades before. Ginger had been fascinated by the rolling beads and had helped her grandmother to gather them up.

It had been that night when they realized that the white gold on Gran's wedding ring had been corroded to nothing by the mercury that she'd gathered in her left hand.

Ginger didn't dare touch the toxin, but she wanted to upset the bowl. Spilling the contents would rid the *Slayers* of at least this much of their precious Elixir. It would get their attention.

And maybe, from that, would come an opportunity.

Ginger would have liked to have had a better plan, but she had to work with the only thing she had.

One big bowl of Elixir.

A blush of heat touched her shoulder suddenly, as if the sun had come out from behind the clouds. It was still overcast, though, the sky still gray overhead. The snow continued to fall with relentless speed, steadily filling her footsteps.

Ginger looked up in confusion.

She caught her breath when she saw three dragons high in the sky overhead. They were too far away for the colors of their scales to be distinguished, but Ginger's heart leapt with hope that she knew who one of them was.

She felt the firestorm, after all.

Two of the dragons abruptly recoiled and turned their course back in the direction they had come. They twitched convulsively and Ginger remembered Thorolf's comments about dragonsmoke's burn. The house must be surrounded with the smoke.

One dragon flew closer though, moving with steady persistence. She smiled when she saw that his scales were copper and emerald, even though they looked to be blackened on one side.

Delaney was alive!

And even better, he wasn't abandoning her to whatever fate Magnus had in store.

Ginger's elation was short-lived. She had to warn Delaney of the danger to him. She had to tell him that Magnus had a dark scheme for him. She glanced at the glass walls surrounding the atrium but couldn't see any shadows moving in the adjacent rooms. The glass was tinted, so she had no idea whether she was being watched.

She didn't want to contribute to Delaney becoming Elixir fodder. All the same, she was glad to see him. She watched him fly closer, her heart hammering, the firestorm sending a welcome heat through her body. She pretended to be studying just the bowl, stealing as many upward glances as she dared.

There wouldn't be many, as much as she would have loved to have stared at him openly. She loved how

Delaney flew, with smooth grace and power, the same way—she realized suddenly—that he walked. Crowds on dance floors parted for him, people sensing his quiet authority. It was also the way he made love, all confidence and power. He exuded grace and strength, like a trained athlete, and one certain of his abilities.

She stole another peek skyward. He was much closer, which explained why she felt as warm as she did. His scales were blackened, as if they had been burned, his beauty diminished by recent battles.

She still thought he was gorgeous, though. There was a cut on his shoulder that she could see, and the ruby scab of his crimson blood was in stark contrast to the dark dark green of his wings. She savored the sight of his allegiance to the *Pyr*, the truth of his heart's inclination, then recalled that was why Magnus wanted him so badly.

Then he grimaced and turned, recoiling from some invisible foe. With each of the circles he flew over the atrium, his moves became more taut. He had to be in agony from the dragonsmoke and he clearly couldn't come all the way to her.

But he endured pain to let her feel the heat of the firestorm. Ginger welcomed its heat and its implications, knowing that she had been too quick to assume his selfishness.

After the third circuit, Delaney turned out of the curve, moving backward in an erratic pattern. Ginger watched and understood that smoke not only burned, but could give chase. She bit her lip as Delaney struggled to evade it, and admired how he never made a sound of protest.

He retreated, but she knew he wasn't gone.

He'd come once, enduring the pain of dragonsmoke. Ginger recognized a reconnaissance mission when she saw one. The very fact that he'd come to check on her gave her new strength and confidence. She might not be able to escape this prison on her own, but she had three dragons on her side, one of whom was ready to put himself in danger to help her.

Delaney would be back.

And Ginger would be ready.

She eyed the Elixir and made her plan.

Chapter 11

"**I** don't get it," Thorolf complained as he dropped another bag of fertilizer into the backseat of Delaney's rental car.

Delaney and Niall each dropped a bag into the trunk and the car sat lower on its shocks. "One more each?" Niall asked.

"Let's overengineer it," Delaney agreed with a nod. "We're not going to have a second chance with this plan."

"But I don't get it," Thorolf repeated, following the two *Pyr* back to the barn. There was a large stack of fifty-pound bags of fertilizer at the back of the barn, a stash that Delaney had suspected would be there.

All the same, he was glad to have found it.

He was even more glad to be putting it to work.

"It's got a lot of nitrogen," Niall said, as if that explained everything.

"So?" Thorolf grunted as he lifted another bag to his shoulder.

"Nitrogen is explosive," Delaney said.

Thorolf still looked confused.

"Remember the Oklahoma City bombing?" Niall asked, his tone becoming impatient. "A load of high-nitrogen fertilizer, some kind of spark, and you're good to go."

"Go where?" Thorolf asked.

Delaney fought a smile at Niall's exasperation. "Sky-high."

"I still don't get it."

"We're going to blow the front off Magnus's house," Niall said, his tone reflecting his opinion of Thorolf. "Ginger is smart enough to run once there's no physical barrier to her freedom. When she gets out of the dragonsmoke, Delaney will be able to snatch her up. You and I will meet fire with fire and cover the escape."

"Oh!" Thorolf eased the bag he carried into the backseat. The undercarriage of the car was nearly scraping the ground. He glanced at Ginger's pickup truck. "We should have used the truck. It would carry more."

"I can't destroy Ginger's vehicle," Delaney said in a tone that allowed no argument. "The renter will do."

"Good thing you haven't got any emotional bonds here," Niall said mildly, and Delaney glared at him.

"It wouldn't be fair to her."

Niall didn't looked persuaded. "You like her."

Delaney ignored that and shut the car door.

Thorolf ran a hand over his hair. "So, who's driving?"

"I am," Delaney said. "I can get closer, despite the smoke."

"You're getting fried, you know," Niall said, his manner worried. "One of those bastards is going to wise up and make a conduit of the smoke, then steal some of your energy."

"It's not so bad," Delaney argued.

Niall rolled his eyes.

"Maybe it's the Elixir that lets him take the smoke better," Thorolf suggested.

Niall and Delaney looked at each other. "The smoke still burns," Delaney admitted.

"But you can take some of it," Niall said. "And I can't take any."

"Me neither," Thorolf said.

"There are a lot of things you can't do," Niall observed, and the two looked daggers at each other.

"I can take a lot of pain, but not that," Thorolf admitted. "It feels like the dragonsmoke is sucking me dry."

"That's because it is," Niall said.

Thorolf shuddered, then eyed Delaney. "Maybe a sip of the Elixir isn't such a bad idea."

"It's a rotten idea," Delaney said sharply. "It ruins your life and destroys your will to live. It gives you nightmares and leaves you writhing in a field like an animal when there's even a partial eclipse. You're always hungry for more of what's killing you." He met Thorolf's astonished gaze. "Trust me. Do not go there. Nothing that stuff promises is worth what you get."

Then he got in the car, started the engine, and backed out slowly. Thorolf looked alarmed.

"Be careful," Niall counseled.

"I'll do whatever has to be done," Delaney said, seeing that his answer didn't please his old friend.

"You can count on us," Niall insisted. *"Just give us a shout when you're close."*

"Will do."

As much as Delaney hated to admit it, he might need help and he was glad of the presence of these two. He saw in the rearview mirror that the two *Pyr* stayed in the driveway, watching him make his way toward the main road. Niall had his hands shoved in his pockets, his expression grim. Thorolf glanced between Niall and Delaney, his uncertainty about the plan more than clear.

Delaney, though, knew exactly what he had to do.

*   *   *

It took Delaney a long time to get to Magnus's driveway, what with the road conditions and the car riding so low. He was afraid to hit a bump and damage the gas tank when the car was full of explosive fertilizer. Darkness was falling when he turned into the driveway, although night came early this time of year.

He hoped Ginger was still okay. It had taken far longer than he'd hoped to get this far.

Delaney felt the first twinges of dragonsmoke as soon as he turned down the driveway, but he forced himself to ignore it. The house was surrounded by a brick wall, one that enclosed a couple of acres as well as the house itself. It had to be a dozen feet tall and was capped with spikes.

Delaney wondered what the locals thought of Magnus's need for security in such a quiet place.

There was a steel gate halfway down the driveway, securing the only breach in the wall. There was an intercom on a pillar just before the gate, but Delaney didn't press the button.

He knew the *Slayers* wouldn't let him in.

Instead he got out of the car. The dragonsmoke assaulted him as soon as he opened the door, burning his skin in a thousand places simultaneously. It slipped beneath his clothes, but he shifted shape quickly.

That only increased its effect upon him. It eased beneath his scales, scorching every bit of skin it touched. It might have driven Delaney mad with the pain, but he'd fought off madness before.

And this pain was external. The battle he'd fought against the Elixir had been for his heart and his mind. He recalled an expression about anything that didn't kill a man making him stronger, and concluded the same logic applied to the *Pyr*.

Meanwhile, he flew to the gate, grasped its icy steel, and ripped. In three tries, he barely bent the gate, revealing that Magnus had invested in high-quality steel.

It was nothing compared to Delaney's motivation, though. He felt the first tickle of the firestorm, weaker in intensity than he'd felt before, but strong enough to empower him.

Ginger was in there, trapped in a situation of Delaney's creation. She had no chance of escape or survival beyond his efforts. He'd endangered her without meaning to do so, but he still had to fix the mess he'd made.

He thought of her, freezing in that atrium without her coat, and roared with anger. He clenched the gates and wrenched them open, casting one broken piece of steel aside. An alarm began to ring, but he shifted shape and drove the car toward the house as quickly as he could. The dragonsmoke increased in intensity, the pain so excruciating that he wanted to scream aloud.

He didn't.

He drove, his expression grim, his resolve unshakable. Delaney had gotten Ginger into this and he was going to get her out of it.

Even if it was the last thing he did.

Ginger hooked her hands beneath the rim of the bowl filled with the Elixir and lifted with all her might.

It didn't budge.

She wasn't truly surprised. The basin had to be six feet across and almost two feet deep, and looked like it was carved of stone. Maybe it was made of poured concrete. At any rate, she hadn't expected it to be light.

She bent down and considered the point where the underside of the basin met the pedestal. It was possible that the whole fount had been made in one piece, but a lot more likely that it was two. The seam should be a weak point.

It was worth a try. If nothing else, Ginger just had to make enough ruckus to distract the *Slayers* from whatever scheme the *Pyr* had planned.

She backed across the courtyard into one corner, then did some deep knee bends to warm up a bit. She eyed the basin with its evil contents and built up her resolve. She'd never done a high kick before, but this was a good time to try.

She didn't have much to lose.

Ginger ran directly at the basin, leaping into the air toward it. She kicked high and hard with both feet, her boots connecting with the rim of the basin.

It shook hard but didn't fall.

She, however, fell right on her ass.

The Elixir sloshed over the back rim of the basin, and the hoarfrost broke around the edge. Ginger peered under the basin and thought she could see a hairline crack between the basin and pedestal.

Encouraged, she brushed herself off and repeated the exercise, launching her attack from the next corner. She reasoned that she'd break the seal faster that way, but really wasn't sure. She ran harder, having a better idea of the distance, and kicked harder, punctuating the impact with a shout. She landed harder too and knew her hip would be black and blue.

But there was a cracking sound, and the basin shifted slightly. It wasn't level anymore, but slightly tipped. The Elixir sloshed over the edges, staining the snow on the patio a vivid red. Ginger got to her feet, sensing triumph.

"What the hell do you think you're doing?"

The man's voice was low and quiet, the kind of voice that carries over a surprising distance and launches a shiver down the spine of everyone who hears it. Every syllable dripped with threat and intimidation.

Ginger recognized that voice. She swallowed and pivoted to face the *Slayer* with the accent, the one who had brought her here.

In human form, he was tall and fair, but now his hair

was shaved to a bare bristle. He was buff and could have been considered handsome, but his eyes were such a cold blue that he could have been made of ice.

Ginger knew he had a block of ice for a heart. She took a step backward. Even if she'd never met him before, she would have recognized danger when it stood right in front of her. One glimpse would tell any thinking person that this was a man who would kill and maim, and probably enjoy every moment of it.

He came closer and Ginger realized his leg was in a cast. She remembered that Delaney had cut off the *Slayer*'s back claw to free her.

Did *Pyr* and *Slayers* carry their injuries between forms?

She took another step back, jumping when a second man cleared his throat behind her.

"You can't get away," he said, and she spun to find him smiling at her. Ginger didn't know this man—he had dark hair and very dark brown eyes, and his accent was French. There was a cut at the outside corner of his eye, one that must have been painful.

She glanced back at the first *Slayer*, who had come even closer. The two moved steadily into the atrium, forcing Ginger to move closer to the Elixir.

"I'm just cold," she said. "I wanted to get your attention."

The blond smiled and it only made him look more unfriendly. "You have it."

"Well, then maybe we could go inside." Ginger glanced brightly between the pair of them. "After all, my being frozen isn't going to help you much."

The dark one chuckled and the fair one smiled more broadly. "Don't you understand?" he asked softly. "You've outlived your usefulness, even for bait."

"What do you mean?"

"Delaney knows where you are. He'll come here."

The blond opened his eyes slightly in emphasis. "We don't need you anymore."

"But, but, Magnus wants me alive."

The blond looked across the atrium, visibly scanning it, then met her gaze again. "You'll notice that Magnus is conspicuously absent."

They moved even closer and Ginger backed up, knowing from the chill that the Elixir was right behind her back. "But isn't Magnus the boss? You wouldn't want him to be angry with you."

The blond *Slayer* sneered. "Magnus grows old and feeble. Right now, he's having his nap. Soon he'll be begging me for more of the Elixir." He nodded at his partner. "Grab her. Let's have some fun while we wait for Delaney."

The dark-haired *Slayer* snatched Ginger from behind, holding her easily off the ground. Ginger panicked and struggled, making absolutely no difference in her situation. "What are you going to do?" she demanded, hearing her voice rise.

The blond eyed her. "We're going to find out whether the Elixir truly is toxic to humans, and in what quantities." His eyes glinted. "Consider it a little experiment." He beckoned, his right index finger changing to a dragon talon as he grinned.

"Low exposure over time is the best way to start," Ginger said wildly.

He laughed. "We're not interested in human laboratory protocols," he said with a sneer. "Let's find out what happens when you drink it. That's the really interesting proposition."

"You can't make me!"

"You'll find that we can be very persuasive."

The dark one carried Ginger toward the Elixir as she squirmed and fought. He was stronger and much bigger than she. The blond watched, his amusement not reach-

ing his eyes. This guy would be able to torture anyone—
he might even enjoy it.

That wasn't a good sign.

The blond knew, Ginger guessed, that she was about
to die a horrible death. It wasn't her favorite idea, but
the dark-haired *Slayer* held her in a relentless grip. He
caught the back of her neck in one hand and pushed her
face toward the Elixir. It appeared to swirl more quickly,
as if it responded to her presence.

Ginger held her breath, not wanting to smell the
Elixir. She averted her face, not wanting to look at it.
She felt its chill, though, felt as if she'd develop frostbite
on the tip of her nose.

If she lived long enough for that. She shuddered and
struggled, which only made the blond laugh.

"Do it, Mallory," he said, and Ginger blinked.

Mallory. The *Slayer* holding her captive was Mallory.
He was the *Slayer* Delaney had struck down that morning, the garnet red and gold one whose body had been
defended by the agate dragon.

He had been dead, or as good as, just hours before.
He held Ginger tightly and she heard his breath rasp. He
seemed pretty lively to her in this moment.

Which meant he'd drunk the Elixir.

He was undead.

Yuck. She was in one of those midnight ghoul
movies.

But Jorge's cast proved that the *Pyr* and *Slayers* carried their injuries between forms. Mallory had had his
eye torn that morning, but he'd also had a major gash on
his shoulder. Ginger couldn't remember which one, but
she knew she'd only have one chance to fool him.

She went limp, as if she'd passed out from the fumes.

"No fun," the blond had time to say, before Mallory's
grasp loosened just a little bit.

It would have to be enough.

*   *   *

There was a porte cochere before Magnus's front door and Delaney turned into it, taking the curve too fast. The car swerved and slid, the passenger side slamming into the front of the house.

There was an announcement of his presence, if they'd missed the first one.

Delaney leapt out of the car even as Balthasar flung open the front door. He'd been about to send a message to Niall in old-speak, but didn't want the *Slayer* to overhear it.

He'd have to hope for the best.

"How rude," Balthasar said. He had a black eye from being chucked head to head against Mallory that morning, and looked resentful.

"I didn't think Magnus was taking visitors," Delaney retorted, backing away from the driver's side door. He'd already popped the flap on the gas tank from inside the car. "Given the wound he got this morning."

The alarm rang and rang, but Delaney was busily unscrewing the cap from the gas tank, holding his hand behind his own hip. His fingers fumbled as the dragon-smoke flooded his body with pain and he feared that he was taking too long. He shoved the gas-soaked rag he'd brought into the opening and knew he had to tempt Balthasar to come around the vehicle.

"No one walked away unscathed," Balthasar said, stepping out of the doorway. "Especially you. Have you come for a restorative sip of the Elixir?"

Delaney let him take two more steps closer. Balthasar was in front of the car, and just a couple more steps would do it. "No, I came to finish you off, since you were the last one left standing." He shrugged and stepped backward, moving toward the trunk of the car. "I dislike loose ends."

Balthasar took the bait, following Delaney down the driver's side of the car. "In your dreams," he hissed.

"Sorry, but when I dream, it's not of you." Delaney shifted shape, knowing Balthasar would follow suit.

The *Slayer* did, becoming an agate and gold dragon. Delaney retreated as quickly as he could. Balthasar lunged toward him, furiously breathing dragonfire.

He was right beside the driver's door when the rag lit. The gas tank was half empty, ensuring that there was a lot of oxygen at the ready. The gas tank exploded instantly, and the car burned like a Roman candle.

Delaney retreated as quickly as he could, but his tail was still singed by the fire. Balthasar swore and followed right behind Delaney. His feathers were in flames, his scales blackened from the explosion.

But that quick pursuit was the only thing that saved Balthasar's life. Just a heartbeat after the gas tank, the fertilizer exploded. The explosion destroyed the porte cochere, sending chunks of brick flying in every direction.

It also decimated the front of the house, reducing it to rubble.

Perfect.

Ginger didn't wait for a better chance. As soon as Mallory loosened his grip, she wriggled. She twisted and dug her fingers into his shoulders as hard as she could.

It was the left shoulder that had been wounded. Ginger could feel the scab beneath her hand and she burrowed her fingers into it, trying to inflict as much pain as possible.

It had healed quickly but not completely, and she showed no shame in ripping the wound open again with her nails.

Mallory screamed and tried to pull from her, stumbling against the basin of Elixir. His momentum was enough to tip the bowl, and the Elixir spilled over the patio.

Ginger dug the fingers of her other hand into his injured eye. She was fighting for her life and it was no time to be squeamish.

Mallory shouted in rage and backed across the atrium, trying to pull her off him. She felt his fingers change to talons and feared he would rip her to shreds right then and there.

But she didn't stop.

"Fool!" the blond shouted. Mallory hauled Ginger free of him and cast her against one glass wall. Her body hit so hard that the glass vibrated. The impact left her dizzy. She slid down the glass, landing heavily in the snow, as Mallory shimmered blue before her.

He didn't look happy.

The blond was on his hands and knees in the middle of the atrium, lapping up Elixir as it spilled from the bowl. "Straighten the basin!" he commanded, evidently having no intent of doing that himself when he could devour more Elixir.

"Do it yourself," Mallory snarled. A puff of smoke came out of his nostril as he eyed Ginger. His lip curled, his eye and his shoulder bled black, and he stepped toward her with purpose.

There was nowhere to run. Ginger had time to think that she was in even bigger trouble than before, when an explosion shook the house.

The sliding glass door behind Ginger cracked right in half. She stumbled backward, falling through the broken pane. Mallory roared and snatched after her, his claw scattering the glass.

Ginger didn't wait for an embossed invitation; she ran.

Out in front of the destroyed house, Balthasar screamed and swore. He raced after Delaney, his eyes blazing with fury. Delaney took flight as the *Slayer* closed fast.

To Delaney's delight, Niall dove out of the sky and attacked the *Slayer* from behind. Surprise gave Niall the upper hand, then the two locked in furious combat.

Delaney caught his breath at the fiery caress of the firestorm. It was a different kind of heat that the burn inflicted by dragonsmoke. It was sensuous and warm, sending desire through his body and making his heart pound with anticipation.

He knew why he was feeling it. Delaney turned and saw a small redhead picking her way through the smoking rubble with remarkable speed.

Ginger!

He didn't know where the other *Slayers* were and he didn't care. He pivoted in flight as he headed directly for his mate.

"On your back," Thorolf declared, and Delaney started at the sudden appearance of the moonstone and silver dragon. Thorolf's coloring gave him good camouflage in a snowstorm.

Once again, he was glad of the *Pyr*'s assistance. The pair swept toward the house together, Thorolf muttering at the pain inflicted by the dragonsmoke. *"It's getting worse!"*

"It will."

"I can't take any more."

"You don't have to. Just cover my back and take care of yourself."

Thorolf hung back, hovering vigilantly behind Delaney. Ginger, to Delaney's delight, was clear of the house and running for the broken gate. He saw no signs of pursuit by the *Slayers*, which was odd, but he'd take any break he could get.

Ginger glanced up, maybe guessing at his presence because of the heat of the firestorm. She smiled, telling him that she wasn't so furious anymore. The sight of her pleasure made the pain easier to endure.

It made him glad to be alive.

Delaney held his breath and dove toward her. He snatched Ginger up in one claw and sparks flew into the snow as his grip closed around her. The heat of the firestorm raged through him, kindling his desire. Ginger felt small and feminine in his grasp, so vulnerable and precious that his breath caught in his throat.

He rocketed into the sky, getting both of them out of harm's way as quickly as possible. She cheered and shivered, and he held her more tightly against his chest. The firestorm's heat teased and beguiled him, reminding him of what they had done together.

And what they hadn't done. He recalled the heat of her surrounding him, her sweetness and passion, then glanced down to find her eyes twinkling. That she could have a sense of humor even in a dangerous situation amazed him.

Then it fed his admiration and his desire.

"You're a mess, hotshot," Ginger said lightly. She glanced over him, clearly assessing the state of his singed scales. "What have you been doing while I've been freezing my butt off?"

Delaney found himself smiling, liking that she felt sufficiently confident of his motives to give him a hard time. "That's the effect of dragonsmoke."

"The perimeter mark," she said, and he knew someone had told her about it.

"We use it to mark territory. It burns any *Pyr* or *Slayer* who crosses it uninvited."

"I didn't see any smoke."

"It can't be detected by humans, although some feel a chill when they walk through it."

"More of those superperceptive senses?" she asked, her tone teasing.

Delaney nodded. Ginger shivered again as she nestled closer to his heat and he closed his claw more protectively around her. He was fiercely glad she was all right.

He wanted to celebrate that fact, alone with Ginger.

"They were going to make me drink it," she admitted quietly, her words sending a stab through his heart. He didn't have to ask what she meant.

"Who?" Delaney was angry enough to go back and demand penance from the *Slayers* for what they'd tried to do to his mate, but he knew he had to ensure her safety first.

"The blond and Mallory."

"Jorge." A cold resolve settled within Delaney and he knew that he'd ensure somehow that Jorge paid for even threatening Ginger with that possibility. He could feel the galloping pace of her heart and knew she had been more afraid than she let on. It was like her to disguise her vulnerability and her fear. He held her closer, relieved that he'd come in time.

Who would defend his mate if he died destroying the Elixir?

It was a question Delaney would have preferred to evade, but it echoed in his thoughts with unwelcome persistence. Could he expect his fellow *Pyr* to take her cause as vigorously as he would? Why would they, without the firestorm's insistence driving them back to Ginger, over and over and over again? Why would they, without this fierce admiration for her strength and audacity, one that made Delaney believe she was the most perfect mate possible?

But what choice did he have?

Niall and Thorolf appeared on his flanks again, neither of them obviously wounded.

"Piece of cake," Thorolf said at Delaney's glance.

"They'll all be drinking the Elixir now," Niall said, more rueful than triumphant.

"Why was Delaney the only one to fly through the

dragonsmoke?" Ginger asked. Delaney smiled at her need for information.

Niall laughed. "He was the one with the motivation."

Delaney felt Ginger watching him and wondered how much she guessed of the obligation he felt toward her. He wouldn't sweeten what he had to do with an emotional confession—that really wouldn't be fair. He knew his fate, although its price was feeling higher with every passing moment.

"I got you into it," he said gruffly. "I got you out."

She eyed him for a long moment and he avoided her gaze. She ran the flat of her hand across his chest, a casual gesture of affection that sent a pang of lust racing through his veins. Delaney *wanted* as he had never wanted before.

But he had to respect Ginger's plan for her own future.

"Was that your rental car?" she asked finally.

"I'm guessing the deposit is forfeit," he said deadpan, delighted when she laughed.

"And what was in it?"

"A whole lot of your fertilizer."

"Right." She nodded, thinking about the plan. "Well, that's a good use for it. Luke and I have been arguing about it for a while."

Luke?

Who was Luke? Delaney felt a stab of jealousy that caught him by surprise. He didn't feel he had the right to ask questions about Ginger's personal life, given his own plan to leave, but he wanted that right.

Badly.

Delaney looked down at her in surprise, but Ginger was frowning in frustration. "Luke refuses to buy anything organic. He refuses to spread anything organic on the fields that he rents from me, because it's not the way he's always done it. It drives me crazy. I refused to let him use that crap on my land, so it's been sitting there ever since."

"He works for you?"

Ginger made a little sound of annoyance. "So to speak."

"Luke," Niall murmured in old-speak, taunting him. *"Lots of energy there."*

Thorolf snickered.

"I wonder what Luke knows about raising Pyr *babies,"* Niall mused, and Delaney thought about decking his old friend for unwelcome commentary.

Ginger looked between them. "What are you talking about?"

"It doesn't matter," Delaney said.

Ginger bristled. "We had a deal. . . ."

"I'm razzing him about Luke," Niall supplied, and Delaney could sense Ginger's pleasure that he was concerned. He felt a whole lot less pleasure over Niall's interference, but that didn't make any difference. He was being drawn into a web of connections with Ginger, one that would only make it harder to do what he had to do.

Too bad he couldn't stop thinking about the pleasures of seducing her.

"My neighbor," Ginger said lightly, evidently unaware of the storm within Delaney. Maybe she didn't feel the same urge, even with the firestorm radiant between them, sending lust through Delaney's body and feeding his amorous thoughts. "Well, he's Silas's son, actually. They rent my fields and work them, and Luke helps me with the girls."

That told Delaney everything and nothing, but he refused to ask more. He didn't want to give Ginger any ideas about him sticking around. He was getting enough ideas on his own.

"Seems to me that anybody planning to commit suicide shouldn't be worried about your employees," Niall said, his manner sly.

"Seems that way to me, too," Ginger said.

They both eyed Delaney, consideration in their expressions.

Delaney ignored them both.

He concentrated instead on checking the horizon for signs of pursuit. He didn't want to think about what Ginger might read into his curiosity. He didn't want to think about why he even resented this Luke guy, and he wasn't going to wonder about Ginger's relationship with him.

He certainly wouldn't ask for details.

The silence seemed to be filled with questions, questions that Delaney didn't dare answer or ask. The last thing he needed was more temptation.

Having Ginger pressed against his chest was dangerous enough. As if she knew the effect of her touch on him, she ran her hands over his chest and shoulders lightly, caressing him almost absently, her touch driving everything else from his thoughts.

If that wasn't treacherous, Delaney didn't know what was.

Chapter 12

"Thanks for not using my truck," Ginger said as they approached her farm and the red pickup became visible through the falling snow. There was impatience in her tone, although Delaney was fighting to keep his hold on her casual.

Brotherly.

Instead of the passionate embrace he wanted to share.

"I've been presumptuous enough," Delaney said. "We need to fix the roof on that barn, too."

"Damn that Jorge!" Ginger said. "It's a new barn, too."

"We'll fix it as well as we can, then I'll leave you money to have it repaired properly."

"Leave nothing but a footprint, huh?" Ginger asked, wry amusement in her tone. "Oh, and a baby."

Delaney was embarrassed, and Niall's chuckle didn't improve his mood. He sounded so callous when Ginger put it that way.

Worse, he was starting to feel callous. He felt Ginger watching him, probably trying to read his thoughts, and kept his expression neutral as the *Pyr* descended in unison.

"Close your eyes," he advised Ginger, his tone terse.

"Forget it. I know what to expect, and I want to see all of it."

Delaney knew from her stubborn tone that he wouldn't change her mind. He tried to shift quickly to make it easier for her, noting that again she didn't even allow herself to blink.

When his feet were on the ground and he was in human form, he held her in his arms. She was pale but hadn't passed out.

"Ha! I did it!" she said, grinning in triumph.

The firestorm burned with greater intensity as Delaney looked down at her, sending sizzling heat from every point they touched. Was it stronger because he was in human form, or stronger simply because they hadn't satisfied it? Either way, it burned with more vigor, pushing thoughts of anything other than Ginger out of his mind.

Ginger flushed a little as she smiled up at him and he knew their thoughts had turned in the same direction.

"Maybe you guys have somewhere to be," he said to the *Pyr*.

Niall chuckled again. "That's the thanks we get."

"Thank you very much, now go away," Thorolf said with a grin.

"How about thank you very much, now let's fix the roof of the barn," Delaney countered. "Ginger isn't going to bear the expense of our time here." Even though he was defending her interests, he felt her withdraw from him. She put one hand on his chest and the heat from her palm shook him to his core.

He wanted to kiss her.

He wanted to seduce her.

He wanted to hear her sigh with satisfaction all over again.

But she didn't want to have his child alone. He had to respect her wishes; he wanted to respect her concerns, but his body was driving him to do what needed to be done for the *Pyr*.

Ginger wriggled until Delaney put her on her feet, although he was reluctant to do so. There was something marvelous about the languid rush of desire that the firestorm sent through his veins, and he didn't want there to be any distance between them. He tried to keep an arm around her waist, but Ginger stepped away from him, her own inclination more than clear.

Delaney knew he shouldn't have been surprised. He'd as much as said he wouldn't be staying. He knew he shouldn't have been disappointed, but he was.

And he knew it wasn't just because his firestorm remained unsatisfied, a mark of his failure to play for the team.

Even without a firestorm, he'd have been fascinated by Ginger Sinclair.

He thought about forgoing his mission. He thought about leaving the Elixir where it was and walking away from the task he'd chosen for himself. He thought about taking the time to know Ginger, to slowly seduce her and savor the firestorm, to build a future together.

But that future would always be tenuous. His past would come to destroy them, to steal his child, to endanger Ginger. So long as the Elixir existed, his nightmare could come true.

He couldn't condemn her to that.

He was caught, snared between his duty and his desire, between his reality and his dream. He knew what he had to do, but his determination to do it was eroding quickly in Ginger's presence.

Still, he had to make things right between them.

He had to try to make amends.

Niall and Thorolf headed toward the barn to assess

the damage. Ginger might have marched after them, but Delaney caught her elbow in his hand. Those sparks danced and he swallowed at the fresh surge of desire that rolled over his flesh.

"Wait," he said quietly. "I need to apologize to you first."

The problem with Delaney was that he was just too sexy.

No, the problem with Delaney was that he had both power and vulnerability, all rolled up in a tasty package, and Ginger had a weak spot for strong men with, well, a weak spot. She could see the shadows in his eyes and felt sympathy for whatever he had suffered. The fact that he had endured the pain of dragonsmoke in order to save her was enough to undermine her determination to avoid him.

That wasn't fair.

It also wasn't fair that his presence made her think about repeating their activities of the night before. The man was too yummy for words, and Ginger had to remind herself that having his child—never mind raising it alone—was not on her agenda. She'd gotten lucky once, according to Rafferty, and should have known better than to push her luck.

Even if dragging Delaney back to her room again was a very tempting idea.

But the last complication she needed in her life was a child.

Ginger might have put distance between them, just to save herself from her own weak impulses, but Delaney touched her arm. She looked back and was lost in the appeal in his eyes. It wasn't the spark of the firestorm that made her knees and her resistance melt to nothing—it was the fact that he wanted to apologize.

He grimaced and shrugged, as awkward with words

as she might have expected of a man whose deeds spoke the loudest.

"I wasn't fair to you last night," he said, his voice low. "And I'm sorry. It's not a justification, but we're taught all our lives that if we have the gift of a firestorm, we have to consummate it. We're taught that we have an obligation to create more *Pyr* if the opportunity presents itself."

He smiled at her, his expression so tentative that it tore her heart, and shrugged. "I didn't think beyond that." He exhaled, then laced their fingers together. "And really, I don't think I could have thought about much of anything last night except you."

His philosophy didn't sound that different from her own, when phrased that way, and she felt that sense of common ground again. Ginger took a half step closer to him, and had to admit the truth. "Ours was a pretty strong connection, right from the start."

"And it was a magical night." He kissed her fingertips, his warm gaze locked on hers. "And I'm sorry that the *Pyr* knew we'd spent the night together."

"But you had to tell them that you'd fulfilled your obligation—or tried to do so—before going on a suicide mission," Ginger concluded. "I get it. You guys play as a team."

Delaney frowned and looked down at their entwined hands. His words were husky. "I'm glad, though, that the firestorm wasn't satisfied."

"You mean that I'm not pregnant."

He nodded.

"Even though you're supposed to knock me up?" she teased.

He didn't smile. "It's primal, the urge to satisfy the firestorm. It's a call to breed and one that's hard to ignore."

"I know something about primal urges," Ginger said.

He looked at her again, his confusion clear. "I own a farm. I raise and breed dairy cows. I make a good buck selling primo bull semen."

His smile was quick then, transforming his features for a tantalizing moment. She had a glimpse of the man he might have been, or maybe the one he once was, and despised Magnus and his scheme all the more. She wished Delaney would smile more often, but knew that wouldn't happen soon.

"Okay, I guess you do understand that then," Delaney said quietly. His gaze clung to hers for a long moment and Ginger wished he would touch her. He swallowed. "I understand your reservations, and I respect them. I know what I have to do, and what I should do." He looked up then and the light in his eyes made her chest tight. "But you mess with my resolve, Ginger Sinclair."

Ginger found herself smiling in response, the warmth that spread around her heart having nothing to do with the firestorm. "I know exactly what you mean," she said softly. Their gazes clung and held for a moment, his intensity leaving Ginger dizzy.

And yearning for his touch again.

Then Delaney's tone changed, becoming more brusque as he stepped away from her. "We should fix the roof of your barn. Why don't you go in the house and get warm?" He might have left her then, but Ginger caught at his arm.

She couldn't fully explain the strength of her desire to help him, but she was accustomed to running on her intuition. And she was pleased by his determination to fix whatever fallout the *Pyr* had left in her life. She dared to trust her gut again.

"Here's something else I understand," Ginger said, her words falling quickly. "The firestorm is a mark of a *Pyr* needing to breed, right?"

"That he's met his destined mate, yes." That wariness

was back in Delaney's eyes and Ginger wanted to know whom he distrusted more—her or himself. She could have guessed the answer, which made her more determined to persuade him of his own merit.

"So, there's a big *Pyr* breeding program, a lot like the one I manage with spreadsheets in my office."

"I guess so."

"And someone's making the matches that count."

"Rafferty would say it's the Great Wyvern." Delaney shrugged. "Our god."

"Okay. I can live with a divine breeding plan," Ginger acknowledged. "We all believe what we need to— that's what my gran used to say. The point is that there is a breeding plan, and someone—maybe this Great Wyvern—has chosen you and me to be a breeding pair."

"Yes." Delaney was watching her closely, listening to her every word. His eyes had brightened, another sign of his interest. The firestorm seemed to heat an increment more, or maybe it was just the effect of Delaney's watchfulness that made Ginger simmer.

She wanted him all over again, this grim fighter so convinced that he had no worth himself. Ginger could see lots of merit in Delaney Shea, from his nobility of purpose to his strength, from his sense of honor to his passion. His friends saw it, too.

Ginger smiled at him. "Well, in my view of the world, that means there has to be a point. Why you and me? Why not you and my friend Tanya? Why not me and her fiancé, Steve?"

Delaney almost smiled. "I'll guess that you have an idea."

"I do. I'm thinking that the firestorm is kind of like love at first sight, that it's an instinctive recognition of a connection. Maybe a connection that's good for both of us." She hooked a finger into his collar and tugged him closer, letting challenge fill her tone. "So I think you owe it to me, if not to the Great Wyvern, to figure what the point is before you kill yourself in destroying the Elixir."

His gaze flicked over her and she knew she had pushed him, maybe a bit too far. His tone was firm, as if he'd put a wall between them. "You don't understand what you're asking." He tried to step away, but Ginger hung on.

"Maybe I want to. Maybe that's the point." Ginger swallowed. "Maybe I just want to have a chance to find out."

"I'm not that special, Ginger. I have a taint—"

She put her finger over his mouth, silencing him in a flash of light. That predictable heat rolled through her body, emanating from her fingertips against his lips, weakening her knees, and making her wonder what would be so bad about having Delaney's son. "I'd like to have the chance to decide for myself about that."

Delaney was silent beneath her fingertip.

The snow swirled around them, surrounding them in a cocoon of dancing white. Ginger swallowed. "Magnus plans to kill you. He has a scheme. . . ."

"Magnus always has a scheme," Delaney said quietly. "I don't want you to get sucked into the *Pyr*'s troubles."

"But he wants to kill you."

"He's tried to kill me a number of times and hasn't succeeded yet." Delaney spoke with familiar resolve. "Don't worry about me."

"But I do! You have to listen to this."

"No, Ginger. You have to forget about us."

"I'll never do that," she said, her tone ferocious.

And Delaney smiled. The curve stole over his lips so slowly that Ginger was transfixed. The smile banished the shadows from his gaze, leaving his eyes clear and focused upon her. His voice dropped low, even as his arm slid around her waist.

The firestorm shimmered and shone, filling the space between them with the golden glow of candlelight. Ginger was warm right to her toes, those toes curling in her boots. Her mouth went dry as she stared up at him, savoring how just his smile could turn her on.

"Thank you," he murmured, studying her as if he'd never get enough of her. "That's more than expected or deserved."

"Wrong," Ginger argued. "It's not nearly enough."

Something flickered in his eyes then, a glimmer that could have been hope. It could have been desire, given the radiant and persistent glow of the firestorm.

Ginger didn't care. She knew what she wanted and wasn't much worried about why.

She eased closer, pressing her breasts against Delaney's chest. She let her hands rise to his shoulders, liking how he simply waited for her to set the pace. She could have her way with him and he would respond in kind, or she could walk away and he, she was confident, would let her go. He was incredibly powerful, but he let her be in control.

That was a seductive gift, perhaps the most seductive gift of all.

And a kiss wouldn't leave her pregnant.

One kiss.

It was a small concession, and one she couldn't resist.

Delaney bent his head, his gaze intent upon hers, and Ginger stretched to her toes to meet him halfway. When his mouth closed possessively over hers, Ginger sighed into his kiss, locked her hands around his neck, and surrendered to the moment.

It was a good one.

*   *   *

Ginger was more than he deserved. Delaney couldn't believe she would give him even a kiss, especially after she had been so angry that morning. He couldn't believe she wanted him to survive, and he was humbled by her concern.

But Ginger didn't understand. She didn't know about the monster that dwelt within him, the one he couldn't control under the light of the eclipse, the one that could destroy everything that was precious about her.

As much as he wanted her kiss and her trust, as persuasive as he found her logic, he didn't want to ever see her face his dark truth. It would be better, far better, that he continue with his plan and even pay the ultimate price. It would be better to leave her with a fond memory of him.

Rather than a nightmare.

He knew too much about nightmares.

Delaney savored her kiss, uncertain whether it would be the last taste of her he ever had. She was sweet and hot, so giving that he yearned to have the opportunity to spend time with her.

But the Elixir had stolen that from Delaney.

And eliminating the Elixir was the only way Delaney could even the score. He had to be certain that no other *Pyr* ever suffered as he had.

He broke his kiss with reluctance, Ginger's soft flush making everything within him tighten. He wanted her, over and over again. He wanted to carry her to that prim bedroom and make her moan a thousand times before the morning. He wanted to feel her shiver and see her tremble and feel her heat close around him.

But she was right—he had no right to leave her pregnant and alone.

He stepped away from her and it wasn't easy. That minute distance didn't make the firestorm much easier to ignore, its sparks dancing between them with a vehemence that stole his breath away. Ginger eyed him, the golden light of the firestorm making her look precious.

"Go inside," Delaney said, his voice husky. "Have a shower and get warm."

"Are you leaving?"

"We'll fix the roof of the barn, then be in."

Ginger smiled. "I suppose you'll all be hungry."

Delaney frowned. "You shouldn't be put out by us, or feel obligated to spend on our behalf. I'll give you money to cover the groceries and to have the roof fixed professionally. . . ."

Ginger stepped closer and put her hand on his chest. White heat jolted him at her touch, nearly stopping his heart and making him close his eyes against the tide of desire. "Are you leaving?" she whispered, urgency in her tone.

"No." Delaney shook his head. "I have to stay here and defend you. The heat of the firestorm will attract others to your farm, but I'll make sure you're safe tonight."

"And tomorrow?"

"Let's focus on one challenge at a time."

It wasn't a real answer, but he saw she understood his intent.

"You're wrong," she said with vehemence, then shivered. "But if you promise you're staying tonight, I'll save that argument for later."

"I promise."

She stared at him for a long moment, then stretched up to brush her lips across his. Delaney closed his eyes against the tingle of heat launched by her touch, bracing himself against the way his body grew taut. He lifted his hands, a beat from snatching her up against him and claiming another kiss, but Ginger stepped away from him.

"I'm going to hold you to that, hotshot." She grinned

then, all confidence and vitality, then strode to the porch. He watched her go, feeling the hunger to possess her again. He could easily lose himself in the sweet perfume of Ginger's skin, the study of her freckles, the caress of her curves.

Once hadn't been enough.

Delaney wondered whether it was possible to have enough of the ray of sunshine that was Ginger Sinclair.

"So, are you helping with this project, or just standing around?" Niall shouted, recalling Delaney to the moment. The door shut behind Ginger, and Delaney checked the resonance of his unbroken smoke ring.

No one had violated it except the *Pyr*, and he hadn't sealed it against them. He couldn't smell *Slayer* on the wind, which was no guarantee of their absence.

He thought the injuries they had sustained were a better guarantee that Ginger's farm would be quiet for the next few hours.

But he wasn't going to count on that. Delaney remained vigilant, even as he went to help Niall and Thorolf repair the damage Jorge had done.

The phone was ringing when Ginger stepped into the kitchen and she ran for it.

"Ginger!" Tanya exclaimed with relief. "Where have you been?"

It was good to hear her friend's voice, a return of the real world that Ginger welcomed after the day she'd had. "Um, out in the barn."

"Right. Cows don't wait, do they?" Tanya teased, and Ginger felt guilty for not having mucked out the barn yet. She'd have to do that before nightfall. "I guess Luke didn't make it over today."

"No. No sign of him. And really, that's a good thing."

Tanya agreed but for a different reason. "No point in anyone going far in this crazy weather. Are you okay?"

"Everything's fine here."

"I thought maybe your power would be out."

"No. Everything's fine." So to speak. Ginger sat down at the kitchen table when she realized her knees were shaking. "The freezer's full, after all."

"So, if your power does go out, you'll be working your way through everything we made for the wedding."

Ginger laughed, although the prospect of two thousand handmade organic hors d'oeuvres going to waste wasn't that funny. She noticed that the sheet of paper was still on the table, Rafferty's firm handwriting across the back of it. It looked like a verse.

She frowned and turned the paper so she could read it.

"I'm so glad we couldn't get the hall for Valentine's Day," Tanya said, her excitement bubbling through the phone. "Having the wedding today would have been a complete nightmare. What if your power does go out?"

"Luke checked the backup generator a few weeks ago. It'll start automatically. No need to worry."

"Now I feel silly for worrying about self-reliant Ginger." Tanya laughed. "I should know better. You always have a plan for every contingency. I've been trying to call you all day, with no luck. Your cell phone even says you're unavailable."

"It ran out of juice," Ginger admitted. "I'm sorry you were worried. I forgot to charge it last night."

Tanya giggled. "Hmm, I wonder why. What distracted you, Ginger?"

Ginger knew where Tanya was going with this, and felt herself blushing. Unfortunately, she couldn't think of a clever way to change the subject. She looked away from Rafferty's verse and tried to divert Tanya's train of thought.

She wasn't nearly fast enough.

"Could it have been Mr. Hunky Stranger?" Tanya teased.

"Well, okay, he did give me a ride home."

"Uh-huh," Tanya said. "And what happened after that? I want *details*."

"Not on the phone," Ginger said. She was stalling and she knew it, but with Tanya's wedding the following Saturday, the week would be too busy for the two friends to exchange secrets. The happy couple were headed to a resort in Mexico for two weeks after the wedding, so Ginger would have the better part of a month to figure out what to tell her friend about Delaney.

And what *not* to tell her.

"I'm going to hold you to that," Tanya teased. "In fact, I've decided that you should bring him to the wedding. Steve agrees."

Ginger was shocked. "But you maxed out on the guest list already."

"We're making an exception. We talked about it this morning, when we thought you were both too, um, *busy* to answer the phone."

Ginger's blush deepened. "Oh, I don't know if that's a good idea. It's kind of late notice."

"Garbage! Everybody in the place last night knew that Ginger Sinclair had finally met her match. The two of you were lost in your own world and oblivious to everyone."

Ginger had nothing articulate to say about that. She twirled the phone cord in her hand and thought about going to a wedding with Delaney. The prospect of him in a tux—or even a suit—was enough to make her mouth go dry.

Never mind the idea of dancing with him again.

On the other hand, taking a date to Tanya's wedding would practically be a public declaration of another wedding to come. Ginger certainly wasn't ready to commit to that—and she doubted Delaney would be, either.

He might be dead by the end of the week.

She swallowed the lump in her throat. "He could be busy."

"Uh-huh," Tanya said, still not taking no for an answer. "Well, here's the deal, Ginger. We left one spot on the guest list for the best woman to have a date, identity TBD. So, tell me now that you'll bring Mr. Hunky Stranger or I'll invite Luke."

"That's dirty!" Ginger protested. Luke had made his plans to merge the two adjoining farms clear, in quite unromantic terms, and was as fixed on the idea as he was on doing things as he always had. No matter what Ginger said or what she did, Luke never got the message that his plan was unwelcome.

If Tanya invited him to be Ginger's date at the wedding, Ginger would never get rid of Luke.

And Tanya knew it.

Tanya laughed. "I just know what's good for you."

"But you'll give Luke the wrong idea."

"He already has the wrong idea. It'll just convince him he's right."

"He's already convinced of that," Ginger admitted.

"Those Hargreaveses are as stubborn as mules, but Luke is the most stubborn of all. That's why he's exactly wrong for you. Bring the new man on Saturday," Tanya commanded. "We need to interrogate him and decide whether he's good enough for our Ginger."

"I'm not sure that will happen. . . ."

"No excuses. Turn on the charm, girl, and *make* it happen. You're the queen of can-do, after all, and we have expectations now." Someone said something in the background, someone Ginger was pretty sure was Steve, and Tanya laughed. "Steve has a plan to find out Mr. Hunk's secrets. It involves a lot of beer."

"You have a wedding to organize," Ginger retorted, knowing her friend meant well. "Isn't that enough to keep you too busy to mess with my life?"

Tanya laughed. "There's always time to take care of your friends." Ginger could have argued that perspective, but Tanya spoke first. "Gotta go," she said, then dropped her voice to a conspiratorial low. "We have a crisis between the moms about the color of the table napkins."

"That was decided months ago."

"It was, but Steve's mom just found out that we didn't go with her choice. Hostilities have been exchanged and cruel comments made about both the sage green and the dusty rose. Nukes have been armed and treaty negotiations begin in five minutes."

"You're joking."

"I'm not. Wish me luck!"

"Luck!" Ginger grinned, knowing that Tanya was in her element. She and Steve were good together and Tanya was so happy—she'd have solved any obstacle with cheerfulness and ease.

"Call if you need anything," Tanya said. "You have forty-eight hours to give me Mr. Hunk's name for the place cards."

"You're merciless."

"And charge your cell phone!"

"Yes, Mom," Ginger said. Then the line clicked and Tanya was gone. She smiled as she hung up the receiver, glad to have such a good friend.

Then Ginger pulled Rafferty's notes closer and read what he had written.

She'd been right—it was a poem.

But not one she knew.

The Outcast patrols shadows deep,
Defending the Pyr while they sleep.
When darkness becomes his domain,
He risks losing his path back again.
Vigilant in the endless night
Yet drawn by the firestorm's light.
But can one so at ease in dark
Surrender fully to love's spark?
Will he dare to leave his task,
Choose himself first instead of last?

What was the poem about?

Ginger read it again and thought it sounded like a prophecy, one about Delaney. If so, it confirmed her sense that he had been injured, and his own conviction that the Elixir he'd been forced to ingest had pushed him from the world of the *Pyr*. He was choosing to defend his fellows by trying to destroy the Elixir.

But the verse carried an interesting message about the firestorm, one that meshed perfectly with Ginger's own ideas about love. It seemed to imply that the firestorm—that Ginger—could heal Delaney.

If he chose to accept that healing.

How could she persuade him to believe in the possibility of their having a future, if the firestorm on its own didn't do so?

It was a puzzle she couldn't solve herself, not without knowing more about the *Pyr*. She was encouraged, though, by the suggestion that she was on the right track. That restored her characteristic optimism.

Ginger got up, feeling energized once more. She faced more important and more immediate issues on this night. She opened the freezer, and two thousand handmade hors d'oeuvres peered back at her.

What was she going to feed three hungry *Pyr*?

* * *

The firestorm didn't play fair.

The golden heat tickled at the edge of Delaney's consciousness, even when Ginger wasn't within close proximity. It teased him, arousing him to the point that he found it hard to concentrate on anything beyond the possibility of seducing Ginger again.

Worse, it tempted him with promises and possibilities, ideas that could not fit into his future as he knew it must be. The firestorm tormented him with the notion of accepting Ginger's challenge.

And in so doing, the firestorm weakened Delaney's resolve. He fought against its temptation, knowing that he had to do what he had to do. The possibilities presented by both Ginger and the firestorm were impossible for him to pursue.

He had no future. He knew that was the best possible outcome from the toxin of the Elixir, and he didn't dare be seduced by empty promises.

By possibilities he'd end up destroying himself.

He would not be responsible for eliminating the sparkle in Ginger's eyes.

He worked in stoic silence, repairing the roof along with Niall and Thorolf. It could never be as good as new, but they managed to bend the beams back so that the cattle were sheltered from the storm. When it was done, they sat on the rafters and looked down into the barn.

"It should be mucked out," Delaney said, wanting to keep himself busy in the hope that he'd think less. "Let's do it."

"You just don't want Luke making you look bad," Niall teased.

Delaney ignored that.

"I don't know how," Thorolf said.

Niall rolled his eyes.

Delaney had more patience than his friend, at least

this time. "It's not hard. The cows just have to be moved into those far sections so that the floors can be cleaned where they are now."

"Why don't we just put them all together?" Thorolf asked.

Delaney gave him a look. "Cows and bulls together?"

Niall started to laugh.

"Hey, I'm a city guy," Thorolf protested. "Milk comes from cartons and beef comes from little Styrofoam trays with plastic wrap over top."

Niall laughed so hard that he choked.

"They're separated on the basis of gender so they can be bred for specific traits," Delaney said. "There are no accidental romances."

"Kind of like the firestorm," Niall said, all false innocence.

Delaney ignored him. "The ones in their own stalls are bulls. It looks like the cows are separated into those that are pregnant and those that aren't."

Niall peered down into the barn. "Do you think they have to be milked?"

"We can check with Ginger, but I don't think so." Delaney noted that the udders of the cows that weren't pregnant didn't appear to be full. He remembered the cycle of the year from the farm where he'd worked before. "The end of the winter can be the dry season, when those that are pregnant stop lactating because the calves are coming, and those that aren't pregnant run out of milk."

"Can be?" Thorolf asked.

"Some farmers ensure that some cows are always lactating to guarantee milk production all year round," Delaney said. "But others breed all the cows at once, to have all the calving at once."

"And that means a dry season before calving," Niall

said with a nod of understanding. "There are shovels by the door."

"Don't shift," Delaney advised. "It might freak them out."

Thorolf looked alarmed. "Freak them out? Like, start a stampede?"

"Cows like routine," Delaney said. "I'll guess that dragons in the barn aren't part of their regular plan."

Thorolf laughed and Niall grinned, then gave Delaney a nudge. "Good to see the old Delaney back again," he said, then headed for the ladders.

Delaney blinked. He did feel lighter and more like his old self. Was that Ginger's power over him?

Had anything else changed?

Chapter 13

Niall moved toward to the exterior wall of the barn. There were ladders mounted on the inside of those walls, presumably to allow maintenance of the roof from the inside. Delaney followed him, noting that several of the bulls were watching them.

A large black-and-white one by the back door had his gaze fixed on Thorolf. The bull stamped a foot when Thorolf moved and exhaled audibly.

"We're, like, going to go in the paddocks with the cattle?" Thorolf asked with some nervousness. He looked at the bull.

The bull looked back.

"They're just *cows*," Niall said with disdain.

"Why do you always talk down to me?" Thorolf asked, his resentment undisguised. The trio had reached the floor of the barn and Niall was heading for the shovels. The cows watched with curiosity, their tails swishing.

"I'm not," Niall argued, his tone not carrying conviction.

"Sure you are. You talk to me like I'm stupid, and I'm tired of it. Show some respect."

"Respect?" Niall gave Thorolf a look and Delaney knew his old friend was going to speak his mind.

"Maybe we could review this later. . . ." Delaney tried to intervene but to no avail. He was warm again, probably from the exertion of fixing the roof, and could have done without the *Pyr* squabbling among themselves.

He was out of luck on that.

Niall pushed Delaney aside and pointed at Thorolf. *"Respect?"* His question was soft, a hint of the coming storm. "What exactly should I respect? That you're centuries old, older even than me, and have no understanding of your powers? That you've learned just about nothing about your body or its abilities? That you haven't honed your innate talents in any way or practiced what we've tried to teach you in the past year?" Niall's eyes flashed. "That you just party and fight and screw, day after day after day?"

Thorolf smiled. "Hey, I'm not that bad."

"I didn't say you were *bad*. You asked why I didn't respect you, and I told you. You have no ambition. You have no goals and you have no initiative and you're lazy, too."

Thorolf fidgeted. "Jeez, you sound just like Rox."

"Rox?" Ginger asked from the doorway. Delaney saw her silhouetted against the falling snow, bundled up in a heavy coat and gloves. Her hair could have been aflame as it spilled over her shoulders.

She looked warmer again and she was smiling just a little.

His heart skipped a beat.

Had she taken his advice and had a shower?

It would have been smart not to try to envision that scene, but Delaney's imagination was off and running before he could stop it. He could see Ginger in the steam, the water flowing over her curves. . . .

"Give me that broom, please," she said.

"Shut the door," Thorolf said. "You're letting the cold in." He moved to get the broom that was leaning against a stall as he spoke, presumably intent on proving that he wasn't lazy.

There was a sudden squawk and a flash of bright feathers, then Thorolf yelped in shock. He scurried backward with his hands over his head, yelling and shouting.

A colorful rooster, meanwhile, attacked Thorolf's shoulders. The rooster pecked and scratched, while Thorolf yowled.

It was enough to bring Delaney back to the moment.

Niall started to chuckle when Ginger grabbed the broom and gave the rooster a swat. The bird cackled in frustration when the broom connected, then sailed through the air, landing in the paddock with a thump. The hens scattered, clucking. The rooster stood up and shook himself in indignation, then began to strut and crow.

"Coq au vin," Ginger said, threatening the rooster with the broom.

The rooster crowed in defiance. Niall laughed and laughed.

Ginger glared at the rooster, brandishing the broom.

It glared back, then tipped back its head and crowed louder than ever.

"Damn bird," Ginger growled. "You'll see the inside of my stewpot before the spring at this rate."

The bird took exception to that idea. Ginger wagged the broom and the rooster launched another assault. They were obviously accustomed to facing off like this, the rooster pecking and scratching while Ginger swung the broom. She missed and missed again. Thorolf sank to the floor of the barn with his hands clasped over his head, moaning.

"If Gran hadn't been so crazy about you, you'd have been soup years ago!"

The rooster flapped, trying to land on Ginger, as Thorolf cowered. Niall laughed. Delaney felt his own lips twitch.

Ginger finally thwacked the bird once more with the broom, dispatching him into the pen again. She brushed her hair out of her eyes with satisfaction. "Ha!" she told the bird. She shook the broom at the pen. "Stay put this time, Reginald."

He crowed and strutted, clearly convinced he was victorious.

"Usually we only go one round," she said, giving the rooster one last look before putting down the broom. "Gran thought Reginald was a looker. He's really just a pain in the neck."

Thorolf peeked out from between his fingers. "Is it safe yet?"

"Afraid of a rooster," Niall said, wiping away a tear. "That's really something."

"He didn't attack you!"

"I think I could have taken him," Niall said with a roll of his eyes.

"You never told me who Rox was," Ginger reminded Thorolf.

"His *sister*," Niall and Delaney said in unison, their doubt of that claim clear in their tone.

Thorolf flushed scarlet. "Okay, so maybe she's not my sister, but she's not my boss, either."

"Honesty," Niall said so sharply that Delaney winced. "There's another trait I admire."

"So what? I should be like you?" Thorolf challenged, glaring at Niall as he got to his feet. He was a good foot taller than Niall, but Niall was muscular, and neither was backing down. "Always at the gym? Always working out? Always *working*? Life is supposed to have some pleasure, you know!"

"But it isn't supposed to be *all* pleasure," Niall retorted. The pair glared at each other and Delaney met Ginger's gaze. He saw understanding there, then a glint of mischief just before she handed Thorolf the broom.

Delaney grinned at her perceptiveness, unable to stop himself. The two *were* squabbling like a pair of roosters. Niall's glare didn't help. Delaney had to turn away, to look away from Ginger's dancing eyes.

"Maybe you two need to find a middle ground," Ginger suggested lightly. "A balance of opposites."

"Maybe they just need to muck out the barn together," Delaney said. "Find harmony in teamwork."

Ginger sobered as she reached for a shovel. She walked toward Delaney, her eyes darkening as she drew closer. "Funny you should suggest that," she said quietly, "when you're the one who wants to do everything alone."

"Ouch," Niall said, but Delaney grabbed a shovel and turned away. His mate's perceptiveness no longer seemed so praiseworthy.

Trust Ginger to find the inconsistencies in his argument—and to be unafraid to point them out to him.

On the other hand, he liked that she wasn't afraid of him.

He caught a waft of that lotion she used and knew she had had a shower. His body went taut at the confirmation of his theory, and he knew that everything was aligned against what he knew he had to do.

"What I need to do is more than just dirty work," he said, his foul mood fully restored.

Delaney didn't wait for the inevitable argument, just set to work. He headed for the far end of the barn, where there was a gate to the empty section. The cows trailed beside him, clearly knowing this ritual. When he opened the gate, they filed into the space.

"The fresh hay is over there," Ginger called. "Put half

a dozen bales on each side." Niall did as she instructed and Delaney started to shovel the floor of the stalls the cows had left.

Thorolf hung back and Niall muttered something about laziness.

"I'm not lazy!" Thorolf shouted, and the cows shied away from the sound.

"Calm," Ginger scolded. "Quiet and routine. That's what they like."

"Get a shovel already," Delaney said with impatience.

He looked up in time to see Thorolf's dismayed expression. "You mean, like, go in there, close to them?"

Ginger laughed. "They're mostly cows!"

"You go in the stall next to them, not with them," Niall said.

Thorolf held his ground. "Hey, I'm a city dude." He put a hand over his heart. "I do mongrels and stray cats, sparrows and pigeons. Raccoons and skunks, maybe. Bats. Rats. Pigeons and crows. Bulls are a whole other thing."

"You do steak," Delaney couldn't help noting.

Thorolf's eyes lit with enthusiasm. "Well, yeah! But it's not going to attack me from the plate."

"Just don't annoy them," Ginger advised. "Move slowly and talk to them in a calm voice. They like having the stalls mucked out, so they should be cooperative."

"Should be," Thorolf repeated with a shake of his head. "Did anyone else hear the uncertainty in that? How much do these things weigh, anyway? They're huge!"

"Move it," Delaney said. He'd already shoveled a quarter of one large paddock.

"Courage," Niall mused as he leaned into it. "Another admirable trait."

Thorolf swore.

Niall smiled.

Ginger seemed to be trying to hide a laugh as she came toward Delaney, challenge in her expression. Delaney could have watched her eyes dance for the rest of the day—never mind the sway of her hips—but he focused on his job. He remembered the satisfaction of heavy work, of using his body to make a difference.

Honest work.

Ginger joined him, showing that she was far from frail in the way she put her shoulder into it, too. "Chute at the back right corner," she instructed. "Luke can move it from out there whenever he gets through the snow."

Luke. There was the mention of that man again. Delaney felt a hot stab of jealousy, one more like dragonsmoke than the firestorm, and resented this man he didn't even know.

"Moo," Thorolf said to a small dark bull in a paddock by the door. The blond *Pyr* was holding a shovel, obviously uncertain of the wisdom of proceeding further.

"That's Darian," Ginger said. "He's quite gentle."

"Uh-uh," Thorolf had time to say before Darian bellowed.

Thorolf bolted toward the door of the barn, his eyes wide with terror. "He's going to kill me!"

"He knows about the steaks," Delaney said deadpan. "He wants to get even."

Niall laughed. Ginger giggled. Thorolf lifted the shovel high in self-defense as Darian bellowed again.

Reginald took exception to Thorolf's quick move and flew to the rail of the paddock, squawking and flapping furiously. Thorolf swore and grabbed the broom, holding both the broom and the shovel aloft.

"Don't hit him with the shovel," Niall advised. "I think Ginger's teasing about the coq au vin."

Thorolf looked momentarily confused, glancing between broom and shovel, rooster and bull. Reginald made his move, flying at the *Pyr* with his talons extended. Thorolf bellowed and retreated. Darian charged the rim of the paddock. Thorolf dropped both tools and bolted from the barn.

The snow spiraled through the open door. Reginald crowed with pride as he strutted along the rail. Darian exhaled, the incident already forgotten as he bent to nuzzle his fresh hay.

Niall cracked up. Ginger joined his laughter, the two of them doubling over. The sound of Ginger and Niall's laughter was so infectious that Delaney found his own smile forming. When he laughed himself, the sound was so unfamiliar that he didn't recognize it as coming from him.

Ginger caught his arm and leaned against him, her voice low with merriment. "You have a great laugh," she said, her eyes glowing and her curves pressed against his side. Delaney caught his breath at the sudden intensity of his desire for her. "You should laugh more often."

When he looked down into her sparkling eyes, Delaney could almost believe it possible that he could have the future he craved, that he could learn to laugh again and to sleep without fear.

Almost.

But not quite.

Something changed after Delaney laughed. Ginger sensed it but couldn't understand the reason why. She'd thought he would kiss her, but something had changed his mind. He'd sobered abruptly and set to clearing the barn floor, working with a diligence that left the rest of them in his dust.

So to speak.

If nothing else, the girls had a clean barn in record time.

Even if Ginger was yearning for the kiss she hadn't gotten.

The three of them headed back to the house together, a restless silence between them. Even Thorolf was quiet—sheepish maybe—where he waited on the porch. Ginger noticed how Niall stole glances at Delaney, who remained grim, but said nothing more. She figured that Niall knew his friend best, and followed the blond *Pyr*'s example.

Back in the kitchen, the ground beef had thawed and Thorolf made a joke about not wanting to make new enemies by eating it.

"Neighbor's cows," Ginger said. "My girls are all dairy." Then she got to work. "Spaghetti okay?"

"Sounds great," the men said in unison.

The *Pyr* made good sous-chefs, Delaney dicing onions and garlic while Niall browned the meat. They did whatever she asked, promptly and without complaint. Ginger opened home-canned tomatoes and tomato paste while Thorolf—clearly motivated by the prospect of food—set the table. She had a lot of dried pasta in the cupboard, which was a good thing.

The silence lasted until they were at the table, and Thorolf was putting away spaghetti with impressive speed. "This is really good," he said again, sparing her an appreciative smile.

"Nothing like working up an appetite," Niall observed, and the tall *Pyr* flushed scarlet.

The comment didn't slow him down, though.

"You wouldn't let me tell you about Magnus," Ginger said to Delaney, wondering whether he would listen this time.

"I know all I need to know about Magnus," he said flatly, and focused on his food.

"I don't think so," Ginger argued.

He cast her a dark look. "I do."

She put down her fork, annoyed with him and unafraid to show it.

"So much for charm," Niall said, glancing at Delaney.
"Maybe you should try bullshit again."

"Balls didn't work, either," Thorolf noted.

The back of Delaney's neck turned red, but he didn't
make any concessions.

Niall shrugged and turned to Ginger. "I don't know
everything I need to know," he said with an encouraging
smile. "What did you learn?"

"Well, he told me about the Elixir, about Cinnabar."

"Who or what is Cinnabar?" Thorolf asked between
mouthfuls.

"He's a *Pyr*. He used to be a slave named Sylvanus
Secundus, and I think he was Magnus's slave." Ginger
watched Delaney, pretty certain that he was listening to
her despite his claim.

"Magnus lived in ancient Rome," Niall said with a
nod. "Rafferty mentioned that once."

"Didn't everyone in ancient Rome have slaves?"
Thorolf asked.

Delaney glanced up and nodded, then his gaze fixed
on Ginger. "I don't know anything about Cinnabar," he
said quietly. "I'm sorry. You were right."

The low timbre of his voice nearly finished Ginger.
She felt Niall watching the two of them, and was well
aware of the firestorm's seductive tingle.

Could Delaney control its magnitude? It seemed to
burn hotter when he was apologizing or asking her for
something.

Maybe she was just a sucker for a man unafraid to
admit that he'd been wrong.

She frowned and tried to focus on her story, instead
of the lean strength of Delaney's fingers on the fork.
Her voice was higher than usual and she was definitely

speaking more quickly, but she hoped the *Pyr* didn't notice.

Even with their keen senses.

"Sylvanus Secundus was caught for some crime—violating a corpse, I think—but I had the feeling that Magnus set him up. Then he was sentenced to work in the cinnabar mines in Almadén, which was a death sentence because the workers all died of mercury poisoning."

"Mercury?" Niall asked with surprise.

Delaney straightened, his eyes revealing his interest.

"But Sylvanus Secundus didn't die, and when Magnus went to see why, he discovered that his former slave had turned red."

Delaney pushed away his plate, his face pale. Niall looked between the two of them while Thorolf stole glances between bites.

"What did I say?"

Delaney's mouth tightened, and his eyes were dark again. "Don't worry about it. Keep going. Please."

"Was he red in human form or dragon form?" Niall asked.

"Both. His skin had turned ruddy and his hair had gone red; then, in dragon form, his scales had turned red. And Magnus said there was some old idea of a *Pyr* exposed to excessive mercury becoming the source of an elixir for immortality."

Delaney frowned at the floor, but said nothing.

Ginger shivered and put down her fork. "I think he made the Dragon's Blood Elixir out of Cinnabar, and that it gets its power from his body dissolving in that big vial. They're drinking his life force, a glass at a time."

"Nice." Niall pushed his plate away, grimacing at the red tomato sauce.

"But Magnus says he's weakening and running out of power." Ginger swallowed and looked at Delaney, who held her gaze steadily. "I think he intends that you should take Cinnabar's place."

"That's just a story," Delaney said, and pushed to his feet. He paced the width of the kitchen, then back. "He's playing with your mind, telling you stories that you'll tell to me."

Niall cleared his throat. "Whose mind is he playing with again?"

"We don't need to review the past," Delaney said with force. "I've overcome his commands before and I'll do it again."

"Have you?"

"I didn't hurt Ginger when he wanted me to."

"What if that was the easy command to deny?" Niall demanded. "After all, who ever heard of a *Pyr* being able to injure his mate?"

"Who ever heard of a *Pyr* being driven to snatch a *Pyr* fetus from the womb of a mate?" Delaney retorted.

"You didn't do that, either," Niall argued. "Maybe Magnus is messing with you, giving you commands that are red herrings. That way, you can feel good about beating him. You can think you have him licked, but meanwhile, you're doing exactly what he really wants you to do."

"That's crazy."

"No, it's Rafferty's idea," Thorolf said. "That you're so distracted by these commands you can deny that you don't even realize your deeper motivation is from Magnus."

"And Magnus wants you to come and try to destroy the Elixir," Niall concluded. "You're just following his plan."

"That's the craziest thing I've ever heard." Delaney's eyes were flashing. "The last thing Magnus wants anyone to do is destroy the Elixir! It's the source of his power and key to his own longevity. He met me at the sanctuary this morning to stop me."

"He met you there to mess with your thoughts," Niall argued.

"You don't know that!"

The pair were shouting at each other now, though Thorolf was still eating with gusto.

"Magnus is manipulative—you know that!" Niall said. "How can you believe that he's not still manipulating you?"

Delaney drove his finger into the table, making it jump. "Why me? If this story is true, why not sacrifice one of the *Slayers* so desperate to win his pleasure? Why not?"

"I don't know," Niall muttered. The pair glared at each other. Niall sat down heavily, clearly displeased.

"I beg your pardon?" Delaney said.

"I don't know why!" Niall shouted. "But he's controlling you. I know it. I might not know all of the reasons, but I know what I see with my own eyes."

"Your eyes are wrong," Delaney said, pulling out a chair and sitting down. Antagonism snapped between them, although it didn't affect Thorolf's appetite. Ginger knew the root of Niall's anger was his affection for Delaney.

"Actually," she said softly, clearing her throat, "I know the reason." The three *Pyr* stared at her and she shrugged. "Magnus told me that the dragon who provides the source of the Elixir has to have blood that flows red. Don't *Slayers* have black blood?"

"They do!" Niall cried in triumph, then jabbed a finger at Delaney. "I'm right! Rafferty was right. If you try to destroy the Elixir, you'll be playing right into Magnus's plan."

Delaney stood up again. He looked haunted to Ginger, as if he were halfway lost already.

"No," he said quietly. "You're wrong. He's trying to make me abort my plan because he knows I can do it.

He'll say anything to protect the Elixir, and tell any lie to keep anyone from attacking it." He looked at each of them in turn, his determination clear, then spoke quietly. "I'm still going."

With that, he pivoted and left the kitchen. The kitchen door slammed behind him and Ginger saw his silhouette on the porch outside. She glanced back as Niall swore.

"That went well, don't you think?" the fair *Pyr* said, his frustration clear. "It doesn't sound to me like he can deny Magnus at all."

"What do you mean?"

Niall frowned and leaned toward Ginger, so intent on helping his friend that she found it easy to take sides with him. "Magnus had a dark academy, where he created shadow dragons by treating their bodies with the Elixir. When Delaney was imprisoned there, he was force-fed the Elixir, and evidently Magnus hypnotized him. Since his release, Delaney has felt a compulsion to act against his own will several times. He exiled himself from us to ensure that he couldn't harm any of us or our mates. He told me last year that his life wasn't worth living, but that he'd make it count."

Ginger's mouth went dry. "By destroying the Elixir."

Niall nodded, then sighed. "But Rafferty thinks this impulse to go on a suicide mission is Magnus's real command. We couldn't figure out why he'd want Delaney to try to destroy the Elixir, not until now."

"We can't let him do that to himself," Ginger said. "We have to help him."

"It's gonna be tough if he doesn't want to be helped," Thorolf contributed, then reached for the serving dish.

Exasperation lit Niall's eyes as he watched the tall *Pyr*; then he got to his feet in turn. "I'll try to talk to him."

"He said he'd stay here tonight to protect me."

Niall forced a smile and Ginger felt a common bond with him. "We've got that long to try then, at least." Then he went out on the porch. Ginger heard the rumble of thunder and assumed the pair had switched to old-speak.

Thorolf appeared to be listening for a moment, then polished off the last bite in his plate. "This was really good," he said, smiling at Ginger.

"There's more in the pot."

"Mind if I help myself?" he asked, already on his feet, his eyes alight with anticipation.

Ginger didn't care if Thorolf ate it all.

She did care about reaching Delaney before he condemned himself. But did she care enough to offer him the one thing he truly wanted of her?

Did she care enough about making him believe in his own future to agree to have his child? That she was even considering the possibility was scary.

She pushed back her chair and grabbed her coat, heading out to the porch where the two *Pyr* stood.

She assumed they were talking, because she could hear thunder, but Niall glanced her way when she stepped outside. He winked at her, then began to speak aloud. "Glad you're here," he said, making space for her beside him. "We could use the firestorm's heat."

Delaney said nothing, just kept his arms folded across his chest and stared into the pastures. Niall glanced at Ginger, shrugged, then continued the conversation.

Ginger listened, and was surprised by what she heard.

Delaney would have preferred that Ginger stay inside. Not only was it too cold for her to be standing on the porch, but he needed a break from the firestorm's insistence to think.

How could he reconcile these two demands?

How could he fulfill the firestorm without taking the time to court Ginger?

How could he destroy the Elixir if he didn't do it immediately? He was caught between two goals, unable to decide which was more imperative. He still wanted to satisfy both.

Soon.

"You should come back," Niall said, but Delaney wasn't interested in his argument. "I'll sell you back your share of the company at the price you sold it to me last year."

The offer was more tempting than it should have been. Delaney had no use for shares in a company when he was going to die.

And yet, and yet, he had enjoyed it so much.

"No, thanks," he said, taking a step away.

"Why not?"

"Why?" Delaney asked when the silence grew too long.

"Because I miss you, of course." Niall was gruff and fidgety, even less comfortable with discussing emotions than Delaney. "Because you were good at it."

"'Were' being the operative word."

Ginger cleared her throat. "What company?"

Niall was happier answering her question than making his own case. Delaney fought a smile at his former partner's evident relief in not having to discuss feelings anymore.

"Delaney and I started an eco-travel company years ago, back before it was fashionable," he said. "We had a hard time at first persuading people to do hard travel, but slowly built up a reputation."

"What kind of travel?"

"We'd take people to the Galápagos, to Bhutan, to the Arctic. Initially we arranged trips to all kinds of obscure and exotic places, hikes to Machu Picchu, and kayaking in Thailand, that kind of thing."

"There are a lot of companies doing that now."

"There are. And Delaney had the idea about ten years ago that we should make ourselves distinctive again. We started organizing trips that made a mission. Garbage cleanup on Mount Kilimanjaro, for example, or inventorying bird species in the Amazon basin. We'd join forces with biologists and researchers working in each area, and provide them with some grunt labor."

"I like that," Ginger said. "I like the idea of making a difference in another part of the world while on vacation."

"It was brilliant and people loved it." Niall shrugged. "Of course, other companies started to copy the idea, and even resort hotels got into the possibilities."

"That's a sign of a good idea," Ginger said, and Delaney felt a modicum of pride.

"Delaney is all about ideas," Niall said. "That's part of why I miss him being around. A couple of years ago, he came up with the bucket list idea."

"Places to go before you die?" Ginger asked.

"No, places to go before they disappear forever."

"Oh. Are there many?"

"I wish the list weren't so long," Delaney said.

"There are atolls that are being submerged as water levels rise, entire islands disappearing in the South Pacific," Niall said. "The Amazon rain forest is being chopped down to make lousy farmland. The Galápagos are under siege. The Arctic ice floes are melting. The reefs are dying. We go to see polar bears, while there still are some, and I even put Venice on the list last year."

"Venice?" Delaney asked with surprise. Previously, they'd focused on natural marvels.

"Well, you weren't around to give me a better idea,"

Niall complained. He made a sound of exasperation as he appealed to Ginger. "The trips keep getting more popular. We have regulars who go every year, and each year, we have more people signing up for them. I'm getting buried. It's too much at the office for just one person, even with all the guides we have trained. I'd love to have help again."

Delaney had been proud of that idea and it was exciting to know it was successful. It was also tempting to step back into his former position and add to the idea's success.

He said nothing, though. He had no future to offer his old friend.

"Venice," Ginger said, and he caught her watching him. "Sounds like maybe you should take Niall up on his offer and get involved again. Sounds like your plan is losing focus."

It was a challenge and he knew it, as well as a request. Delaney didn't need any more challenges at the moment. He shivered and rubbed his upper arms, wishing he'd grabbed a coat. "Niall can handle it. He was always the best at organizing the details."

"And you were always the idea man," Niall argued. "That's why we made such a good team. Come on back."

"What about the Elixir?"

"What about the Elixir?" Niall said with impatience. "Why are you so determined to do it alone and die trying? We could all work together—"

"No!" Delaney interrupted flatly. "You're not going to expose yourself to that!"

Niall regarded him with narrowed eyes. "Why are you letting Magnus run you? You're smarter than that."

"Magnus isn't running me," Delaney argued. "I'm making my own choice." He heard his voice rise. "Just because it isn't your choice doesn't mean it's the wrong choice."

Niall wasn't persuaded. "But think of the future! Think of Ginger and your firestorm!"

"I can't think about that!" Delaney shouted. "I don't have the luxury!"

"Sounds like you won't give yourself the luxury."

He almost snarled at Niall in his frustration, in his dawning sense that he might fail at every facet of his plan. "You can't know the hell that the Elixir creates in your mind. Until you've tasted its darkness, until you've writhed in a field beneath the eclipse, unable to control your body, you can't understand."

His voice was rising and he knew it, but he couldn't stop. Niall took a step back and Ginger's eyes widened. The tickle of the firestorm's heat, an indication of another thing denied to him, just made Delaney more angry.

"Until you feel its cold fury inside you, until you feel it eat at your confidence and erode your power, until you're afraid to go to sleep because it will give you nightmares, you can't know how debilitating it is!" He gritted his teeth, seeing the horror in both Niall's and Ginger's expressions, and spoke tersely. "I won't permit any of you to know that, regardless of the cost to myself. If that's the only thing I manage to accomplish in this life, that's plenty." Delaney took a deep breath. "The Elixir has to go."

Ginger swallowed and Niall looked worried.

"It's not that bad of a concept," Delaney argued.

"That's not what's bothering me," Niall said softly. "Look at your hand."

Delaney looked down and he saw the flush of his skin, the red of his cuticles. He glanced in the kitchen window and caught his own reflection, practically flaming red.

And that cold. That pervasive cold went right to his bones and was impossible to shake. His involuntary shudder stirred Ginger to action. She opened the kitchen door and made a sweeping gesture toward him.

"Look at how cold you are. You should be wearing a coat," Ginger scolded, but Delaney knew that wasn't the real problem. He met Niall's gaze and saw that his old friend knew it, too.

He knew he wasn't the only one thinking of Cinnabar's red chill.

Was his body becoming the new source, despite his own plans? Was it a transformation beyond his own control?

What had Magnus done to him?

Chapter 14

They sat in the kitchen for a few hours, the conversation desultory. Delaney was quiet, but as the redness Ginger had glimpsed on the porch receded, she wondered whether her eyes had deceived her.

She certainly wasn't going to think about Cinnabar.

Much less Delaney trapped in a big vial forever.

There was a tingle of awareness between them, one that they both tried to ignore, even as the sparks danced and glowed.

The firestorm was giving Ginger unwelcome ideas.

It was late when she climbed the stairs to the bedroom, tired and yet filled with a curious anticipation.

Her heart skipped a beat when she heard a footfall on the stairs behind her.

She didn't have to look back to know that Delaney was following her. The firestorm warmed her back and fed her desire. She knew she'd be lost if he touched her again, if he showed any desire for her, if he kissed her.

She knew rationally that it would be dumb to get herself pregnant by a man bent on fulfilling a mission from which he wouldn't return. She knew what it was like to grow up without parents.

But there was something about Delaney that got Ginger right where she lived. When his eyes darkened with that tormented look, she wanted to touch him. When he spoke of what he had endured—and he did so only in the most terse tones—she sensed the depth of his pain. She knew she could heal him. The bond she felt with him was strong and irrational, yet perfectly explained by the mythology of his own kind.

When it got right down to it, Ginger wanted to believe in the firestorm. She wanted to believe in destiny and kismet and that there was someone out in the world who was meant to be her partner and lover. She wanted that person to be Delaney.

But he had to believe it, too.

And he refused to do so.

Maybe he was right. Maybe he wasn't the person for her. Maybe she was putting a romantic gloss on raw biological need. Maybe she should prove that she was as smart as everyone said she was, and keep danger—danger like Delaney—at bay.

Ginger stopped at the top of the stairs and turned to face him. He glanced up, halfway up the stairs, and his expression was resolute.

"Don't even think you're coming into my bedroom tonight," Ginger said, speaking more sternly than she meant to.

Delaney didn't slow down. "Don't even think you're keeping me out," he said, his words low. Ginger shivered at the threat in his soft words, all the more potent because he hadn't shouted.

"I mean it."

"So do I." He paused two steps below her and looked her in the eye. "The *Slayers* are tracking us and will be drawn to the firestorm. They try to stop firestorms, in order to stop the *Pyr* from breeding."

Ginger folded her arms across her chest. "Well, they don't have to stop this one. I'm stopping it."

Delaney shook his head. He lifted one hand and that predictable spark danced between her shoulder and his fingertips. Ginger took a step back and the flame made a brilliant arc toward her, sending heat through her veins and lighting Delaney's features. "There's only one way for us to stop it."

"We're not having sex again. Not until I know a whole lot more, and maybe not even then."

"Then the firestorm will continue to burn." He arched a brow, looking unpredictable and dangerous. "And the *Slayers* will continue to come, drawn to its heat."

Ginger's heart leapt. "What about dragonsmoke? Why don't you just make a perimeter mark?"

"I've done that," Delaney said. "I've breathed smoke, woven it high and deep. I did that the first night, before I left."

Ginger was warmed by his protectiveness, but her relief was undermined by his next words.

"But the *Slayers* who have drunk the Elixir are learning to do things that traditionally only the Wyvern could do."

"The Wyvern?"

"The only female of our kind. A prophetess."

"Where is she?"

"She died last year. The story is that another will be born, but there's no telling when that will be." He shrugged, dismissive of the whimsy that Ginger found fascinating. "The point is that the Wyvern could move through dragonsmoke, I think because she had the ability to spontaneously manifest and disappear in different locations. It's possible that she would just manifest inside the dragonsmoke ring. I'm really not sure, but some

Slayers can violate perimeter marks now." He met her gaze steadily and she knew he was telling her the truth. "It tends to be the ones who have drunk more of the Elixir who can do that."

"That would be most of the ones in our vicinity."

"Pretty much." Delaney frowned. "Jorge was in your barn today, without having left any tracks or signs of entrance. I'm wondering whether he has mastered that art of spontaneous manifestation."

Ginger shivered at the prospect of meeting Jorge again, ever. "So, the dragonsmoke barrier is useless."

"Probably." Delaney held her gaze, his determination clear. "The usual way to stop a firestorm is to kill the human mate."

Ginger stared at him in horror. "You're kidding," she said, but she already knew he wasn't.

"I'm not leaving you alone, Ginger, and that's all there is to it."

Was it Ginger's imagination that the light made him look sharper, more like a predator than she'd noticed before? She recalled how his pupil had been shaped like a slit that morning, like a dragon's pupil, even when he was in human form, and couldn't look into his eyes for a minute. He was dangerous.

But, on the other hand, she was being stalked by even more dangerous *Slayers*. It was a good thing to have a *Pyr* prepared to defend her.

"So, what's the resolution? You're staying here forever? When does the firestorm end?"

"It ends when it's satisfied."

"When a child is conceived." At his nod, Ginger felt her lips tighten. "What if that doesn't happen?"

Delaney shrugged. "Some *Pyr* say that the firestorm burns hotter and becomes more demanding as time passes, that it becomes harder and harder to deny."

Ginger folded her arms across her chest and lied.

"I'm feeling very resolute." Her claim was ridiculously untrue, pure bravado, and Ginger knew it. If Delaney touched her, she'd be a goner.

His smile was fleeting, but precious all the same. It made her wonder whether he knew that she was talking big, too.

"There are tides we cannot withstand, Ginger," he murmured, his soft words making her mouth go dry. He met her gaze, his own eyes dark with intent. "If we're destined lovers, how can we evade each other?"

He raised a hand and Ginger knew he would touch her, as surely as she knew that sparks would fly.

As surely as she knew she might be lost.

But she held her ground and waited for the knee-melting surge of desire all the same. She'd never turned and run from anything or anyone, and she wasn't going to start now.

Ginger caught her breath when Delaney's fingertips brushed her jawline. Just as she'd anticipated, a cascade of sparks fell from the point of contact, each one sending an urgent demand through her body. She heard herself gasp, felt her knees weaken, knew her lips parted.

Delaney slid his fingers into her hair and gave her the tiniest tug to bring her closer. Ginger fell against his chest, loosing a shower of sparks, knowing her body was on the firestorm's side.

She didn't have time to regret it, or even to consider whether she should.

Because Delaney kissed her.

It was a sweet and wild kiss, a seductive and slow kiss that turned demanding. Ginger felt the heat emanate between them, flow through her body and feed the inferno that had been within her since meeting him. Her nipples tightened, her breasts lightly crushed against his chest, her mouth sizzling as his kiss teased and tempted.

And he was holding her with only one hand, his long, strong fingers curled around her nape. Ginger let him feast upon her mouth, let her tongue dance with his, let the firestorm melt her reservations and resolutions.

Or maybe it was just Delaney.

Maybe he would have had her number even without the firestorm's magical heat. What would be his effect upon her after the firestorm was satisfied? Ginger couldn't believe she wouldn't still want this man with everything she had.

Ginger broke their kiss, planting her hands on his chest. Delaney let her do it, his eyes gleaming like diamonds in the darkness as he watched her. Ginger took a step backward, caught her breath, and locked her hands together behind her back.

When she spoke, she sounded breathless, even to herself. "The firestorm should have been satisfied already, from what you've all said. So maybe there's something different going on here."

"Maybe it just needs another chance." He was beside her in one step and she backed into the wall, staring up at him as he braced his hands on either side of her shoulders. "I could satisfy the firestorm," he said, his words silky low, "whether you agreed or not. I could extinguish it and make you invisible again to the *Slayers*."

His gaze danced over her, that increment of space between them filled with the golden heat of the firestorm. He was taut, so much larger and stronger than she that Ginger should have been afraid.

She wasn't, though, because she knew Delaney wouldn't force himself upon her. He was asking her for what he wanted.

He spoke in a low whisper, his words making Ginger shiver with desire. "I could ensure that my obligation to the *Pyr* was fulfilled, before I leave on this mission."

It was too tempting to surrender to his request, to give him what he wanted.

But that would make it easy for him to leave her forever.

"No." Ginger didn't give him a chance to argue with her. She knew what she had to say, and she had to say it now, before she was dissuaded of what she knew was right. "You think it's all so easy, that you feel the firestorm and knock up the woman in question; then you carry on with whatever it is you intend to do. You're not thinking about the child. You're not thinking about the future."

His expression set. "I don't have a future."

Ginger wondered whom he was trying to convince. She chose to argue for her perspective. "That's your choice, but any child I bear *will* have a future. I'll guarantee it. And a future without a father isn't a very appealing one for any child."

"I would have been better off without my father."

"Well, I wasn't better off without mine," Ginger said. "Let me tell you a story." She took a deep breath and loosed her story on a tide of words, one she couldn't stop once it had started.

"Once upon a time, there was a couple who fell in love. The man's name was Sean Sinclair and the woman's name was Elena van Vliet. They grew up around here. They went to school together and they went to the same church with their families, and they knew each other all of their lives. And all of their lives, they were smitten with each other, and everyone joked how Elena and Sean were going to get married one day. In high school, they were sweethearts. They went to the same college—Sean for dairy farm management and Elena to become a teacher—and after they graduated, they were married in June."

Ginger pointed out the window on the second-floor

foyer. There was nothing visible beyond the glass but darkness and snow, but she knew what she'd see on a summer's day. "They were married right out there, in Gran's perennial flower garden, and everyone from miles around came to their wedding. Everyone danced and everyone had a good time, and everyone said that Elena was the prettiest bride they'd ever seen."

Delaney watched her, his eyes glinting, and Ginger heard her voice rise. "They moved into this very house." She jabbed a finger in the direction of the back bedroom. "And they slept in that very room. Sean worked the farm alongside his parents, taking on more of the responsibility as his father became more frail. Elena cooked and cleaned alongside Sean's mother, learning to make pickles and bread and all the thousands of bits of wisdom that Gran had to share. When Sean's father had a heart attack shortly after the wedding, Sean ran the farm under his father's supervision."

Ginger took a breath, knowing that the next part of her story was the toughest bit for her to share. "They didn't have a lot. They worked hard and they slept well. But Gran always said this house was filled with love and respect, and that was the best part. And one day, after a number of years and a lot of disappointments, Elena became pregnant."

She looked up at Delaney, aware of his watchfulness, and tried to blink back her tears. "Everyone said she was rosy with her pregnancy, but they were being kind. She was sick every day. She had a hard time keeping much of anything down, and she lived in fear of losing another baby. Gran sent her to bed and cooked for her, going up and down these stairs a hundred times a day. Sean read to her at night, and though they all tried their best, there wasn't a one of them who wasn't surprised when Elena not only managed to hold on to that baby but went past her term. And when old Doc Stevenson delivered a healthy seven-pound baby girl that August, there was quite the celebration on the Sinclair farm."

Ginger swallowed and looked out the window, unable to hold Delaney's gaze. "It was just over a year later, when that baby girl was weaned and Elena had recovered her strength, that Gran insisted the pair take a weekend for themselves. They went to Niagara Falls, joking that they'd make a brother or sister for little Ginger. They never came back."

Ginger took a shaking breath and pushed the tears from her eyes with impatience. "A truck lost a tire on the interstate, and that tire crossed the median and bounced right through their windshield. Their car went off the road and they were both killed instantly. It was night, they were driving late, and the state trooper thought they probably hadn't even seen it coming. Gran thought they were trying to get home early. It was just bad luck."

Delaney was suspiciously silent, though Ginger could feel the weight of his gaze upon her. She didn't want his sympathy or his compassion—she just wanted him to listen. "I respected my grandmother and I loved her with all my heart, but our life wasn't easy and I certainly didn't know the half of it. I decided a long, long time ago that I would never choose to have a child alone. It's not easy for a child to face the world without both parents, without as much love and support as it's possible for a child to have. You never know what Fate will toss at you, but you have to make choices that give you a better chance."

Delaney was still watching her, still silent and intent.

"I won't have your child alone," Ginger said, just to make things completely clear to both of them. She took another deep breath. "Besides, I want what my parents had. I want that kind of love and commitment, for however long it lasts. I think that's the kind of relationship that children should know and I think it's the kind of relationship that is worth waiting for."

Delaney frowned and looked at the floor.

"What about you? Don't you think love is worth working for, or waiting for?"

He shook his head, impatient with the concept. "Love is for other people."

"Love is for *everybody*."

"I don't think so." His conviction was clear and that was enough to persuade Ginger that the heat between them carried an empty promise.

She'd have to make do without him, and without his child, somehow. She knew herself well enough to realize that she'd never manage to keep her own vow if he touched her again.

"I want you to make me a promise," Ginger said, and Delaney glanced up again. There was a suspicion in his eyes that tore at her heart, and she wondered what or who had taught him that love was not for him. "I want you to promise that you won't make any choices for me that compromise what I want for my life."

He shook his head, his manner resolute. "I wouldn't choose for you, Ginger. Last night, I made a mistake and I'm sorry."

"Promise."

He straightened and came to her, moving so quickly that she barely saw him take a step. He was simply in front of her, a mere hand span between them, his gaze blazing into her own. "I promise," he said, his words resonating with conviction.

He didn't move closer, but simply left that increment of space between them. Ginger knew she could have touched him, that she could have reached out and claimed a kiss to seal their wager, but she didn't dare.

She was smarter than that.

"You can sleep in the bedroom, then," she said, keeping her tone resolute. "In the chair, but not in the bed. I'll get you a couple of extra quilts." She moved away from him, heading for the linen closet, but his softly uttered words halted her steps.

"You trust me to keep my word?"

Ginger pivoted to face him and squared her shoulders. She'd heard the uncertainty in his voice and knew that few people had trusted Delaney Shea. Maybe that was the problem. Maybe her trusting him could give their relationship a chance.

Ginger was willing to try.

Either way, she guessed that her trust was new to him, and another facet of his not trusting himself. She heard in his voice that it was important to him that she take him at his word.

Maybe it was even key to making a real bond between them.

"I do," she said, noting only after she spoke that the words were similar to another vow couples made.

Delaney was cold.

Again.

Self-recrimination would hardly keep him warm. He watched Ginger sleep and reviewed her story over and over again. He was ashamed that he'd thought even for a moment about simply sating the firestorm and not so much about the result.

Not about the child.

Not about Ginger.

What was the difference between his father leaving his mother pregnant—twice—and disappearing, and what he had done to Ginger the night before? Ginger had gotten lucky, or birth control had worked. That was it. His behavior was perfectly consistent with that of his father.

Selfish.

Maybe he *was* the shard of his father's talon.

But Ginger knew what it was to grow up without parents and though she had known the love of her grandmother, her story—and the passion with which she shared it—made him want the same things for his own child.

It made him believe things could be different for a *Pyr* child than they had been for him. It had been his brother, Donovan, who had given Delaney hope, who had been the only family he had known.

Donovan, who had endured the same cruel awakening.

Donovan, who now had a son and a mate of his own.

Donovan, who now knew it wasn't safe to trust Delaney.

Delaney sat in the darkness and wondered about Donovan and Alex. He wondered at the possibilities.

He reminded himself that no such possibilities existed for him.

Meanwhile, the cold claimed his body, increment by increment. The chill seemed to emanate from his marrow, seize his muscles, and run like ice along his veins. Delaney was colder than he'd ever been and assumed that he had become too chilled in the sanctuary that morning.

He adjusted his position repeatedly, trying to get comfortable, but no matter how he moved, the draft from the window was too chilly. No matter how much he tucked the quilt around him, he couldn't get warm. He watched Ginger sleep, nestled beneath the faded quilts on her bed, her hair cascading over the pillow like spun gold. He resisted the temptation to join her there, avoided the seductive heat of the firestorm and the allure of Ginger herself, until the wee hours of the morning.

Then the wind stirred, driving snow against the windowpane so that it tinkled. Delaney shivered at the sound and couldn't stop. His skin was cold to the touch. His teeth were chattering so loudly that he was afraid of waking Ginger.

And that was what drove him finally toward the bed. His intention had been to remain wrapped in his assigned quilt, not to slide beneath the covers with Ginger, but the notion didn't survive the caress of the firestorm.

The heat caressed his skin and he was drawn to it by a force greater than himself. A radiant glow lit between himself and Ginger, growing brighter with every step he took toward the bed. The light illuminated her features, stroked her cheek, made her look so delicate and feminine that Delaney's heart clenched. He stood and stared, watching how the golden light slipped over the curve of her neck, the line of her jaw, the fragile curve of her collarbone, and he yearned to follow its course with his fingertips.

He didn't dare to touch her, but he needed to get warm.

He peeled off his shirt and jeans, leaving them both folded on the straight chair. He deliberately kept on his T-shirt and Jockeys, knowing the cotton would be scant barrier against his desire. The clothing reminded him of his vow, though, reminded him that he could choose man over beast.

He cast the quilt Ginger had given him over the bed, then eased beneath the whole pile of quilts. The heat enveloped him instantly, weakened his resolve, and drew him closer to the source of the firestorm.

Ginger.

He gritted his teeth and lay flat on his back beside her, telling himself that the heat he already felt was enough. He knew it was a lie. He thought of Ginger, her softness and her strength, her humor and her passion, and he wanted to reach for her.

But he had promised.

Against all expectation, she suddenly rolled over and nestled against him, fitting her curves against him without waking up.

Delaney caught his breath at the surge of heat that raced through his body, banishing winter's cold. When he realized she still slept undisturbed, he surrendered his fight. He pulled her closer, letting her bury her head against his shoulder.

It was innocent to lie entangled like this. Harmless.

Or maybe not.

Ginger's hair tickled his nose, teasing his senses with the scent of a floral shampoo. She was warm, so warm, and so soft. So giving. Her fearlessness stood in stark contrast to his own doubts and he wished, not for the first time, that things could have been different between them. The firestorm cast the room in gold, like a treasury filled with golden hoard, and Delaney's mouth went dry.

He was warm. He was home. He was at the heart of what had the power to make him happy and make his life worthwhile. She had already given him more than he deserved, but he wanted only more. He was momentarily overwhelmed by the power of his connection with Ginger, and let himself imagine that they did have a future. That they could have a future.

Even though it could not be.

Delaney held Ginger close, savoring the scent of her skin and the feel of her breath against his throat. He stared at the ceiling and understood fully what Magnus had stolen from him.

He checked the resonance of his dragonsmoke ring. He listened to the steady breathing of Thorolf in the kitchen below. He heard Niall, keeping watch on the roof and murmuring to the wind. He listened harder and heard the girls stirring in the barn, their tails swishing. He felt the rhythm of the earth, the warm pulse of spring

growth deep in the earth. He listened to the wind as it howled and whistled around the house, to the tinkling of the falling snow, and felt the depths of the drifts grow around the house.

He sensed a *Pyr* moving closer and guessed that Sloane was returning. He couldn't sense *Slayer*, but he knew better than to believe they had moved out of range. They were all wounded, though, and he imagined they were drinking of the Elixir and healing.

This was a night in which Delaney could do the same.

He conceded to his body's demands and to the seductive warmth of Ginger's bed. He slept, cocooned in what he thought was safety.

The nightmare, which Delaney had thwarted several nights running, snatched his mind as soon he had been lulled into a deep sleep. He sensed its beginning, just as it always began, and fought to wake up.

No luck.

The shadow began to move across the earth, its inexorable path making him panic. He had to stop it. He had to ensure that this vision of the future never came to be. Delaney struggled against his own body to no avail.

He shivered at the cold of the Elixir claiming the planet, feeling that same cold claim his own body once again. He tried to force his eyes open but was powerless in the nightmare's grasp. The earth was eclipsed, cast in darkness, then the light revealed the horrific truth.

Delaney saw the earth encased in silver ice, preserved and dead.

He heard himself roar in fury. He felt himself fly furiously toward the earth. He found the *Pyr*, one at a time, each one snared in the element he knew best.

Dead.

Quinn was blackened by fire beside his cold forge, his body crumbling to ash at the merest touch.

Donovan was frozen in a fighting posture, encased in the ice he could command as Warrior.

Erik was flayed by air, his carcass reduced to bone and sinew.

Niall had tumbled from a mountaintop, blown to the ends of the earth by the wind that had long been his ally. His body was bashed and broken, tossed into a deep crevasse where only Delaney could find it.

Sloane was drowned in the water that had given him understanding, his body trapped beneath a layer of ice.

Rafferty was enclosed in earth, suffocated and crushed, his strength no match for that of a furious Gaia.

Delaney found them all, each in turn, and struggled to free their bodies from the clutch of the elements. Quinn's body disintegrated to ash; Donovan's body shattered into shards of ice; Erik's body crumbled to nothing with Delaney's every touch. Niall's body broke into parts that could never be fused together again; Sloane dissolved when Delaney tried to break him free and Rafferty, Rafferty turned to dust that could not be distinguished from the earth that held him fast.

In trying to help his fellows, Delaney destroyed all that remained of each and every one of them.

He struggled against the nightmare's vision, his horror at his own failure complete.

Then he found Ginger, her body frozen under the ice at Brush Creek, near the entry to the sanctuary. There was no spark between them, no firestorm's light to gild her features. Her eyes were wide and staring, blind to his arrival.

He broke through the ice, using all of his might to free her from her wintry prison. He cast thick sheets of ice to one side and the other, desperate to save her.

But when the ice was broken and the riverbed was exposed, there was no one there.

Ginger was gone, as surely as if she had never been.

"A spark extinguished," a woman declared. Delaney knew that voice, knew it as well as he knew his own name.

He spun in his dream, seeing the house where he had been born, not truly surprised to find his mother waiting there.

"You could have changed the course of destiny," she said, and Delaney hated that she was right. The words settled heavily around his heart, resonant with the truth they carried. "You had the chance to destroy the Elixir, but you were"—his mother sneered—"*afraid* to keep your promise."

Delaney tasted his own failure.

"I had expected better of you," she said softly.

Delaney cried out and reached for his mother.

His hands closed on empty air.

He spun in panic, realizing his own solitude. She was gone. The house was gone. The earth was dead, his friends were dead, and his mate was dead. He was alone, alone with only the knowledge of his own failure for companionship.

He raged at his own inadequacies.

He was infuriated by the injustice of it all.

Delaney tipped back his head and shouted in fury.

Chapter 15

Rafferty dozed in Erik's living room. He felt on edge, as if something changed and demanded his attention. He wasn't certain whether he was simply struck by Chicago's unfamiliar rhythms or whether there were greater issues afoot.

Either way, he didn't sleep.

He lounged on one of the black couches set before the fireplace. Despite the fire and destruction of Erik's loft, many things had been replaced and repaired to the same look. This wasn't the couch where Sophie had lounged, her white blond hair in stark contrast to the black, but it was sufficiently similar to make Rafferty think of her.

He missed her.

He missed Nikolas.

Rafferty turned the black and white glass ring on his hand absently and indulged his thoughts.

He appreciated what Sophie and Nikolas had done and why, but he missed their presences. He missed Sophie's unpredictability and her gentle beauty. He missed her wisdom. He missed the clarity of Nikolas's vision and his conviction in his own choices.

Rafferty often felt that there were too many choices of varying merit, and that no decision was black and white.

So to speak. He glanced down at the ring and the way he was busily turning it, then rose to his feet.

What about Delaney?

What else could Rafferty do to help? He'd left the verse for Ginger to find, sensing that she was in a better position to change Delaney's mind than any of the *Pyr*. The firestorm gave her a certain hold over Delaney's thoughts and, in herself, Ginger had a compelling strength.

What else could he do?

Could the earth tell him more? Gaia hadn't been responsive of late, and Rafferty wasn't entirely certain that it was safe to lie in the street in the middle of the night in this part of town.

He missed his London town house, with its small garden and his neighbors with their high tolerance of eccentricity. They thought little of it when they spied him lying in his garden during the night.

He was aware of Eileen and Erik sleeping in their room, and was unwilling to disturb them. All the same, he was restless, unable to dismiss the sense that he should do *something*.

If only he'd known what it was.

He paced, as quietly as possible.

But then, Erik had nearly paced a hole in Rafferty's own carpets the year before. Rafferty figured that his pacing was fair play.

He found himself on the threshold of the small room they used as a nursery. Erik was convinced that three-month-old Zoë was the new Wyvern. Rafferty wasn't sure—he'd come soon after her birth, hoping to find Sophie's soul resident in the new baby. He'd been disappointed. Zoë didn't strike him as having the same energy that Sophie had. She didn't remind him of the lost Wyvern, and that made him doubt that she was the Wyvern at all. It didn't matter much, not until she was capable of communicating with them and came into her powers.

Zoë, though, had an affection for him. She let out a plaintive cry when he would have turned away, and Rafferty moved into the room instead. He liked children and was said to have a special touch with them. He thought he might save Erik and Eileen another break in their sleep. They were both tired with the challenge of a new baby, although Zoë was comparatively tranquil.

He halted beside the crib, only to find her eyes open and fixed upon him.

"Are you wet?" he asked quietly. Her diaper appeared to be dry, although she kicked with enthusiasm when he checked. "Hungry?" He offered the bottle that Eileen had left in the nursery, but the baby spurned it.

Her left hand opened and closed, and Rafferty had the sense that she was asking him for something.

Maybe she was bored. Lonely. Restless.

He could understand that.

Rafferty picked her up, smiling at her little gurgle of satisfaction when he did so. He tucked a blanket around her and she bounced a little, so clearly showing her pleasure in his decision that he smiled a bit more.

"Some nights, we all need a little company," he said to her, turning to go back into the living room.

She seized his hand, her little fingers locking on the black and white glass ring. Rafferty had a moment to assume that she was fascinated by shiny things, like all children, then she pulled the ring into her mouth.

The vision that assailed his mind left him reeling.

He saw the earth spinning on its axis, the moon orbiting around it more rapidly than it did in actuality. The earth, in its turn, orbited around the sun, until the three orbs were aligned with the moon between the sun and earth.

"A lunar eclipse," Rafferty murmured to himself. The *Pyr* were sensitive to lunar eclipses, seeing as they announced important firestorms.

The planets moved again in his vision, traveling through space at wildly accelerated speed. He saw the earth move through shadow and light so quickly that the continents seemed to flicker. There were other times when the three were aligned for a lunar eclipse, but the rotation didn't stop. He became aware of a ticking, and saw a number imposed on the earth. It became higher and higher, the count accelerating with lightning speed, until suddenly it stopped.

Sun, moon, and earth were aligned again for a lunar eclipse, and Rafferty thought the arrangement looked very similar to the first time this display had halted.

The number imposed on the earth read 6585.322.

Then the vision faded, a silver curtain of liquid beads dripping over the view and obscuring it. Rafferty was left staring into the darkness of Erik's loft. Zoë gurgled again and sighed. Her grip on the ring slackened and when Rafferty looked down at her, she had fallen asleep again.

He stared at the child and wondered.

The Wyvern traditionally had the ability to dispatch dreams to the *Pyr*. Could this child, this new Wyvern, do that already?

If so, what did his vision mean?

He balanced her on his hip as he booted up Erik's laptop. It didn't take long for him to discover—when he searched for lunar eclipses and 6585.322—that eclipses occurred in groups called Saros cycles, and that a Saros cycle was a period of 6585.322 days.

Why was that important?

Rafferty kept reading, his excitement rising as he found

details. A Saros cycle was a period of time in which the positions of the planets were replicated in three ways. A synodic month is the time from one full or new moon to the next, and a full or new moon is a necessary element for a lunar eclipse. A draconic year is the time it takes the sun to travel through the moon's north node to the south and back to the initial starting point. An anomalistic month is the time it takes for the moon to move from perigee to perigee, from the point where it is closest to the earth to the point where it is farthest away and back again.

And all three of these cycles repeat roughly every eighteen years, or every 6585.322 days.

Even more important, when they repeat, another eclipse will occur that is very similar to the one eighteen years before. Thus, eclipses are grouped together and numbered to indicate their Saros family. Each Saros family had an eclipse roughly every eighteen years.

Because nineteen draconic years is eleven hours longer than 223 synodic months, the alignment isn't perfect—thus, Saros families have a beginning and an end. The entire life cycle of a Saros family of eclipses lasts centuries, including seventy or eighty eclipses. They begin as penumbral eclipses, become total eclipses, then diminish until they stop completely.

On impulse, Rafferty looked up the most recent penumbral eclipse, the one that had presaged Delaney's firestorm. It was part of a family assigned the number 143, which had begun in the eighteenth century. That couldn't be it. He looked up the next eclipse, the one that would come in July, and his heart skipped.

It was the second to last eclipse in Saros family 110.

He looked down at Zoë sleeping against his chest and the ring on the hand with which he held her. He thought of cycles, of Sophie's passionate insistence that everything must live and then die. He thought of Ginger's story of Cinnabar, and Magnus's determination to replace Cinnabar in the Elixir, and he looked at the date of the first eclipse in the Saros cycle 110.

May 28, 747.

The Moors had been in Spain by the mid-eighth century. Could the Saros cycle be governing the effectiveness of the Elixir? Was Cinnabar waning because the Saros cycle that had marked his becoming the source of the Elixir was ending? If so, the last eclipse in this cycle, the one that would happen on July 18, 2027, would signal the end of the Elixir.

So why seek a replacement for Cinnabar so early?

Rafferty tapped on the keyboard with one hand, seeking the answer that he knew had to be there. Saros cycles didn't begin very often. A new one would begin in May 2013, then not another before June 2096. Rafferty doubted that Magnus could survive the interval of sixty-nine years without any Elixir.

And it was in Magnus's nature to prefer a buffer. He'd create his new source by 2013, which meant capturing Delaney before that date. Rafferty didn't want to think about how Magnus would ensure that Delaney didn't escape him again.

Somehow, Magnus had compelled Delaney to seek the Elixir, to put himself in the easiest position for Magnus to succeed at his plan.

He remembered the curtain of dripping silver and guessed.

Rafferty glanced up to find Erik on the threshold of his room. The leader of the *Pyr* glanced at his child, and evidently read Rafferty's expression. "The effectiveness is tied to the Saros cycles," Rafferty said.

"And the toxin in Delaney is quicksilver," Erik said. Rafferty knew then they had both had the same dream. "Mercury."

"She sent us the vision," Rafferty said, and his old friend nodded.

"It's not the first time." Erik exhaled. "She's powerful, more powerful than we've guessed." He came into the room to take Zoë from Rafferty's arms. "We have to stop Magnus, no matter the risk. This is too important for any of us to stand aside."

Before Rafferty could agree, Eileen spoke from the doorway. "Then we'll all go," she said. Erik might have protested, but she gave him a stern look. "You're not leaving me behind when interesting things are happening."

"Dangerous things," Erik corrected.

"All the more reason to have Zoë defended by her father." Eileen claimed the child, snuggling her close. "Don't imagine that you'll leave without us." Rafferty could see Erik had mixed feelings about this decision.

"I suppose you want to take commercial flights," he said, his tone tight.

Eileen smiled. "There won't be any with the snowstorm in Ohio, and I can live without being diverted all over the continent. Sleeping in airports isn't good for little people." She tapped him on the shoulder. "If nothing else, you always land where you're planning to land."

Erik rolled his eyes. "At least I have some merit," he said, but there was laughter underlying his complaint.

"More than a little bit," Eileen conceded. "Give me ten minutes."

"I'll go ahead," Rafferty said, and Erik put a hand on his arm.

"Don't take unnecessary risks," Erik said, and Rafferty knew the leader of the *Pyr* had guessed his intention.

Rafferty smiled. "A wise *Pyr* once told me that no risks are unnecessary in these times." The pair stared at each other for a moment; then they shook hands and Rafferty left.

If one of them didn't return, they had parted in understanding.

*   *   *

In the lower peninsula of Michigan, Sara awakened with a start. Snow fell lightly in the meadow outside the window and the house was silent. Her heart was pounding, and she thought at first that she'd heard Garrett. She left Quinn sleeping as she rose to check their son.

The baby was asleep as well, his room tranquil as ever.

Sara, though, couldn't dismiss the sense that something was very wrong. She felt agitated and the hair was prickling on the back of her scalp.

This was how she had felt when Sophie, the Wyvern, had sent her a dream.

But not as vehemently as she had when the Dragon's Egg had been broken.

Sara was the Seer of the *Pyr*, the foretold mate of the Smith who sensed the future through her dreams. Even though the Wyvern was dead, Sara tried to review her dream. There was no telling its source, and really, the source was unimportant. She leaned over Garrett, her heart tight at the perfection of his tiny fingers and the sight of his dark lashes against his round cheeks, and let her mind seek the shreds of her dream.

"What is it?" Quinn asked as she tucked the quilt more closely around their son.

Sara touched Garrett's cheek and he fidgeted, impatient even in sleep with such shows of affection. He rolled over and burrowed into his quilt, his fierce expression easing Sara's mood.

"I woke up, certain that something was wrong."

"A dream?" Quinn asked.

"I was dreaming about Nikolas and Sophie." She swallowed, still overcome by emotion. "It was so sad. He was seeking her everywhere, with that single-mindedness of his."

"Nothing could stand in his way," Quinn agreed quietly, his eyes gleaming like sapphires as he watched her.

"He couldn't find her, Quinn," Sara said, her words husky. "He sought her everywhere, but couldn't find her. She was lost to him forever." Tears rose to her eyes again.

Quinn crossed the room in two steps and pulled her against his heat. Sara closed her eyes as she leaned against him, his quiet strength soothing her fears as it always did. "Maybe not forever. Maybe just for now," he said. "If anyone can find her, it will be Nikolas."

"But he was so upset. He said she was lost forever." She felt Quinn shake his head.

"No. Nothing is truly lost forever, certainly not souls or sparks of the divine." He kissed Sara's temple. "Everything becomes something else. There are transitions, not terminations. The steel melts and is reshaped, but it never disappears."

Sara smiled, knowing she should have anticipated that he would use his forge as a metaphor. "You're so sure."

"I am. Sophie must have something to do, or she must be somewhere Nikolas can't follow her."

"They have to be together, Quinn."

"They have to be together in their own time."

She tipped her head back to ensure that she saw his reaction. "He looked like Donovan's son in my dream. It was Nikolas, but he was a child. He was Nick."

Quinn smiled. "So, maybe Donovan is taking on the job of Seer, too. He said the baby reminded him of Nikolas from the beginning. That's why they named him Nicholas."

"Alex said the delivery was quick, as if the baby had set his own schedule and was going to keep it."

Quinn chuckled and held her closer. "Sounds like Nikolas."

Sara braced herself for Quinn's reaction to the suggestion she had to make, knowing he wouldn't like it. "We have to find Delaney."

He stiffened instantly, though he didn't say anything. He was utterly still, waiting for more information.

Sara stepped out of his embrace to make her appeal. "We have to go. You have to help him."

Quinn looked as resolute as she'd expected. His eyes narrowed. "Have you forgotten that he tried to attack you?" His voice rose slightly. "Have you forgotten that he would have snatched Garrett from inside you? You tried to help him then—"

Sara interrupted him. "In my dream, Nikolas found a scale. He gave it to me. He said I would know what to do with it, and I do."

Quinn swore softly and turned away, but not before Sara saw his features soften. "What color of scale?" He knew the answer, but Sara said it aloud, anyway.

"Copper and emerald, with a red tinge at the root. It was Delaney's scale."

"Has he lost it already?"

"I don't know. Maybe he will lose it in the future. Maybe you need to be there for whenever it happens."

Quinn shoved a hand through his hair and paced in silence.

"You have to fix Delaney's armor, Quinn. You know it. We have to go to him."

Quinn took a deep breath and folded his arms across his chest as he looked out the window. "He's having his firestorm."

"Really?" Sara hadn't known this.

Quinn nodded. "I felt it. I can feel it."

"You weren't drawn to it?"

"I was, but I declined to go." He glanced over his shoulder, protectiveness clear in his eyes. "I'm not going to put you two in danger, firestorm or not. I won't go alone and leave you undefended, and I won't take you with me."

"But it's more than a firestorm, now. It's his scale."

Quinn grimaced.

"It's your inherited duty as the Smith to heal the *Pyr*. We have to go, Quinn. That's why I had the dream."

"He's half lost, anyway. He's already outcast himself."

"No, Quinn. We need to bring him back."

"Or?"

Sara shrugged, unable to articulate the sense of doom that her dream had left with her.

Quinn growled and he paced, caught by the simple truth in her statement, yet unhappy with it. When he didn't argue further, Sara knew then he'd do as she requested.

He paused to point a finger at her. "If we're going, Donovan has to come, too. And Erik." He was so clearly displeased that Sara knew he trusted her instincts enough to put aside his own concerns. He gave her an intense look, his eyes a stormy blue. "We're not going near Delaney without every talon I can muster."

"Fair enough," Sara said, smiling as she used Quinn's favorite expression.

He shook his head and shoved both hands through his hair, irritated yet prepared to do what had to be done. His brow was furrowed and he looked troubled.

His features softened when he studied her. "You're absolutely sure that we need to be there?"

Sara nodded, honored by his trust. "You have to help him, Quinn, or we'll lose him forever." She tried to express the sense of dread left by her dream. "And maybe more than that, too."

"Who sent you the dream?"

"I don't know. It's not quite the same as when Sophie sent me a dream, and not at all like the dream I had when the Dragon's Egg broke." Sara tried to identify the strange sense she had. "Could a different Wyvern have sent it to me? One less subtle in the use of her powers?"

Their gazes met across the darkened room. Quinn swallowed. "Erik said his visions are sharper when he holds Zoë."

Sara nodded. "So, we do have a new Wyvern. We have to trust her counsel, Quinn, no matter how she communicates it." She licked her lips. "We have to believe that if we act as she urges, it will all come right." Quinn held her gaze for a long moment, and Sara knew he was gauging her conviction.

Then he turned away with a terse nod.

"Fair enough." Quinn was decisive then, his choice made. "I'll get my tools."

In Minneapolis, Donovan awakened suddenly, his eyes flying open in the darkness. His heart was leaping as if he had been running. Alex slept deeply beside him and he listened, but Nick was sleeping as well. Their home was quiet. At peace.

It wasn't the first time this had happened to him in the last week.

He knew in his heart what was wrong, but also knew that he couldn't go to his brother's firestorm.

He wouldn't risk his partner and child.

Donovan slipped from the bed and checked the house, following his usual routine.

Nothing.

Everything was as it should be.

Just as he'd anticipated.

He paused in the living room, surveying the park on the opposite side of the street. There was snow on the ground and the trees were dark silhouettes against the night.

Donovan still felt unsettled, his mind flooded with images of the past. He felt as if he stood in the middle of a tumult, a hurricane of memory. Just as the other nights when his sleep had been disturbed, he saw his mother. Her image was as clear as if she had been standing in front of him, although she had presumably been dead for centuries.

A pretty woman, but a poor one, Elizabeth Connaught probably hadn't aged well. Maybe it was kinder to remember her in her youth. Donovan saw her in the act of throwing him out of her house, hurling a pot after him as he strode down the alley. She called him names, but he had never turned around. He'd never gone back.

That had been a mistake, because his father had gone back to Elizabeth. Donovan hadn't known about his younger brother's existence for years, and he hadn't known that he and Delaney were brothers until recently.

But Donovan knew he had made his peace with that. He waited, wondering whether the cycle of memories would continue, maybe tell him why he couldn't sleep.

He saw his father in their last fatal fight, and his hands clenched in recollection of what he had been compelled to do. The shadow dragon Keir had become not only had to die, but Donovan had to give the killing blow. It hadn't been the happiest reunion, but he and Keir had never seen eye to eye.

Donovan had never been afraid to take on the dirty work, and he hadn't shirked from it then. He could wish, though, that his father had made different choices. He could learn from those bad choices and move forward, making better choices himself. He could respect that the Elixir had fed the evil within Keir and made him worse than he ever could have been without its power.

The Elixir.

Keir had been fed the Elixir, his body roused from

the dead by Magnus with his vile substance. Keir had never fully become *Slayer*—he lacked the motivation—but he had possessed tendencies in that direction. Had his blood run black at the end of his wasted life? Donovan wasn't sure, because Keir had had no blood when father and son met again. He shuddered, felt the tingle of a firestorm, and knew that Keir couldn't plague his other son as he had tried to interfere with Donovan's firestorm.

Yes, it was Delaney's firestorm that tickled at Donovan's consciousness, that tempted him closer, that summoned him to help his only brother. Donovan had resisted its summons, knowing that his greater responsibility was to Alex and Nick.

Was that why his sleep was disturbed? Because he wasn't helping Delaney?

But Delaney had been forced to drink the Elixir as well. And even though Delaney had been drawn to Donovan's firestorm, even though the heat of Donovan's firestorm had pulled Delaney from the deepest pit of darkness, he was still infected with the Elixir's toxin. He still responded to commands Magnus had slipped into his subconscious, one of which had been a compulsion to harvest the children in Sara's and Alex's wombs.

They had tried to help Delaney, they had tried to ensure his healing, and he had turned on the two pregnant women. Donovan's lips set in a tight line. A firestorm couldn't last forever, and he would not go to this one. He wouldn't risk Alex and Nick by taking them along, and he wouldn't leave them alone and undefended.

He evidently also wouldn't sleep. His resolve unwavering, he pivoted to return to bed before his absence awakened Alex.

Then the power went out.

The streetlights winked out, leaving only the light of the stars beyond the window. Donovan looked out the window at the park again. The darkness was startling after the ambient light of the city. The hair on the back of Donovan's neck prickled, portentous of something he couldn't name.

"Power's out," Alex said, and Donovan heard her footsteps on the hardwood floor. "Did you get the flashlight?" She went into the kitchen and returned a moment later. There was a click, and an arc of yellow light spilled across the floor.

And Donovan saw his own reflection in the wide pane of glass that was the living room window. His hand seemed to lift of its own accord, his fingertips meeting those of his own reflection.

A third memory assaulted him, the power of the visual reminder weakening his knees. He had encountered Delaney centuries before on a Dublin street, and even though neither of them knew any others of their kind, they had immediately recognized each other as *Pyr*. They had sensed the common ground they held and they had faced each other, just as he faced his reflection, in that fateful encounter. Their fingertips had met, each of them touching the other as if encountering a mirror.

They had never talked about it, but Donovan knew it had been a powerful moment of connection for both of them.

It had been when they had each known they were not alone.

Donovan tapped the glass lightly with his fingertips, not liking the message but unable to argue with it. Could he leave his brother alone? Could he truly abandon him?

Donovan realized he couldn't.

Somehow he had to help Delaney.

Then he heard Quinn's old-speak slide into his thoughts.

"Sara says we have to go." Quinn was perfunctory,

resolute. *"It'll be worse if we don't."* Even in old-speak, Donovan could hear his friend's displeasure with this course of action.

But Sara was the Seer.

And neither he nor Quinn had ever avoided what they had to do.

"At your back," he replied.

"Ditto," Quinn replied.

The prospect of going to Delaney with Quinn eased Donovan's uncertainty and he was filled with conviction as he turned to meet the question in Alex's eyes.

"Delaney needs me," he said. "We have to go to his firestorm."

She froze, her gaze dancing over him. "Even with Nick?"

"Especially with Nick," Donovan said, convinced of his choice. "Our firestorm helped Delaney before. We need to finish what we started. Sara says so."

"I thought I heard thunder."

He smiled at Alex to reassure her and she came a step closer. "You know that I'll do anything to defend you."

"Yes," Alex agreed softly. "I know."

They stared at each other for a long moment, each drawing strength from the other. Donovan reached for Alex and caught her close. She wound her arms around his neck and tipped her head back. He liked that she didn't argue with him, but trusted his judgment and his ability to defend her. He'd summon every element to protect his small family and the sight of Alex's trust made his heart skip a beat.

"What's wrong?" she asked.

"I've been sensing his firestorm but didn't want to go to it. If Sara dreamed that we need to go, I'll guess that it's going wrong."

Alex nodded. "Then we do have to go. If anyone ever

needed love in his life, it's your brother. Where are we going, anyway?"

Donovan listened and inhaled slowly, gathering a sense of what was in the wind. He felt the tingle of Delaney's firestorm again, its heat a bit more intense than it had been. This time, he explored it, letting it fill his senses and tinge his tongue. It was a hot one.

"South," he said quietly, striving to pinpoint the heat. "Not that far, but I'll know better as we get closer. Maybe Ohio."

"Snugglies for Nick then," Alex said, and touched her lips to his. Her tone lightened as she teased him. "You *Pyr* could have firestorms in Fiji in the winter, you know. Maybe at a nice all-inclusive resort with hunky bartenders."

"What do you need with a hunky bartender?" Donovan growled, pulling her closer.

"Nothing but the view," Alex responded, those few words all she had time to admit before he kissed her.

Donovan was sure she wasn't thinking about bartenders, hunky or otherwise, by the time he was done. As always, her touch gave him strength and fortified his knowledge not only of what he had to do but that they would succeed.

As a team.

Chapter 16

Delaney's shout awakened Ginger.

She was surprised to find him in her bed, even more surprised to find him battling a nightmare. He thrashed in his sleep, clearly trying to wake up. Ginger couldn't imagine what haunted him and she didn't really care.

She cared only that he was suffering.

Again.

She had to make a difference. She sat up and gave his shoulder a firm shake.

"Wake up!" she urged, then shook him again.

He mumbled something she didn't understand, then frowned and struggled once more against some unseen foe.

Ginger seized both of his shoulders and shook him hard. "Wake up, Delaney!" she said. When he still writhed beside her, his anguish evident, she slapped him across the face.

His eyes flew open at that, his expression wild. He looked terrified and haunted, and Ginger's heart melted that he should suffer so. He scanned the room, as if uncertain where he was, then his gaze fixed upon her so abruptly that she jumped. His eyes were piercingly green, but filled with those dark shadows. Ginger caught her breath. Delaney was pale and cold, like a man who had seen a ghost.

Or who had walked with the dead.

"Ginger," he whispered, seemingly awed to find her with him. He reached for her and it never occurred to Ginger to deny him. He caught her close and rolled her beneath him, protecting her from some villain that only he could sense. He ran his fingertips across her cheek, then exhaled in relief at the dance of the firestorm's sparks. He swallowed as he met her gaze again.

"I dreamed you were dead," he confessed, his words husky.

"Not yet," Ginger said, smiling in the hope that he would, as well.

"I dreamed it was my fault," he whispered.

Ginger reached to frame his face in her hands. "No," she said firmly. "No. It could never be your fault. You defend me." She smiled at him again, letting her fingers slide over his hair. "Every time."

Some of the tension eased out of his shoulders then and the shadows dimmed in his eyes. Ginger became aware of the way he held his strength over her, the warmth of his fingers tangled in her hair. His T-shirt did nothing to hide the muscled splendor of his chest and she could see that his wounds were healing with record speed. She also saw the cross beneath his T-shirt, its silver gleaming through the fabric.

He smiled ever so slightly, his smile even more precious each time she prompted it, and the firestorm shimmered and glimmered between them. Her bedroom was filled with a magical golden light, a glamour that she would never forget. Ginger swallowed, aware of the press of her breasts against his chest, the heat that the firestorm lit in her body, and a desire that was far from languid. Delaney wore his Jockeys still, obviously having intended to honor his promise to her, but she could feel that his body had other ideas.

He'd never inflict himself on her, though.

Ginger felt powerful and sexy as she slid her hands around his neck. She pulled him closer, smiling into his eyes. "Come here and kiss me," she invited in a husky whisper, and she didn't need to ask him twice.

Delaney dipped his head and caught her lips beneath his. He kissed her thoroughly, his embrace demanding and possessive. Ginger knew he was claiming her and she didn't care. She felt the rasp of a day's growth of whiskers and locked her fingers around his neck, drawing him closer.

Their kiss was open-mouthed, hungry and demanding, hot and fierce. She knew what he was and welcomed his power. Their tongues danced, each of them nearly intent on devouring the other. Ginger's heart began to skip, the firestorm burning hotter and brighter. She arched against Delaney, pulling his strength to her, wanting him as she had never wanted a man before.

She didn't give a damn about the pill or about the chance of bearing his son.

She wanted Delaney inside her.

Immediately.

He groaned her name and pulled away, but she didn't let him retreat. Ginger held on and rolled on top of him. Delaney started to argue, but Ginger straddled him, sat up, and pulled off her nightgown. She was nude, her hair tangled and her cheeks flushed, and had never felt more gorgeous.

Whatever Delaney had been planning to say was never uttered. He fell silent, and swallowed, as he stared at her. He raised one hand to cup her breast. Her nipple tightened as his fingers slipped over her skin, and

a golden spark of light leapt between them as Ginger
arched her back. She caught Delaney's hand in hers and
held his palm against her breast.

She smiled down at him, seeing the wonder in his
eyes. She also felt something against her thigh, his erection revealing that their thoughts were as one.

"Get naked already," she whispered, then grinned.

"But—" Delaney began to argue, but Ginger didn't
give him a chance. She fell against his chest and kissed
him, sliding her tongue into his mouth in silent demand.
He groaned, his hands closing on her buttocks to draw
her closer. Ginger pulled her knees up on either side of
him and Delaney's fingers clenched.

As she kissed him, she could feel the thunder of his
heart against her breasts. She caught her breath as their
heartbeats synchronized. It was a dizzying sensation,
one that gave her an overwhelming sense of union with
him.

One that made her think they could be a team.

One that encouraged her to believe that the firestorm
had it right.

She slid her hands beneath the hem of his T-shirt,
pulling it up to his shoulders. She was naked and she
wanted him to be; she wanted to rub herself against him
and feel every contour of his body.

His skin was smoother than hers, stronger, satin to
her silk. His legs entwined with hers, his all muscled
strength and definition.

She wanted to see everything he had. She wanted to
touch everything he had.

Delaney pushed her hands away, as if he'd stop their
embrace, but Ginger could feel the truth of his desire
for her.

"Don't you want me?" she teased.

He visibly gritted his teeth. "I promised you."

"I'm changing the deal."

"You'll regret it in the morning," he argued.

"I don't think so."

"I do!" Delaney locked his hands around her waist and made to move her to one side. He looked disheveled and irritated and so utterly sexy that Ginger wasn't having any of it.

She pulled down his Jockeys and sat on him.

He gasped and froze, his gaze flying to hers.

Ginger smiled and rolled her hips, pulling him deeper inside of her. Delaney's eyes blazed into hers, then he moved so quickly that she was surprised. One moment she was astride him; the next she was on her back and his fingers were making her forget everything she knew. She reached for him but he evaded her, ducking to caress her with his tongue again.

He was too good at it. Ginger couldn't argue with him, couldn't summon a coherent thought to her lips. She understood that he was keeping his promise to her and she loved that; all the same, she yearned to feel him inside her again. Delaney gave her no opportunity to argue or to challenge his decision. He touched her and teased her with such conviction of what she liked best that they could have been lovers for a dozen years.

Or destined mates.

He brought her easily to climax, then did it again. And again. Tongue and fingers and lips and breath, each was a tool he used to give her pleasure. Ginger was dazzled, both by his creativity and his determination to deny himself.

The sizzle of the firestorm's sparks seemed to be beneath his command as well, a timely tingle driving her over the edge each time. She shimmered and simmered, sizzling in her desire for him. He was taut and persistent, and Ginger realized he meant to sate her at his own expense.

When she was too exhausted to stay awake, she

reached for him. He easily evaded her touch, slipping from the bed and tucking her beneath the quilts again.

"I'll touch you," she said, hearing sleep in her own tone.

Delaney made a rueful sound. "There's not a chance I'd keep control then," he muttered. His fingertips fluttered across her cheek and then he was gone.

And as she dozed, powerless against her own exhaustion, Ginger realized one thing. Delaney had given her all the pleasure she could want, except the one thing she wanted most.

Her heart melted that he did what he did in order to keep his promise to her.

She'd been right—he was a keeper.

And she was going to do her best to persuade him that they had a future, together.

Ginger was confident of her own success until she straightened the bed. She meant to sleep a few more hours, but what she found on the pillow left her wide awake.

It was a bead of mercury, lying on the linen like a perfect silver tear.

Where had it come from?

She thought of the hoarfrost around the bowl of Elixir, the mercury dripping from it into the snow, and was afraid that Delaney's future might not be hers to claim.

Delaney was no better than his father.

He descended the stairs quietly, keenly aware that only his promise to Ginger had kept him from repeating his own family history. That wasn't good enough. He should have been stronger than he had been.

He refused to become an abomination, a puppet condemned to serve Magnus's will. He refused to fulfill his mother's dark condemnation of his future prospects. He owed Ginger better than that, owed more to the woman whose trust was like a shaft of sunlight upon his heart.

Thorolf was sleeping in the kitchen, his feet braced on one of Ginger's kitchen chairs. The tall *Pyr*'s head was tipped back and he was snoring loudly enough to cover the sounds of Delaney's departure.

Although Delaney knew Niall would have enjoyed finding Thorolf so remiss on his watch—and the chance to berate the newest recruit yet again—he crept past the sleeping *Pyr*.

The door to the porch didn't squeak as he opened it, although he feared the gust of cold air would awaken Thorolf. He slipped through the door as quickly as he could, shutting it behind himself.

A moment later, he knew that nothing could have awakened Thorolf. The tall *Pyr* hadn't even stirred.

He wasn't much of a watchman.

The night was cold, the overcast sky as dark as pewter. The snow fell in a relentless rhythm, its volume on the ground increasing steadily. It glittered in the bit of light from the house, making Ginger's fields look as if they were sown with diamonds. It was a cruel beauty, though, one that Delaney was certain had already claimed a number of lives locally.

It reminded him all too well of his nightmare.

He took a breath of the cold air, feeling it pierce his lungs with cold, and knew he had to destroy the Elixir. He had an inkling of a plan and would have stepped off the porch to begin it, but he caught a sudden scent of *Pyr*.

He winced in recognition of the scent, even before he saw Erik's ebony and pewter figure whirling out of the sky.

He had asked Erik to watch over Ginger.

The leader of the *Pyr* had asked Delaney to wait for him.

He might have bolted, putting his own plan into action first, but he realized Erik hadn't come alone. Eileen was clasped against his chest, her hair shining copper against Erik's dark scales.

Delaney frowned, wondering that Eileen would have come without their daughter. Then he saw the bundle she held closely in her arms. Delaney was shocked.

They had brought Zoë.

They had brought their child, the *Pyr* reputed to be the next Wyvern, a child key to the *Pyr*'s survival and triumph. They had brought their precious firstborn into Delaney's presence and had done so willingly.

Knowing the risk.

They knew that Delaney had exiled himself because he had barely been able to resist Magnus's subliminal command to harvest the children of the *Pyr*, that he had nearly assaulted both Sara and Alex a year ago while they were pregnant.

And yet Erik and Eileen came to his firestorm, with their own child, a child more important to the *Pyr* than any other.

Delaney was so humbled by their trust that he couldn't bring himself to move. He watched Erik land, a hard lump in his own throat. The snow stirred and swirled as Erik shifted in the last moment before his feet touched the ground.

"Smooth flight, smooth landing," Eileen said, touching her lips to Erik's cheek with an affection that Delaney found touching. "Despite adverse climactic conditions. I'll fly this carrier again."

"How is she?" Erik asked, his words tight.

"Bundled in tight and sound asleep." Delaney watched Eileen smile as she unfurled layers of scarves and blankets, letting Erik assure himself as to the welfare of their child.

They'd brought the Wyvern into Delaney's presence. Seeing didn't help Delaney believe it.

The leader of the *Pyr* was tall and lean, his hair dark and his temples touched with silver. He wore a black leather jacket and dark jeans. His sweater was thick with intricate cables, knit of a black wool flicked with many colors. Eileen was dressed all in black as well, her silver jewelry shining in contrast to her dark sweater, jacket, and skirt. She had a knitted hood over her shoulders, one that extended into a scarf that she had wrapped securely around the baby. All Delaney could see of Zoë was the top of her head, which was capped with a bright pink hat that looked like a knitted slice of watermelon.

Erik arched a brow at Eileen's comment, then fixed his gaze upon Delaney. "Did you wait or did I catch you in time?"

Delaney flushed and indicated the kitchen door. "Ginger's asleep," he said, not answering Erik's question.

"And the firestorm?"

"Still burns," Delaney had to admit, knowing that Erik would disapprove. "Even though I tried to sate it."

Erik snorted. "Sloane will have ideas about that."

"Have you tried again?" Eileen asked, her eyes bright as she climbed the steps to the porch. These two had a talent for identifying the very core of an issue, and for being unafraid to ask after it.

Delaney gritted his teeth. "She refuses to raise a child alone. I promised not to tempt her to break her word."

"I like her already," Eileen said with satisfaction, heading into the kitchen. "I'll guess that she buys good coffee."

"She's a chef."

"Better and better."

Erik seemed to be stifling a smile. "Rafferty said you might have to decide to live."

"It's impossible," Delaney began with impatience,

but the leader of the *Pyr* laid a paternal hand on his shoulder.

"Nothing is impossible," Erik said. "Come inside and wait for Sloane. We'll find a solution together." Erik frowned at Delaney. "You're too cold."

Delaney swallowed and decided he could meet Erik's trust with some of his own. He pulled his hands from his pockets and spread out his fingers, knowing that Erik would notice the tinge of red on his cuticles. It seemed to be brighter than it had been just hours before.

Erik's eyes glittered as he looked, then he studied Delaney's face. "What's happening?"

"I don't know. Ginger said that Magnus intends to replace Cinnabar in the Elixir, as the source of the Elixir. She thinks he's chosen me."

Erik's tone became stern. "Why would you plan to go directly to the sanctuary to make Magnus's disgusting scheme easier for him?" He didn't wait for an answer, his eyes flashing. "I think not. Inside. Now. We have to talk."

"But . . ."

Erik glared at him. "Defy me in this and you will surely regret it."

Delaney knew when he had lost an argument. He passed the leader of the *Pyr* and headed back into Ginger's kitchen, resigned to the need to wait for Sloane and his counsel.

As much as he appreciated the aid of the *Pyr* and their resolve to save him, he didn't have to like it. He didn't trust how it eroded his conviction to do what needed doing.

Although it had been Ginger who had made the first breach.

Ginger, who was just entering the kitchen, and whose presence sent a stabbing shaft of sunlight through his heart. She smiled at him, then shrugged.

"I guess I should get used to finding strangers in my kitchen," she said, heading for the coffeepot.

Eileen put her diaper bag on the table loudly enough to awaken Thorolf. Zoë stirred, then began to cry.

"Move," Eileen told Thorolf, her disapproval of his pose clear. The tall *Pyr* scurried to sit up straight and brush off the chair where his boots had been. "Count yourself lucky you're not in our lair," she said as she unwrapped her many layers of cloth.

Eileen adjusted Zoë's position and the baby began to purse her lips hungrily in anticipation. Eileen caught her breath as the baby latched on to one nipple and began to suck, then she glared at Thorolf again. "Nobody puts their shoes on my furniture and lives to tell about it." She cast a scarf over her shoulder, cloaking the baby's feeding from view, and sighed as she sank into a chair.

Thorolf flushed crimson. Erik stifled a chuckle, then turned to Ginger. "I am Erik Sorensson, leader of the *Pyr*," he said, offering his hand to Ginger. "And this is my partner, Eileen Grosvenor."

"Not mate?" Ginger asked with an arch of her brow. She reached for the coffeepot, pointedly not taking Erik's hand.

He smiled "Also my mate, but more importantly, my partner and better half."

"You're staying together then."

"For the duration," Erik said.

"Children need a stable home," Eileen interjected.

Ginger smiled as she shook Erik's hand and Delaney didn't miss the glance she cast his way. "I thought you *Pyr* just left women pregnant and went on with your lives."

It was Erik then who gave Delaney the stern look. "There are those among us who subscribe to that view, but the more enlightened *Pyr* see the merit of a permanent relationship."

"We won't say who persuades them of that merit," Eileen said with a smile, and the two women exchanged a glance.

"More of your friends?" Ginger asked Delaney, and he nodded agreement.

"I particularly like these ones," she said, and went to fill the coffeepot with water. Once the coffee was on, Ginger went to Eileen and cooed over the baby, who kicked and gurgled. They were all so convinced that Delaney could have all of this, that this could be his future, that he knew he had to set them straight.

Immediately.

Before every last crumb of his determination was eroded to nothing.

He pulled out a chair and sat astride it, knowing his manner was even more intense than usual. For once, he didn't care if anyone could guess his thoughts, or the strength of his feelings. His words came with a force that surprised him. He needed to tell this story, and he needed to tell it now.

"Let me tell you a story," he said, his voice so low and purposeful that he immediately snared every eye in the kitchen. He deliberately echoed the beginning Ginger had used the night before and saw the glimmer of recognition in her eyes. "It's a story of the past shaping the future, of reality determining possibilities. It might even be a story of destiny."

He saw trepidation dawn in Ginger's eyes, but he kept talking. This might well be the story that turned her against him forever.

Maybe that was why he suddenly had to tell it.

Rafferty hesitated in the parking lot of the Serpent Mound park.

He had sniffed and he had listened. Even though there was no evidence of a *Slayer* in the vicinity, Rafferty doubted he was alone. He climbed to the earth mound itself, following its sinuous curve. It was heavy going, the snow as high as his hips, but he liked the shape of the effigy.

He cleared the snow with his hands from the egg beyond the snake's mouth. He sat there, savoring the contact with the earth, opening his thoughts to Gaia. The snow fell all around him, surrounding him with white and silence, and he felt a welcome serenity.

It wasn't long before he heard the uproar within the earth. It wasn't long before he sensed the foul contamination of the Elixir, far beneath the sacred egg where he sat.

It wasn't long before he found the motion in the earth that was Magnus, emanating malice. He felt the consolidation of mercury, he sensed the despair of Cinnabar, and he knew what he had to do. He looked at the ring he had worn for the past year, studied the black and the white entwined together. He recalled Sophie's ability to manifest in other locations, as well as her talent for taking other forms. He knew *Slayers* could master those tricks, knew that somehow the Elixir gave them the power to appropriate the Wyvern's traditional gifts.

Rafferty had never tasted the Elixir and he never would. But he dared to believe that Sophie would help him. He stared into the black and white whirled together, glass and anthracite entwined so completely that they could never be separated. He stared and he let his mind slide, and he refused to believe that anything was impossible.

Then he wished to be where Magnus was, and he wished to be in salamander form.

Rafferty got half of what he requested.

He found himself deep in the earth, with no clear sense of how he had gotten there. He was in his human form, but was amazed to have had any luck with his wish at all.

He was in a cavern with a high ceiling. The massive red vial of the Elixir filled the far wall of the cavern, and it emanated a pulsing red light that reminded him of the light in Magnus's dark academy.

It was paler though, more pink, and the pulse was slower. It snared Rafferty's eye, its cloudy contents swirling as if they would reveal Cinnabar to him.

"How nice of you to join us," Magnus said.

Rafferty spun to find the ancient *Slayer* leaning in the only doorway, still in human form. Magnus smiled. He was looking particularly hale and smug, which told Rafferty all he needed to know about his situation.

He took a step back.

Magnus's smile broadened. "It's so satisfying to have circles come to a close in their own fashion, isn't it?"

"What do you mean?"

"I mean that you and I were once such friends, such comrades in arms, so to speak. And that union waxed and waned in its own time."

Rafferty folded his arms across his chest. "Did it? I thought it ended when you decided to become a killer."

Magnus's smile turned colder. "I have never changed, not in all these many eons. Perhaps what changed was your perceptiveness."

"Or my usefulness."

Magnus was dismissive. "Believe what you need to. I acted in my own best interest and had you been clever, you would have joined ranks with me."

"You never told me about the Elixir. You never offered me that chance to join ranks."

Magnus chuckled. "Well, one can't share all of one's hidden strengths. Would you care for a sip now?"

Rafferty scoffed. "Now that its potency is fading? Why would I bother? I'll live past 2027 without it."

Magnus caught his breath, then nodded slowly. "So, you know."

"So, I know."

The two stared at each other across the space, animosity tingeing the air between them.

"Where are your minions?" Rafferty asked.

Magnus chuckled. "Doing what they've been told to do. For once."

"For the moment."

"What do you mean?"

"I mean that your perch is precarious. They all aspire to take your place."

"And none of them will manage to do so." Magnus's confidence was complete. "You are not the only one who knows a mere fraction of my plan."

"But I am the one who will defy you," Rafferty said. He reached into his pocket and did what he should have done centuries before.

He tossed his challenge coin at Magnus.

The ancient *Slayer's* smile flashed as he snatched the gold coin out of the air. It was an English coin, showing St. George spearing the dragon on one side and a sun with emanating rays on the other. Rafferty thought of it as a *Pyr* in human form giving a *Slayer* the fate he deserved. Magnus studied it and smiled.

He flicked his own coin so quickly that Rafferty had to lunge to catch it. It was a Roman coin, which didn't surprise Rafferty at all. It appeared to be silver, but Rafferty could sense the resonance of brass within its core. The silver was simply a wash on the surface.

"How appropriate that it's been made to look more valuable than it is," he said.

"It's a *follis*," Magnus said haughtily.

Rafferty laughed. "A money bag," he said, recalling the slang term for the coin. "It's doubly apt then." He pocketed the coin, accepting the challenge just as Magnus shifted shape.

The *Slayer* lunged toward Rafferty with a roar, his jade and gold form gleaming with power. Rafferty shifted shape then and dove for Magnus, talons extended. The two of them locked claws in the traditional battle pose.

"To the death," Magnus said, as if there were any doubt about it.

"To the death," Rafferty agreed. *"It's past due."* Then he struck Magnus hard with his tail.

Delaney stared at the tabletop, well aware that the others were watching him closely, and focused on telling the story he had to share.

He was surprised to hear himself start the same way Ginger had, when she'd told him of her past the night before.

But maybe that was fitting.

"Once upon a time, there was a boy who lived with his mother. His mother seldom talked about the boy's father, and when she did, her anger spilled forth unchecked. The toxin of her bitterness could stain the air of their small home for weeks afterward, and so the boy learned not to ask questions." Delaney heard the cadence of Ireland in his own voice, an echo of his mother's speech that had long faded from his own.

The accent was comforting in its familiarity.

"And so it was that they were content, if poor and often hungry. The mother worked when she could get what she called honest work, helping in bakeries and shops. She was pretty and had a certain charm, but would periodically plunge into a despair so dark that she couldn't even be roused from bed. On those occasions, she invariably lost whatever position she had, and when she recovered from her despair, she would begin her search for employment again."

Delaney sighed and frowned, pulling the silver cross from inside his T-shirt. The chain was long enough that he could see it himself, and he turned it in the light, running his thumb across the worked silver. "In those dark times, she recited her prayers repeatedly and always told the boy afterward that it had been God who had carried her through the darkness. The boy knew that his presence had no power over his mother's demons, that she essentially forgot about him in her misery. He did his best to earn a few coins for firewood or gruel when she fell ill, ensuring his own survival when his mother was suffering. He became accustomed to taking care of himself from an early age, and so, perhaps, it was easier for him when the change came."

Delaney pursed his lips, well aware of Ginger's assessing gaze locked upon him. "The boy, unbeknownst to himself, was *Pyr*, the product of a second mating between a *Pyr* and his destined mate. In her dark moods, his mother spoke of having been seduced by the Devil, but the boy thought little of this reference. He also had no knowledge of his older brother, for his mother never spoke of Donovan. He had ceased to exist for her when he showed signs of carrying the same taint as his father. If the boy had known that, the upheaval in their small home when his own change occurred might not have surprised him."

Delaney turned his hand, still amazed by the power of his body. "It began with his thumbnail. He had a bad dream and awakened in a cold sweat, only to discover that his left thumbnail had become a dragon's talon. He was terrified by this, but the nail reverted to its normal shape. He was certain that he had imagined the incident, or that it had been part of his nightmare."

"It was only the beginning of his nightmare," Erik suggested, and Delaney nodded rueful agreement.

"The same thing happened again, when a neighbor's

son made a disparaging remark about the boy's mother. They scuffled and fought in the street, as boys will do, the taunts rousing the ire of this mother's son. The fight halted suddenly, the neighbor's son fleeing the fight. After that, they called the boy Dragon Eyes."

Erik folded his arms across his chest, his tone reasonable and encouraging. "Because the fight roused your ire, and your body began to shift to its fighting pose."

Delaney nodded. "I had no idea what was happening to me or why." He realized he had shifted from using third person to first, acknowledging that the story was about himself, but knew the pretense had been a thin one all along.

"Puberty can be challenging for even the most informed *Pyr*," agreed Erik when Delaney hesitated.

"Which wasn't me. The third incident was the most terrifying. I hauled kegs for a quartermaster who was provisioning a ship in the harbor. It was hard work and an endless day. He was known to not pay fairly, but my mother was in her bed and we needed to eat. I feared for her health that time, and wished to have the healer call. The healer demanded to be paid in advance.

"And so, I spent a day and the better part of a night loading his ship. Backbreaking work, with him always insisting that it had to be done faster. The only other boy who'd taken the job collapsed on the pier in exhaustion and the quartermaster insisted he wouldn't be paid. I was determined to not be cheated, so I kept working. When I was done, he dared to say it had been done too slowly. He cast me a penny, one penny for a shilling's work, and made to leave."

Delaney took a deep breath. "I thought of my mother, alone all day and night and in who knew what state, and I was furious that I should fail her because this man was a cheat. My body shifted shape before I knew what was happening. It was dark on the pier, late and quiet, with only the sound of the lapping of the sea against the wharf and the moon casting its silver light. The change didn't seem real to me then, but the power of the dragon form was overwhelming. My rage filled me and with my newfound strength, I attacked the quartermaster to collect my due."

He swallowed. "He had no chance to scream."

Delaney heard Ginger catch her breath and didn't even glance her way.

"I doubt anyone missed him," Niall said quietly.

Delaney couldn't look at Ginger, couldn't face the condemnation he knew he'd see in her eyes. His words fell more quickly. "I took his purse. I went to the healer and paid her in advance. I went home to my mother. She had worsened and there was no fire in the grate, since she hadn't had the strength to tend the one I'd left. I rekindled it to a blaze, indifferent to the cost of the fuel, and turned to find her gaze upon me.

"'You are just like him,' she said, hatred in her tone. I told her I didn't understand what she meant, but she pointed to my hand. The quartermaster's blood was under my nails. She sat up, finding new strength in her terror, and pointed at me. 'Just like him!' she cried. 'The Devil's own spawn!'

"I still didn't understand her, but she dared me to show her what I truly was. And then I knew; I knew that she had known about this power of mine but had chosen to leave me in ignorance. And I, fourteen years of age, resented bitterly that she had not told me all she knew. I was angry that she had kept me in darkness and left me to discover the truth in my own fear."

He played with the cross. "So I did what she asked. I thought it the least that she deserved. In anger I shifted shape again, liking the power of my coiled tail, the gleam of my scales, the majesty of my own appearance. I turned to look upon her and she screamed in terror.

By the time the healer came running, I had changed to
my normal shape again. My mother was babbling about
demons, only coherent when she insisted that I leave her
house. The healer eyed the quartermaster's velvet purse,
the red stain under my nails, and turned her face away
as she told me I'd best leave."

He traced a pattern on the table with one fingertip,
his chest tight with the heartache of that night. "And so
I did, certain I'd never go back."

"But you must have," Ginger said.

Delaney glanced up, surprised to find encouragement
in her expression.

"You have her cross," she said. He was surprised that
she had guessed the origin of the necklace.

"I always wondered why you wore it," Erik said.
"It's not a common symbol for the *Pyr* to choose for
adornment."

Delaney looked down at the silver emblem. "It means
something different to me. It reminds me of a promise
I made."

"What happened when you went back?" Ginger
asked.

"Why did you go back?" Niall asked.

"I heard that my mother was failing. It was years later
and I had surreptitiously ensured that I knew about her
health. She had borne me. She had raised me. She was
my mother and I loved her, even if she couldn't love
what I was. I worried about her periods of darkness, and
how she would survive them with no one to help her.
So I had those I would visit and ask, and I had those
who would take some coin to her or sit with her at my
behest."

Delaney frowned. "The story spread that I had killed
the quartermaster, which was true, although the details
embroidered on the tale had little resemblance to the
truth. The neighbors were somewhat afraid of me, then,

and quick to comply with my requests. I always ensured that there was some consideration for them in it, and so I had several wary allies. The boy who had first called me Dragon Eyes was one of the most helpful."

He shrugged. "And so I heard when she fell more seriously ill, and so I went to her when I believed she was at her last. I had hoped we could reconcile before it was too late. I had met Donovan by then, but it would be centuries before I learned that we were more than two of a kind, that we were in fact brothers. Knowing that there were other *Pyr* had given me a kind of confidence and a new life, but still I yearned for my mother's blessing. So I returned to our small home in the night, shocked after my absence by its simplicity."

"It hadn't changed," Erik guessed, "but you had."

Delaney nodded and swallowed. "She was sleeping when I arrived, her breath so shallow that I thought I was too late. Her hair had turned to gray and her face was creased, her knuckles swollen on her lined hands. I could see that she was smaller beneath the blankets, that she had worn to sinew and bone in this last illness, and I blamed myself for the fading of her rose. The cross was clutched in her hand, her fingers closed over it so ferociously that I knew she yet lived."

"I sat by the fire, listening to her sleeping breath, and waited. I was more richly attired in those days, a man where once I had been a boy. The beams seemed lower to me, the space more confining than once it had been. Twenty years had passed, but when she awakened, she knew me instantly." He smiled sadly. "She looked me over, then asked if I had come to claim her soul."

Delaney paused and Ginger leaned closer. "She thought you were evil?"

"She thought my powers were the mark of the Devil. Years before I hadn't been able to argue with her."

"But by then, you had learned," Erik said softly.

Delaney nodded, aware of the way Ginger looked avidly between them. "I told her then that I had found others of my kind, that I was learning the powers of my body. I told her the story of the *Pyr*, or at least as much as I knew of it then."

"What's that?" Ginger asked, and there was no denying her interest.

The fact that she hadn't held his nature against him before, and that she was unlikely to do so in future, warmed corners of Delaney's heart that even the firestorm couldn't reach.

And that was why he had to tell her the rest of the story.

Chapter 17

Delaney nodded at Erik, who smiled slightly. "In the beginning," Erik said, and the others straightened. They all knew this passage as well as they knew their own names.

"In the beginning, there was the fire," the *Pyr* said in unison.

Delaney watched Ginger look between them in amazement, enjoying the opportunity to study her while her gaze was averted from him. Her amber earrings flashed as she moved, seemingly lit by some internal fire.

Just as Ginger was illuminated by her inner spark. The firestorm flattered her coloring, caressing her features and illuminating the sparkle of her eyes, but Delaney knew she would always have that radiance he found so attractive. She was vital, and alive, and chose to live her life actively and engaged.

He wished with everything within him that things could have been different for them.

"And the fire burned hot because it was cradled by the earth," Thorolf continued.

"The fire burned bright because it was nurtured by

the air," Niall said. "The fire burned lower only when it was quenched by the water."

Erik continued. "And these were the four elements of divine design, of which all would be built and with which all would be destroyed."

Eileen smiled, rocking Zoë as she spoke. "And the elements were placed at the cornerstones of the material world and it was good."

Erik surveyed Eileen, his eyes gleaming. "But the elements were alone and undefended, incapable of communicating with one another, snared within the matter that was theirs to control." They looked as one at their sleeping child.

Niall continued. "And so, out of the endless void was created a race of guardians whose appointed task was to protect and defend the integrity of the four sacred elements."

"They were given powers, the better to fulfill their responsibilities," Thorolf said.

Erik nodded. "They were given strength and cunning and longevity to safeguard the treasures surrendered to their stewardship. To them alone would the elements respond."

He paused pointedly, then Delaney and the others concluded the story in unison. "These guardians were—and are—the *Pyr*."

"Wow," Ginger said, her bright gaze flicking to Delaney again. Her smile made his heart skip a beat and his chest clench. "What did she say to that?"

"Not much, at least not initially," Delaney admitted. He felt uncharacteristically expansive and leaned closer to Ginger. "She told me that my father had seduced and deceived her. She told me about wickedness and the wages of sin. She told me to repent, but then she faltered to silence, perhaps aware that I couldn't repent of my body's powers."

Delaney frowned in memory. "We sat together as the fire died to embers, only the crackle in the grate interrupting the silence between us. Her eyes closed and her breath became softer, so hard to discern that I feared she was gone. I went to her side, touched her hand, and found it colder." He sighed. "Even after all she had said, I couldn't imagine her being gone, despite the differences between us."

His words stumbled and Ginger reached for him, her hand closing over his. It was meant to be a gesture of encouragement, but the brilliant spark of the firestorm that emanated from the point of contact made Delaney close his eyes.

He couldn't think about his failures, not now.

He couldn't help but savor the sweet heat of desire that rolled through his body, and his mouth went dry. He thought of Ginger's softness against him, her pale smooth curves, her laughter in bed, and he wanted her with a ferocity that startled him.

He opened his eyes to find her flushed and smiling at him. *Wow*, she mouthed, then pretended to fan herself with her other hand. *Hot stuff.*

Delaney found himself smiling at her, liking that she didn't pull her hand away. He turned his own hand, closing his fingers over hers. The firestorm's heat pulsed and throbbed, radiating from their interlocked hands and bathing the kitchen in golden light. He felt the delicacy of Ginger's fingers, knew they were stronger than they appeared.

Just as she was both delicate and strong.

"Of course, you were sad," she said. "She was your mom and the one who knew you best."

Delaney nodded. "She had loved and nurtured me as a child; she had gone without to give to me; and I hadn't wanted our estrangement to be permanent. I held her cold hand in mine and bowed my head and regretted that things had been as they were, regretted that I had failed her and could not have done otherwise. I might have wept, but I realized that her eyes had opened and she was watching me."

"She hadn't yet gone," Erik murmured.

"And she knew that monsters don't have compassion," Ginger whispered.

Maybe that had been it. Delaney didn't know. He swallowed, that bittersweet parting still vivid in his thoughts. "Her hand tightened every so slightly over mine, then she shook her head. 'I cannot know the mind of God,' she said. 'I cannot say I know why each of us is given the burdens we carry. I cannot explain why I was so plagued by darkness in my own life, or why I found your father alluring, or how it is that I bore a son with such a taint as yours.'"

Delaney could see that room again with startling clarity, only the firm grasp of Ginger's fingers keeping him in the present. "She reached for the cross that hung around her neck. 'But I must trust in the wisdom of God. I must trust that all has a purpose and that there is a divine plan. That conviction is the only thing that has carried me through the shadows. My faith has been the light in the darkness. I did my best with you. I tried my best and I can only believe that He did not assign a greater burden to me than what I could carry.'" She removed the chain she had always worn and gave it to me, insisting that I put it around my own neck."

"So that's when you got it," Ginger murmured. Delaney saw approval in her eyes.

"I don't know what she expected, but no one smote me and the cross didn't melt on contact. She looked and she waited, and then she spoke again. 'I do not know what you are, or why you are, Delaney, but you are my son, and I have loved you best of all. I have taught you what I know, and I cannot believe that you are truly wicked, or that you are forever lost. I must trust that there is a purpose, and that maybe this tale of guardians is your truth. I cannot know. But you must promise me one thing.' And I vowed to pledge anything to her. 'You must wear my cross, you must remember my faith, and you must use whatever powers you have in service to goodness.'"

"I like that," Ginger said. "She tried to accept your nature and accommodate it at the end. That's love at work."

Delaney didn't know. He only remembered the power of his relief, and his determination to keep that vow. "I made that promise and then she fell back, exhausted. I would have talked more, but her eyes closed. I sat with her as the fire burned down to nothing."

He rose to his feet and turned away, feeling vulnerable in the strength of his grief. He kept his back to the others as he composed himself, feeling the weight of Ginger's gaze upon him. "She didn't awaken again," he said finally, his voice husky.

"And you've never taken it off," Ginger guessed.

He pivoted to face her, knowing that he looked defiant. "And I never will, not until I keep my pledge to her." He squared his shoulders. "And this is the point. You're all so certain that you understand, that Magnus is driving my choices, that I don't have the will to live, that you can persuade me to follow the course you would choose."

Delaney moved back to the table, and tapped his finger on it. Sharing his story had restored his resolve and made him determined to succeed, and he needed his fellows to see his conviction. "But this is the choice I want to make. Eliminating the Elixir is what I can do to be of service to the *Pyr* and to the world at large: it's how I can be a guardian of the elements and how I can use my powers for goodness. It's how I can fulfill that promise to my mother. And that's why you're not going to change my mind. I halfway think I was born to do this."

He let them look, let them realize the extent of his conviction, then left the kitchen before they could argue with him. Delaney headed for the barn, for livestock and manure and an opinionated rooster, for simplicity and clarity and honesty.

It was, he knew, exactly what he could have from Ginger, if he had the audacity to ask for it. If his life had been different. If his destiny had shaped him in another way.

But as it was, he had to have the same kind of faith his mother had possessed, and he had to do his best to make a difference.

It was all over for Ginger.

Resistance was futile. Any man who could act with honor and decency, to surrender his own life to keep a promise made to his mother on her deathbed, was a man she could love with all her heart.

Delaney might have thought that his story would turn her against him—because he had killed the quartermaster in cold blood—but to her, the story showed that his mother had instilled good in her son. Delaney had taken care of his mother, even when they were estranged. He had gone back to see her at the end, in an attempt to reconcile. He had made the promise she'd asked of him, and he was trying to keep it.

Delaney had been so vehement, so obviously under duress that Ginger was reminded of a wound rubbed raw. He chose the same phrases she had used the night before, but she would have known just by his manner that he was sharing his own past.

For the first time.

As fearful as she'd been of what he'd say, she was honored by his trust.

And in the end, his story simply reaffirmed Ginger's conviction that Delaney was a keeper. His mother's acceptance of his nature—inasmuch as she had been capable of coming to terms with his reality—and his obvious relief at their reconciliation also showed her the power of love.

Ginger liked that a lot.

It also reminded her of her grandmother's ability to find the good in things, to overcome adversity, to accept things as they were and to strive for something better. It made her think about accommodating a concession to ensure the greater good. It made her realize that she hadn't done so badly growing up without her parents— she'd had love, and maybe that was all a child needed to flourish.

She was also sure the *Pyr* needed more in their company who were like Delaney. Her mouth went dry when she considered how Delaney was denying his own desire and impulse to keep his promise to her. She thought about Rafferty's poem and Magnus's plan and knew she was the only one who could change Delaney's mind.

And there was only one way to do it. She had to take a calculated risk and satisfy the firestorm. She had to conceive his son and believe in the future. She had to trust in a higher power, in the wisdom of their Great Wyvern maybe, and follow her own instinct to trust Delaney.

Ginger was sure that Delaney wouldn't be able to abandon his son, that he wouldn't condemn another *Pyr* to grow up without a father as he had done. She was sure not only that he would be a wonderful father, but that she could have the kind of love with him that her parents had shared.

They had an instinctive connection, one that Ginger had sensed immediately. The firestorm heightened it, but wasn't the root of it. Ginger, like Delaney's mother, chose to believe that she'd been given the chance to meet

Delaney for a reason. She chose to believe she would be the light that pulled him back from the shadows.

And if she lost Delaney, somehow in some way, and was compelled to raise his child alone, well, she'd do her best to tell the boy about his father and his legacy. She had a feeling that the other *Pyr* wouldn't abandon her or the child, that she wouldn't be left alone to face this challenge.

She believed that Delaney was her destined mate, in every possible way, no matter how things might shake out after she surrendered to the firestorm. Had her parents regretted having so little time together? Ginger couldn't believe they would have chosen differently, even knowing their marriage would be cut short by tragedy.

She was in. She had to take a chance. She was going to make the most of opportunity, and she was going to do that immediately.

Ginger decided all of this in a heartbeat after Delaney's departure. The door had barely shut behind him when she was on her feet.

"Where are you going?" Niall asked. "We need to make a plan. Delaney isn't going to change his mind. . . ."

"I have to talk to him," Ginger said, grabbing her coat.

"I don't think talking is going to make any difference," Niall noted.

"You never know." Eileen smiled, hiding her expression as she bent to kiss her baby. Ginger knew that the other woman understood that Ginger's plan didn't just include talking.

"We should all talk to him," Erik said as he rose to his feet, but Eileen nudged his foot with her own.

Sit, she mouthed to him.

Ginger was amused as the leader of the *Pyr* glanced

between Ginger and his own partner, his inclination clear. "But—"

"Sit," Eileen said aloud, and raised her eyebrows to emphasize her command. Erik sat, his manner cautious and watchful as he tried to understand.

Eileen smiled approval, which only seemed to mystify him. "I thought you were the one with foresight," she teased.

Erik frowned.

"And the one who believed every firestorm should be satisfied," she murmured, and Erik's features lit with understanding.

"I'll go with Ginger," Niall said.

"No, you won't," Eileen said sternly.

"Sit," Erik commanded. "Leave this to Ginger."

Niall looked at Erik, then at Ginger as he rose to his feet. "But two of us together—"

"Will just be in the way," Eileen said firmly. "Men," she muttered, rolling her eyes. "Go ahead, Ginger. I'll make sure you have your privacy."

"Oh!" Niall said, and sat down heavily.

"Why don't you *Pyr* do something useful and breathe some smoke?" Eileen asked brightly.

Ginger flushed that they all knew her intention, but she didn't care. She practically flew out the door, her coat open in the cold, and followed Delaney's tracks.

He'd chosen the old barn, which made her smile. It was her favorite place and the loft was full of fresh hay.

Perfect.

Delaney felt raw.

He'd never told anyone about his mother's death. On one hand, he felt as if he'd exposed something sacred and left it undefended; on the other, he knew that he'd had to share the story to make the *Pyr* understand the depth of his conviction.

He hadn't anticipated how powerfully Ginger would respond, much less how her response had affected him. That connection between them kept getting stronger, independent of the firestorm's increased heat. He still wanted her, but he wanted more than sex.

He wanted to be partners.

He wanted to conceive that son, and stay with Ginger to raise him. He wanted to build a life together with her, learn precisely what made her laugh, hear her stories and tell her more of his own. He wanted to help her convert the farm to an organic operation and watch her persuade people to make changes with her own passion for local produce.

He wanted a future, more than he had ever wanted one before.

Was this a dangerous temptation? Ginger was the only one who threatened the strength of his resolve. She was the only one who tempted him to find another solution.

But there wasn't one. Delaney knew it. He knew what he had to do, but he realized that he had to collect his thoughts first.

He went into the old barn, needing more of a link to the past than the new efficient barn offered. There were no animals in this structure, which had to be more than one hundred years old. The foundation was field-stone and the roof was steel, the barn itself built of wood that had weathered to a silvery patina. The doors were painted dark red. It was precisely as a barn should be, in Delaney's estimation.

He forced open the door against the drifted snow and took a deep breath once he stood in the darkened interior. The barn smelled of manure and earth, but mostly of fresh hay. Light came through the walls like slivers of white, the old wood planks having shrunk as they aged.

He'd entered in the basement, where livestock had

once been kept and the walls were of exposed fieldstone. It was clean, but had a welcome organic smell. Delaney ignored the few lightbulbs hanging from the ceiling, preferring to move in the darkness. He climbed the stairs to the main floor, and found an old red tractor parked in the middle. There were double doors opposite and he knew that the earth must be mounded into a ramp on the side away from the house.

There was a loft and the scent of fresh hay was stronger. Delaney climbed the ladder and smiled at the neatly stacked bundles of golden hay. The loft was only half full, but redolent of that sweet scent of late summer. The wind whistled a little through the cracks, and the air was chilly. He thought he could hear the snow falling ceaselessly outside, blanketing the building in pristine white.

He stood and simply listened, loving this place.

Delaney glanced over his shoulder at a slight sound in the barn below. He heard someone walk closer, following his footsteps. The glow of the firestorm told him who it was, even as he recognized the sound of Ginger's steps.

She'd come to console him. He'd already guessed at the strength of her compassion and couldn't deny himself one last taste of it. He waited, still and silent, guessing that she'd find him easily.

Because of the firestorm?

Or because she'd instinctively guessed where he'd gone?

Ginger appeared at the top of the ladder, her hair framing her face like a golden halo. She smiled and something melted within Delaney, something that spelled disaster for his plan.

"You can't change my mind," he said, not nearly as convinced of that as he wanted to be.

Her eyes danced. "Don't be so sure of that, hotshot."

Her confidence shook him, but he couldn't turn away
from her.

The firestorm's spark danced in her eyes, flushed her
cheeks, and was reflected in the amber of her earrings.
She was so alluring that he knew he'd never be able to
resist her.

She reached the top of the ladder and swung her
leg around—he instinctively stepped closer to offer his
hand to help her. She clasped his fingers, her own icily
cold, and they gasped in unison at the hot spark of the
firestorm's demand. It sizzled through Delaney, sending
a white heat through his veins that was matched only by
the intensity of his desire.

Their gazes caught and held, the firestorm electric in
its intensity. He knew he should step away. He knew he
couldn't risk even one kiss. He knew that sating the firestorm would be unfair to her.

But Ginger undermined his every conviction. She was
warm under her coat, warm and soft and inviting. She
leaned against him, her breasts crushed against his chest.
They fit together as perfectly as they had the first night,
the sparks of the firestorm dancing from their entwined
bodies with glittering intensity. The heat took Delaney's
breath away.

"I came to offer you a deal," Ginger whispered, and
Delaney ached to give her whatever she wanted of him.

"What kind of deal?" His voice was husky, the sizzle
of heat between them making his throat tight.

Ginger licked her lips and took a breath. "I know
what you believe you have to do and why you believe it.
I'm not nearly so sure you're right about the price you'll
have to pay."

Delaney frowned, but she reached up and touched a
fingertip to his lips to silence him. His lips warmed beneath her touch. "Rafferty left a verse on the kitchen
table. I saw him writing it, but I thought it was just

notes." She pulled a sheet of paper out of her pocket and showed it to him. "I read it before and didn't understand, but I think it's about you."

> *The Outcast patrols shadows deep,*
> *Defending the* Pyr *while they sleep.*
> *When darkness becomes his domain,*
> *He risks losing his path back again.*
> *Vigilant in the endless night*
> *Yet drawn by the firestorm's light.*
> *But can one so at ease in dark*
> *Surrender fully to love's spark?*
> *Will he dare to leave his task,*
> *Choose himself first instead of last?*

Delaney read it twice, surprised at how accurately it told of his struggle. His heart began to pound with the promise offered by the verse—if he trusted his instincts, if he allowed himself the chance to be with Ginger, he might have a different fate than the one he'd envisioned.

He might have a future.

They might have a future.

"I think you have a choice," Ginger said, then her voice hardened. "I have to believe that you have a choice. It's just the way I am."

Delaney found himself smiling. He couldn't think of anyone more inclined to make her own choices and make them work than Ginger.

She smiled at him. "Did you ever think," she said softly, "that there was a reason why you didn't die and why the Elixir didn't turn you bad?"

"All the time," Delaney said. "It's so I can destroy the Elixir."

"Maybe." She looked him in the eye. "Or maybe it's because you were given a second chance."

"What does that mean?"

"That most people who cheat death try to make the most of life, not to figure out how best to commit suicide."

He stared at her in surprise.

"You're thinking you need to die to make everything come right, but I'm thinking you were given the chance to live again in order to make a difference by living."

It was a tempting possibility.

"So my offer is that if you'll choose to try to come back, to try to give us a chance, then I'll surrender to the firestorm right now." Ginger swallowed and squared her shoulders. "I'll have your son and raise him as well as I can, no matter how it works out with the Elixir."

Delaney was awed by the magnitude of her gift. "But what about you? You grew up without your parents and you said—"

"I was thinking of only half the story. I was conceived in love, and I was raised with love, and that really is what matters." Her smile turned mischievous. "I think I came out all right, all things considered."

"You certainly did."

"So, what do you say, hotshot? Want to make a deal?"

"It's an offer I can't refuse," Delaney said, surprised at the way hope surged through him at his agreement. He felt lighter and stronger, tempered into something greater than he had been.

Because of his choice.

Delaney pulled Ginger closer before he could stop himself. She came willingly, winding her arms around his neck and pulling him down for a kiss. Delaney heard her heart pound against his own, felt her breath on his cheek, and was surrounded by her sweet perfume. He felt her stretch to her toes, then his lips were on hers and he was lost.

Lost and—for the moment—unwilling to be found.
The firestorm shot through him like a beam of white
light, cauterizing, cleansing, purifying. He felt the Elixir's grasp upon him weaken. He felt the shadow of his
nightmares shrink from that brilliant light and disperse.
He felt the spark of the divine within him kindle to new
brightness and burn brighter and hotter than it had ever
before.

And he knew that even after the firestorm was sated,
its heat would sustain him forever.

Because of Ginger.

Something changed the moment that Delaney accepted Ginger's offer. In fact, it changed when he read
the verse. She saw the spark leap in his eyes and wondered what had happened to those shadows of pain.

They were gone.

Then he kissed her with such ardor that every coherent thought was driven from her head. The sheet of
paper with the verse fell to the floor of the loft and Ginger didn't care. Ginger didn't want to think; she wanted
to feel. She'd made her choice and she wanted to remember this moment forever.

Regardless of what happened next.

Delaney's kiss was hot yet reverent, and she sensed
that he was amazed by her choice. Ginger didn't want
him to think about it too much, didn't want him to stop
as he had the night before. She pushed him back toward the piled hay bales. He shrugged off his jacket and
spread it across the hay, then Ginger flung hers beside it.
Delaney fell backward, taking her with him but bracing
her against the fall with his body.

He was protective.

He was honorable.

He had promised to try to come back.

Ginger fell across his chest, framed his face in her

hands, and kissed him as if this would be the last kiss ever. His hands locked around her waist and he held her on top of him, even as their tongues danced. Sparks were flying, leaping from her fingertips, emanating from their lips. Every point their bodies touched was radiant and warm, dispelling the chill of the barn and ensuring there was nothing in Ginger's world but Delaney.

She had her hands beneath his shirt in a heartbeat, pulling the hem loose from his jeans. She ran her hands over his ribs and up his chest, watching at the sizzle of golden light that followed her caress. His nipples were taut and Ginger bent to kiss one, teasing the peak with her teeth and tongue until he squirmed. He was all muscle, solid strength, and she thought about his power to change into a fearsome and beautiful dragon. His body was a marvel to her, alien and beautiful even in human form.

She wanted to see all of it.

She tugged his shirt over his shoulders, smiling as the silver cross bounced against his tanned skin. He lay back against the hay at one push from her fingertip and let her look. There wasn't a spare ounce of flesh, every inch of him tanned and powerful. His eyes gleamed as he watched her climb astride him.

He was magnificent, especially as he was determined to use his power for good. She liked his story, liked his love for his mother, liked that he had not only tried to reconcile but that he had succeeded. It was no wonder his mother had seen the good in him—Ginger could see it, too.

"Now I have you right where I want you," Ginger growled, bracing her hands on either side of his shoulders. Delaney's smile flashed with sudden brilliance. His eyes shone a clear green, filled with purpose and reverence.

"Is that right?" he teased, and Ginger knew he intended to turn the tables on her. Before he could move, she put her hands on the front of his jeans, his erection large and hard beneath her hands. He gasped at her sure touch and froze for a moment.

That was all the time Ginger needed to peel open his jeans and take him in her mouth.

She loved his groan of surrender.

She had Delaney naked and ready, and right where she wanted him. Ginger teased and tormented him, using the firestorm's sparks to drive him to distraction. He got larger and harder and less coherent, the sheer power of his body amazing her. When she thought he couldn't take any more, she knelt over him and pulled off her own shirt.

She let him look at her lacy bra and lifted his hands so that he caressed her breasts. They shared an incendiary kiss, then she removed the bra and flung it away. She was treated again to his smile.

"It's what's inside that counts," he murmured, his words sending a low rumble through Ginger.

"You've got that right," she agreed, seeing that she'd surprised him again. She lay down beside him and wriggled out of her jeans, kicking them aside. She reached for her underwear, but he moved quickly to catch her hands in his.

"Let me," he whispered, his eyes glowing with intent.

Ginger's mouth went dry and she nodded mutely, unable to summon a word of protest. She knew what he was going to do, and arched her back as his mouth closed over her. She saw her panties fly across the loft as he flung them aside and couldn't have cared less. There was nothing beyond the intoxicating caress of Delaney's tongue and the magic he made with his hands.

She'd never forget this, no matter how long she lived.

And she'd never regret this choice.

She saw the radiance of the firestorm change hue, becoming whiter as Delaney roused her passion to a fever pitch. Her blood simmered, turning to molten lava in her veins. She tingled and shimmered, desire escalating moment by moment until she was sure she'd explode. She tasted the salt of sweat on her upper lip and felt the sheen of perspiration on her skin. Delaney was relentless, his sure touch inciting her desire as nothing else could have done. Ginger heard herself moan. She felt herself writhe. She ached to have him inside her, stretching and filling her. She didn't want to find her own release alone, but only with him.

Together.

"Delaney," she gasped. "Together," she managed to say, and felt him move immediately. He held himself over her, running his tongue over the length of her body. The contact point sizzled, shooting brilliant yellow sparks as he eased his length atop hers. He braced his elbows on either side of her shoulders and bent to kiss her deeply. Ginger welcomed his kiss, then locked her knees around his waist, urging him to make their union complete.

He lifted his head, holding her gaze as he eased into her. Ginger swallowed at the size of him. She saw his concern. She saw his admiration of her. She felt a keen sense that both of them had been coming toward this point in time, this point of union, this nexus of choice.

There was no turning back.

This moment would change them both forever.

And Ginger welcomed that as surely as she welcomed Delaney's heat. When he was fully inside her, he closed his eyes and sighed, bending to touch his lips to her shoulder. Ginger caught him close and blinked back her tears, overwhelmed by the power of the connection she felt with him.

"I'll never forget," she vowed, and he kissed her ear.

"No. Never," he agreed, his voice rough with emotion.

Then he began to move within her. His expression was intense, almost fierce, and when his gaze locked with hers, Ginger's heart pounded. His eyes were bright green, devoid of shadows or doubt.

The firestorm flickered and heated, burning with new fervor, hotter and brighter than ever it had been. It was radiant between them, making their skin glisten and their hearts race. Ginger could have been on a sunny beach, or even merging with the sun itself. She'd never felt such heat, or burned with such desire, but she couldn't imagine declining its pleasure.

She kissed Delaney instead.

She felt his heart match its pace to hers and caught her breath at the sensation. He smiled, and she felt the rhythm of his breath, realized that it too matched her own. His eyes glittered, reminding her of all he was, and Ginger dug her nails into his shoulders, only wanting more.

Delaney moved slowly, his strokes sure, and Ginger was sure he meant to prolong the moment as long as possible.

But the sensation was too much for her to last. She was too aroused and too emotional, and Ginger felt the crescendo rise within her all too soon. As soon as she trembled, he smiled. That was the sight that sent her over the edge. Ginger felt the tide roll through her—she gripped Delaney's shoulders, saw the sparks fly, and hung on as long as she could.

When she shouted with the force of her release, Delaney exploded, too. She felt his body go taut not a heartbeat after hers, heard his shout of joy. She could have sworn she felt the hot cascade of his semen inside her, then he leaned his head against her shoulder. They were both panting and when she kissed his temple, she tasted salt. Ginger smiled and held him close, recognizing that he still braced his weight over her.

Protective.

Dragons were supposed to protect and defend their treasures, weren't they? Ginger's smile broadened as her eyes closed. She let herself sleep, safe in Delaney's embrace.

Chapter 18

Delaney slowly caught his breath and steadied his pulse. He stared down at Ginger, her hair spread across the hay. She wore nothing except those amber earrings, and it occurred to him that they might have meaning to her. It would be like Ginger to wear something from her family, or jewelry that had been a gift from someone she loved. She was filled with more love than anyone he had ever known, and she shared it willingly.

She was a marvel.

And she had made him whole again. He wanted to pick up that piece of paper and read the verse again, but he didn't want to move away from Ginger. How could he have ever resisted her?

Delaney traced a fingertip along the satisfied curve of her lips, admiration and affection vying for the upper hand in his thoughts. He was so busy studying her that it took a moment for him to realize what had changed.

There was no spark.

No light leapt between his fingertip and Ginger's skin.

In fact, the loft was feeling a bit chilly. The light had changed, taking on a cold, bluish tinge instead of the warm gold of the firestorm.

Impossible.

Delaney touched her again, his eyes widening in shock at the evidence before him. There was no spark.

Which meant the firestorm had been sated.

Which meant Ginger would bear his son.

He remembered Rafferty's conviction that Ginger's pills would fail, and knew that his choice was the change that had made it possible.

For a moment, his chest tightened in awe of what they had done. He could envision Ginger with their baby, and he could imagine how she would take the challenge of pregnancy—or anything else—in stride. He knew she would always have a smile and a positive attitude, as well as a determination to find a solution.

He wanted with all his heart and soul to be beside her every step of the way.

But his thumbnail had turned almost completely red. It wasn't a natural red. It was a pulsing, angry red, the red of the Elixir. It was the taint of something other than the Elixir, because Delaney could feel that the Elixir had been banished from his body. There was no shadow in his thoughts, no dread in his view of the future, no dark terror of what would be.

No conviction that a dire future awaited them all.

He stared at his nail and wondered what Magnus had done to him. Ginger had said that Magnus had intended to replace Cinnabar with Delaney, and he wondered now what Magnus might have done to prepare for that possibility. He was turning into Cinnabar, turning as red as that *Pyr* had so many centuries before. The red was claiming his body in steady increments.

Delaney pushed to his feet in his agitation. He was still tainted, but in his body instead of his soul. He still posed a threat to Ginger and their son. He still had to destroy the Elixir, and though he would try to return to her and keep his vow, he had to ensure that his mate and son had a better future than they would if he did nothing.

If anything, the fact that she would have his son redoubled his determination to do whatever was necessary to destroy the Elixir forever. Delaney couldn't father a child, only to let that young *Pyr* inherit a toxic legacy. He wouldn't let his nightmare come true in his son's life. The *Pyr* were charged to defend the treasures of the earth, and both Ginger and Delaney's unborn son counted.

He had to do what only he was capable of doing.

He had to meet his fate.

Whatever it proved to be.

Delaney tucked Ginger beneath her coat with care, then kissed her cheek. He dressed quickly, then paused at the top of the ladder for one last look. He wished he could talk to her one last time, wished he could explain, but he didn't want to awaken her.

With sudden clarity, he knew how to tell her that he wouldn't forget his vow. Delaney removed his mother's cross, cradling the silver chain in one hand. He poured the silver into Ginger's open palm, ensuring that the cross was on top.

She stirred slightly in her sleep, but he held his breath and she didn't awaken.

Then he was gone, as swift as the wind, intent on doing what had to be done.

His resolve redoubled, Delaney headed for the barn and the rest of the fertilizer that Ginger didn't want anyway. He picked up the broom inside the door, ready for Reginald, but the rooster didn't rouse himself to attack. The hens were all piled up in one corner, their feathers fluffed out and their heads burrowed down low. Regi-

nald was on the perimeter of the group, his head buried
in his colorful feathers.

The barn was chilly but not frigid and the animals
didn't seem overly troubled by the temperature. Delaney halfway thought it was getting warmer—he could
hear water dripping from the roof.

Delaney moved bags of fertilizer out of the barn,
stacking them out of sight of the house. He'd appropri-
ated a heavy tarp and spread it across the snow, then
stacked the fertilizer bags on top of it. The cows didn't
seem to mind his movement in their space. They stood
with their heads down, tails swishing, and appeared to
be sleepy. The bulls were more curious, but even they
seemed content to simply keep an eye on him.

Delaney didn't touch the rails of their paddocks, and
slipped past them as stealthily as a shadow. He worked
quickly, ignoring the scent of his fellows.

When he had moved as much fertilizer as he thought
he could carry, he shifted shape. He gathered the corners of the tarp in his talons and took flight, lifting the
burden with some effort.

Then he headed toward the sanctuary, his flight low
with the weight he carried. The wind was warmer and
the sky was clearing, and Delaney's heart was full of a
conviction bolstered by his promise to Ginger.

Delaney could choose to do better than his father,
and he could choose to keep his promises.

Both of them.

Magnus was strong, stronger than Rafferty had recalled, but Rafferty was fueled by anger and a passion
for justice. They battled with ferocity, flinging each
other back and forth across the stone chamber. The
rock walls vibrated with each strike, and stone crumbled all around them. Rafferty deliberately cast Magnus against the vial of the Elixir every time he could,

but as he had suggested earlier, it couldn't be shattered with force.

Rafferty felt himself tiring, just as he was struck by Magnus's apparent invincibility. The old *Slayer* was stronger and more resplendent than ever, cocky in his confidence. That bare spot on his chest had grown a twisted partial scale, one that looked more like a nail than a scale. It was thick and gnarled but diminished the size of his weak spot.

Rafferty knew he would have only one chance to strike.

He also noticed that Magnus seemed to be listening for something. Or someone. Either way, the *Slayer* was slightly distracted.

Rafferty had a good idea who Magnus expected to arrive. He knew then that he couldn't risk being injured when Delaney came to the sanctuary, as the younger *Pyr* would likely need his help. Magnus's minions might have been charged to seal off the entrance to the sanctuary after Delaney's arrival.

That meant the *Pyr* wouldn't be able to follow and help him.

Rafferty took a blow deliberately then. He stumbled and let himself fall, feigning a greater injury than he'd had. He endured a flurry of blows from Magnus, pretending to be too feeble to fight back.

"Weakling!" Magnus chortled in old-speak, then breathed dragonfire at Rafferty's fallen form. Rafferty fought the urge to defend himself. *"You should have accepted my offer when you had the chance."*

Rafferty groaned and let his body go limp. Magnus landed beside him, cautious in case it was a feint. Rafferty never moved. The *Slayer* poked at him, then forced open his eye with his gold talons. Rafferty let his eye roll backward.

Then he shifted to human form, flickering rapidly between his two forms. It was a sure sign of distress among his kind and not easily done by choice, but Rafferty did it.

And Magnus was persuaded.

He snorted, then kicked Rafferty. He grabbed the *Pyr*'s leg and dragged him into another chamber, one that was colder. Rafferty guessed it was on the path to the entrance to the sanctuary. The *Slayer* dumped Rafferty behind a pile of rubble, pivoting suddenly at a slight sound.

"Yes!" Magnus hissed, then darted out of sight to hide.

Rafferty barely dared to breathe, suspecting as he did that everything was coming to a culmination.

It was warmer in the barn. Ginger was aware of the change in the temperature even in her sleep. She smiled to herself, amused that she was so attuned to the land and the weather that influenced it. She'd known that the cold and snow couldn't last, and liked that the storm was breaking at roughly the same time that Delaney had made his promise to her.

She took it as a good sign.

She sighed and stretched, feeling very good. There was a moment of surprise when she realized she was alone—again—then she heard a man's tread on the floor of the barn below. Maybe he'd gone to get coffee.

Ginger snuggled beneath her coat, content to be surprised. The hay prickled against her skin, but it was fun to be naked in the barn.

Almost as much fun as having great sex in the barn.

With Delaney.

Ginger sighed and nestled more deeply into her coat's warmth. That was when she realized there was something in her hand. She felt the weight of the silver, and the sinuous tangle of the chain, and knew exactly what she held. Her eyes flew open and she gasped to find Delaney's cross in her grip.

His tread sounded on the ladder, coming steadily closer.

Ginger sat up then, surprised and confused. Why had he given her his mother's cross? Did he mean he was going to keep his promise to her? Ginger had a bad feeling, one that got worse when she saw blond hair appear at the top of the ladder.

Delaney had auburn hair.

She squeaked and drew her bare legs beneath her coat, just in the nick of time. Niall appeared at the top of the ladder. He looked determined and irritated, especially when he saw that Ginger was alone.

"Sorry to interrupt."

Ginger felt herself blush, but she had to ask. "Don't tell me that you heard that we were done."

Much less that the *Pyr* had heard everything.

Had she shouted? Ginger couldn't remember.

Niall averted his gaze and the back of his neck reddened, telling evidence that Ginger had guessed correctly. "Keen hearing," he mumbled. "I heard that you were sleeping." Ginger got dressed quickly while Niall retreated to the ground floor. "Where's Delaney?" he called just as Ginger started down the ladder.

"He must have gone into the house." To her dismay, her bra was slung across a bale of hay, impossible to miss.

Niall frowned. "I guess I could have missed him," he mused, sounding unconvinced. Mostly he appeared to be fascinated with the view of hay bales in the opposite direction of Ginger's bra. "Erik is making a plan, because Sloane's back. You should be part of it, too."

Ginger grabbed her bra and shoved it into her coat pocket. Niall gestured and Ginger stepped out of the barn ahead of him. The wind was much warmer, the snow already melting quickly. There were puddles on the driveway and the sky was clearing overhead. It was late afternoon, but there was a glimmer of sunlight on the horizon.

There was a big black pickup truck and a red sports car parked beside Ginger's pickup. The *Pyr* were gathering to help Delaney, and Ginger liked that a lot.

Niall looked back, scanning the horizon and sniffing the air. Ginger wondered what he was sensing, but before she could ask, he urged her toward the house. "Hurry!"

Thorolf was in Ginger's kitchen, sprawled on the tile floor as he played with two toddler boys. Eileen had made coffee and the kitchen was filled with its enticing scent. Sloane was back, flipping through what looked like an old book, his brows pulled together in a frown. He seemed more intense than previously, his dark hair mussed from his stabbing his fingers through it, and Ginger sensed that he was preparing an argument. Erik was right beside him, his eyes gleaming with purpose.

There were others, though. A tall man with similar coloring to Delaney paced the width of the room. A dark-haired man with blue eyes and broad shoulders leaned against the counter and tapped his toe as he watched the others.

Delaney wasn't in the kitchen, but Ginger assumed he was upstairs, maybe having a quick shower.

There were also two more women in her kitchen. Eileen held her baby against her breast, although Zoë was sleeping soundly now. A boy who looked to be about a year old was playing peekaboo with Thorolf. The tall, athletic-looking woman with dark hair watched and smiled. That boy shared the auburn hair of Delaney and the pacing *Pyr*. A dark-haired boy crawled across the floor, touching the box of tools at the feet of the still man who shared the child's coloring. A blond and petite woman bent to whisper to the child, smiling when he left the box of tools alone and returned to Thorolf.

Ginger's kitchen was full to bursting.

She had no doubt that these men were more *Pyr*. Delaney had said they could sense one another's firestorms. The fact that they were more drawn to the firestorms of those they cared about indicated to Ginger that Delaney had better friends than he realized.

"More *Pyr*?" she asked by way of greeting.

Eileen nodded agreement and smiled. "I hope we're not too much trouble."

"We have to help Delaney," contributed the petite blonde. She smiled in turn. "I'm Sara."

"Alex," said the dark-haired woman. She crossed the kitchen with purpose and offered Ginger her hand.

Ginger appreciated how direct she was and shook hands with her. Alex had a firm grasp and a no-nonsense glint in her eyes that Gran would have liked. "Ginger."

"It's weird, isn't it?" Alex said with a smile that Ginger immediately returned.

"So, you're all . . ." Ginger's voice faltered over the *Pyr*'s preferred choice of term for their partners. It seemed so biological to call women "mates."

"Mates," Alex said firmly.

"Survivors of the firestorm," Eileen added.

Sara slid her hand into the crook of the dark-haired *Pyr*'s elbow. "But not just breeding machines. We're partners for the duration. We provide balance to the *Pyr*, making them more than they can be without us."

Ginger liked the sound of that.

So did Sara's partner. He nodded and smiled slowly, his affection for her clear. "Quinn Tyrrell," he said, offering Ginger his hand. "I'm the Smith."

"Should I know what that means?" Ginger felt an amazing strength in his grip.

"Quinn repairs the armor of the *Pyr*," the man who

resembled Delaney said, offering his hand in turn. "I'm Donovan Shea, Delaney's older brother."

"Drawn to his firestorm?"

Donovan's smile was a quick flash. "You'd better believe it."

Ginger felt that everything was coming together for Delaney. She eyed Quinn. "You mean that you fix the *Pyr*'s dragon scales?"

Eileen answered before Quinn did. "They don't like to admit it, but losing a scale leaves them vulnerable. Quinn can replace a missing scale, for example."

"We have more pressing matters than the surrender of our secrets," Erik said quickly.

Ginger recalled that he was the leader of the *Pyr*. "Do you all have roles?"

"No," Niall said, then shrugged. "Or perhaps we don't all know of our destiny as yet."

"Some of us have affinities for specific elements," Donovan said. "Rafferty has a strong bond with the earth."

"While Niall has a connection with air, and thus the wind," Quinn contributed.

"Quinn, as the Smith, has the closest bond with fire," Erik said.

"While Erik's connection with air gives him the gift of foresight," Donovan contributed.

Ginger sat down, feeling a bit overwhelmed. "What about Delaney?"

Erik exhaled and frowned. "That's why we're here," he said quietly, and Ginger knew they were just as worried about him as she was. "Sloane is the Apothecary of our kind, and he has tried to heal Delaney since he was compelled to ingest the Elixir."

"The firestorm is part of it," Sloane said. "Delaney made the first big step in his recovery when he was drawn to Donovan's firestorm."

Alex cleared her throat and folded her arms across her chest. "*Donovan*'s firestorm?" There was a twinkle in her eyes, though, and Ginger understood that this group knew one another well.

Delaney was lucky to have such a group of friends.

"Alex and Donovan's firestorm," Sloane clarified, and Donovan chuckled. "And I think Delaney has a chance for a complete recovery because his own firestorm has come."

"But?" Ginger asked, hearing the implied qualification. She perched on the lip of a kitchen chair that seemed to have been left vacant just for her. Niall slid a mug of coffee onto the table beside Ginger and she spared him a smile of gratitude.

They were welcoming her to their company, each in their own way, and she appreciated their thoughtfulness.

"Ginger is some kind of cook," Thorolf said.

"Later," Niall chided, and went to make another pot of coffee.

"Well, she is."

"Thanks," Ginger said, smiling at Thorolf.

"Best spaghetti sauce ever," he said with approval.

Erik cleared his throat, managing to sound stern. Thorolf flushed and became quiet.

"There's a piece of the puzzle missing," Sloane said, and Ginger knew what it was.

She gave him the verse Rafferty had written down and his eyes lit with excitement. He passed it around to the *Pyr*, each reading it in turn. There was tangible excitement in the room.

"Something changed," Ginger said. "He promised me that he'd try to come back from destroying the Elixir, and something changed."

"What?" Sara asked, leaning closer.

"The shadows in his eyes. They were gone."

"But what of the red in his nails?" Erik asked.

Ginger was uncertain what he meant.

"He showed me last night," Erik said. "His scales were turning red. And he was cold, so cold."

"Oh!" Ginger said, remembering Magnus's tale. "Magnus said Cinnabar had turned all red when he went to find him. He also said he made Cinnabar be the source of the Elixir, and that Cinnabar was fading."

"What else?" Sloane asked.

"He said Cinnabar had to be replaced, and I had the sense that he was planning for the replacement to be Delaney."

"But he wasn't counting on the firestorm," Sloane said with satisfaction. He opened the book. "This is an old treatise," he said. "It was in code, the kind of letter code that people have always used to hide their secrets. I've broken the code, but the meaning is still pretty elusive. What you said about Delaney shooting blanks made me wonder whether it's about the Elixir."

"Why?" Ginger asked.

"Where is Delaney, anyway?"

"I thought he was in the barn, with you," Erik said, blinking in surprise.

"Ginger thought he came back into the house," Niall said.

Ginger had her bad feeling again. "It's been at least an hour since I've seen him," she said, knowing what that meant.

She dug into her pocket as the *Pyr* exchanged looks.

"He wouldn't have," Eileen said, but her words lacked conviction.

"Delaney left me this," Ginger said, pulling the silver chain from her pocket. "I think he's gone to the Elixir."

"Why would he give you that?" Sara asked.

"I asked him to promise to try to come back." Ginger shrugged. "I think he means he's going to try to keep his promise to me, just as he's trying to keep his promise to his mom."

She felt the ripple of panic slide through the company of *Pyr*.

Erik immediately began to delegate. "We need to find Rafferty and we need to help Delaney. Quinn and Donovan, I want you—"

Before he could say more, there was a shout from the other side of the room.

"No!" the auburn-haired toddler cried with surprising volume. "No, no, no!" He was pointing at the counter and backing away. "No!"

A garnet red salamander appeared over the lip of the sink, its tongue flicking. Ginger was amazed. It must have come up the drain, although that made little sense. The toddler shouted in fear, and both Ginger and Alex moved toward the boy.

Neither managed to take two steps before Donovan intervened.

Chapter 19

The sanctuary was silent.

There was no fresh scent of *Slayer* at all.

Still, Delaney was wary. He knew Magnus could disguise his scent and he wouldn't have been surprised if others had learned the trick.

He waited.

He listened.

He strained his senses, but was certain he was alone.

Delaney didn't imagine that situation would last. He seized one bag of fertilizer, ignoring the cold that permeated his body, and descended into the sanctuary.

It was silent and dark, only the red light of the Elixir itself illuminating the cavern. Delaney paused, certain that the light was more faint than it had been the day before.

More pink than red.

Did the Elixir have an expiry date of its own? He didn't know, and didn't have time to find out.

Reasoning that his stash of fertilizer would be less likely to draw attention once it was within the cavern, he climbed up the rocky incline to the entrance again.

Again and again and again, he brought a bag of fertilizer into the cavern. He was panting from the exertion and soaked with sweat, but he didn't dare to rest. Each trip to the creek side revealed that the sky was an increment darker. Delaney didn't doubt that evening would bring visitors to the Elixir.

That pervasive cold left his hands shaking and his teeth chattering. He didn't let it stop him.

If anything, Delaney worked more quickly, aware of the press of time. His solitude in the sanctuary couldn't last and he had to make this opportunity count.

He wished he had help, because the work would have gone more quickly, but he knew he couldn't have condemned his fellow *Pyr* to this job.

It was his responsibility.

When there were only half a dozen bags left, Delaney was so exhausted that he was dizzy. He eyed the narrow opening and had an idea. He pushed the tarp into the opening, loaded those remaining bags onto it, then let the underground river carry the weight to the bottom. He scurried after it himself.

Two bags slipped from the wet tarp and fell to one side, but Delaney lugged them to the bottom as well. He piled the bags on the tarp again and hauled them to the first opening. He was soaked with perspiration and so cold, but he had to get all of this to the inner sanctuary.

He'd pile it around the vial that held Cinnabar, then ignite it with his dragonfire. The cave would probably collapse and it was likely that he'd be challenged in the last minutes. Delaney didn't expect to stroll out of the sanctuary.

It took precious time to move the fertilizer, time that Delaney resented bitterly. The tarp with its burden wouldn't fit through the portals between chambers and he had to carry each bag individually through the gap.

Then he piled the bags on the tarp again and pulled the entire load to the next portal.

The outer chambers weren't large enough that he could take flight and use the strength of his dragon form to get the task done more quickly.

The minutes ticked by with alarming speed. He was certain every minute noise was the sound of Magnus and the *Slayers* arriving to intercept him, to stop his efforts. He feared he'd get this close to success and fail.

The sanctuary itself was filled with a sickly pink light, one that Delaney found troubling. The Elixir seemed to move with agitation—because it sensed his intent or because something else was changing?

Delaney didn't know and he didn't want to know.

That baleful eye appeared more frequently against the crystal and Delaney had the sense that Cinnabar was watching him. The eye never blinked, though, and he was sure he was too tired to think straight. If he got through this alive, he'd hole up with Ginger, make love, and sleep for a week.

That was motivating enough to give him new strength.

Still, Delaney was exhausted when he finally had the fertilizer stacked around the vial of rock crystal. He stood back and eyed the arrangement, checking for gaps, and his whole body shook.

The cold had seized him in an icy grasp. It didn't help that his clothes had gotten wet on the descent into the cavern. He looked down at his hands, noting that his skin was much redder than normal. It was odd—he would have expected it to be pale. His fingertips could have been frozen, but to his surprise, his nails weren't blue.

They were tinged crimson.

"Perfect timing," a man said, and Delaney spun to find Magnus leaning in the last doorway. He was in human form, his smile as untrustworthy as ever. He was tossing a grayish stone in one hand.

Delaney was wary. "You came to watch the show?"

"I came to clean up the details." Magnus strolled into the sanctuary, so calm that Delaney grew more suspicious. Didn't the *Slayer* see the fertilizer? Didn't he understand what Delaney intended to do?

Delaney stepped back, working his way toward the fertilizer he intended to ignite.

Magnus didn't intervene. "I feel it's only fair to explain everything to you," he said with a cool smile. His gaze flicked to the Elixir, then back to Delaney. "Even though I'm not certain how capable you'll be of thinking about your situation."

Delaney decided to keep Magnus talking. "What situation would that be?"

"Haven't you guessed? Cinnabar is moving past his 'best before' date. That's why the Elixir is turning pink. It's losing its potency, as he ceases to be a useful source."

"So you need another source," Delaney said. "Ginger thought you meant for it to be me."

"You would be ideal," Magnus said. "After all, you've been prepared for the responsibility."

"What do you mean?"

Magnus smiled. "What do you think happened to you in my academy?"

Bitterness nearly choked Delaney. "You forced the Elixir into me."

Magnus wagged a finger at him. "That was only the first part of it. I chose you for this task then, and I made the necessary preparations."

"I don't understand."

"I needed a *Pyr* with blood that ran red. You sufficed as none of the *Slayers* would. I needed a *Pyr* exposed to mercury at consistent levels. Repeat doses of the Elixir took care of that."

"Even though it turned my blood black."

Magnus waved one hand. "A temporary setback. Sigmund believed a firestorm would clarifiy your blood, and he was right. Finally, I needed a *Pyr* with pure quicksilver in his veins."

Delaney was horrified. "That's what you injected into me."

Magnus's smile broadened. "It was Sigmund's experiment, and a pity he didn't survive to follow up and compile his results. Did you have nightmares? That was his suspicion and you had several within the academy before we released you. Such an interesting notion, but one that we have no further time to explore."

"What does time matter?"

"The Elixir is tied to a family of eclipses called a Saros cycle. It grows in potency and diminishes along with the cycle begun when it was created. It took me centuries to figure this out as the records are somewhat elusive—or should I say deceptive—in their explanations."

Magnus strolled into the chamber, waxing eloquent in his explanation, clearly delighted to have an audience. Delaney folded his arms across his chest and let the *Slayer* talk, welcoming the chance to catch his breath before their inevitable fight. "An eclipse can only occur when there is a full moon for a lunar eclipse or a new moon for a solar eclipse, as the moon, sun, and earth must line up for the eclipse to occur."

"The *Pyr* are only affected by lunar eclipses," Delaney said.

"Indeed. So the moon must be full for there to be a lunar eclipse. In order for the eclipse to be visible from the earth, the moon and sun must be near one of the moon's nodes; otherwise the shadow isn't visible to the earth."

"All right."

"Finally, the difference in distance between the moon and the earth determines the totality of the eclipse. At perigee, when they are closest together, the moon's shadow can form a total eclipse. At apogee, when they are farthest apart, the eclipse will be only partial or annual."

"And that follows a regular routine."

"Yes!" Magnus could have been a teacher, proud of his student's perception. Delaney wondered whether there was a gold star in this for him. "All of these are regular cycles: one full moon to the next is a synodic month, which is about twenty-nine and a half days. The sun takes about three hundred forty-six days to travel through all the signs of the zodiac, moving from north node to south and back." Magnus smiled. "I do enjoy that being called a draconic year."

"But less than a solar year."

"Because the moon moves backward through the zodiac. An illusion but one that informs the calculation. Eclipses are all about the perception of the sky from our specific vantage point."

"And the cycle of the moon?"

"Roughly twenty-seven days from perigee to perigee. Which means the entire cycle repeats roughly every eighteen years—6585.322 days, to be precise, which is called a Saros cycle. Any eclipse will occur again, with very similar geometry, in 6585.322 days. All of the eclipses within a family sharing the same geometry are called a Saros cycle." Magnus cleared his throat. "Despite their many frailties, humans figured this out thousands of years ago and have predicted eclipses with great accuracy since the time of the Babylonians."

Magnus strolled closer. "The Saros cycle governs the effectiveness of the Elixir—it waxes and wanes, like the moon each month. I understood when I put the final fatal dose of quicksilver in Cinnabar's veins that it was necessary to create a batch of Elixir at the start of a Saros cycle. Of course."

"Of course."

"Cinnabar formed the Elixir in May, of the year 747."

Magnus smiled. "Allowing for adjustments in the Julian calendar. Of course."

"Of course."

"That was the beginning of Saros series 110, a cycle of seventy-two eclipses." He held up two fingers. "Just two left, one in July of this year and one in July of 2027."

"Then Cinnabar will be useless."

Magnus sighed. "His effectiveness is already fading quickly, which is why I didn't want to leave anything to chance."

"Is there another Saros cycle beginning?"

"How clever you are! The next begins in May 2013, Saros cycle 150, so you see there is a period of overlap." Magnus chuckled. "A window of opportunity, as it were. If I find a recruit by that first eclipse, I will have Elixir through the year 3275."

"You were prepared to wait."

Magnus glanced toward the vial and its pinkish contents. "Yes, but I'm persuaded that sooner is better. You've been quite accommodating, I must say."

"You did hypnotize me to destroy the Elixir."

"It makes it so much more convenient to harvest you, if you are right at the source, so to speak." Magnus stepped closer, his eyes gleaming. He tucked that stone into his pocket again, and Delaney wondered what it was. "It was very obliging of you to comply with my scheme. And now, let's secure the future supply of the Elixir, shall we?"

But Delaney wasn't complying.

"It's not going to be that easy," he said, and shifted shape with lightning speed.

Magnus's eyes flashed and he followed suit, roaring as he took his jade and gold form. He was splendid, bigger than ever, and more robust than ever. His wounds of the day before had healed completely and his eyes shone with pride as Delaney surveyed him in surprise.

"Oh, it still works," he hissed, then laughed.

Delaney wasn't daunted. He took flight and charged.

The leader of the *Slayers* laughed in triumph at the sight of him. "Look at you!" Magnus crowed. "Halfway to becoming the source already!"

Delaney glanced down to find his scales tinged red, as if they had been dipped in blood. Terror made his flight falter. He was changing color—just as Ginger had said that Magnus had told of Cinnabar changing color. The quicksilver in his veins was changing his metabolism.

Could the change Magnus had inflicted upon him be reversed?

Delaney intended to find out. He wasn't down yet, and he certainly wasn't trapped in a vial. He raised his claws and attacked Magnus, intent on teaching the ancient *Slayer* a few things before he died.

The fight erupted in Ginger's kitchen with startling speed. One minute Donovan was stepping between Alex and Nick, and the next moment, there was a ferocious lapis lazuli and silver dragon in his place, breathing fire at the small red lizard.

The dragon snatched up the boy and flung him toward his mother. Alex caught Nick and retreated behind the *Pyr*, holding her son close. Eileen held Zoë tightly and Sara tugged her son into her arms, the three women retreating behind Sloane and Thorolf. Niall pulled Ginger back, shoving her roughly behind him.

The red salamander hissed at Donovan, then leapt for the window.

The small creature shattered the glass on impact, then shifted shape to a garnet red and gold dragon in the air beyond the window. Donovan changed to a man just long enough to get through the door, then flung himself into the sky in pursuit.

"Mallory," Erik murmured. "But why?"

"I'm at Donovan's back," Quinn said, kissed Sara's

cheek, and followed his friend. Thorolf moved to the door to watch the fight.

"Good." Erik turned on Sloane, evidently trusting that the two *Pyr* could defeat the single *Slayer*. "Tell us what you found."

Sloane spoke quickly. "There are two riddles bracketing the text, one at the beginning and one at the end."

"Alpha and omega," Eileen said.

"My thought exactly," Sloane agreed. "The beginning and the end." He read carefully.

> *I am the mirror that both heals and kills*
> *false silver and burning red;*
> *the stone that flows*
> *the blood that breathes;*
> *the source of an immortality*
> *without breath or pulse.*

"The Elixir," Ginger guessed, remembering the way Cinnabar floated in the liquid.

"No," Alex said firmly. "It's mercury."

Everyone looked at her in surprise.

Alex ticked off the clues on her fingers. "Mercury is silver, but not sterling. It was called quicksilver for a long time and is a reflective surface like a mirror. It was known to kill germs and consuming it was believed in the Renaissance to confer immortality."

"Paracelsus?" Erik asked, as if remembering.

"He said he cured syphilis with it. I remember that." Alex smiled. "Maybe that made him feel immortal."

"Why *burning red*, then?" Sara asked.

"Mercury poisoning is characterized by flushed skin and a burning sensation," Alex said. "And mercury is the only element that is liquid at room temperature."

"Delaney was turning red," Erik said.

"And Cinnabar *is* red," Ginger agreed.

"*The stone that flows*," Sloane mused.

"Doesn't mercury come from cinnabar?" Ginger asked, remembering Magnus's story.

"Yes!" Alex said. "That's one source, and it supposedly bleeds from the stone. That's how the ancients found the deposits."

"*Blood that breathes*?" Niall asked.

"Another old name for mercury and quicksilver is dragon's blood," Sloane said.

"And I remember that it's said to breathe when it's heated," Alex said, her excitement clear. "That's how they discovered the element of oxygen. You heat mercury and it takes in oxygen, then heat it more and it expels it all."

"What about the immortality bit?"

"Cinnabar," Ginger said. She quickly told the *Pyr* the story of Magnus's slave and his work at the cinnabar mine in Spain, as well as his current state. She was quite certain that Sloane was right about the rhyme, then remembered something else.

"What's wrong?" he asked, evidently seeing her dismay.

"There was mercury on the pillow last night, right where Delaney's head had been."

"And a bead of it fell from one of his wounds yesterday morning," Niall supplied with urgency.

"He's gone there," Ginger whispered. Sara gripped her shoulder and the *Pyr* stirred with concern. Ginger could feel their impatience.

Erik raised a hand. "We need a plan."

"What can we do?" Thorolf asked.

"Read the last riddle," Alex demanded, and Sloane did.

Elusive as water
Strong as earth

I work change inexorably
Fire takes blood to stone
The cycle can only end
with my sacrifice.

"Nice," Niall said flatly.

"You dislike the word *sacrifice*," Sloane said.

"When it applies to my friends, yes."

"But it doesn't necessarily," Sloane argued, leaning forward. "It depends upon the riddle's solution."

"Okay. It could mean the wind," Niall allowed. "The wind erodes rock over time, so that could be the change. You can't grab it, so that's like water, and it can be strong."

"But how do you sacrifice the wind?" Sara asked.

"We don't want to pursue that," Erik said as Niall straightened with alarm.

They all looked at Alex with hope. She frowned and worried her bottom lip with her teeth. "I don't remember that anything destroys mercury, but chemistry wasn't my specific area of study. Do you have an Internet connection?"

"Elusive earth. Elusive strength. Water earth. Strong water," Sloane mused; then his eyes lit. "Wait. Strong water is a literal translation of *aqua fortis*."

"Should that mean something to us?" Eileen asked.

"It's the old name for nitric acid!" Alex said with a snap of her fingers. "Of course!"

"Of course?" Sara echoed.

"You put two things together in a chemical reaction, and you get something else," Alex explained. "So, I'll bet that mercury and nitric acid together make another mercury compound—by that logic, the nitric acid appears to have been sacrificed, because it's gone."

"What about the fire?" Sloane asked.

Alex waved a hand dismissively. "How much you want to bet that it's a reaction that requires heat?" She turned to Erik. "Did you bring your laptop?"

"I have a high-speed connection in my office," Ginger said, and Alex practically ran behind her in her excitement.

In a matter of moments, she shouted in triumph. "Yes! If you heat mercury in a nitric acid solution, mercury oxide crystals precipitate out of the solution."

"What does that mean?" Eileen asked.

"Crystals form and fall out of the solution," Alex said. "Like, um, sugar crystals forming in the bottom of a bottle of maple syrup. In that case, the sugar has precipitated out of the solution." Her face appeared around the door frame, her eyes alight. "And yes, those mercury oxide crystals are considered in many traditions to be therapeutic, not toxic."

"So, all we have to do to destroy the Elixir is mix it with *aqua fortis* and boil it." Erik ran a hand over his forehead at that prospect. "Where are we going to get that much *aqua fortis*?"

"Pour sulfuric acid over saltpeter," Alex said from the other room, obviously reading a reference.

"Of course," Thorolf said, his tone skeptical. "Doesn't everybody carry saltpeter in their luggage?"

"Or we could just buy the nitric acid," Alex said, and Sloane chuckled. "I'll figure out how much. We'll need cash. . . ."

"Beguiling will be quicker than answering questions," Erik said.

"What's beguiling?" Ginger asked.

"It's a kind of hypnosis," Niall said. "We use it to persuade humans that they haven't really seen dragons in the vicinity, for example. Easier for everyone."

Ginger bristled. "It wouldn't be easy for any *Pyr* who decided to beguile me."

"Relax," Sara said, putting a hand on Ginger's arm. "None of us volunteer for that."

"And we watch out for one another," Eileen added with a wink.

"There's a plant in Cincinnati," Alex said, looking out the window as she returned to the kitchen. Quinn and Donovan were descending quickly and there was no sign of the garnet red dragon.

"He ran," Donovan said with disgust once he entered the kitchen.

"But why was he here?" Sloane asked.

"And how did he get into the drain?" Ginger asked.

"What's most important is that he's gone." Erik was dismissive. "We have to find Rafferty and help Delaney at the sanctuary. I'll look for Rafferty. Donovan and Quinn, take Alex and get the nitric acid. Sloane and Niall, you take Ginger and follow Delaney."

"Are you sure she'll be safe?" Alex asked.

Erik gave her a hard look. "She is his only chance."

"What about me?" Thorolf asked.

Erik surveyed the tall *Pyr* and Ginger sensed he had found Thorolf lacking on occasion. "Until I return with Rafferty, you must guard Sara and Eileen and Alex and the children."

Thorolf swallowed and stood a little taller.

Erik looked skeptical. "Are you fit for this task?"

Thorolf put his closed fist over his heart and spoke with force. "I am the son of Thorvald, who was the son of Thorkel, and you ask me this?"

The barest smile touched Erik's lips. "You remembered. Good. It is a start." He touched his lips to Eileen's temple and she closed her eyes, squaring her shoulders. "Be strong," were his murmured words, so softly uttered that Ginger barely heard them.

Then Niall offered her his hand. "Come fly with me," he invited. Ginger put the silver cross around her neck before she put her hand in his.

"Can't hurt," she said, checking that her lucky earrings were tightly fastened. She had a glimpse of Thorolf shifting shape, becoming a massive moonstone and silver dragon, his tail coiled across her kitchen floor. His blue eyes glinted dangerously and he exhaled slowly, watchful and alert.

Then Niall caught Ginger around the waist, leapt off the porch, and shifted shape, flying toward the sanctuary across a clearing sky. Ginger felt the rain in the warming wind. She trusted Delaney's friends completely, trusted in her own faith, and hoped it was enough.

It was thrilling to fly with the dragons. Erik led the way, Niall and Sloane on his flanks. Ginger was amazed by how quickly the snow was melting, then by how fast the trio could travel. In moments, they were over the parking lot at Serpent Mound.

It was still devoid of cars.

Niall hissed in displeasure as they came close to the sanctuary's entrance.

"What is it?" Ginger asked.

"Mallory and Balthasar and Jorge," he murmured.

"I can't see them," Sloane said.

"I can smell them," Niall insisted. "They're waiting for us."

"Because Delaney is in the sanctuary," Erik said. "Probably with Magnus."

"So is Rafferty," Niall added.

"Good," Erik said, then the three *Slayers* erupted from the line of trees. Ginger had time to see that Jorge led the way, his topaz and gold dragon form marred by the scar on his back leg. She shuddered in recollection of how he had snatched her and the coldness in his eyes.

Mallory was garnet red and gold with pearls on his chest, his eye and shoulder still marked with a scab. Ginger knew she didn't imagine that his eyes gleamed with malice when he saw her.

The third dragon was agate and gold and his tail was

burned. He also looked angry and she knew this had to be Balthasar.

"Hang on," Niall said, but Ginger didn't need any such advice. These *Slayers* had tried to kill her before and she didn't doubt they'd be glad to try again.

Then Niall locked claws with Balthasar. He breathed a brilliant stream of fire at his opponent and Ginger closed her eyes as she hung on.

Niall pivoted in the air, taking a blow on his back. He ducked and feinted, showing a muscular agility that amazed Ginger.

She could hear him murmuring, as if he spoke an incantation. He punched Balthasar in the face, then ripped his talons across Balthasar's gut. Balthasar bellowed and leapt on Niall's back. Ginger heard Niall's cry of pain as the *Slayer*'s talons dug into the top of Niall's wings.

Then he writhed and pivoted and struck the *Slayer* hard enough with his tail to send him tumbling through the sky. Balthasar hit the ground heavily and didn't immediately move. Ginger recalled that he was the only one who hadn't drunk the Elixir.

Sloane and Mallory were locked in a bitter battle, tails entwined and claws locked. They snapped and bit at each other, tumbling end over end as each tried to damage the other. They looked to be equally matched in strength, and Ginger heard the thunder of old-speak. Did they taunt each other? She wouldn't have been surprised.

Niall landed on Mallory's back, shredding the *Slayer*'s wings with sure strokes. Mallory screamed in pain and writhed, caught as he was between the two *Pyr*. At Sloane's nod, Niall released the *Slayer* and carried Ginger out of harm's way.

Sloane loosed a fearsome torrent of dragonfire on his opponent, burning the beautiful red of Mallory's scales and blackening his inset pearls. The *Slayer* attacked with new rage.

Niall sang outright, the vibration of his voice resonating throughout Ginger's body. It was a call of urgency, one that made her want to do *something*.

How much power did he have over the element of air? It seemed intent upon responding to him. Ginger watched dark clouds gather on the horizon, swirling with violent intent and building like thunderclouds. Niall chanted steadily, cajoling and commanding, his song unwavering in its demand.

Balthasar picked himself up and shuddered from head to toe. He glared at Niall, then took flight, moving swiftly toward the amethyst dragon.

Meanwhile, Erik was battling fiercely with Jorge, the *Slayer* seeing the worst of the exchange. Jorge kept taking dirty shots, but none of them surprised the leader of the *Pyr*. Erik fought grimly and effectively, reopening Jorge's leg wound so that the foot fell to the earth again.

Jorge leapt at Erik, talons extended and teeth bared. Erik struck him across the face with his tail, then snatched the end of Jorge's tail as the *Slayer* spun from the force of the blow. Erik swung him around and cast him into the trees below.

Then she saw figures appear on the horizon. They were dark, like specters but dragon-shaped. They looked like dragons made of dark smoke, or of shadows, and there were three of them on the approach.

"Shit," said Sloane, and fought with greater vigor.

"What's going on?" Ginger demanded, watching those ominous shapes approach. Their features became more clear with proximity and she could see that they really did have those zombie eyes. Niall sang more loudly and with more force, and the wind was whipped into a frenzy.

"Shadow dragons," Sloane supplied when no one else answered her.

"Dead *Pyr* raised by Magnus with the Elixir," Ginger remembered, fearful of the odds facing her *Pyr*. "Don't they have to be dismembered and burned to be killed?"

No one had time to answer her.

Ginger quietly panicked. Could the three *Pyr* take on three more opponents? Niall's chanting became more vehement, as if he shared her concern. Ginger felt the wind mustering. What could she do to help?

The clouds rolled closer and the wind became stronger. It lifted Ginger's hair and tossed the trees, unsettled and verging on violence. The sky took on a yellow tinge that Ginger had learned young to distrust.

Niall chanted more insistently, calling disaster closer, urging it to greater speed. The shadow dragons approached rapidly, their colors becoming visible just as the first funnel cloud appeared. One looked like a copy of Niall, all amethyst and silver, but the silver of his scales seemed tarnished and the amethyst appeared to be clouded with smoke.

"Phelan," Niall hissed under his breath.

"Who's that?" Ginger demanded.

"My twin."

Phelan snarled and leapt at Niall, talons extended.

"To me!" Erik cried, and Niall tossed Ginger to the leader of the *Pyr*. She didn't have time to be afraid before Erik's claw closed protectively over her. He held her away from Jorge as that *Slayer* attacked again.

Meanwhile, Niall roared with rage. He raised his own claws, then engaged with his twin. His song was lost and Ginger felt the wind easing. The *Slayers* attacked with force, the other two shadow dragons targeting one of the other *Pyr*.

Six against three, and half of the bad guys didn't die easily. Ginger winced. Surely the good guys couldn't lose?

·   *   *

Eileen couldn't figure out why Zoë was fussing so much. She tried to settle the baby, without success. Nothing worked. The breast and the bottle were both rejected. Zoë was neither too warm nor too cold. Her diaper was dry. Yet she wailed and cried and made more fuss than she ever had.

They'd made another pot of coffee, but it seemed that every time one of them stood up to pour a round, Zoë had another fit of hysterics.

"The kid's got lung power," Thorolf said. "You've got to give her that."

Alex moved to try to pour coffee again, but Zoë had a screaming fit longer and louder than any of the previous ones, the sheer volume leaving them wincing as Alex stood, pot in hand.

"They have no way to tell us what they really want," Sara said sympathetically.

"That's it," Eileen said. "She's trying to tell us something."

"You've covered all the options," Alex said.

"No, no," Eileen said, studying her child. "She gave Erik a vision and sent Rafferty one, too. She's trying to do something Wyvern-like."

"But what?" Sara said. The three women watched the baby's frustration mount as they tried to understand. The toddlers even came closer, as if fascinated by someone who could make more trouble than they could.

"Baby," Garrett said with conviction.

"Yes, she's a baby, just as you're not," Sara agreed. He smiled, showing some of his father's solemnity, then reached for Zoë.

She flailed and caught his hand, her crying stopping as soon as they touched. Garrett's eyes widened as she held fast to his fingers, then he released her and headed for the porch.

"Garrett!" Sara cried. "Don't leave the house!"

He didn't stop, fumbling with the door with such determination that Eileen got to her feet. The hair was prickling on the back of her neck. "She told him something," she said. "See where he goes."

Thorolf accompanied the boy outside. He went straight to a terra-cotta planter at the end of the porch, one that had been swept free of the snow. Thorolf didn't let him touch the matching saucer, but brought it back into the house.

"This is what Niall took from Delaney's wound yesterday. That's what he wanted to get." He set it on the table, the silver bead within it rolling with the motion.

"It's mercury," Alex said.

Zoë hiccuped and sucked her own fist, watching them solemnly.

"She's been upset since the *Pyr* left," Eileen said.

"No," Sara corrected. "She's been upset since Mallory showed up on the lip of the sink."

"And she doesn't want us to drink the coffee," Thorolf said. "Kid's a health freak."

"That's it!" Alex pushed to her feet.

"That's what?" Thorolf asked.

"That's what she's trying to tell us."

"What?" Thorolf asked, looking confused.

"What if mercury poisoning in people is what makes a *Pyr* become the source of the Elixir?" Alex asked. "What if Cinnabar is red and Delaney is turning red because of mercury poisoning? And what if the way to prepare a candidate to replace Cinnabar is to poison him with mercury?"

"What are you suggesting?" Sara asked.

"That Mallory was here to put mercury in the well, mercury that would turn all of the *Pyr* present into candidates to replace Cinnabar."

"If they drank the water," Thorolf said, then poured the contents of the pot down the drain.

"We've got to check the well," Alex said, and headed for the basement.

"I wonder whether there's bottled water," Sara said, making for the pantry. "Ginger seems to be the kind of person who is prepared for everything."

Zoë, Eileen noticed with surprise, had fallen asleep against her breast, her expression so angelic that she might have been a different child than the one who had raged for the past hour. "I could use a cup of decaf," Eileen said, and Thorolf chuckled.

The fight outside the sanctuary had become more violent. Ginger watched as Sloane was slashed across one shoulder by Mallory and his red blood fell in a torrent, staining the snow. Sloane spun and attacked the shadow dragon behind him, slicing one arm at the elbow. The limb fell, splashing into the river far below, but there was no blood.

The shadow dragon didn't even seem to notice the loss.

It just kept on fighting.

Jorge had sunk his teeth into Erik's chest, leaving a nasty gash in the armor of the leader of the *Pyr*. Erik slashed at the *Slayer*, reopening his earlier wounds in systematic succession. Jorge breathed dragonfire at Erik, but Erik turned his back on the stream of fire. Ginger closed her eyes. To her surprise, Erik laughed and seemed strengthened by the attack. He turned and slashed Jorge across the face, then spun to decapitate the shadow dragon with one heavy slash of his talon.

Then Jorge leapt on Erik from behind, sinking his teeth into the shoulders of the leader of the *Pyr*. Erik screamed and lost altitude, and Ginger hung on in terror.

Niall was fighting hard against Phelan, that shadow

dragon taunting him. Niall sliced one wing of the shadow dragon, cutting deep, and Phelan fell toward the earth. Niall swooped toward Erik, scooping Ginger from Erik's grasp, then exhaled dragonfire at Jorge. Erik pulled out of his dive and attacked Jorge from behind, just as Balthasar slashed at Niall's back. Niall fought hard but Ginger could see him fading.

It didn't look good.

Ginger had time to panic when two more dragons appeared in the distance. They seemed to be heavily burdened and their flight pattern was both erratic and slow.

The brilliant hue of their scales soon became clear, and Ginger recognized them as Donovan and Quinn. They were carrying large plastic drums.

Ginger would have bet they contained nitric acid.

She wanted to cheer.

The *Slayers* and shadow dragons must have seen the *Pyr* coming, because they attacked with new fervor.

Balthasar attacked Niall again, the pair grappling as they tumbled through the air. Ginger felt a bit sick but Niall held fast to her, defending her from the *Slayer's* dragonfire. When Niall shook free of the *Slayer's* grasp, the claw that had been wrapped around her was burned and blackened.

Donovan dove into the battle with a roar. He dropped two heavy plastic canisters by the entry to the sanctuary, then spun in the air to help Sloane against Mallory. It looked as if he had metal talons, and Ginger winced as he slashed Mallory's gut. Black blood flowed from the wounds, steaming as it dropped into the creek below.

Donovan slashed at the shadow dragon that had been attacking Sloane, dismembering the abomination with measured strokes. Sloane incinerated each piece as it fell to the earth and soon there was nothing left but ash of that shadow dragon.

He turned to attack Phelan, but the shadow dragon snarled and retreated. "I will find you, brother!" he cried to Niall.

"Not unless I find you first," Niall murmured with heat. He decked Balthasar, then began to sing loudly. The wind mustered on cue, responding more quickly to Niall's summons than it had the first time.

Ginger knew the import of that yellow-tinged sky. The storm was raised with alarming speed, but the shadow dragons and *Slayers* seemed unaware of its approach.

Or indifferent.

Phelan was the first to be sucked into the maelstrom, his shadowed form disappearing into the swirling gray of the funnel cloud. His shout was lost in the wind, as Niall continued to sing, his voice as resonant as a clarion call.

Meanwhile, Jorge came raging upward toward Erik, fury making his eyes blaze. Erik, confident and calm, waited for him, looking amused even in dragon form. Ginger saw Jorge falter, look for what he had missed, then spot the funnel cloud.

Jorge shouted a warning and dove down into the trees. Balthasar bolted, flying as quickly as possible in the opposite direction of the gathering storm. Mallory screamed as he tried to disengage from Sloane's claws without success. Sloane held fast, thrashing the *Slayer* repeatedly with his tail.

The funnel cloud swallowed those who fled. Ginger heard the screams of Balthasar and the other shadow dragon as the powerful column of wind touched down to the ground. It swirled and churned, giving her glimpses of claws and tails.

Niall sang and sang as the wind swirled to his command. Sloane cast Mallory into the swirling maelstrom, then Niall softened his song. The wind eased almost instantly, Niall's power filling Ginger with awe.

The funnel cloud receded and the clouds turned a normal stormy gray. It began to rain as the trees stopped tossing. The rain was icily cold and Ginger shivered under its assault.

Jorge erupted suddenly from the forest, his every move filled with anger and purpose. Two new *Slayers* took flight from Magnus's compound, heading directly toward the *Pyr*.

It wasn't over yet, and the *Pyr* were tired. Ginger held on to Delaney's mother's cross and said a little prayer.

Chapter 20

Delaney finally got a good strike on Magnus, catching the *Slayer* by surprise. Magnus hit his head against a stalactite and lost the rhythm of flight.

This was his chance.

Delaney pivoted in the air as the *Slayer* fell and dove for the vial instead of his opponent. He summoned every vestige of strength within himself as he spiraled toward the stacked fertilizer. He exhaled mightily, intending to breathe a torrent of dragonfire to ignite the blast.

But he exhaled only air.

Cold air.

How could that be?

Delaney turned at the last minute, heading for the vial again. He fought the panic rising within himself, refusing to admit defeat. He drew from the core of his strength, willed the fire to burn hot and bright, and aimed at the bags of fertilizer.

Once again, only cold air flowed from his lungs.

That was when he heard Magnus laughing.

The old *Slayer* laughed so hard that he could barely

speak. He braced himself against the wall of the cavern and howled with his amusement.

Delaney didn't appreciate the joke.

He landed on top of the fertilizer, not caring whether he was eliminated in the blast, and raged.

The cold air from his lungs seemed to encourage the growth of hoarfrost on the outside of the crystal vial. The Elixir swirled and Delaney glared at Magnus.

"Your fire is extinguished," the *Slayer* said, his confidence so complete that Delaney wanted to shred him alive. "It's the next step in the progression. You're almost mine."

Delaney leapt from the pile and flew at Magnus, furious as he had never been before. They locked talons and tumbled through the air, landing on the floor of the cavern with a crash. Delaney struck the *Slayer* with his tail until Magnus collapsed, then dragged the *Slayer*'s body toward the fertilizer.

Maybe Magnus would exhale the necessary spark.

The old *Slayer* was bleeding black all over the floor, weakening steadily. Delaney taunted him, trying to draw his fire, but Magnus fell silent. He apparently was unable to move.

Delaney was certain he hadn't hit him hard enough for this. But Magnus looked as if he were having a heart attack. His eyes widened as he gasped in pain, and his features contorted. A spasm shook his body and he seemed unable to speak, his claw outstretched to Delaney.

Delaney had no mercy to spare for Magnus. He scanned the chamber, desperate for some way to ignite the fertilizer.

Magnus meanwhile exhaled steadily and slowly, filling the cavern with the haze of his dragonsmoke. It was silvery, like a snake, and it wound through the air toward Delaney so deliberately that it might have had a target. He wasn't worried about it as much as he would once have been, given that he'd been able to endure it for Ginger.

Until the dragonsmoke touched him.

The dragonsmoke hit Delaney like a jolt of electricity, and he screamed at the pain that rocketed through his body. The smoke stung and burned, like a dagger of ice that went straight to his heart. His ability to challenge it had eroded to nothing, and he was more vulnerable than ever.

His body was changing, and not in a good way.

Delaney saw the dragonsmoke make a conduit between himself and Magnus, and felt the steady reduction of his energy as Magnus grew larger. The *Slayer* rose to his feet once again, brushing off his injuries, his eyes gleaming as he watched Delaney stumble. The smoke sucked at Delaney's power, stealing it and feeding it to Magnus, reversing the balance of power between them. Delaney struggled to get away from the dragonsmoke, to break the line by which it destroyed him, but it was unshakable. He backed into the wall of the cavern and fell to his knees.

And Delaney saw the hole in his own armor, the dragonsmoke winding into it with merciless precision.

He was missing a scale in the middle of his chest, one that hadn't been missing before. He saw the exposed skin, unprotected and already burned bright crimson, and knew what had happened.

He had already come to care for Ginger, but his affection and admiration had only weakened him.

Fatally.

He wanted to fight. He wanted to rise up and rip Magnus apart. He wanted to destroy the Elixir. But his body failed to respond to his command and the dragonsmoke steadily claimed the power within him. He was already on his knees, then braced himself on all fours. The dragonsmoke encircled him, surrounded him, isolated him, and sucked him dry.

It wasn't the Elixir that would be destroyed.

It would be Delaney.

The quicksilver was stifling the divine spark within him. He was leaving the land of the living *Pyr*, destined for some dark realm occupied by shadow dragons and pawns like Cinnabar. He had no choice over his future, though he wanted one desperately.

Was this how Cinnabar had felt?

Delaney wanted nothing in common with the *Pyr* who had become the Elixir. He hoped only that he would be unaware of his circumstance.

For Magnus's plan seemed destined to come to perfect fruition, ensuring the *Slayers'* survival and power for millennia into the future. Delaney wanted to scream in frustration but he collapsed instead, his eyes closing to the peal of Magnus's laughter.

He shifted shape, without meaning to do so, and recognized it as a sign of his body's demise. He felt a tear slide from his eye as Magnus shifted to human form beside him. He tried to rouse himself, without success, then Magnus bent. Delaney saw the syringe and felt the needle slide into his vein.

He felt the cold shock of quicksilver moving through his body, turning him to deadened ice like the earth in his nightmares. The mercury stole his strength and numbed his mind, making it impossible to defend himself.

"Just a taste," Magnus murmured. "Just a little sample of what is in store for you in 2013."

No doubt about it, Delaney had failed.

And his only regret was that he hadn't kept his promise to Ginger.

Delaney felt Magnus put a round stone in his mouth, but couldn't stop him. He was powerless to move. He then heard the old *Slayer* chant a verse that he couldn't understand. It wound its way into his ears, slithering toward his heart, turning him to ice like Gaia in his nightmare. He was failing in his quest and abandoning Ginger.

The worst part was that there was nothing he could do about it.

Donovan began to sing a different song than Niall's, a potent tune that seemed like a call to war. Ginger could almost feel the earth responding to his battle cry. Her own blood pounded in rhythm, making her believe that victory was possible.

"Can Donovan command the wind, too?"

"He can summon weapons from the elements," Erik said, just as pellets of ice began to fall from the sky. They slanted down upon the fight, and Ginger cried out at their impact. The pellets could have been little arrows of ice.

The *Slayers* in the distance lost altitude and seemed to hesitate beneath the assault of the elements.

Donovan seized Jorge from behind, digging those metal talons into the *Slayer*'s wings as he continued to sing. Jorge pivoted with a snarl and Donovan struck him open-clawed across the face. Four long cuts appeared, black blood falling fast. Jorge screamed and Donovan flung the *Slayer* across the sky.

The two other *Slayers* decided to retreat.

Ginger cheered.

One of Donovan's canisters rolled down the sloped entry and Sloane moved to give the second a nudge. Quinn landed with his cargo, more deliberate in his actions. The *Pyr* landed beside the entry to the sanctuary, the new arrivals less wounded than those who had fought longest. They were all well, though, and Ginger was glad to feel the ground beneath her feet again. She thanked Erik and Niall for their protection, and they each nodded acknowledgment.

"Phase two," Quinn said, pushing one of his canisters

into the opening. It rolled down the hidden slope, into the darkness below.

Then both Sloane and Quinn twitched. Ginger knew what their involuntary starts meant. "There's dragonsmoke!"

"I smell it," Niall said, backing away.

"Magnus," Erik murmured, and Ginger remembered Delaney telling her they could identify who had breathed a territory mark.

"It's coming from inside the sanctuary," Sloane said.

Ginger was frightened. "Is Delaney in there?"

The *Pyr* didn't answer, which was all the answer she needed. She headed for the opening, but Erik caught at her arm.

"The *Slayers* will target you."

Ginger shook off his grip. "None of you can go in there to help Delaney, right? None of you can cross the dragonsmoke, but I can. You need me to move those drums and pour that acid into the Elixir." Again they said nothing.

"Don't you?"

Erik visibly gritted his teeth and nodded once. "The risk, though . . ."

Ginger didn't wait for further discussion. There was nothing they could do to change her mind, and Ginger suspected they didn't have another answer.

Because she was right.

And even Erik knew it.

She was halfway down the chute when she heard another song begin.

Rafferty waited until Magnus was confident of his victory before he revealed himself. He knew that as soon as he made a sound, the *Slayer* would be aware he had been tricked, and he didn't want to do it too soon. He heard Magnus fall, heard him laugh, sensed the unfurling of dragonsmoke.

Then he crept from his hiding place.

He was shocked to see Delaney not only down, not only surrounded by dragonsmoke, but immobile. He feared the *Pyr* was dead and concluded he had waited too long. Magnus, in contrast, had become large and powerful again, fueled by the conduit of dragonsmoke.

He was adept at stealing the life force of others. Rafferty turned the black and white ring on his hand, wondering how many Magnus would sacrifice to his own dream of immortality. He turned the ring and he wished for Sophie's clarity in knowing what to do. He turned the ring and he wished for Nikolas's focus and determination. He turned the ring and he wished for Delaney's powerful heart.

Then he interrupted Magnus's charm.

Magnus spun to face Rafferty then, so triumphant that his features seemed lit from within. His selfishness and indifference to anyone other than himself awakened a rare rage in Rafferty. "It's too late!" he crowed.

"It's never too late," Rafferty retorted.

Rafferty leapt into the sanctuary, shifted in midair, and roared. He flew toward Magnus, the ring like a radiant beacon on his talon. It spiraled around his finger, flashing black and white as it turned. The Elixir stopped swirling and Cinnabar seemed to press his snout against the rock crystal to watch.

And the two old adversaries locked talons in battle again.

The challenge was only half done.

They thrashed each other with their tails and Rafferty threw the old *Slayer* into the wall of the cavern. The rock shook, and Rafferty began to sing, not caring if he brought the whole world down on Magnus. He'd die happily himself, knowing he'd killed Magnus.

Rafferty sang and the earth jumped. Chunks of rock fell from the ceiling, shattering on the ground and raising a cloud of dust. The Elixir sloshed and vibrated, but the vial held firm. Magnus fought viciously, perhaps sensing Rafferty's determination. He sank his teeth into Rafferty's hide, tearing the flesh wherever he could. He slashed with his talons and struck with his tail. The blood flowed both black and red, mixing but never mingling, sizzling on the floor of the sanctuary. The floor heaved and buckled, long cracks opening across its width.

The sanctuary was falling into ruin and Rafferty didn't care. He cared only that Magnus died first.

Neither of them saw the small redhead roll four good-sized canisters, one at a time, across the floor beneath them. Neither of them saw her heave those canisters, one at a time, up the stairs that wrapped around the rock crystal vial. Neither of them saw her sweat at her exertion or noted how she paled as she passed Delaney.

Neither of them saw her reach the summit one last time and pull the plug on the first industrial canister. She pushed it into the vial, then repeated the action with the other three.

They saw her when she straightened and whistled. It was a good, loud wolf whistle, one Ginger had learned to make early, and it echoed through the crumbling cavern.

"Hey, Magnus!" Ginger shouted at the incredulous *Slayer*. "Aren't you leaving something unfinished?" She waved with a cheerfulness that struck Rafferty as painfully human. He knew exactly what she was doing and admired her for it. "I hear you guys like *Pyr* mates well-done." She snapped her fingers as Magnus seethed. "I'm pregnant, you know, just in case that affects your calculations."

Magnus sputtered.

Magnus roared.

Magnus tore himself free from Rafferty and lunged toward Ginger, breathing a torrent of dragonfire all the way.

Rafferty saw what was going to happen and couldn't get there in time to do a thing about it.

Delaney was dead.

Ginger fought against her tears as she struggled with the canisters. Just because Delaney was dead didn't mean he had to become the source of the Elixir that would keep Magnus alive for the next thousand years. An anger burned within Ginger, a fury at injustice that gave her more strength than she could have believed possible.

It also gave her the audacity not to care what it cost to fix what Magnus had done.

She challenged him, casting him a dare she knew he'd take.

And she stood at the top of the rock crystal stairs, waiting for his worst. She saw the flames approaching, but she refused to flinch. She held Magnus's angry gaze and taunted him, letting him see that she wasn't afraid.

It wasn't going to be pretty and Ginger didn't care.

But in the last moment before Magnus's dragonfire reached her, something lunged out of the vial of the Elixir. Something large and pink flung itself from the depths of the vial, making a massive wet barrier between Ginger and the dragonfire.

Cinnabar screamed as the flames hit him.

He writhed and fell from the top of the enormous vial, surrounding Ginger with his wet self. She was disgusted and she fought against his slimy grip.

Suddenly she realized that the smell of the Elixir had changed. It had become less fetid.

And Cinnabar was saving her. She stopped fighting him.

There was no more time to think. The fertilizer lit and its explosion filled the cavern with dust and flame. The Elixir boiled, releasing a thick crimson cloud of smoke that filled the cavern to bursting. The Elixir changed color, losing its redness as the smoke roiled and rose.

Magnus screamed in fury, but he didn't come any closer—Rafferty jumped him from behind. The pair locked in battle again. The ring on Rafferty's left talon shone like a light in the darkness. It also seemed to be guiding Rafferty's blows—he couldn't seem to miss. She saw Rafferty sink that same left talon that bore the ring into Magnus's chest and knew that the *Pyr* had found the *Slayer*'s vulnerable spot.

Good.

She didn't watch any more of that fight because the rock crystal vial abruptly cracked. Cinnabar swooped down and lifted Delaney from the floor, grimacing as he held him high.

The liquid that had once been the Elixir spilled in a torrent, flooding across the floor of the cavern and into the crevasses that had opened in its floor. It looked like water as it slipped away, disappearing, absorbed by the earth.

Once the tide had passed, Cinnabar almost dropped Delaney, then set Ginger on her feet. "Thank you," she said, and she was certain he smiled at her.

Cinnabar moved, languidly but deliberately, sinking to his knees beside Delaney. He touched the unconscious *Pyr* with a tenderness that astonished Ginger. He glanced her way, then laid himself protectively over Delaney, spreading himself like a blanket over his fallen body.

And Cinnabar began to hum.

As Ginger watched, silver beads began to drip from Delaney's fingertips. Cinnabar grew paler with every passing moment, but she could see that he was drawing the mercury out of Delaney's body. The tiny beads grew in number, pooling around Delaney's fingertips until their extrusion slowed to nothing. Cinnabar hummed another bar of his tune with force and one last single bead fell out of Delaney's left index finger.

The nail on that finger was no longer red.

Then Cinnabar sighed, exhausted. He had faded almost to transparency, looking ghostlike in the cavern's light. He turned to Ginger, moving slowly as if his strength were gone, and beckoned.

Ginger went to his side immediately, unafraid. "You helped him," she said. Delaney didn't look ruddy anymore, or flushed, or dead.

He looked like he was sleeping.

Cinnabar had given him the gift of life. A lump rose in her throat, because she guessed the cost of his gift.

"The last of me," Cinnabar whispered, his words no more substantial than the wind. "So there will be no more."

Ginger reached out to take his talon. She could barely feel his presence within her grip, could barely sense his chill.

But she had something to say to him before he was gone.

"Thank you, Sahir," Ginger said, her words husky and sincere. "Thank you with all my heart."

He seemed shocked when she said his name, the name that had been his before he had had the misfortune to meet Magnus. Then he shifted in a rosy haze. Ginger had a glimpse of a young man, tanned and golden, a man with a tentative smile. He turned his hand in hers, gave her fingers a minute squeeze, then faded.

And Sahir was gone, gone forever.

Ginger choked back her tears. She knelt beside Delaney, reassured at the even flow of his breathing. She took off his silver cross and put it in his hand. "You forgot something, hotshot," she whispered, and kissed his cheek. "I'm thinking your momma would be proud of you today."

Delaney's eyes opened immediately, so clear and green that Ginger couldn't hold back her tears any longer. He opened his mouth and removed a round gray stone, about the size of a chicken egg, but covered with mysterious carvings. Then he sat up and caught Ginger close, letting her cry against the solid strength of his chest.

Delaney was back.

And he was fully healed.

The red cloud that had billowed out of the vial when the nitric acid reacted with the Elixir began to rain red crystals. They bounced and scattered across the floor, looking like a harvest of rubies. The mercury was precipitating, just as Alex had said it would. Ginger remembered Sloane's interest in the therapeutic quality of the mercury oxide crystals and grabbed a handful for him.

Magnus screamed in agony; then there was a thunderclap and a cloud of dust.

Rafferty landed beside them, the red stones bouncing off his opal scales. "An old job finally done," he said, the gleam in his eyes telling Ginger that he was very pleased with the situation.

"Where's Magnus?" Delaney asked as he got to his feet.

"Trapped in the earth," Rafferty said with satisfaction. His smile flashed as he tossed a silver coin, his pleasure unmistakable. "Gone forever."

"Because now there's no Elixir to heal him," Ginger said.

Rafferty only smiled. "And there will never be more Elixir," he said with resolve. "The secret of its creation is lost with Magnus." He reached out and took the round stone from Delaney, sparing it a glance before he grimaced in distaste.

"What is it?" Ginger asked.

"An old piece of wickedness," Rafferty mused. "So

many stories that we had thought no more than myths are proving to have their roots in truth." He arched a brow. "Eileen will have a lecture for us on that, no doubt." He winked at Ginger. "But maybe she'll never need to know that this one was real."

Then Rafferty closed his hand around the stone and sang a low thrumming song, one that made Ginger's bones hum. She saw the stone vibrate within his grasp, saw the lines carved on its surface blur, and then it crumbled to dust.

Rafferty brushed it from his hands, then glanced up. "Time to go," he said softly.

The ceiling of the cavern made an ominous crack, as if responding to him. Red crystals continued to fall all around them, as deep as Ginger's ankles across the floor. Delaney shifted shape, picking up Ginger and flying to the other side of the ruined sanctuary. The three hurried out the door, then through the other two caverns. They were climbing that wet tunnel when Ginger heard the roar and crash of collapsing stone behind them.

Rocks began to fall all around them, but the *Pyr* were there, hauling them back out into the open air.

Where the sun was setting, in a brilliant orange display.

Chapter 21

Delaney couldn't believe his luck, the power of his firestorm, and the strength of his friends' loyalty. He felt blessed to be alive. He swung Ginger into his arms and leapt into the air, shifting shape as he took flight. She held on to him, her hair flowing wildly around them both. When she laughed, he felt his heart skip, as if a bit of sunlight danced in his veins.

Delaney felt the *Pyr* following him and was glad to lead the way. He turned high over the Ohio countryside and spied Ginger's farm immediately.

Home.

It was home to him, because it was Ginger's home. He spiraled out of the sky, landing with a flourish, then tossing her in his arms.

"Show off!" she teased, and he laughed.

She smiled at him and he laughed longer. Joy bubbled inside him, a joy fed by Ginger. He laughed more than he could ever remember laughing, then he kissed the woman who had given him back his life.

Against all expectations, Delaney Shea was finally home. When he lifted his head, she smiled up at him.

"Hey, hotshot, you want to go to a wedding?"

"Are you asking me on a date?"

Ginger grinned. "Even better—the worst kind of date possible. A wedding date, where I'm maid of honor and have all sorts of official duties to fulfill, plus you won't know anyone but me. You'll probably be bored out of your mind."

Delaney had no qualms. "Yes."

Ginger glanced up at him. "It's Saturday, the wedding of my friends Tanya and Steve. You know that stag-and-doe was for them. You're probably leaving town by then."

"I'll stay," Delaney said. "Unless you're trying to talk me out of accepting."

She blushed. "No, I just thought it was fair to warn you what you would be getting into."

"I know exactly what I'm getting into." Delaney caught her hand in his and held her gaze as he kissed her palm. He watched her swallow as he bent closer. "And I wouldn't miss it for the world."

"Why?" she asked quietly.

Delaney smiled. "Because you'll be there. Of course."

"There's something I've got to ask you." She frowned and glanced at their entwined hands, and he knew that this woman would never be afraid to speak her mind. He liked that a lot. "Just how long are you intending to stay, hotshot?"

"For as long as you want me to."

She laughed then and leapt toward him. He caught her close and swung her around, loving the vivid sparkle of her eyes. He kissed her deeply again and swung her around as the *Pyr* landed all around him. The women and Thorolf came out of the house with the children, but Delaney didn't care who saw his happiness.

Ginger was his sun, always shining brightly, always

giving more to those around her. She'd made him whole once more and he'd happily spend the rest of his life proving his gratitude to her.

He hoped she knew that.

If her famous intuition didn't tell her that, he would.

In no uncertain terms.

Gran had always insisted there were things a person didn't need to be told, that there were truths we all knew in our hearts. It had been her habitual defense of her own taciturn nature. Ginger had never thought much of that view, until Delaney brought her home.

He looked right on her farm.

He felt right on her farm and in her life.

And he said he would stay.

He fit so well that he might always have been there. Or maybe Ginger had always known she was waiting for him. Maybe she had recognized him on sight as the missing piece in the puzzle of her life.

She fully expected that life with a *Pyr* committed to the *Pyr*'s goal to save the earth would be one of surprise and challenge.

But that was what life was about.

She knew that she and Delaney would face adversity better together than alone, and that over time, they would work even better as a team than they did now. She knew they could make a difference to the *Pyr*'s objectives on a smaller scale, by taking the farm organic and educating others by their example.

He didn't put her down, just held her in his arms as the other *Pyr* descended out of the sky to land beside him. There was water running on the ground and into the fields, the snow disappearing with remarkable speed. Erik headed for the house, meeting Eileen halfway there.

Ginger liked how these *Pyr* took care of their own.

Thorolf came out with the other women, Nick riding on Thorolf's shoulders and Garrett in Sara's arms, and Donovan and Quinn went to them immediately.

Then everyone looked at her, expectant.

Ginger looked at Delaney and he just smiled as he set her on her feet, his expression mysterious.

Ginger knew she was missing something. The *Pyr* were waiting for her to do or say something.

"Don't they know the firestorm is satisfied?" she whispered to Delaney.

He nodded with satisfaction. "They can feel that."

"And the Elixir is destroyed."

He nodded again, his gaze bright upon her.

"And you're healed."

He smiled as he nodded this time. Ginger loved the look of his smile and the gleam of intent in his eyes. "So why don't they go?" she whispered very quietly, thinking a private celebration would be ideal.

"Because our task here is not yet done," Erik said, proving once again that the *Pyr* had keen hearing.

"I don't understand," Ginger said.

Sloane opened his hand, revealing the copper and emerald dragon scale that he held. "It was outside the entry to the sanctuary."

"That's yours!" Ginger said to Delaney. He nodded agreement, so watchful that she knew there was a point. She took the scale from Sloane, amazed that it was so light and strong. She thought about the fight, then turned to face Delaney. "It was missing. You had a bare spot in your armor, and that's how Magnus took you down."

Delaney folded his arms across his chest and watched her. "That's right."

She was supposed to figure this out herself. Ginger knew it. She could feel the expectation of the *Pyr*, but she'd always been up to a challenge. She must know all of the pieces—she just had to pull the solution together.

Then she remembered. She turned to Quinn. "You're the Smith. You repair the armor of the *Pyr*."

"True," he acknowledged, without moving.

"Can you fix this?"

"Not alone."

"Do you need tools, or a forge?" Ginger tried to solve the riddle. "Because if you need my help, just tell me. Whatever I've got, you can use to heal him."

"I think that's good enough, don't you?" Eileen said.

"It's rather vague," Erik demurred.

"But heartfelt," Niall argued.

"I think it should count," Sloane said.

"Be serious," Alex said impatiently. "She already surrendered to the firestorm and helped destroy the Elixir. You're not going to let this go on a technicality."

"She was prepared to die to avenge him," Rafferty said.

"What do you need from me?" Ginger asked, turning to Delaney.

"Nothing," he said. "I'll fight as I am and defend you to the end."

"That's not good enough," Ginger argued, waving the scale. "I want this fixed and I want to know how."

Sara smiled and passed Garrett to Quinn before coming to Ginger's side. "First you have to understand why he lost it."

Ginger shook her head.

"It makes him vulnerable. It's a metaphor," Sara said.

"A pretty tangible one," Quinn commented.

"What makes a man vulnerable?" Sara asked quietly.

"Caring for someone. Or something," Ginger said quickly, then turned to Delaney. His eyes were glowing and his look so intense that her heart went thump. "It's because you made that promise to me, isn't it?"

"I think so."

"And so you need a promise from me, or some kind of reciprocation."

"The pairing of a *Pyr* and his mate makes him complete. It counters his weakness with strength, so that the pair together are stronger than either can be alone," Eileen said.

"Complete how?"

"Complete in terms of the elements that the *Pyr* are charged to defend," Sara said.

"Each has an affinity; you told me that," Ginger said with excitement. She gestured to Delaney. "What's your affinity?"

"I'm not sure. Not fire."

"No, you were so cold," Rafferty said. "Until the firestorm drove the chill from deep inside you." He smiled. "Ginger is the fire in this partnership."

"Ideas are associated with air and the wind," Niall said. "Even though I have a strong bond with the wind, Delaney always has the best ideas."

"That's two," Sara said with approval. "What about water?"

"Swimming?" Ginger asked.

"It's often shown by empathy and understanding," Eileen said. "Compassion, an attempt to reconcile or create unions, soothe troubled waters." She shrugged and smiled. "Or other things."

Ginger was already shaking a finger at Delaney. "That's you. You went back to your mother, and you were worried about the planet in your nightmare. You're air and water."

"And you're earth," Delaney agreed. "You're completely in touch with the land and its cycles, with the rhythm of life."

"You said you missed that feeling," Ginger said, and he nodded agreement.

"Practical, problem solving," Alex mused. "I think we can agree that Ginger has an affinity for the earth."

"So we need a token, willingly given, that represents the earth and the fire that you bring to this union," Sara said. "That's what will heal Delaney's scale."

Ginger knew instantly what it had to be. She pulled off her mother's amber earrings and offered them along with the scale to Quinn. "Can you use these? They look like fire to me, and they come from the earth, and they were my father's first gift to my mother."

"Ginger!" Delaney protested. "You don't have to do this."

"Yes," she said with conviction. "Yes, I do."

Quinn took the earrings in his broad hand and turned them over as he examined them. "Set in silver," he said. "They resonate beautifully."

"What do you mean?"

He smiled at her. "They continue to be given in love. Gems know these things."

Ginger could believe that. "Can you use them?"

"I'll go one better," Quinn said. "I can work the sterling easily. I'll use just one for the scale."

"What will I do with one earring?"

"Quinn can make the other one into a ring," Delaney said, coming to Ginger's side. He took her hand in his. "Make a ring that I can give back to Ginger."

She looked at him in surprise and his crooked smile made her chest tighten. "Wear it on your right hand for now. By the time the baby comes, you'll know whether you want to move it to your left hand or not. Either way, it'll always be yours."

And this man would always be in her heart.

*   *   *

They stood in the old barn, its scents and history filling Delaney's senses. Evening was falling and the twilight slid through the cracks between the boards, filling the barn with a velvety darkness. Delaney heard the meltwater dripping from the roof. He heard the girls moving restlessly and knew there was work to be done. He sensed the earth thawing, and knew spring would come, with more work. And he knew there would be a bountiful harvest on Ginger's farm in the coming year.

He stood in her old barn, surrounded by his friends and the power of the bond between them all, and stared into Ginger's sparkling eyes.

"What do I do?" she whispered, this woman who had already given so much to him, yet was always ready to give more.

"Close your eyes," he advised as Quinn inhaled deeply. "We're all going to shift."

Ginger, predictably, kept her eyes wide open.

Quinn changed shape first, shimmering brilliant blue around his perimeter, then becoming a sapphire and steel dragon. He breathed fire, the flames licking the earrings in his grasp and making Delaney's lost scale glow a vivid copper pink. Sara stood beside him, holding Garrett, who watched his father with awe.

Donovan changed next, resplendent in lapis lazuli and silver. He lifted his own son, Nick, in one arm and Alex in the other, holding them high so that they could see the proceedings.

The barn was going to be full. Sloane shifted next, taking his dragon form of tourmaline and gold, then Erik shifted into ebony and pewter. There was a flurry of scales and talons and feathers, as Niall, Thorolf, and Rafferty shifted shape almost in unison. Niall was amethyst and silver; Thorolf was moonstone and silver; Rafferty was opal and gold. Their dragon forms gleamed as if they were jeweled, and the children's eyes were round with wonder.

Delaney noted the jet pin that marked his brother's repaired scale, the runestone that had been Erik's, and the iron fusing Quinn's own damaged scale. He was honored to be entering this company of scarred but strengthened warriors, and he knew that it was Ginger who gave him this gift.

"Ready?" he asked, feeling tender and protective of her. She nodded without hesitation, which made him smile. He held her gaze as he let himself begin to shimmer, as his body did what it did best. She didn't flinch; she didn't blink; she didn't evade his reality.

Because she had accepted him as he was, both good and bad mingled together. She knew his truth and didn't hold it against him—in fact, she had a habit of seeing the good in him.

And that made him a better *Pyr*.

The change gained in momentum then and he tipped back his head to roar as it claimed his body fully. He felt triumphant and strong, potent as he hadn't been in years. He stretched, showing the spot where he had lost the scale and where Magnus had driven deeply.

"Fire," Quinn said, breathing his own fire to merge scale and gem. The scale looked like it was burning, the edges so brilliant that the light reminded Delaney of his firestorm. The copper was almost pink, so radiant and fluid, and the emerald shone like a beacon in the night.

"Earth," Sara whispered as the amber earring glinted in the light of the dragonfire. Quinn worked the setting of the stone with remarkable agility, reshaping the hook to make a triple circle around the oval gem. He set it in the middle of the scale, deftly attaching it with his dragonfire.

"Air," the *Pyr* said, and exhaled as one, their breath

making the flames surrounding the scale dance high. Quinn stepped forward and pressed the scale into place, deliberately and firmly. The heat sent a stab of pain through Delaney and he felt it illuminate every corner of his being.

But then, Ginger had already sent her sunshine through his darkness. He was awed by his own good fortune and his heart was full enough to burst.

He had never expected to be whole again.

Delaney felt his single tear of gratitude slide down his cheek and hiss as it landed on the scale. Then Ginger put her hands over the repair, her fingers light and warm on it. She bent and touched her lips to the repaired scale, her breath making him shiver.

"Will it come loose?" she asked, her expression so worried that Delaney feared he'd lose another scale over her.

"Never," Quinn said, and shifted back to human form. He took Garrett out of Sara's arms and tossed the boy high. "We should get going."

"No use overstaying our welcome," Eileen said. "We'll be seeing you."

"We'll fly home," Donovan said, and tossed Delaney a set of keys. He caught them out of the air, acting instinctively, as his brother grinned. "I knew you sold the Viper, so I found another one when I felt your firestorm. I figured that if you had a mate, you might be sticking around, and you'd probably want some decent wheels."

"My pickup truck is *decent*," Ginger said, and Donovan laughed.

"I thought the Viper was yours," Delaney argued. "I can't take this from you."

"You're my brother. It's a firestorm gift."

"Now there are firestorm gifts?" Niall muttered. "I've got shopping to do."

"Besides, I am a Ducati man through and through," Donovan said.

"Except for the minivan," Alex teased, and Donovan rolled his eyes.

"Don't tell them that!"

Alex laughed. "Let's go. These people want some privacy."

"I gotta get back to my greenhouse," Sloane said, heading for the door.

"And I've got bookings to manage," Niall said, pausing beside Delaney. "If you want back into the partnership, just say the word."

Delaney smiled down at the woman in his arms. "I'm going to invest in another partnership," he said, watching Ginger's eyes light. "I hear that Sinclair Farms needs some help, some more cooperative help. I'm pretty interested in learning more about organic farming."

Ginger's eyes danced. "Don't come crying to me when you find out how hard it is."

"Not a chance," he said, and caught her close. He bent to kiss her, willing his fellows to disappear, and by the time he lifted his head, they were gone.

"Better than beguiling them," Ginger said with satisfaction.

Delaney was startled. "What do you know about beguiling?"

"Only that if you ever do that to me, you'll be toast, hotshot."

"Burned toast."

"You should be so lucky."

He flicked a glance to the loft, then back to her. "Maybe we should look for your lingerie."

"Maybe we should try the bedroom this time."

"Don't tell me you're going to get all predictable on me."

"Not a chance!" Ginger laughed. "No stockings or garters today, for example."

"As if I care," he said, his voice low as he reached for her. "It's just wrapping, Ginger, and the outside isn't what counts."

By the way she kissed him, Delaney was sure they were in agreement on that.

Don't miss the next paranormal romance
in the bestselling Dragonfire series
from Deborah Cooke,
featuring Niall's story. . . .

WHISPER KISS

Coming from Signet Eclipse in August 2010

His intruder was female.

Niall suddenly felt warm in the entry to his studio. It was because he was out of that crazy wind; he knew it because the building was folded protectively around him. It had a stillness about it that he liked a lot, maybe because it was so old. He narrowed his eyes, noting that the intruder was at the top of the stairs.

She had great legs.

She rounded the corner without looking back, taking the route to Niall's apartment.

He followed her silently, his suspicion growing even as he wiped a bead of perspiration from his lip.

Who was she?

Why was she here?

What did she intend to steal from him?

She went to the third floor. He heard the steps creak, just as they always did, and was surprised at her lack of hesitation. She moved decisively, quickly, knowing her destination, and certain she wouldn't be interrupted or caught.

Maybe she didn't care.

Interesting.

He climbed the stairs, finding it warmer with every step he took. The heat always rose in the stairwell, wafting up from the radiator just inside the exterior door, but Niall couldn't remember it ever being this hot. And the furnace should be off at this time of year.

Niall heard her knock once on his door, then try the knob. He smiled at her expectation that anyone would leave a door unlocked in Manhattan. She jiggled the knob, then again, more vehemently, and he thought she swore.

Then she kicked the door.

He frowned, reached the top of the stairs, and eased around the last corner. She was trying to peer through the lock, her skirt rising high in the back. She was short, but her legs were lean and muscled. Remarkably so. Niall shook his head at his own awareness of her gender, then eased around the corner.

The spark that leapt between the two of them shocked Niall in more ways than one.

He froze at the sudden brilliance of it, and felt dizzy at the heat it sent rocketing through his body. He understood immediately that he was experiencing his firestorm.

The woman at his door, the woman who must be his destined mate, pivoted to glare at him. Niall knew instantly that she was as unlikely a companion for him as could be imagined.

Could the firestorm be wrong?

She was petite, her hair dyed black with fuchsia tips and moussed into spikes. She wore a black leather biker jacket liberally embellished with studs, a black and yellow tartan skirt, biker boots, and black fishnet stockings. He could see her tattoos through her stockings and at the edges of her chain-mail gauntlets. Her eyes were lined with black, her lips painted burgundy, and her gaze filled with hostility.

"What the hell was that?" she demanded. Her voice was her only asset, the low throaty purr of a jazz singer.

"What do you think you're doing?" Niall said at the same time.

"Who are you?" She put her hands on her hips and confronted him, her eyes flashing. He was surprised that she was undaunted—she couldn't have weighed one hundred pounds, and he was fully pumped after his workout. "Don't tell me that you're Niall Talbot?"

"Who else would I be?"

Her sudden laugh took him completely off guard and transformed her features. She fell against the wall as she laughed. She looked young then, mischievous and unpredictable. Sexy. Niall checked her legs again without meaning to do so. He felt something tighten within him, something he wasn't inclined to heed.

Firestorm be damned.

"You mean that you really exist?" She shook her head in rueful amusement. She wore a long silver earring on her left ear, and it sparkled as she moved. Niall couldn't see a mate on her other ear. "Because that would really take it, if that big dope wasn't lying to me."

Then she swore with an eloquence that made him blink.

Niall took a step closer and the firestorm's heat flared between them with unmistakable intensity. "Why wouldn't I exist?" he asked, wondering what she knew about him and his nature.

As he drew near to her, he noted the curve of her jaw, the soft line of her throat, the fairness of her skin, and he swallowed. She was pretty, more pretty than he had initially realized.

Her perfume teased him, making him keenly aware of her femininity—even if she tried to hide it. She would have been undeniably alluring if she were dressed conservatively, wearing pearls, her hair flowing loose instead of sharpened into spikes.

"I just thought T was lying to me, that's all."

He saw her grimace, as if hurt, before her expression turned insouciant once more. It was astonishing to Niall that any woman could care enough about Thorolf to be hurt by anything he said.

"I guess T—I mean Thorolf—was telling the truth after all. There really is a Niall Talbot."

That glimpse of vulnerability, and the fact that she'd struggled to hide it, made Niall wonder what other secrets she had. He was surprised by how much he wanted to know. He took another step and a spark flashed between them.

"Holy shit," she whispered as she stared at it. "You gotta do something about the wiring in this place."

"It's not the wiring," Niall said flatly, and she met his gaze with surprise. "So, who are you and what do you want?" His tone was more challenging than he'd meant it to be, but she didn't appear to be intimidated by him.

She straightened and lifted her chin, her gaze sliding over him. "I'm Rox," she said with pride, and another piece of the puzzle slid into place for Niall. Thorolf had mentioned someone named Rox before—in another time and place, Niall might have found it amusing that he'd assumed no person named Rox actually existed.

"What do you want with T?" she demanded. "Because, you know, if you're intending to take advantage of him, you're going to have to deal with me first. He might not be the sharpest guy, but he means well, and he trusts people too easily. . . ."

Niall shook his head at her fervent defense of Thorolf. There was something particularly bittersweet about the notion of his destined mate being smitten with Thorolf—the bane of Niall's existence—but Niall had no time to express his irritation or defend his own position.

Because the earth heaved.

He remembered that sense of pending doom and cursed himself for being distracted by Rox and the firestorm.

It was too late. Whatever was chasing him had arrived. Rox squeaked in surprise as the floor rippled beneath their feet and they fell against the wall together. Niall was sure he heard the wind roar with fury. He heard the pavement crack in the street below. There was the crash of windows breaking, and sirens going off. The building tipped and moaned.

He threw himself protectively over Rox just as a long jagged crack opened like a zipper in the opposite wall. That crack rose to the ceiling and a gap opened there, yawning ever wider. Plaster began to fall all around them and Niall feared the worst. He heard the beams rip in the attic and instinctively shifted shape.

Niall changed to his dragon form to protect his mate from the threat against her. Only after the transformation was done did he worry about the repercussions. Some humans went insane when they witnessed the change, but it was too late to worry about that.

He heard Rox gasp as he folded himself over her and hoped for the best. She was small, delicate, and achingly feminine. The firestorm flared as he pulled her closer, making his blood simmer, giving him other ideas.

Seductive ideas.

Untimely ideas.

The roof fell in chunks, landing on his back and shoulders, filling his lungs with dust from who knew what illicit building material. He thrashed his tail and roared, deflecting the falling debris, snarling as the building fell into rubble.

Rox curled tightly against him, but she didn't shake and she didn't cry. He heard the quick rhythm of her breathing. She didn't scream, which he liked a lot, but she definitely hung on. Her tiny hands slid across his chest, and he realized she was exploring his dragon form.

Not driven crazy at all. Niall's eyes widened with surprise that she was checking him out.

She flattened her palm and slid it across his scales, her caress coaxing his blood to a boil. She ran her hands over his claws and across his belly, leaving him dizzy with the firestorm's demand. He felt her catch her breath, heard the pulse of her heart and nearly forgot everything except his mate.

The firestorm simmered, bathing them both in golden light that teased their bodies to awareness, tormenting Niall with possibilities. He smelled dust and felt the ripping wind yet couldn't ignore the sweet scent of Rox's perfume.

Or turn his thoughts from the temptation of the firestorm.

In a way, he was oblivious to the chaos around them even as he listened to it. It felt separate from him. Irrelevant. He was more aware of Rox, sweetly pressed against him, of the cocoon of the firestorm surrounding them.

That was dangerous, but he couldn't tame his errant thoughts.

He looked down at her and his desire surged. Her burgundy-stained lips were so close, so soft and full, and he was tempted to taste them, to take advantage of the opportunity to satisfy his curiosity.

He reminded himself that she wasn't the kind of woman for him.

If nothing else, Niall Talbot had principles.

Could the firestorm be wrong? He'd never heard of such a thing, but there was no doubt that this woman was the wrong one for him.

Niall was tempted to sate the firestorm and worry about the details later.

The upheaval lasted less than two minutes, although it felt as if it would go on forever. When the shaking finally stopped, Niall felt Rox trembling a little bit. He didn't doubt that she would try to hide her fear with bravado.

He shifted quickly, hoping she didn't watch the

change. Maybe she'd forget about it. Maybe he should beguile her, although Niall was not a fan of beguiling humans. It seemed particularly rude to consider the possibility of beguiling one's mate.

He doubted that Rox was susceptible to suggestion. She seemed to be very much in touch with reality.

In human form, he angled over her, his fingers in her hair. Niall cupped her head and held her face against his chest, protecting her small figure from the last of the tumbling debris. Before looking into her eyes, he hoped for the best.

He lifted his head and looked down at her cautiously, startled by the knowing gleam in her eyes.

"You are the same as him." Her lips twisted. "Who would have believed there could be another one?"

There was no question in her tone. She knew. Rox wasn't just in touch with reality—she knew about *his* reality. Niall wasn't sure what to say, but she was watching him, waiting for his agreement. It would have been wrong to lie during his firestorm, to deceive his mate or beguile her.

Niall nodded once.

"So, you are mentoring him, just as he said." Rox licked her lips and looked away, then met Niall's gaze again. Her eyes were a vivid blue, snapping with intelligence. "He didn't lie about that."

Niall shook his head. "If that's what he said, it wasn't a lie. I am supposed to be mentoring him."

Her lips quirked. "You don't sound very enthused."

"He's not an attentive student."

Rox laughed. "I guess that must mean you're not as screwed up as he is."

Niall struggled to be polite about Thorolf, although he wasn't sure why. Maybe because Rox had tried to hide her dismay about Thorolf's departure. "I like to think that I'm not."

To his dismay, he ended up sounding exactly like his father. Stuff and inflexible.

Rox considered him. Niall wondered what she saw other than a guy in a T-shirt and jeans, covered in plaster and fallen wood. He wondered what she was thinking or feeling—he knew what he was feeling.

The firestorm wasn't interested in being ignored. He knew it would be inappropriate to pursue it, yet he couldn't seem to let go of Rox. His body had definite ideas about how things should proceed, ideas Niall had no intention of pursuing. Rox wasn't the kind of woman for him, and he wasn't one to just do the deed and leave. He'd never abandon a woman if she was pregnant with his child, and he'd never have a child with a woman like Rox.

Period.

The firestorm had it wrong.

Rox smiled suddenly, almost as if she'd heard his thoughts, and he blinked at the change in her. She looked softer when she smiled, less cynical, more alluring. "Then you know how he is," she said in that husky, confidential tone, " and you won't be surprised that I thought he was lying to me." She lifted one dark eyebrow, her eyes shining. "I thought he didn't have the balls to tell me the truth."

Niall smiled despite himself. "Yeah, I can see Thorolf doing that." It was conceivable that the tall *Pyr* would be terrorized by an outspoken woman like Rox.

"I've seen him do it a lot in three years." She heaved a sigh and brushed some debris off Niall's shoulder, pausing to look him in the eye. Her lips looked soft and full. Inviting. She wrinkled her nose. "Sorry if I came across too strong. I was sure that someone was taking advantage of him. He's not really good at assessing people's motives, you know. He's not stupid, but he's too trusting."

"He just doesn't pay attention," Niall said, hearing his father's stern judgment in his own tone. "He thinks he can fight his way out of anything."

Rox nodded ruefully. "Fighting's not always the best answer."

"Sometimes avoiding a fight is smarter."

She met his gaze and nodded again, their agreement surprising Niall a bit. "But he's not the sharpest tack. He needs someone to watch over him."

"And that was you?" At her shrug, Niall grimaced and sighed. "So, I guess now it's me."

"And we have something in common, despite appearances," Rox said, an enticing thread of laughter in her tone.

Niall was surprised to hear his own thought on her lips. He saw the glint of awareness in her expression and knew he should stand up. He was still angled over Rox, but the earthquake had ended. His body was just reluctant to move. He felt her breasts against his chest, her legs beneath his own, and he wanted something he knew he shouldn't be tempted to take.

"Imagine—I thought you might be a woman," Rox whispered, then laughed again. Her laughter sounded even better the second time. Niall felt his own lips twitch.

"Not many named Niall."

"Oh, I assumed the whole business-card trick was bogus, that he'd found your card and was lying to me."

"And you came after him, even so?"

She grimaced. "He's not a bad guy—just suffers from a lack of focus. And I finally found him a job, too."

"So you weren't happy to hear that he'd found one on his own."

Their gazes locked and held, her eyes so filled with stars that Niall couldn't look away. Rox slid her hands across Niall's shoulders and curved her fingers around the muscles there, then cast him a wicked smile. Her approval of what she saw was more than clear. Niall's heart skipped a beat as she arched her back, bringing her breasts into collision with his chest.

"I'm pretty sure, though, that you are a guy," she whispered.

"Pretty sure?" Niall teased.

Rox grinned. "You can't be faking these biceps." She ran her hands across his chest again, launching an array of little sparks and making Niall catch his breath. "And the usual suspects are absent and unaccounted for."

"Excuse me?"

Rox's smile turned coy as she slid her breasts across his chest. He glanced down into her cleavage, saw the creamy curves of her breasts, and his mouth went dry. He saw appreciation light her eyes and knew he should stand up, put some distance between them.

Before it was too late.

But Rox caught his neck in her hands. Niall froze, uncertain of what she would do but wanting to know. The firestorm was messing with his usual clear thinking, sending an insistent message through his body that was impossible to ignore.

"Thanks, Niall," she whispered, eyes shining. "I would have been squished like a roach without you."

Niall had no chance to answer because Rox kissed him. It wasn't a sweet kiss or a shy kiss—it was a kiss that knew where it was going and why.

It was going exactly where the firestorm wanted to lead.

And that kiss shorted Niall's circuits. It got right to where he lived, routed his doubts, and undermined his hesitation. It filled his body and his mind with an urge to consummate the firestorm, with a sense of urgency and demand.

It made him want.

It made him need.

It made him forget the merit of duty and logic and deliberate choice. It made him appreciate the call of passion and impulse.

And one cheeky little brunette named Rox.

Author's Note

In writing the Dragonfire novels, I've come to rely upon the Web sites provided by Fred Espenak of NASA, which offer comprehensive information about eclipses, past and present. Extrapolations regarding the *Pyr* and eclipses are, of course, my own, as are any errors made in interpreting the data provided.

If you are interested in learning more about eclipses and Saros cycles, visit http://eclipse.gsfc.nasa.gov.

About the Author

Deborah Cooke has always been fascinated by dragons, although she has never understood why they have to be the bad guys. She has an honors degree in history with a focus on medieval studies, and is an avid reader of medieval vernacular literature, fairy tales, and fantasy novels. Since 1992, Deborah has written more than thirty romance novels under the names Claire Cross and Claire Delacroix.

Deborah makes her home in Canada with her husband. When she isn't writing, she can be found knitting, sewing, or hunting for vintage patterns. To learn more about the Dragonfire series and Deborah, please visit her Web site at www.deborahcooke.com and her blog, Alive & Knitting, at www.delacroix.net/blog.

Also Available

THE FIRST NOVEL IN THE DRAGONFIRE SERIES

KISS OF FIRE
A Dragonfire Novel

by DEBORAH COOKE

For millennia, the shape-shifting dragon warriors
known as the Pyr have commanded the four
elements and guarded the earth's treasures.
But now the final reckoning between the Pyr, who
count humans among the earth's treasures, and the
Slayers, who would eradicate both humans and the
Pyr who protect them, is about to begin...

When Sara Keegan decides to settle down and run
her quirky aunt's New Age bookstore, she's not
looking for adventure. She doesn't believe in fate
or the magic of the tarot—but when she's saved
from a vicious attack by a man who has the ability
to turn into a fire-breathing dragon, she questions
whether she's losing her mind—
or about to lose her heart...

**Available wherever books are sold or
at penguin.com**

Also Available

KISS OF FURY
A Dragonfire Novel

by DEBORAH COOKE

Scientist Alexandra Madison was on the verge of releasing an invention that could save the world—until her partner was murdered, their lab burned, and their prototype destroyed. When Alex learns that her recurring nightmares of dragons have led to a transfer to a psychiatric hospital, she knows she has to escape to rebuild her prototype in time. And that she must return to the wreckage of the lab for one last thing...

Handsome, daring, impulsive Donovan Shea knows the Madison project is of dire importance to the ongoing Pyr/Slayer war, but resents being assigned to surveillance of the lab. He's surprised by the arrival of a beautiful woman in the middle of the night—not that she's being followed by a Slayer, not that she won't admit her name, but that she's his destined mate. As the sparks of the firestorm ignite and the Slayers close in on their prey, Donovan knows he'll surrender his life to protect Alex—even risk his heart, if that's what it takes...

Available wherever books are sold or at penguin.com

Also Available

KISS OF FATE
A Dragonfire Novel

by DEBORAH COOKE

Haunted by dreams of a lover who takes the form
of a dragon, Eileen Grosvenor searches for the
truth. She never expects to find a real dragon
shape shifter, let alone one who awakens her
passion and ignites memories of a forgotten past.

Erik Sorensson is focused on leading the Pyr
against the Slayers when a powerful ancient relic
reveals itself. Erik tries to retrieve it from Eileen's
possession—and is shocked by a fury of passion.
Her presence touches him in unexpected ways,
reminding him of mistakes he's determined not to
make again, and Erik is forced to make a choice—
duty or love.

Available wherever books are sold or